HORIZON™

VOLUME 03 REVEAL

HORIZON CREATED BY
BRANDON THOMAS AND **JUAN GEDEON**

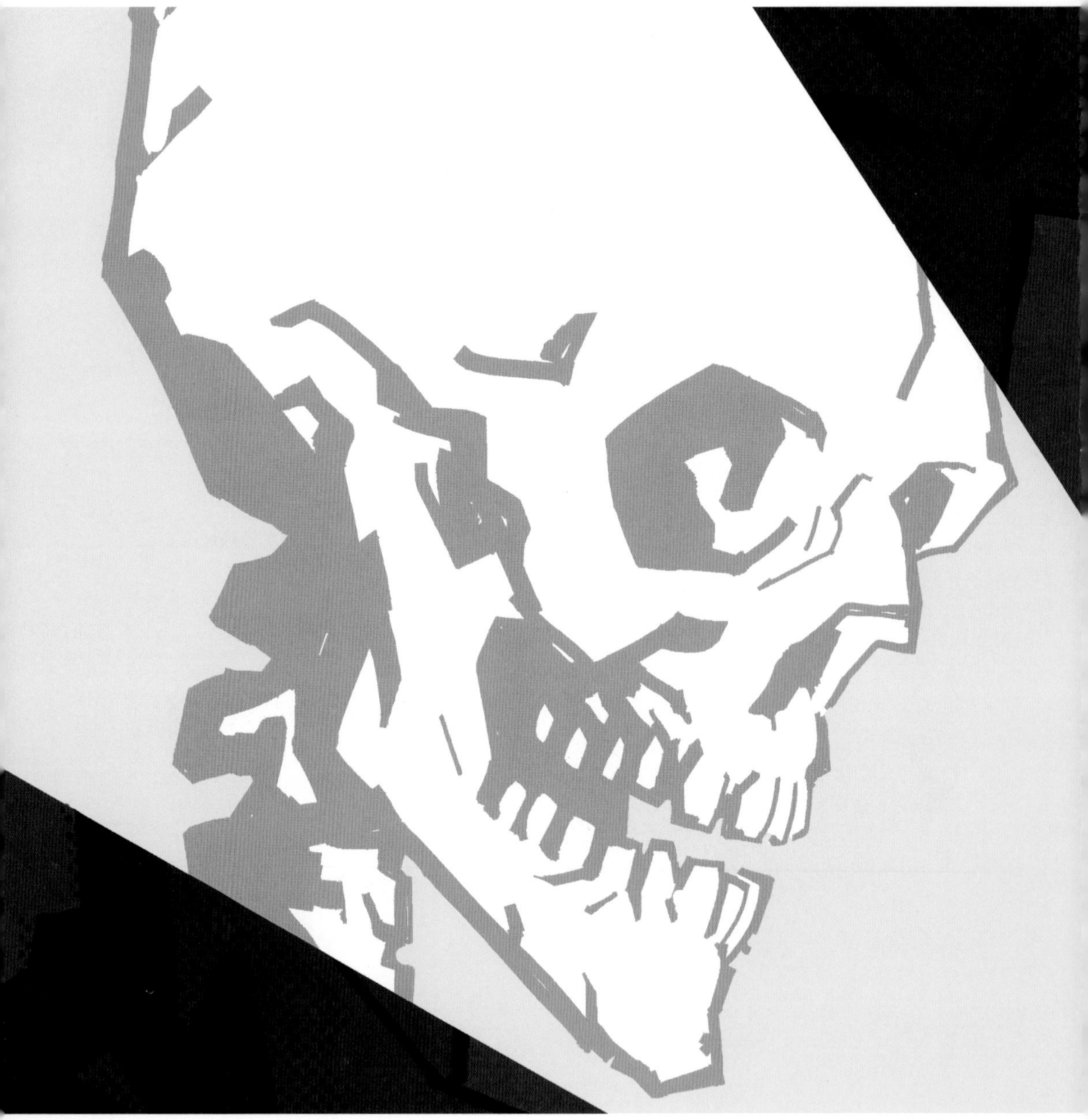

FOR SKYBOUND ENTERTAINMENT

ROBERT KIRKMAN *CHAIRMAN* // **DAVID ALPERT** *CEO* // **SEAN MACKIEWICZ** *SVP, EDITOR-IN-CHIEF* // **SHAWN KIRKHAM** *SVP, BUSINESS DEVELOPMENT* // **BRIAN HUNTINGTON** *ONLINE EDITORIAL DIRECTOR* // **JUNE ALIAN** *PUBLICITY DIRECTOR* // **ANDRES JUAREZ** *ART DIRECTOR* // **JON MOISAN** *EDITOR* // **ARIELLE BASICH** *ASSOCIATE EDITOR* // **CARINA TAYLOR** *PRODUCTION ARTIST* // **PAUL SHIN** *BUSINESS DEVELOPMENT COORDINATOR* // **JOHNNY O'DELL** *SOCIAL MEDIA MANAGER* // **SALLY JACKA** *SKYBOUND RETAILER RELATIONS* // **DAN PETERSEN** *DIRECTOR OF OPERATIONS & EVENTS* // **NICK PALMER** *OPERATIONS COORDINATOR*

INTERNATIONAL INQUIRIES: AG@SEQUENTIALRIGHTS.COM
LICENSING INQUIRIES: CONTACT@SKYBOUND.COM

WWW.SKYBOUND.COM

IMAGE COMICS, INC.

ROBERT KIRKMAN *CHIEF OPERATING OFFICER* // **ERIK LARSEN** *CHIEF FINANCIAL OFFICER* // **TODD MCFARLANE** *PRESIDENT* // **MARC SILVESTRI** *CHIEF EXECUTIVE OFFICER* // **JIM VALENTINO** *VICE-PRESIDENT* // **ERIC STEPHENSON** *PUBLISHER* // **COREY HART** *DIRECTOR OF SALES* // **JEFF BOISON** *DIRECTOR OF PUBLISHING PLANNING & BOOK TRADE SALES* // **CHRIS ROSS** *DIRECTOR OF DIGITAL SALES* // **JEFF STANG** *DIRECTOR OF SPECIALTY SALES* // **KAT SALAZAR** *DIRECTOR OF PR & MARKETING* // **DREW GILL** *ART DIRECTOR* // **HEATHER DOORNINK** *ART DIRECTOR* // **BRANWYN BIGGLESTONE** *CONTROLLER*

WWW.IMAGECOMICS.COM

BRANDON THOMAS
WRITER

JUAN GEDEON
ARTIST

MIKE SPICER
COLORIST

RUS WOOTON
LETTERER

ARIELLE BASICH
ASSOCIATE EDITOR

SEAN MACKIEWICZ
EDITOR

JASON HOWARD
COVER

HORIZON VOLUME 3: REVEAL. FIRST PRINTING. ISBN: 978-1-5343-0487-1. PUBLISHED BY IMAGE COMICS, INC. OFFICE OF PUBLICATION: 2701 NW VAUGHN ST., STE. 780, PORTLAND, OR 97210. COPYRIGHT
© 2018 SKYBOUND, LLC. ALL RIGHTS RESERVED. ORIGINALLY PUBLISHED IN SINGLE MAGAZINE FORM AS HORIZON #13-18. HORIZON™ (INCLUDING ALL PROMINENT CHARACTERS FEATURED HEREIN), ITS LOGO
AND ALL CHARACTER LIKENESSES ARE TRADEMARKS OF SKYBOUND, LLC, UNLESS OTHERWISE NOTED. IMAGE COMICS® AND ITS LOGOS ARE REGISTERED TRADEMARKS AND COPYRIGHTS OF IMAGE COMICS, INC. ALL
RIGHTS RESERVED. NO PART OF THIS PUBLICATION MAY BE REPRODUCED OR TRANSMITTED IN ANY FORM OR BY ANY MEANS (EXCEPT FOR SHORT EXCERPTS FOR REVIEW PURPOSES) WITHOUT THE EXPRESS WRITTEN
PERMISSION OF IMAGE COMICS, INC. ALL NAMES, CHARACTERS, EVENTS AND LOCALES IN THIS PUBLICATION ARE ENTIRELY FICTIONAL. ANY RESEMBLANCE TO ACTUAL PERSONS (LIVING OR DEAD), EVENTS OR PLACES,
WITHOUT SATIRIC INTENT, IS COINCIDENTAL. PRINTED IN THE U.S.A. FOR INFORMATION REGARDING THE CPSIA ON THIS PRINTED MATERIAL CALL: 203-595-3636 AND PROVIDE REFERENCE # RICH - 778332.

LANGUAGE KEY

NATIVE VALIAN

EARTH ENGLISH

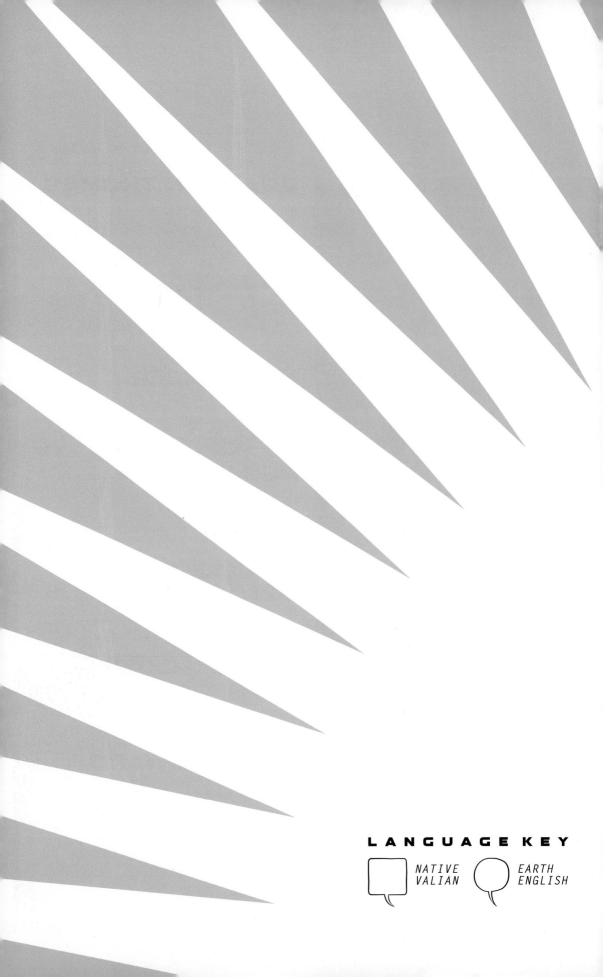

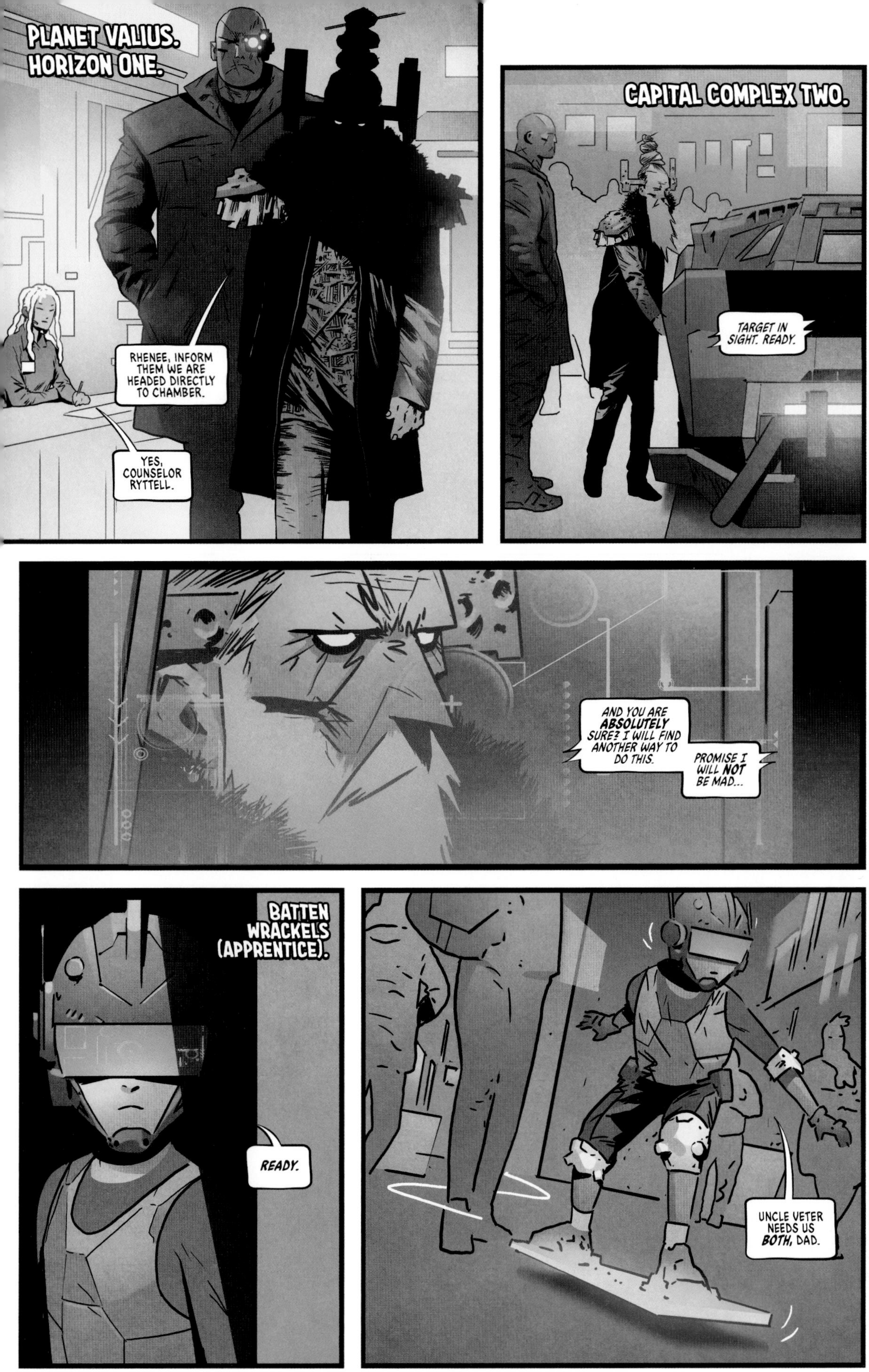
PLANET VALIUS. HORIZON ONE.
RHENEE, INFORM THEM WE ARE HEADED DIRECTLY TO CHAMBER.
YES, COUNSELOR RYTTELL.
CAPITAL COMPLEX TWO.
TARGET IN SIGHT. READY.
AND YOU ARE ABSOLUTELY SURE? I WILL FIND ANOTHER WAY TO DO THIS.
PROMISE I WILL NOT BE MAD...
BATTEN WRACKELS (APPRENTICE).
READY.
UNCLE VETER NEEDS US BOTH, DAD.

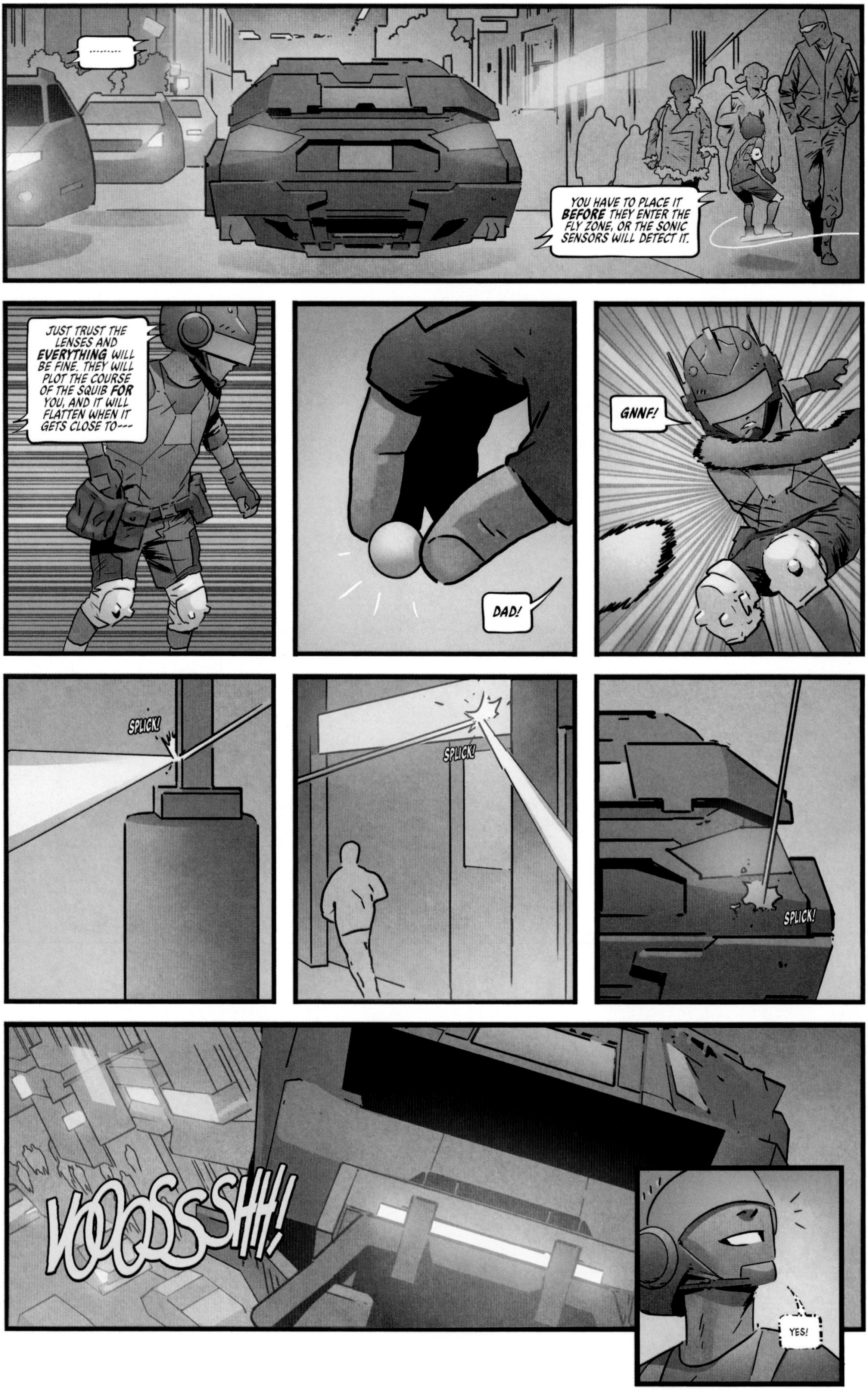

....
YOU HAVE TO PLACE IT BEFORE THEY ENTER THE FLY ZONE, OR THE SONIC SENSORS WILL DETECT IT.
JUST TRUST THE LENSES AND EVERYTHING WILL BE FINE. THEY WILL PLOT THE COURSE OF THE SQUIB FOR YOU, AND IT WILL FLATTEN WHEN IT GETS CLOSE TO---
DAD!
GNNF!
SPLICK!
SPLICK!
SPLICK!
VOOOSSSHH!
YES!

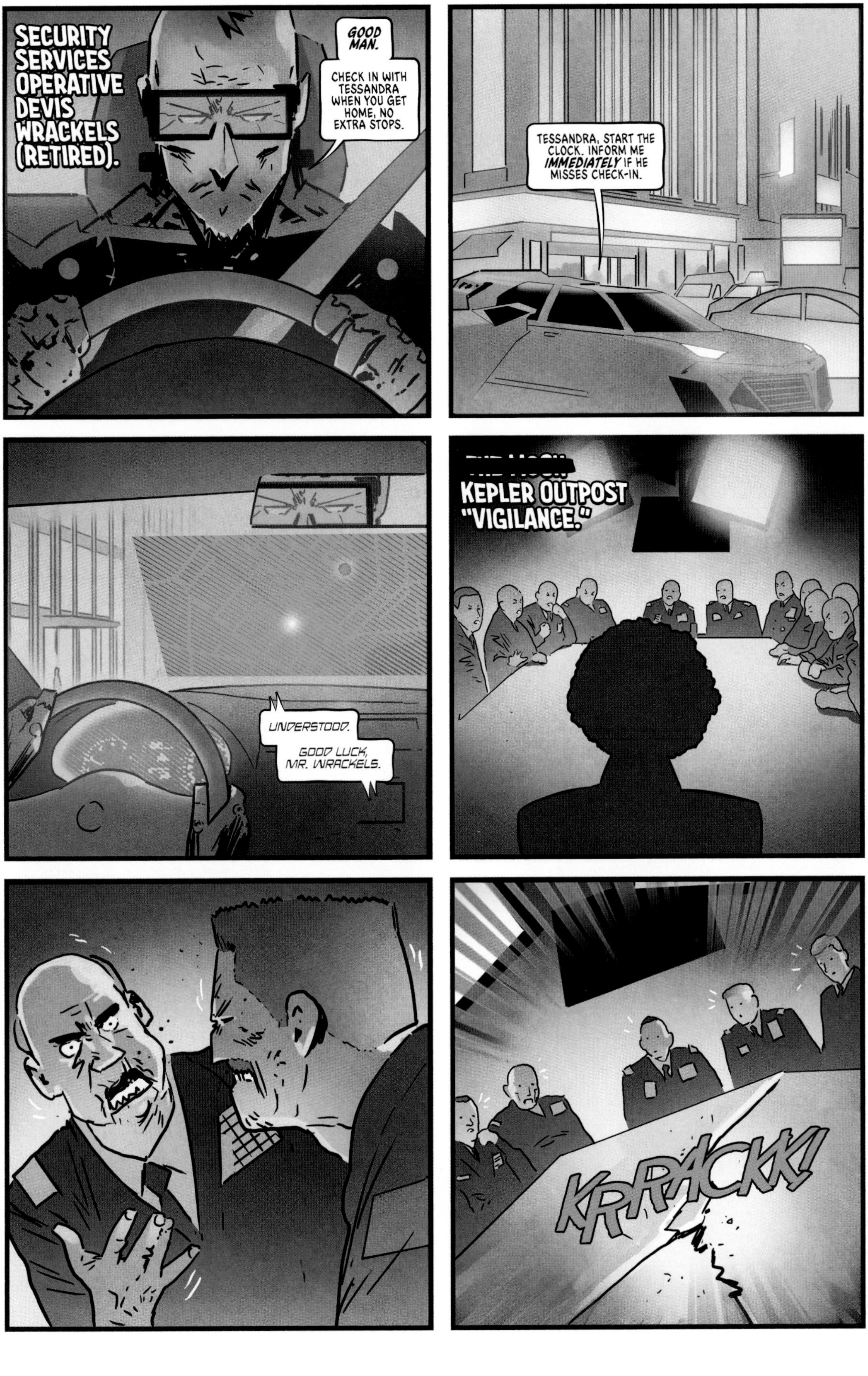
SECURITY SERVICES OPERATIVE DEVIS WRACKELS (RETIRED).
GOOD MAN.
CHECK IN WITH TESSANDRA WHEN YOU GET HOME, NO EXTRA STOPS.
TESSANDRA, START THE CLOCK. INFORM ME IMMEDIATELY IF HE MISSES CHECK-IN.
UNDERSTOOD.
GOOD LUCK, MR. WRACKELS.
[redacted]
KEPLER OUTPOST "VIGILANCE."
KRRACKK!

DOES ANYBODY ELSE HERE REMEMBER WHAT MY RECOMMENDATION WAS ON VALIUS?

PLEASE. SPEAK THE *FUCK* UP.

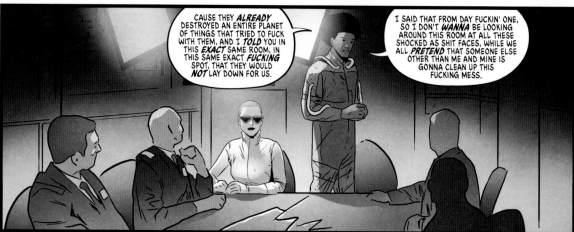

CAUSE THEY *ALREADY* DESTROYED AN ENTIRE PLANET OF THINGS THAT TRIED TO FUCK WITH THEM, AND I *TOLD* YOU IN THIS *EXACT* SAME ROOM, IN THIS SAME EXACT *FUCKING* SPOT, THAT THEY WOULD *NOT* LAY DOWN FOR US.

I SAID THAT FROM DAY FUCKIN' ONE, SO I DON'T *WANNA* BE LOOKING AROUND THIS ROOM AT ALL THESE SHOCKED AS SHIT FACES, WHILE WE ALL *PRETEND* THAT SOMEONE ELSE OTHER THAN ME AND MINE IS GONNA CLEAN UP THIS FUCKING MESS.

THEY ARE *RECRUITING* NOW, LADIES AND GENTLEMEN, AND PEOPLE ARE LISTENING BECAUSE THEY KNOW WE'VE BEEN BULLSHITTING THEM FOR WAY TOO LONG.

PEOPLE WILL HAVE TO DIE VIOLENTLY TO SET THIS ALL RIGHT AGAIN, MADAME PRESIDENT.

....

PLEASE, LINCOLN. PUT AN END TO THIS.

YES, MA'AM.

NOW, IF YOU'LL EXCUSE US...THIS LEMONADE AIN'T GONNA FUCKIN' MAKE ITSELF.

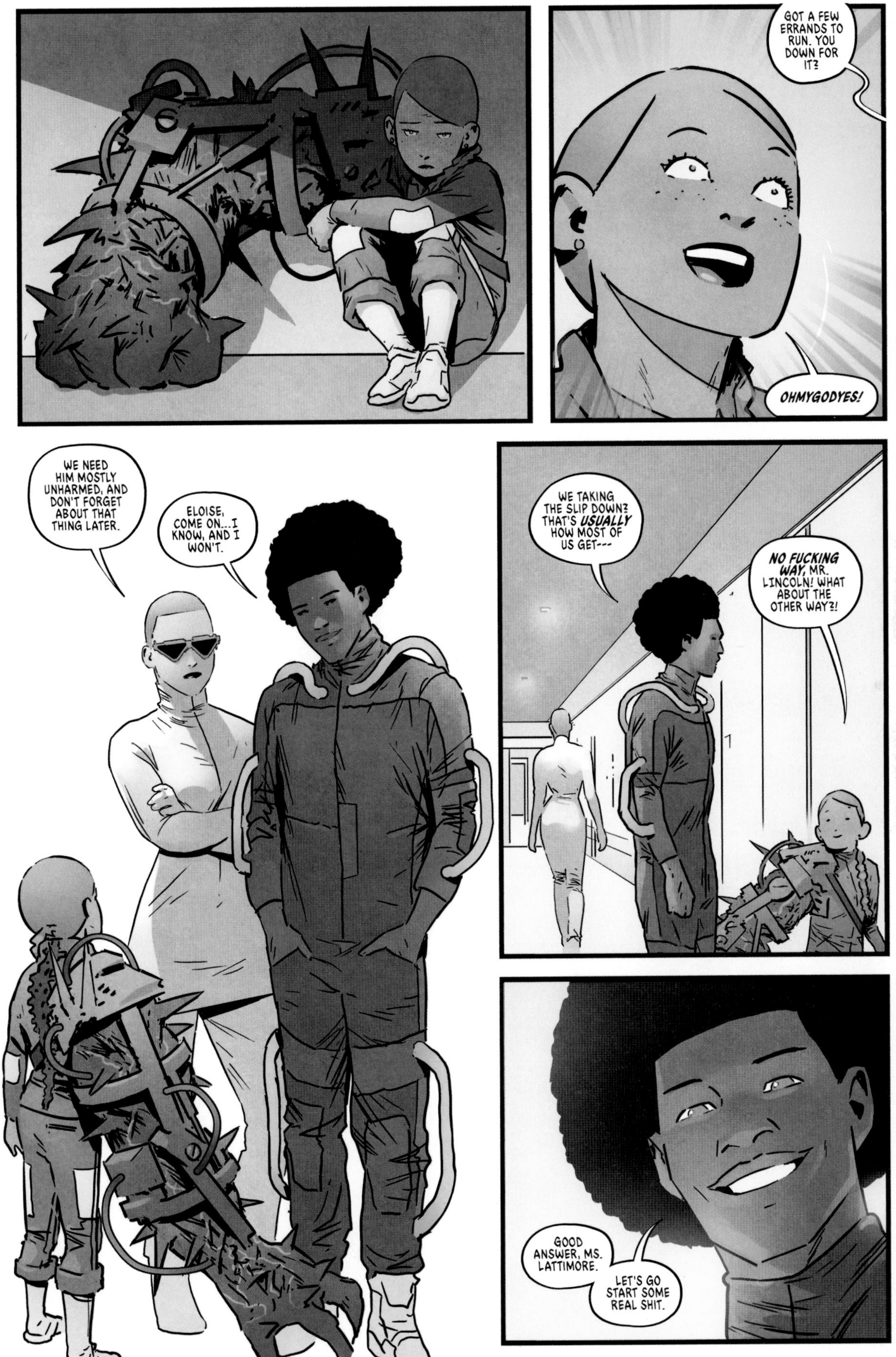

GOT A FEW ERRANDS TO RUN. YOU DOWN FOR IT?
OHMYGODYES!
WE NEED HIM MOSTLY UNHARMED, AND DON'T FORGET ABOUT THAT THING LATER.
ELOISE, COME ON... I KNOW, AND I WON'T.
WE TAKING THE SLIP DOWN? THAT'S USUALLY HOW MOST OF US GET---
NO FUCKING WAY, MR. LINCOLN! WHAT ABOUT THE OTHER WAY?!
GOOD ANSWER, MS. LATTIMORE.
LET'S GO START SOME REAL SHIT.

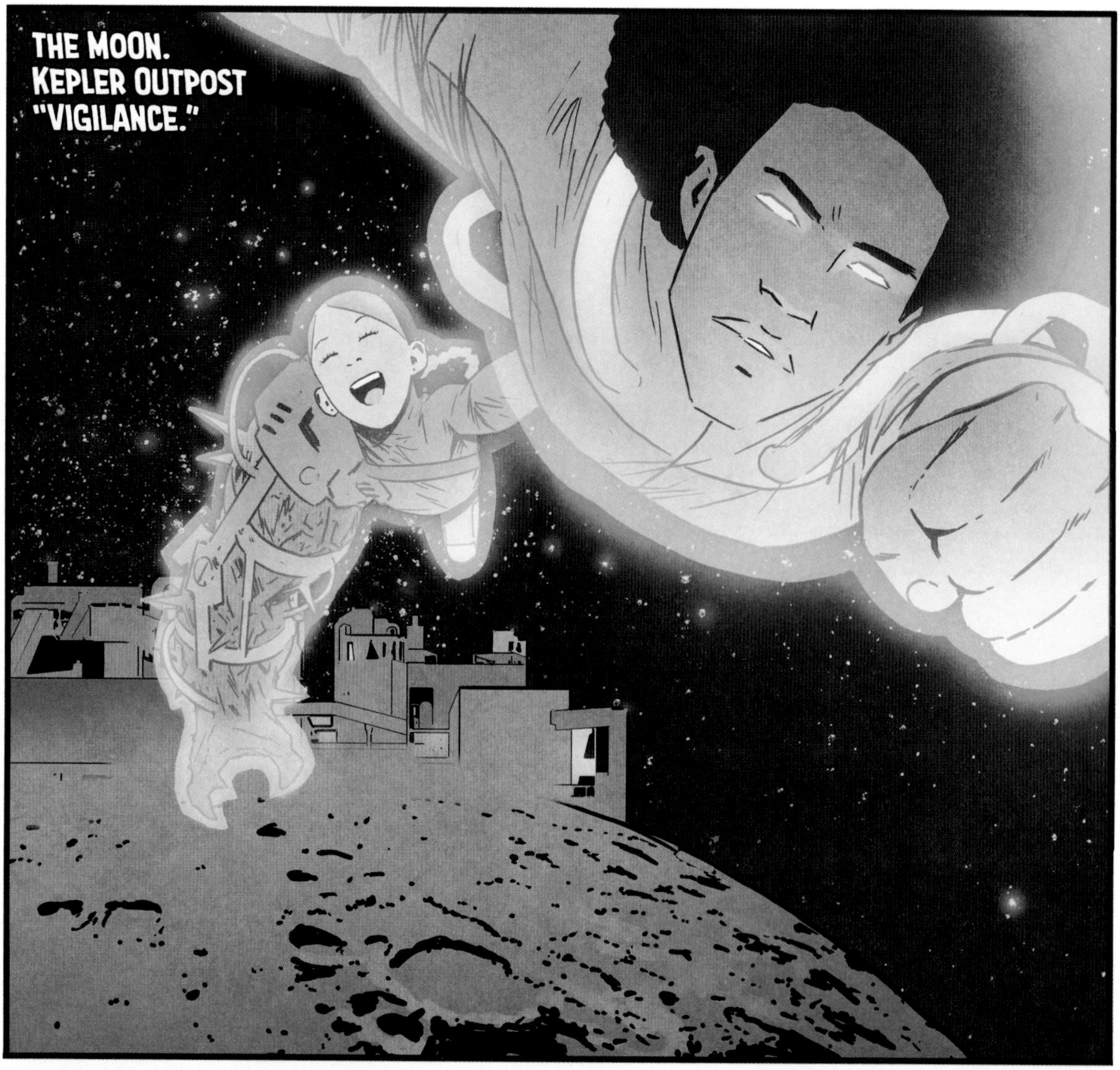
THE MOON.
KEPLER OUTPOST
"VIGILANCE."
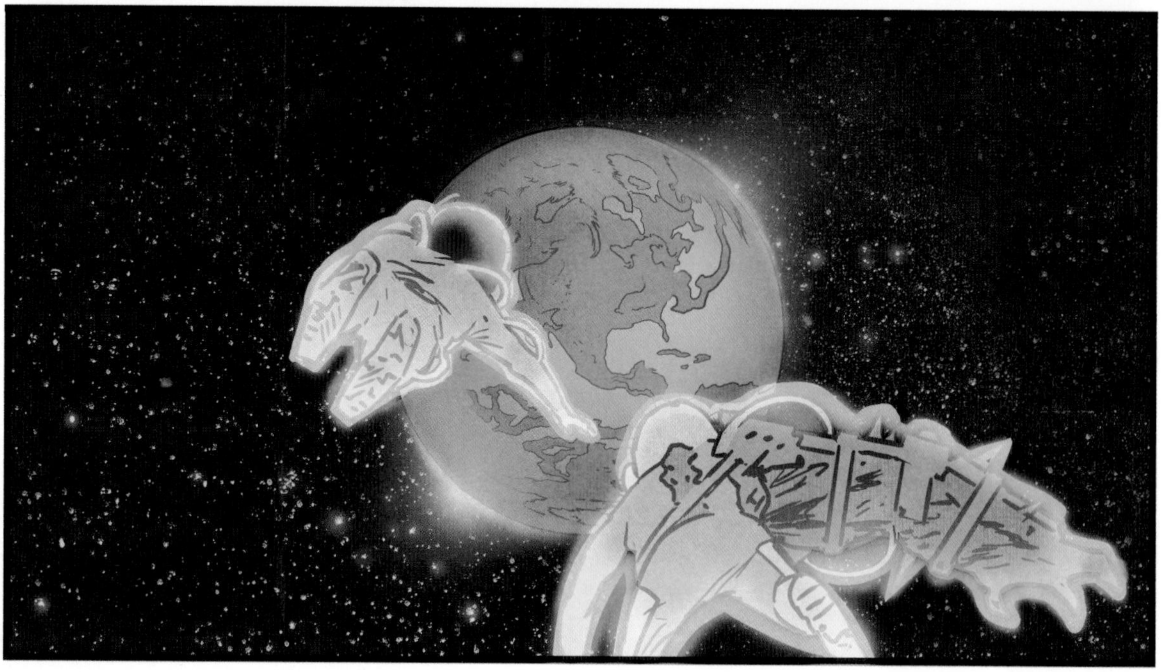

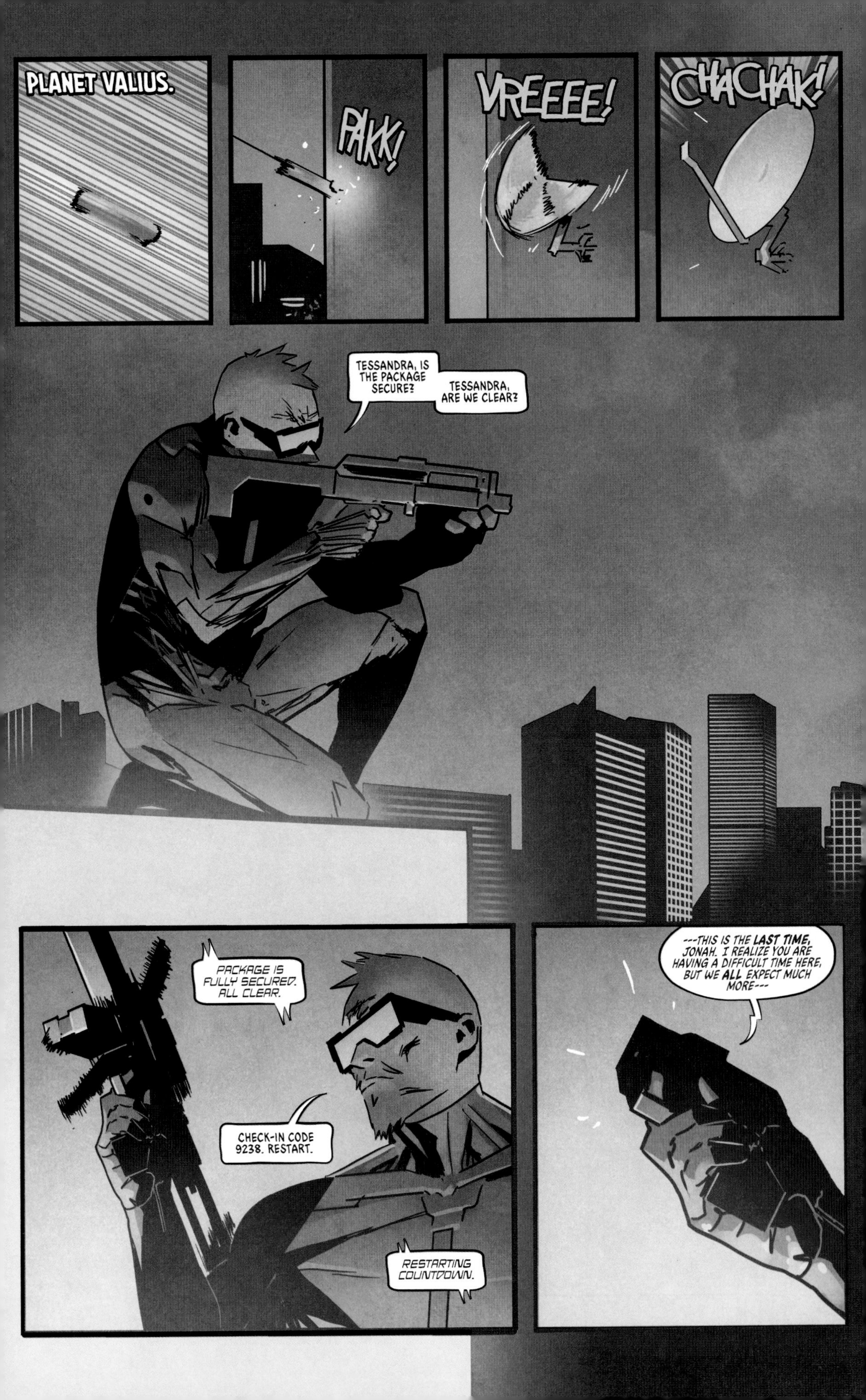
PLANET VALIUS.
PAKK!
VREEEE!
CHACHAK!
TESSANDRA, IS THE PACKAGE SECURE?
TESSANDRA, ARE WE CLEAR?
PACKAGE IS FULLY SECURED. ALL CLEAR.
CHECK-IN CODE 9238. RESTART.
RESTARTING COUNTDOWN.
---THIS IS THE **LAST TIME,** JONAH. I REALIZE YOU ARE HAVING A DIFFICULT TIME HERE, BUT WE **ALL** EXPECT MUCH MORE---

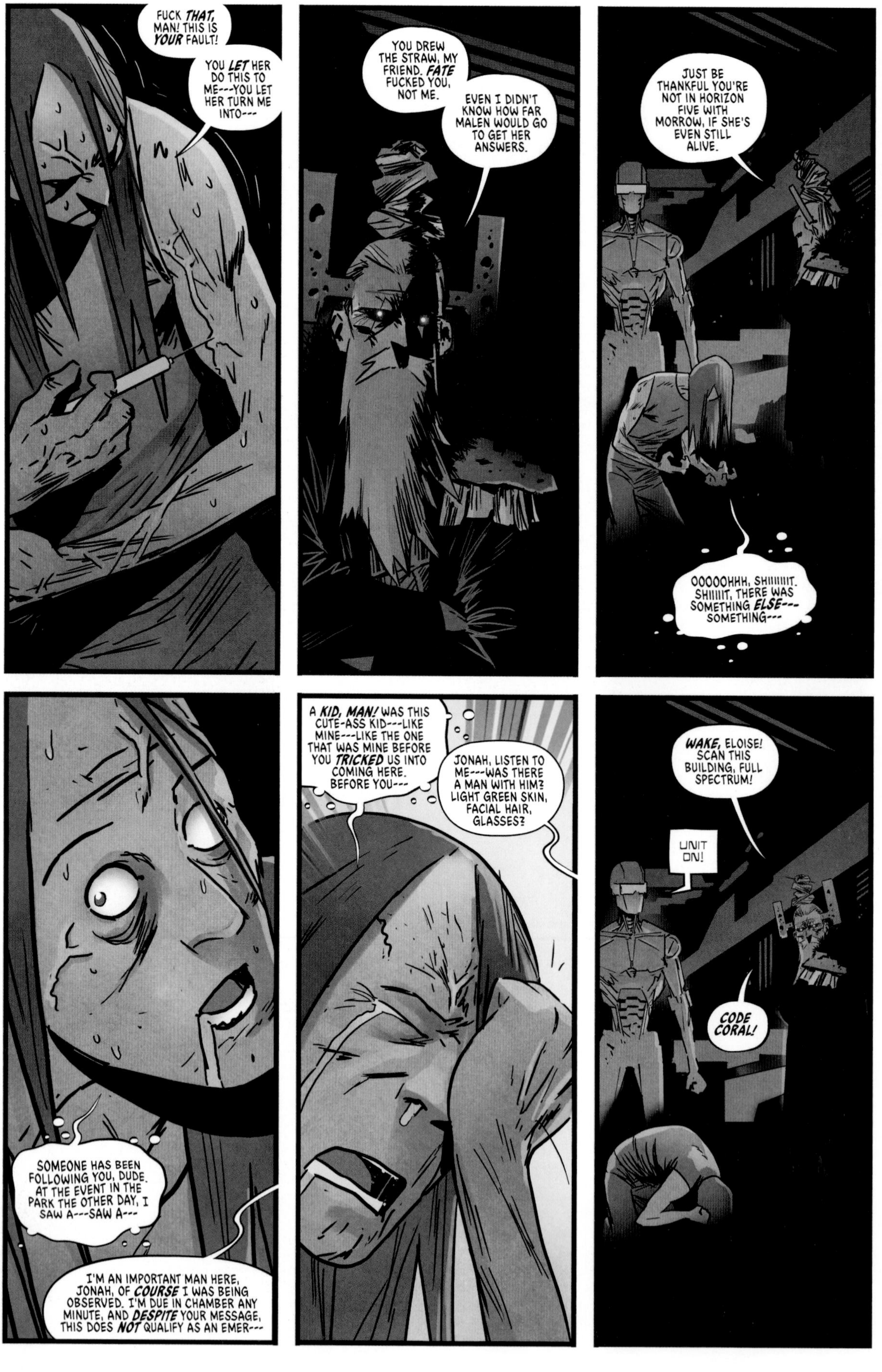
FUCK THAT, MAN! THIS IS YOUR FAULT!
YOU LET HER DO THIS TO ME---YOU LET HER TURN ME INTO---
YOU DREW THE STRAW, MY FRIEND. FATE FUCKED YOU, NOT ME.
EVEN I DIDN'T KNOW HOW FAR MALEN WOULD GO TO GET HER ANSWERS.
JUST BE THANKFUL YOU'RE NOT IN HORIZON FIVE WITH MORROW, IF SHE'S EVEN STILL ALIVE.
OOOOOHHH, SHIIIIIIT. SHIIIIIT, THERE WAS SOMETHING ELSE--- SOMETHING---
SOMEONE HAS BEEN FOLLOWING YOU, DUDE. AT THE EVENT IN THE PARK THE OTHER DAY, I SAW A---SAW A---
I'M AN IMPORTANT MAN HERE, JONAH, OF COURSE I WAS BEING OBSERVED. I'M DUE IN CHAMBER ANY MINUTE, AND DESPITE YOUR MESSAGE, THIS DOES NOT QUALIFY AS AN EMER---
A KID, MAN! WAS THIS CUTE-ASS KID---LIKE MINE---LIKE THE ONE THAT WAS MINE BEFORE YOU TRICKED US INTO COMING HERE. BEFORE YOU---
JONAH, LISTEN TO ME---WAS THERE A MAN WITH HIM? LIGHT GREEN SKIN, FACIAL HAIR, GLASSES?
WAKE, ELOISE! SCAN THIS BUILDING, FULL SPECTRUM!
UNIT ON!
CODE CORAL!

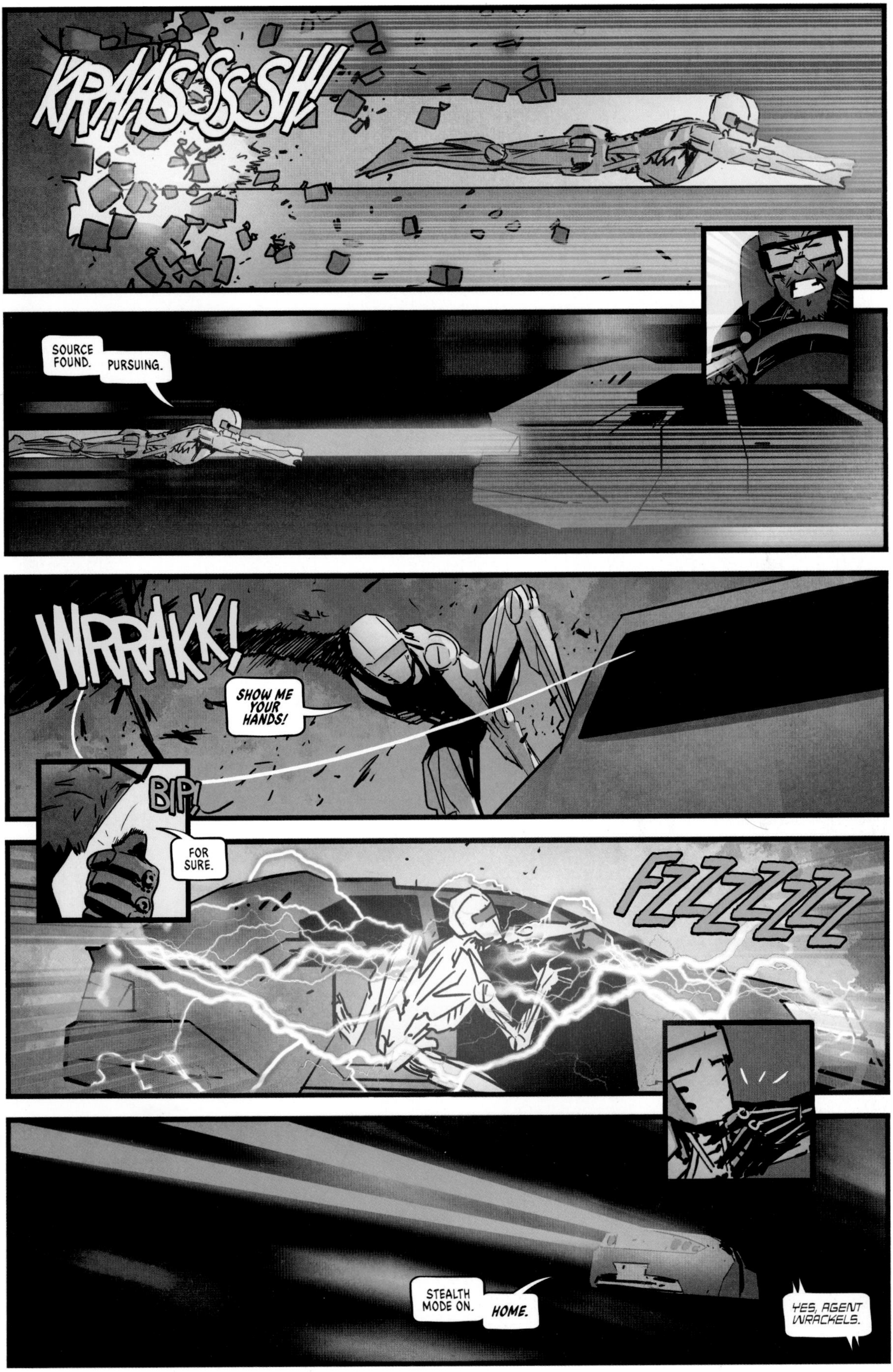
KRAASSSSH!
SOURCE FOUND.
PURSUING.
WRRAKK!
SHOW ME YOUR HANDS!
BIP!
FOR SURE.
FZZZZZZZ
STEALTH MODE ON.
HOME.
YES, AGENT WRACKELS.

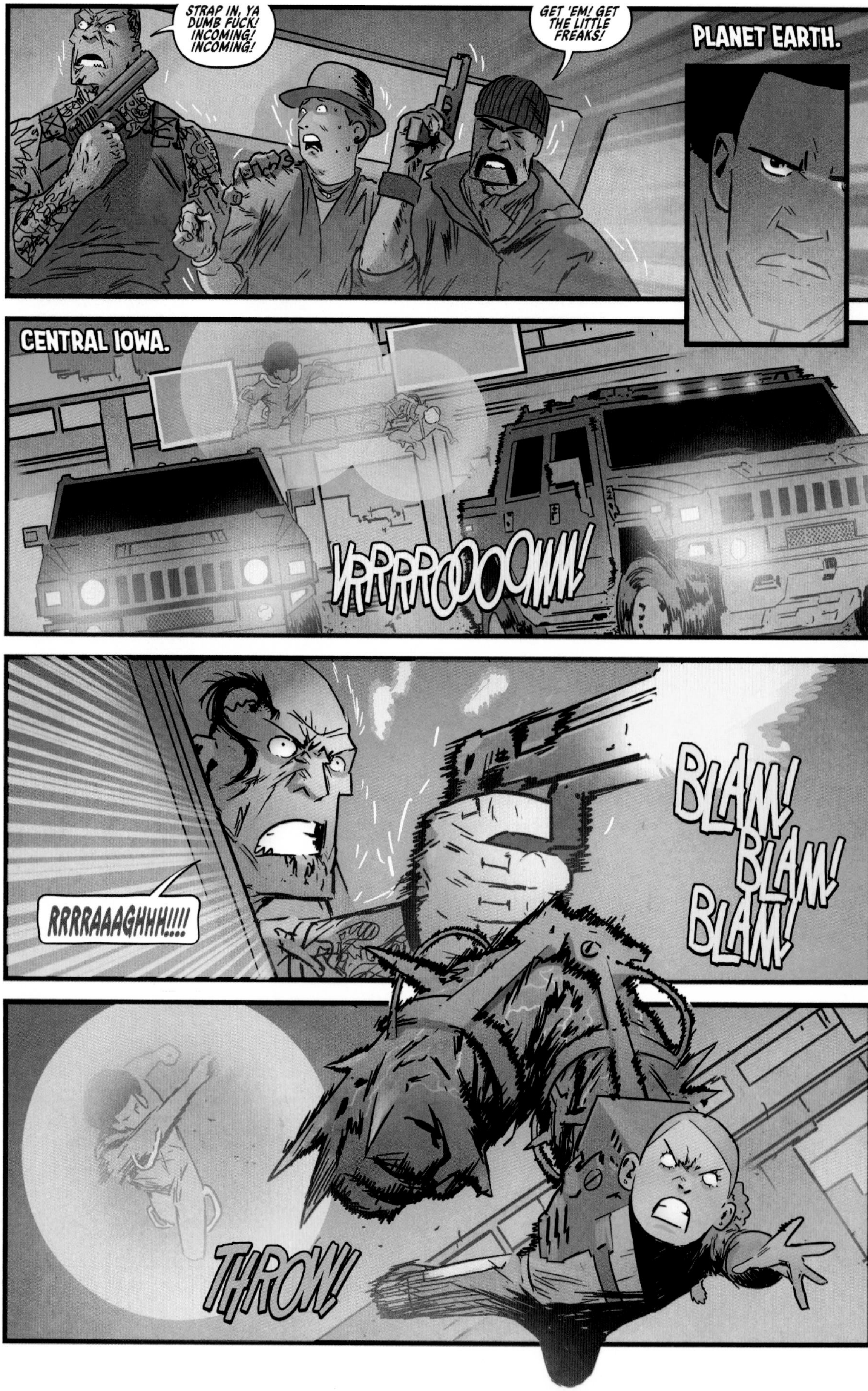
STRAP IN, YA DUMB FUCK! INCOMING! INCOMING!
GET 'EM! GET THE LITTLE FREAKS!
PLANET EARTH.
CENTRAL IOWA.
VRRRRROOOOMM!
BLAM! BLAM! BLAM!
RRRRAAAGHHH!!!!
THROW!

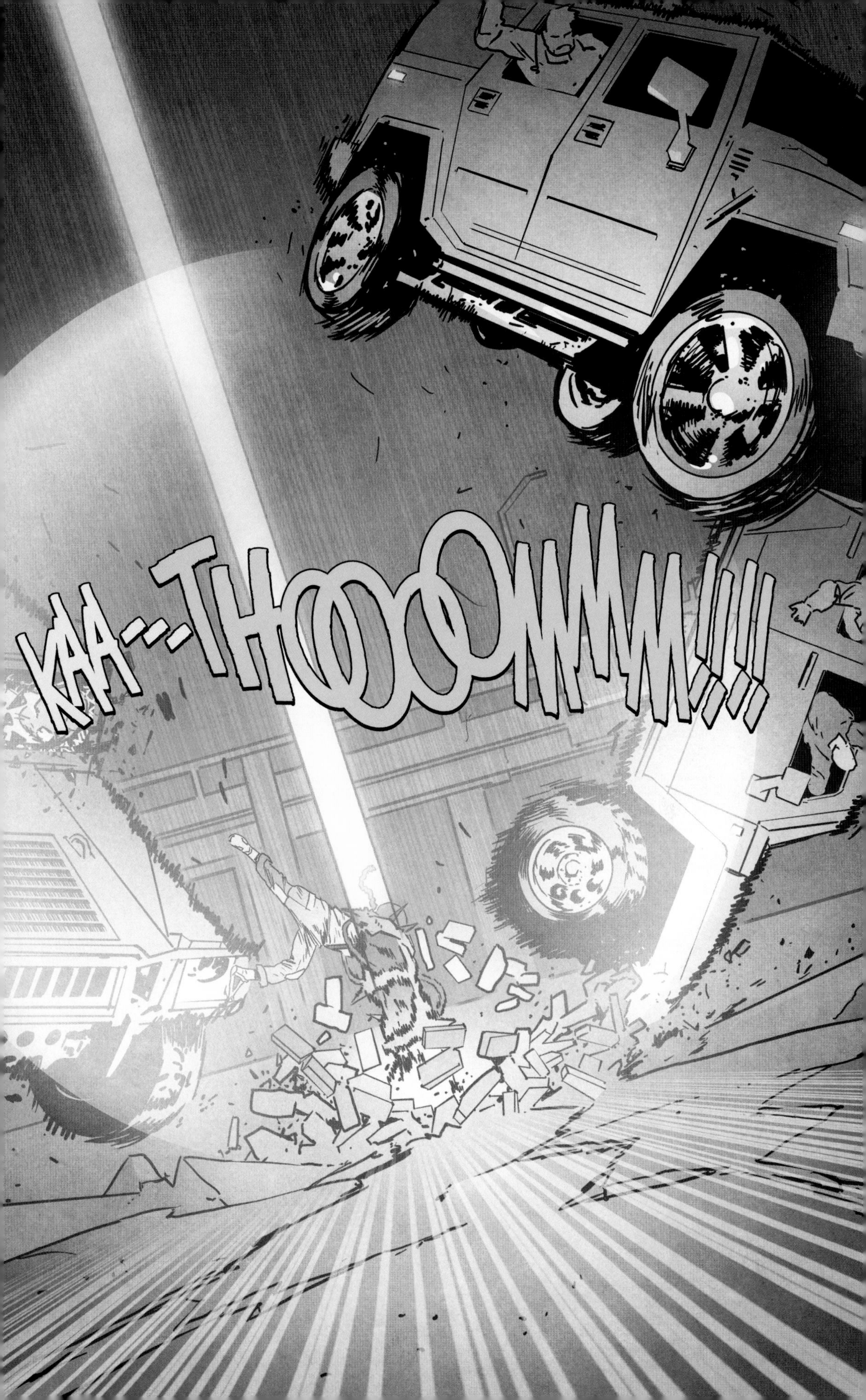
KAA--THOOOOMMM!!!!

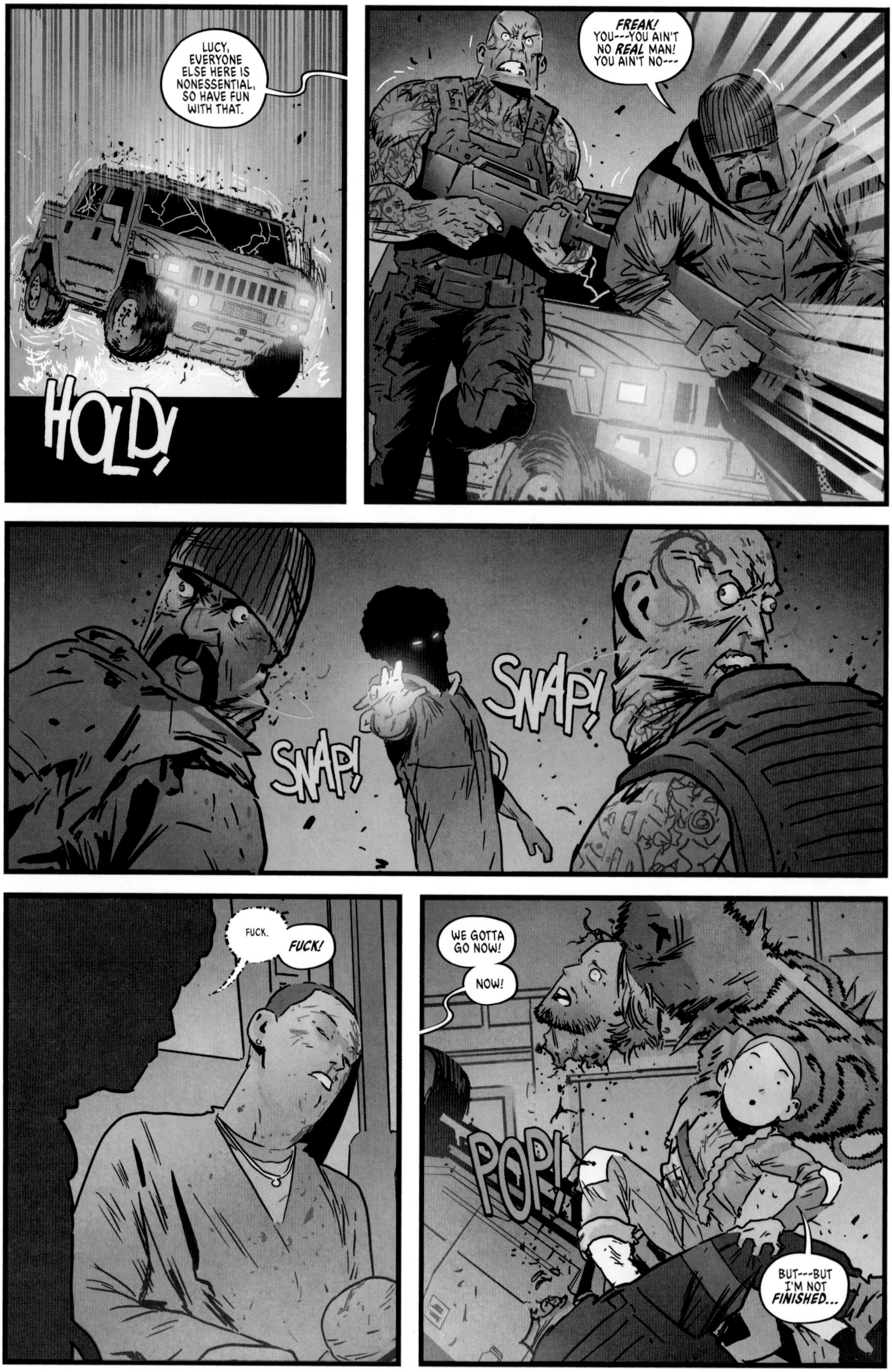

LUCY, EVERYONE ELSE HERE IS NONESSENTIAL, SO HAVE FUN WITH THAT.
HOLD!
FREAK! YOU---YOU AIN'T NO REAL MAN! YOU AIN'T NO---
SNAP!
SNAP!
FUCK.
FUCK!
WE GOTTA GO NOW!
NOW!
POP!
BUT---BUT I'M NOT FINISHED...

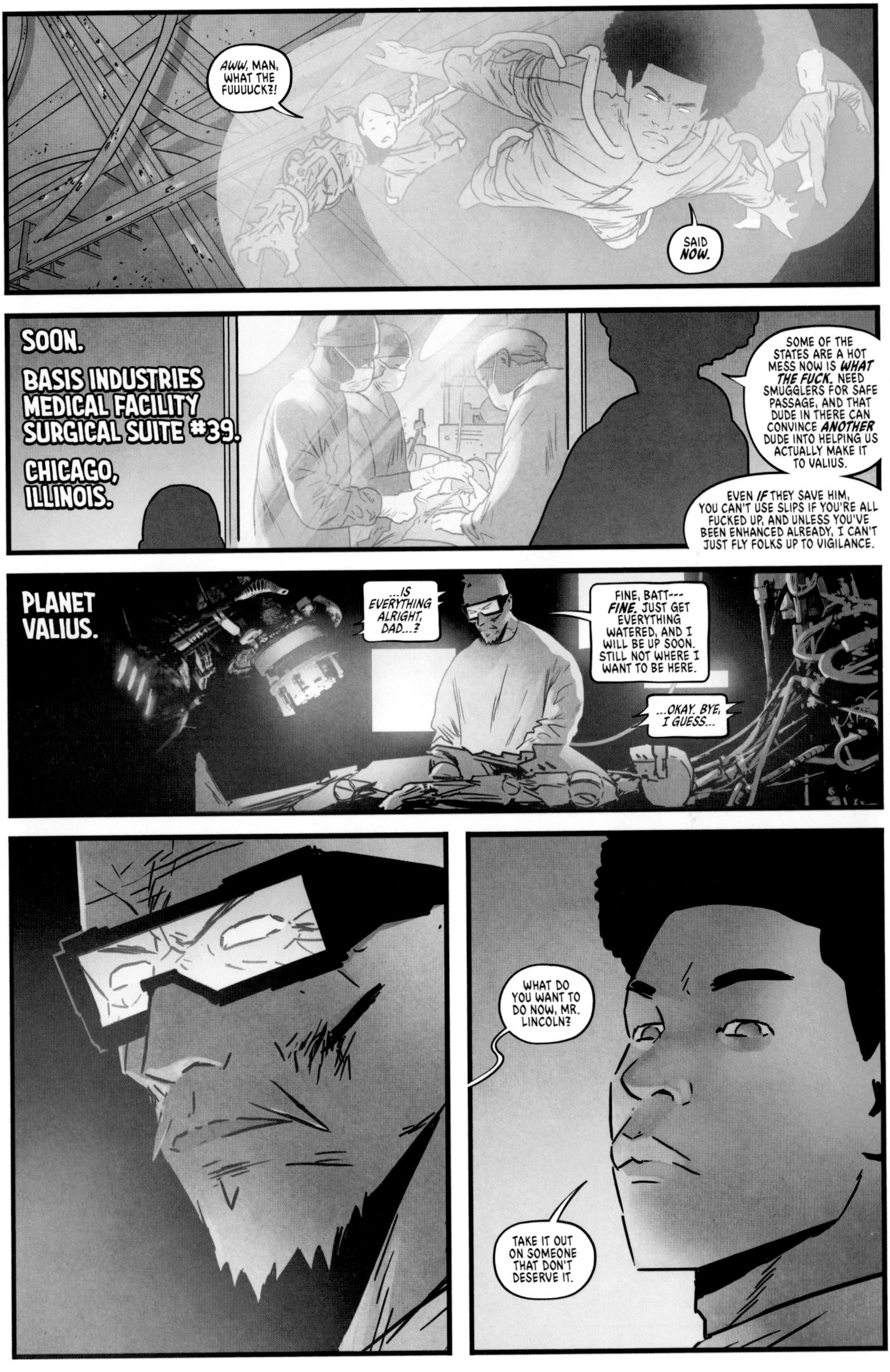
AWW, MAN, WHAT THE FUUUUCK?!
SAID NOW.
SOON.
BASIS INDUSTRIES MEDICAL FACILITY SURGICAL SUITE #39.
CHICAGO, ILLINOIS.
SOME OF THE STATES ARE A HOT MESS NOW IS WHAT THE FUCK. NEED SMUGGLERS FOR SAFE PASSAGE, AND THAT DUDE IN THERE CAN CONVINCE ANOTHER DUDE INTO HELPING US ACTUALLY MAKE IT TO VALIUS.
EVEN IF THEY SAVE HIM, YOU CAN'T USE SLIPS IF YOU'RE ALL FUCKED UP, AND UNLESS YOU'VE BEEN ENHANCED ALREADY, I CAN'T JUST FLY FOLKS UP TO VIGILANCE.
PLANET VALIUS.
...IS EVERYTHING ALRIGHT, DAD...?
FINE, BATT--- FINE. JUST GET EVERYTHING WATERED, AND I WILL BE UP SOON. STILL NOT WHERE I WANT TO BE HERE.
...OKAY. BYE, I GUESS...
WHAT DO YOU WANT TO DO NOW, MR. LINCOLN?
TAKE IT OUT ON SOMEONE THAT DON'T DESERVE IT.

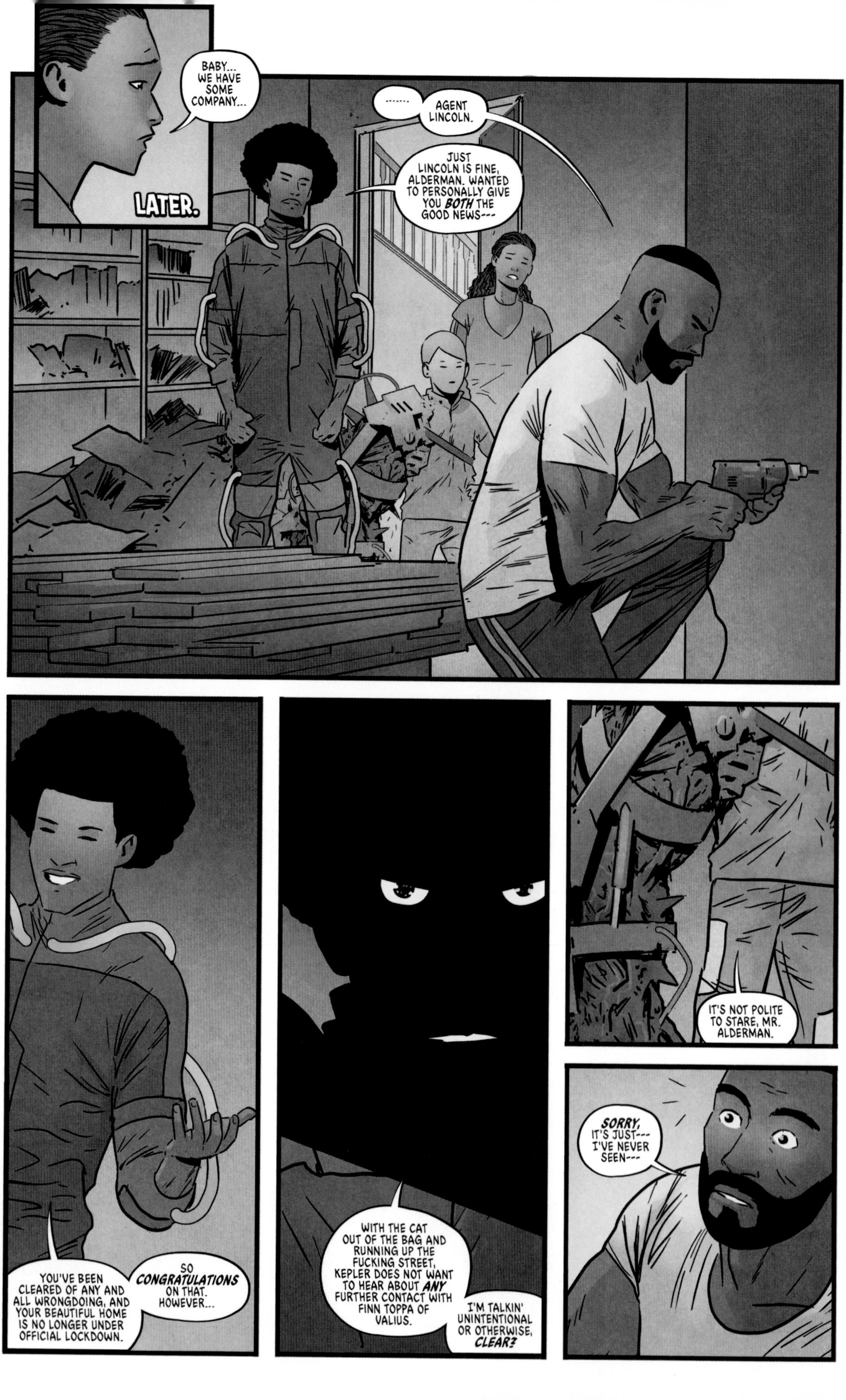
BABY... WE HAVE SOME COMPANY...
LATER.
....
AGENT LINCOLN.
JUST LINCOLN IS FINE, ALDERMAN. WANTED TO PERSONALLY GIVE YOU BOTH THE GOOD NEWS---
YOU'VE BEEN CLEARED OF ANY AND ALL WRONGDOING, AND YOUR BEAUTIFUL HOME IS NO LONGER UNDER OFFICIAL LOCKDOWN.
SO CONGRATULATIONS ON THAT. HOWEVER...
WITH THE CAT OUT OF THE BAG AND RUNNING UP THE FUCKING STREET, KEPLER DOES NOT WANT TO HEAR ABOUT ANY FURTHER CONTACT WITH FINN TOPPA OF VALIUS.
I'M TALKIN' UNINTENTIONAL OR OTHERWISE, CLEAR?
IT'S NOT POLITE TO STARE, MR. ALDERMAN.
SORRY, IT'S JUST--- I'VE NEVER SEEN---

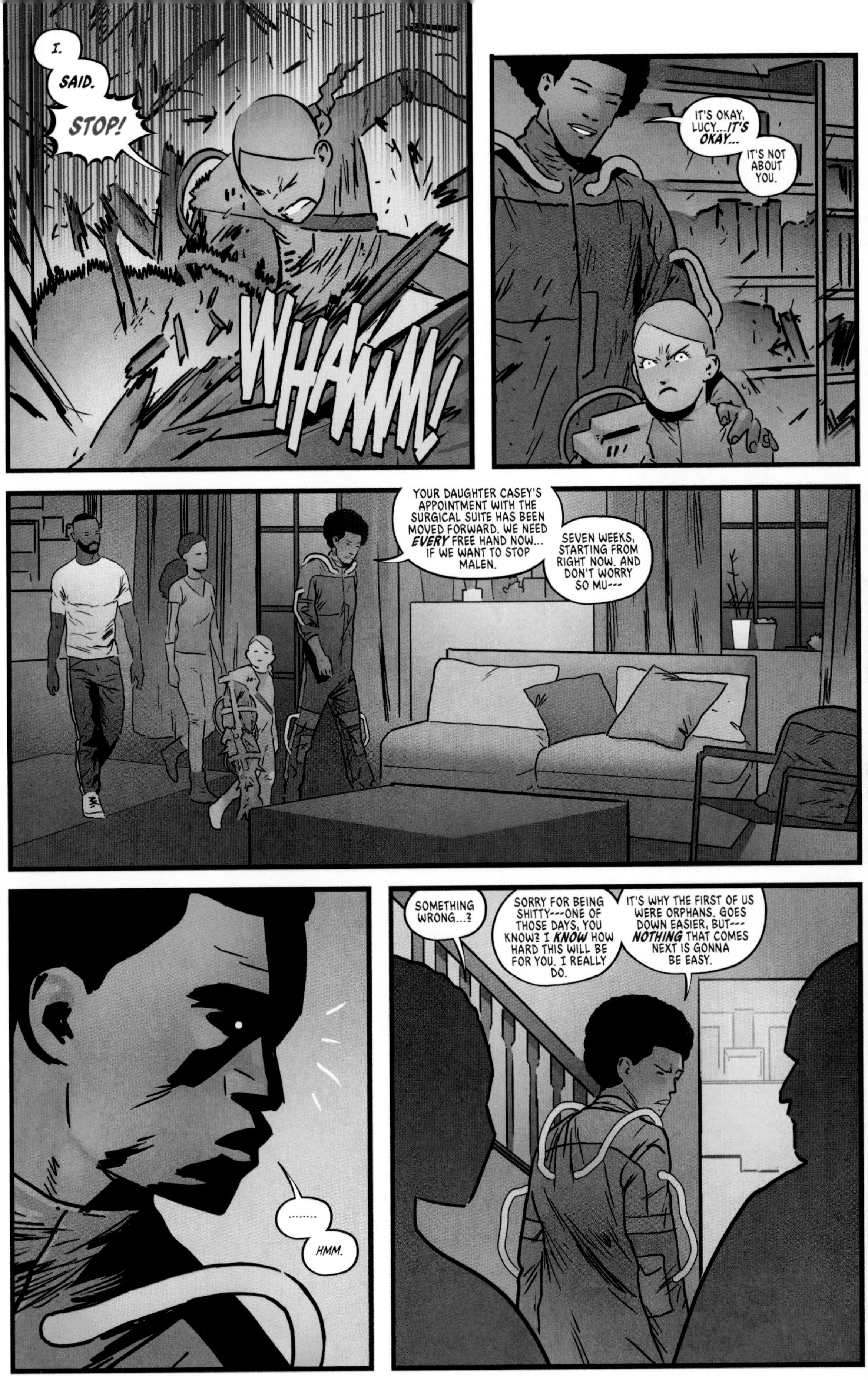
I.
SAID.
STOP!
WHAMM!
IT'S OKAY, LUCY... IT'S OKAY...
IT'S NOT ABOUT YOU.
YOUR DAUGHTER CASEY'S APPOINTMENT WITH THE SURGICAL SUITE HAS BEEN MOVED FORWARD. WE NEED EVERY FREE HAND NOW... IF WE WANT TO STOP MALEN.
SEVEN WEEKS, STARTING FROM RIGHT NOW. AND DON'T WORRY SO MU---
....
HMM.
SOMETHING WRONG...?
SORRY FOR BEING SHITTY---ONE OF THOSE DAYS, YOU KNOW? I KNOW HOW HARD THIS WILL BE FOR YOU. I REALLY DO.
IT'S WHY THE FIRST OF US WERE ORPHANS. GOES DOWN EASIER, BUT--- NOTHING THAT COMES NEXT IS GONNA BE EASY.

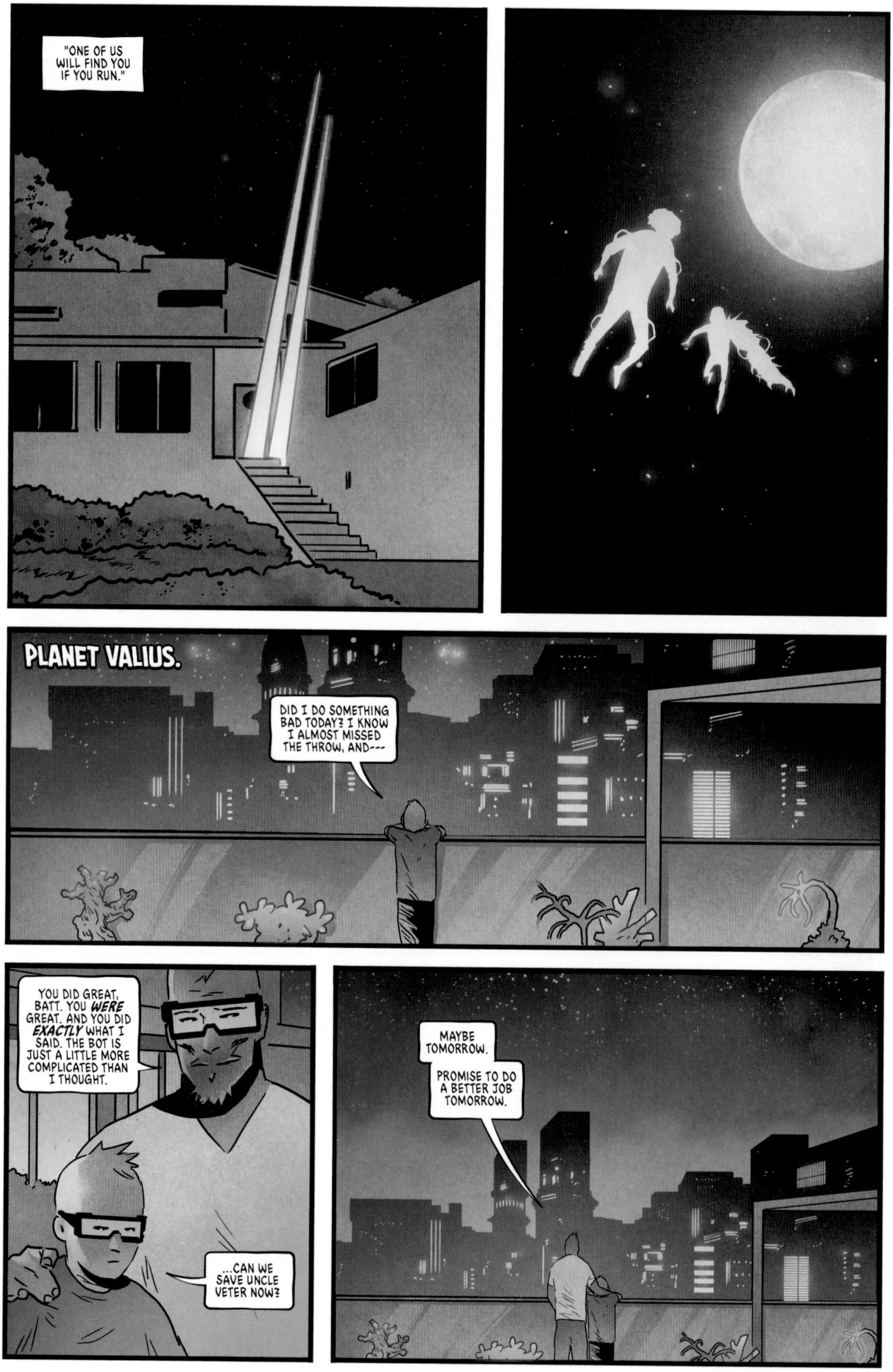
"ONE OF US WILL FIND YOU IF YOU RUN."
PLANET VALIUS.
DID I DO SOMETHING BAD TODAY? I KNOW I ALMOST MISSED THE THROW, AND---
YOU DID GREAT, BATT. YOU *WERE* GREAT. AND YOU DID ***EXACTLY*** WHAT I SAID. THE BOT IS JUST A LITTLE MORE COMPLICATED THAN I THOUGHT.
...CAN WE SAVE UNCLE VETER NOW?
MAYBE TOMORROW.
PROMISE TO DO A BETTER JOB TOMORROW.

WE NEVER KNOW WHEN WE MIGHT NEED ANOTHER EXTRA PIECE, AND---WELL, THERE ARE SOME *OTHER* REASONS, TOO.

NO EYE CONTACT UNLESS I SAY SO.

THIS ONE IS OKAY TO LOOK AT...POWER SET IS ENHANCED STRENGTH, AGILITY, SENSES---LAYS EGGS, TOO, BUT WE PUT A STOP TO ALL THAT.

LIKE I SAID, THOUGH...MAYBE ONE DAY WE CHANGE OUR MINDS.

JUST TELEKINESIS AND SOME OTHER SMALL THINGS, SO YOU'RE COOL HERE, TOO.

THIS IS MY GUY, AND I'LL ALWAYS OWE HIM IN A REAL, REAL WAY. COMING UP RIGHT HERE THOUGH---

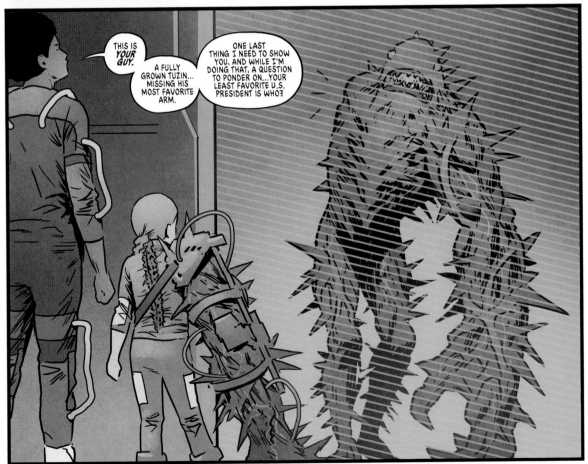

THIS IS *YOUR GUY.*

A FULLY GROWN TUZIN... MISSING HIS MOST FAVORITE ARM.

ONE LAST THING I NEED TO SHOW YOU, AND WHILE I'M DOING THAT, A QUESTION TO PONDER ON...YOUR LEAST FAVORITE U.S. PRESIDENT IS WHO?

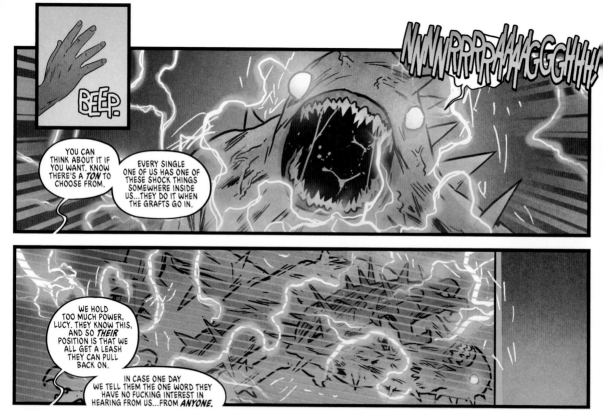

BEEP.

NNNNRRRRAAAAGGGHHH!

YOU CAN THINK ABOUT IT IF YOU WANT. KNOW THERE'S A *TON* TO CHOOSE FROM.

EVERY SINGLE ONE OF US HAS ONE OF THESE SHOCK THINGS SOMEWHERE INSIDE US...THEY DO IT WHEN THE GRAFTS GO IN.

WE HOLD TOO MUCH POWER, LUCY. THEY KNOW THIS, AND SO *THEIR* POSITION IS THAT WE ALL GET A LEASH THEY CAN PULL BACK ON.

IN CASE ONE DAY WE TELL THEM THE ONE WORD THEY HAVE NO FUCKING INTEREST IN HEARING FROM US...FROM *ANYONE.*

NNNNRRRRAAAA--

ENOUGH.

THAT'S WHAT KEPLER IS. NOT FUCKING PEOPLE UP AND THEN LAUGHING ABOUT IT.

I'LL TELL YOUR DAD YOU'RE READY TO HEAD ON HOME, AND FOR THE RECORD---DON'T YOU EVER IN YOUR LIFE DISOBEY AN ORDER FROM ME AGAIN.

SEE YOU SOON, KID.

THIS LAST THING YOU CAN'T BE NO PART OF.

AAAAAAAAOOOOOHH!!!!
AAAAAAAAAHH---
HHHHH...
VNNN--VNNN--VNNN--
LEAVE IT, LINCOLN... LEEEEAVE ITTT---
VNNN--VNNN--VNNN--
MIGHT BE IMPORTANT. JUST BREATHE.
HMMM.
WHAT IS IT...?

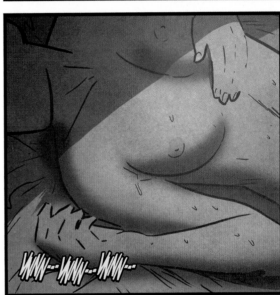

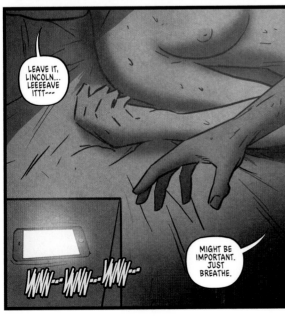

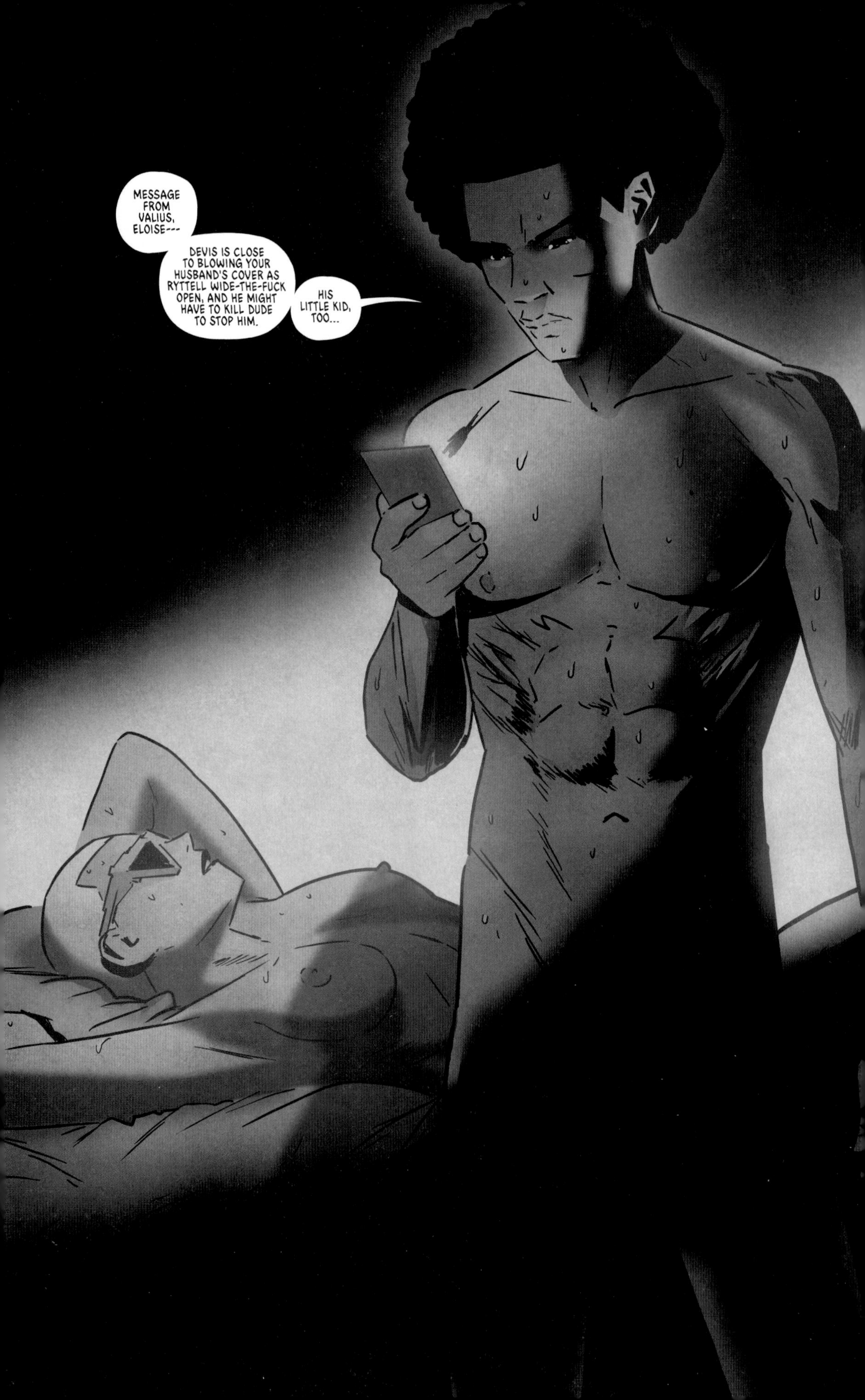
MESSAGE FROM VALIUS, ELOISE---
DEVIS IS CLOSE TO BLOWING YOUR HUSBAND'S COVER AS RYTTELL WIDE-THE-FUCK OPEN, AND HE MIGHT HAVE TO KILL DUDE TO STOP HIM.
HIS LITTLE KID, TOO...

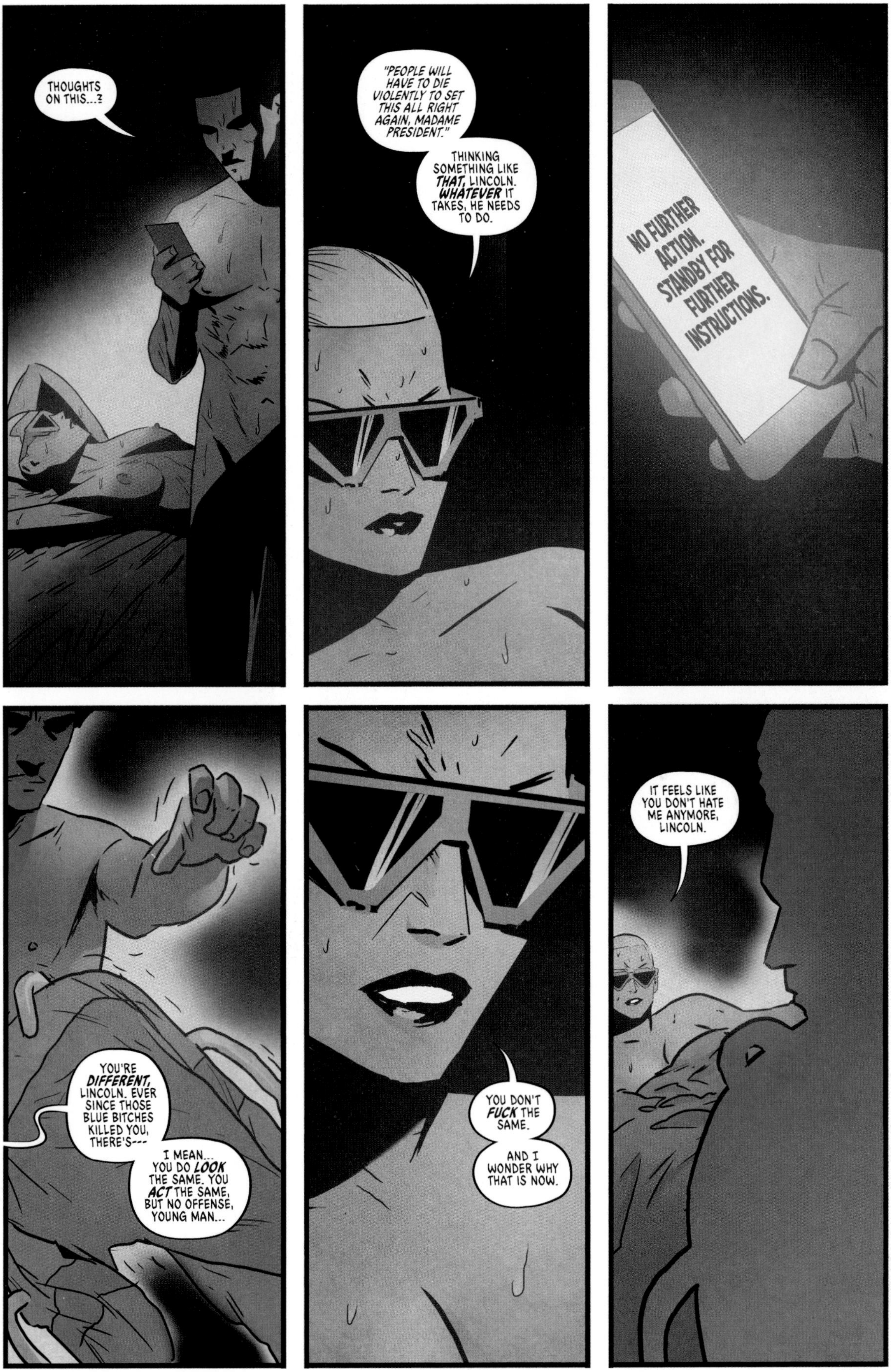
THOUGHTS ON THIS...?
"PEOPLE WILL HAVE TO DIE VIOLENTLY TO SET THIS ALL RIGHT AGAIN, MADAME PRESIDENT."
THINKING SOMETHING LIKE THAT, LINCOLN. WHATEVER IT TAKES, HE NEEDS TO DO.
NO FURTHER ACTION. STANDBY FOR FURTHER INSTRUCTIONS.
YOU'RE DIFFERENT, LINCOLN. EVER SINCE THOSE BLUE BITCHES KILLED YOU, THERE'S---
I MEAN... YOU DO LOOK THE SAME. YOU ACT THE SAME, BUT NO OFFENSE, YOUNG MAN...
YOU DON'T FUCK THE SAME.
AND I WONDER WHY THAT IS NOW.
IT FEELS LIKE YOU DON'T HATE ME ANYMORE, LINCOLN.

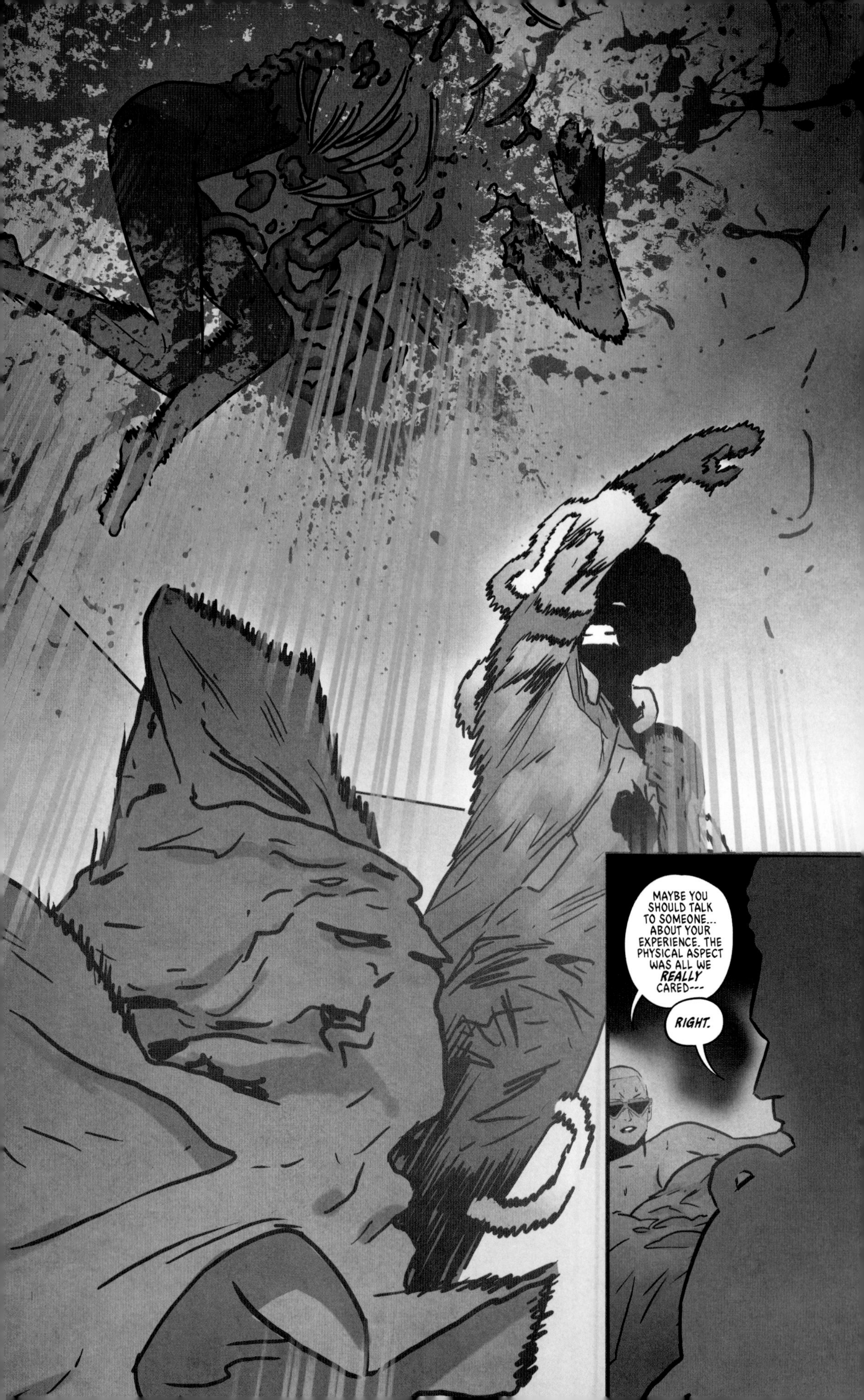
MAYBE YOU SHOULD TALK TO SOMEONE... ABOUT YOUR EXPERIENCE. THE PHYSICAL ASPECT WAS ALL WE *REALLY* CARED---
RIGHT.

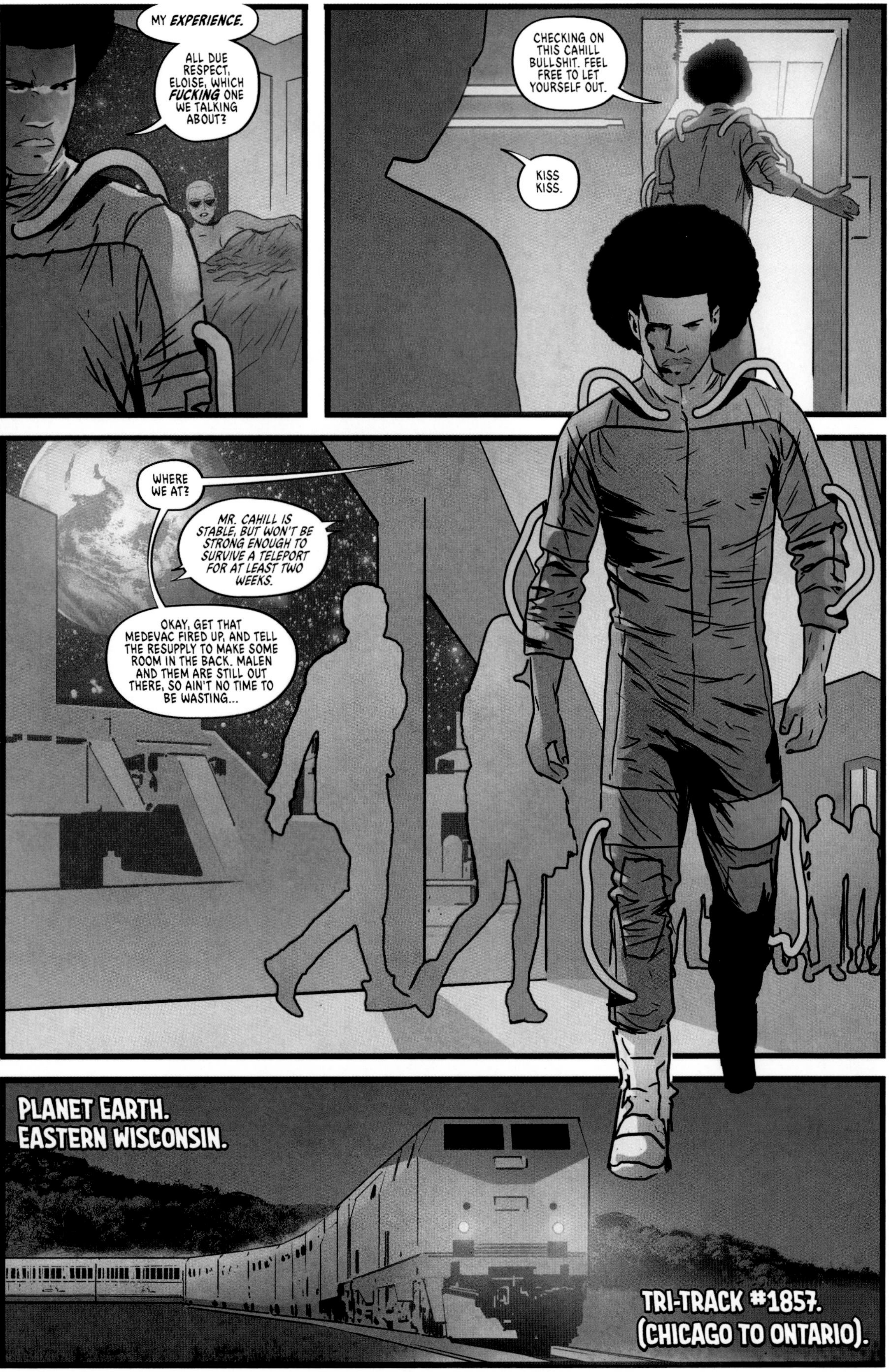
MY EXPERIENCE.
ALL DUE RESPECT, ELOISE, WHICH FUCKING ONE WE TALKING ABOUT?
CHECKING ON THIS CAHILL BULLSHIT. FEEL FREE TO LET YOURSELF OUT.
KISS KISS.
WHERE WE AT?
MR. CAHILL IS STABLE, BUT WON'T BE STRONG ENOUGH TO SURVIVE A TELEPORT FOR AT LEAST TWO WEEKS.
OKAY, GET THAT MEDEVAC FIRED UP, AND TELL THE RESUPPLY TO MAKE SOME ROOM IN THE BACK. MALEN AND THEM ARE STILL OUT THERE, SO AIN'T NO TIME TO BE WASTING...
PLANET EARTH. EASTERN WISCONSIN.
TRI-TRACK #1857. (CHICAGO TO ONTARIO).

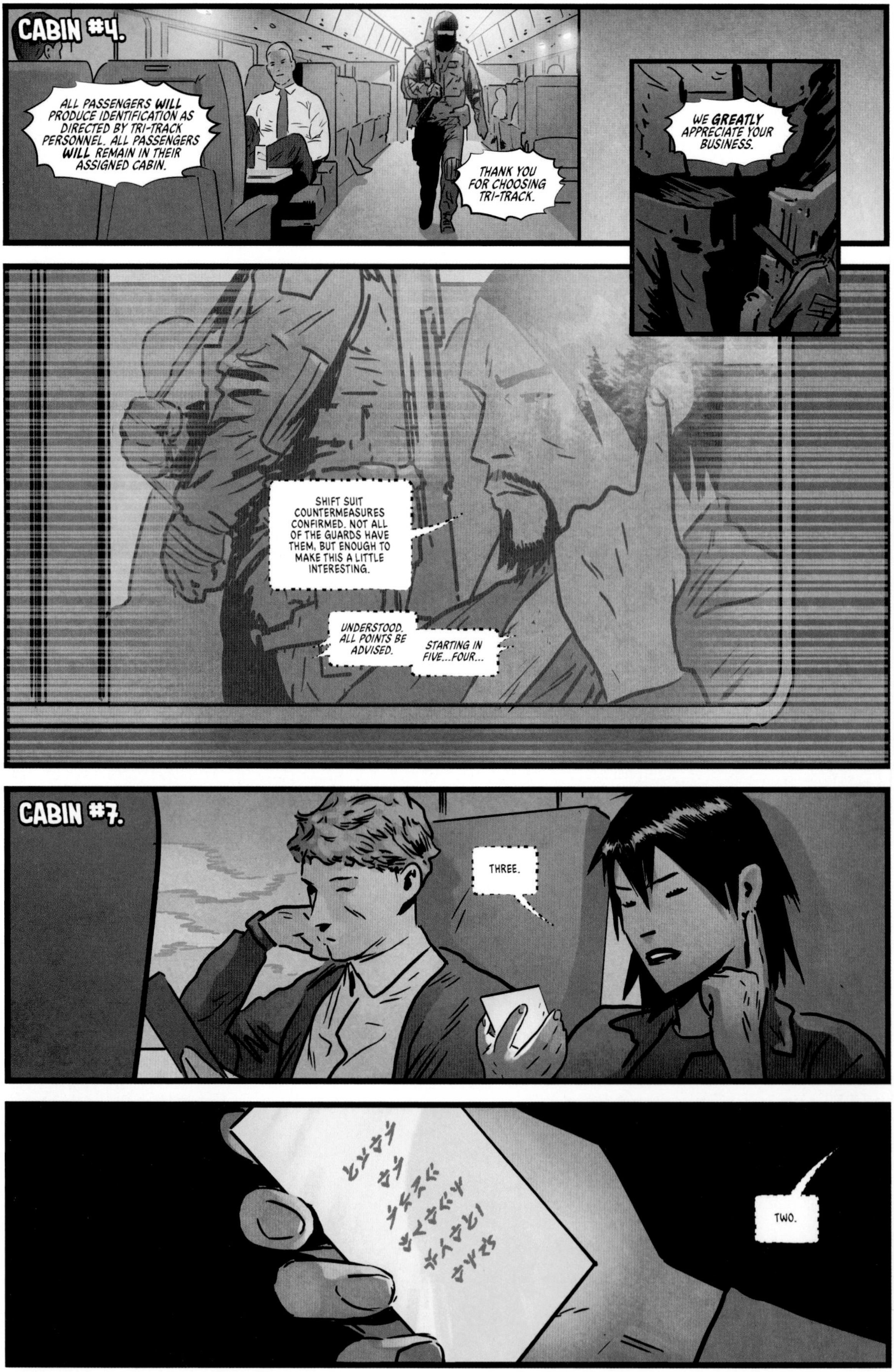
CABIN #4.
ALL PASSENGERS WILL PRODUCE IDENTIFICATION AS DIRECTED BY TRI-TRACK PERSONNEL. ALL PASSENGERS WILL REMAIN IN THEIR ASSIGNED CABIN.
THANK YOU FOR CHOOSING TRI-TRACK.
WE GREATLY APPRECIATE YOUR BUSINESS.
SHIFT SUIT COUNTERMEASURES CONFIRMED. NOT ALL OF THE GUARDS HAVE THEM, BUT ENOUGH TO MAKE THIS A LITTLE INTERESTING.
UNDERSTOOD. ALL POINTS BE ADVISED.
STARTING IN FIVE...FOUR...
CABIN #7.
THREE.
TWO.

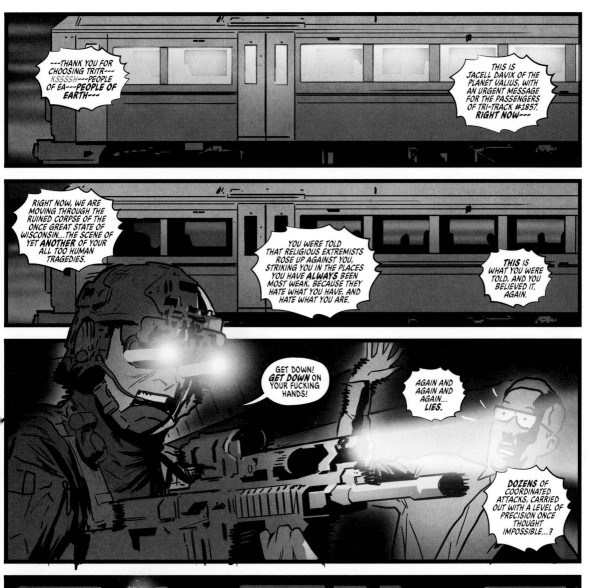

---THANK YOU FOR CHOOSING TRITR--- KSSSSH---PEOPLE OF EA---**PEOPLE OF EARTH**---

THIS IS JACELL DAVIX OF THE PLANET VALIUS, WITH AN URGENT MESSAGE FOR THE PASSENGERS OF TRI-TRACK #1857. **RIGHT NOW**---

RIGHT NOW, WE ARE MOVING THROUGH THE RUINED CORPSE OF THE ONCE GREAT STATE OF WISCONSIN...THE SCENE OF YET **ANOTHER** OF YOUR ALL TOO HUMAN TRAGEDIES.

YOU WERE TOLD THAT RELIGIOUS EXTREMISTS ROSE UP AGAINST YOU, STRIKING YOU IN THE PLACES YOU HAVE **ALWAYS** BEEN MOST WEAK, BECAUSE THEY HATE WHAT YOU HAVE, AND HATE WHAT YOU ARE.

THIS IS WHAT YOU WERE TOLD, AND YOU BELIEVED IT. AGAIN.

GET DOWN! **GET DOWN** ON YOUR FUCKING HANDS!

AGAIN AND AGAIN AND AGAIN... **LIES.**

DOZENS OF COORDINATED ATTACKS, CARRIED OUT WITH A LEVEL OF PRECISION ONCE THOUGHT IMPOSSIBLE...?

THINK. THINK FOR ONE MOMENT IN YOUR WASTED LIVES.

YOU **KNOW** WHO IS RESPONSIBLE. YOU HAVE **ALWAYS** KNOWN.

AS THOSE SO-CALLED INNOCENTS DIED THEIR HORRIBLE AND UNNECESSARY DEATHS--- WHAT WAS KEPLER DOING THEN?

ALL POINTS--- FREE TO ESCALATE.

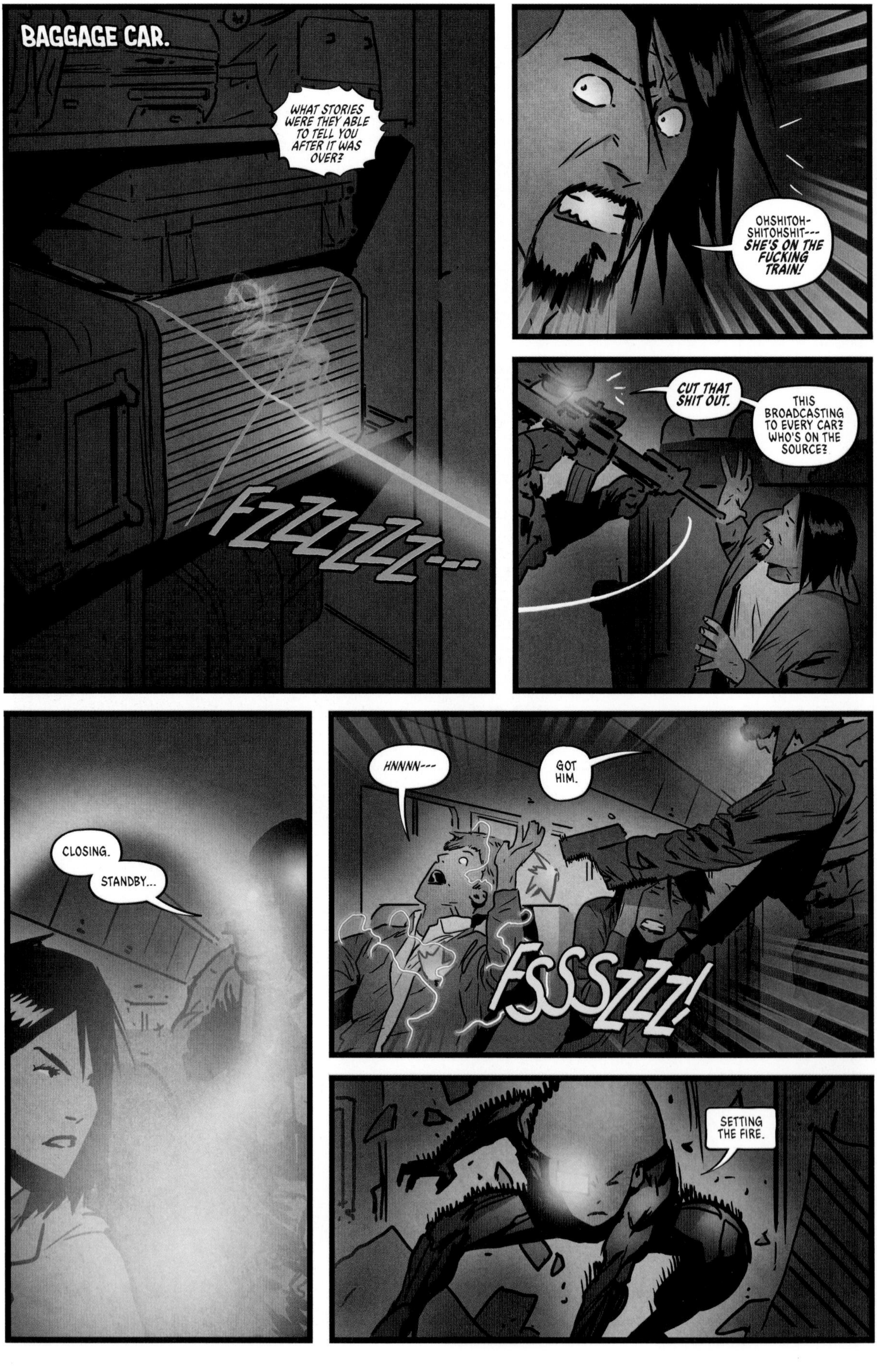
BAGGAGE CAR.
WHAT STORIES WERE THEY ABLE TO TELL YOU AFTER IT WAS OVER?
FZZZZZZ---
OHSHITOH-SHITOHSHIT--- SHE'S ON THE FUCKING TRAIN!
CUT THAT SHIT OUT.
THIS BROADCASTING TO EVERY CAR? WHO'S ON THE SOURCE?
CLOSING.
STANDBY...
HNNNN---
GOT HIM.
FSSSZZZ!
SETTING THE FIRE.

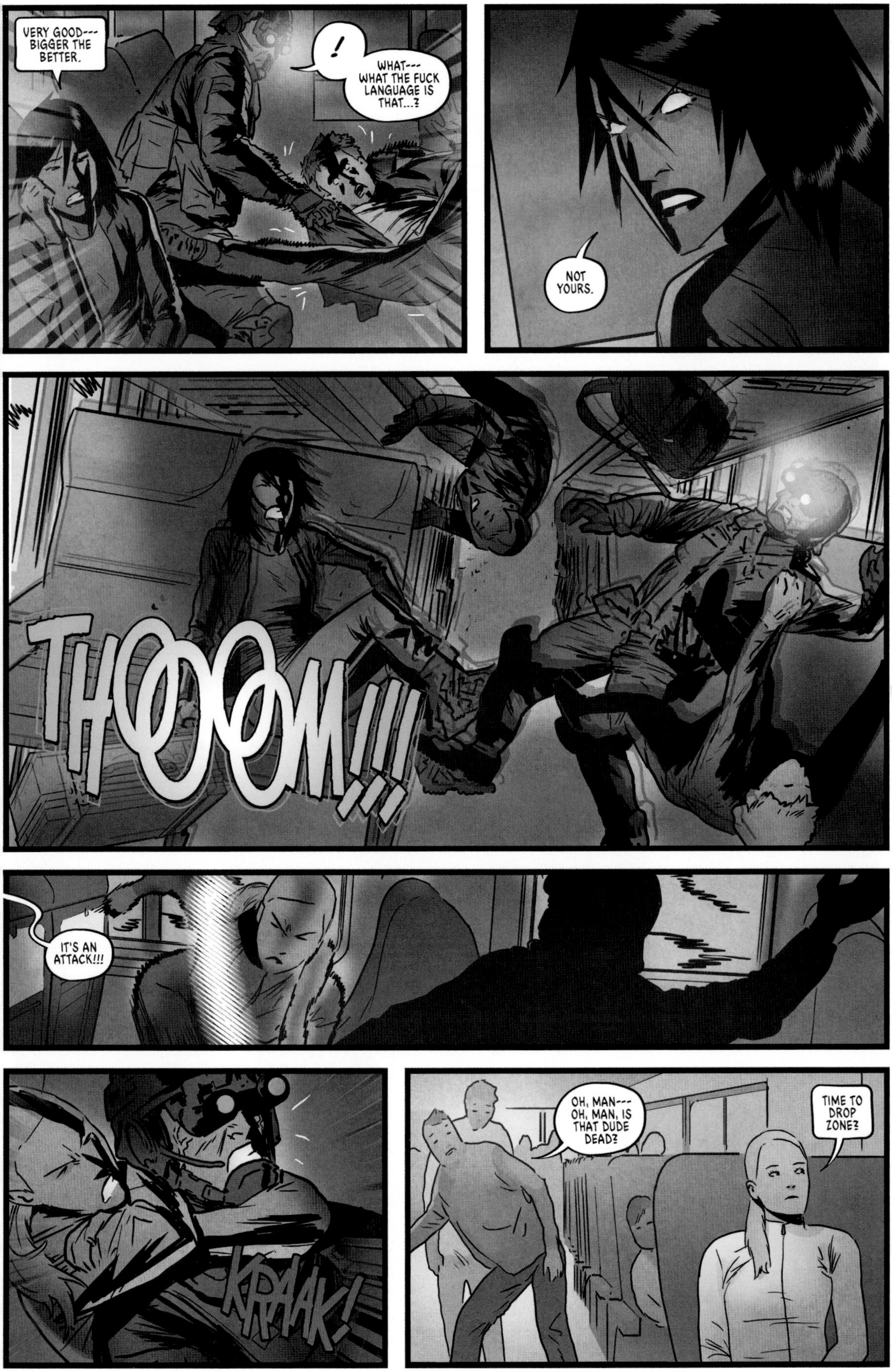
VERY GOOD---
BIGGER THE
BETTER.
!
WHAT---
WHAT THE FUCK
LANGUAGE IS
THAT...?
NOT
YOURS.
THOOOM!!!
IT'S AN
ATTACK!!!
KRAAK!
OH, MAN---
OH, MAN, IS
THAT DUDE
DEAD?
TIME TO
DROP
ZONE?

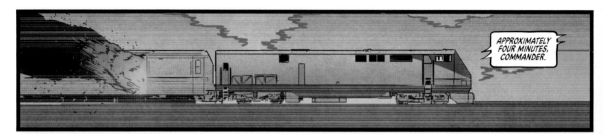

APPROXIMATELY FOUR MINUTES, COMMANDER.

IF THEY DIVERT COURSE.

HOLD THAT THOUGHT, MADAME COZA---

---MOVING IN THE RIGHT DIRECTION THERE.

NO, I *CAN'T* REACH RENDELL, AND *YES* I KNOW WE'RE ON *FIRE.* I DON'T CARE *WHAT* THE PROTOCOL SAYS, GIVE US A FEW MORE MINUTES TO LOCK IT---

THAT'S A *MISTAKE,* MAN---YOU'VE GOTTA GIVE US MORE---

CONDUCTOR'S CABIN.

RE-ROUTING NOW...

KA-CHUKK!

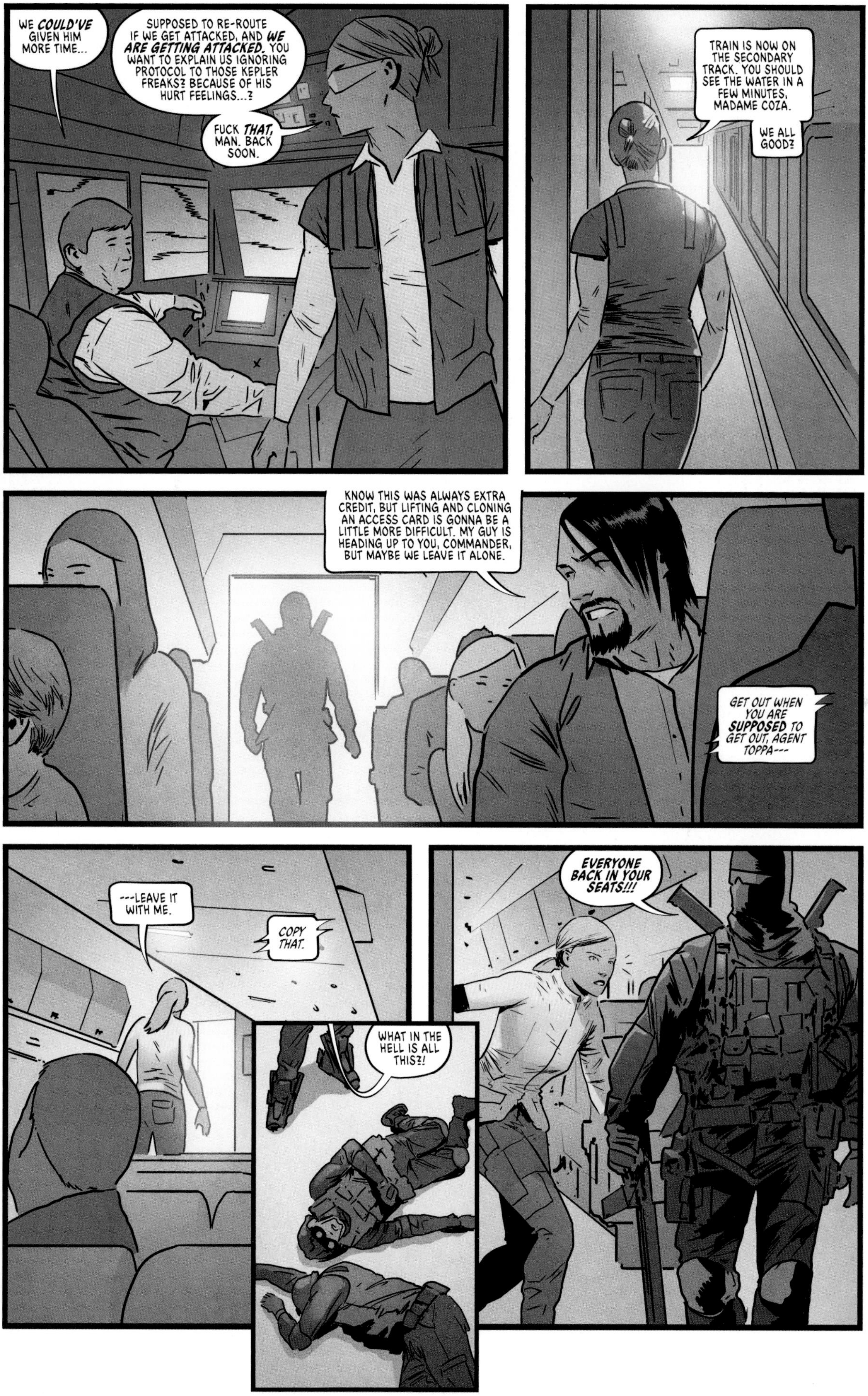
WE COULD'VE GIVEN HIM MORE TIME...
SUPPOSED TO RE-ROUTE IF WE GET ATTACKED, AND WE ARE GETTING ATTACKED. YOU WANT TO EXPLAIN US IGNORING PROTOCOL TO THOSE KEPLER FREAKS? BECAUSE OF HIS HURT FEELINGS...?
FUCK THAT, MAN. BACK SOON.
TRAIN IS NOW ON THE SECONDARY TRACK. YOU SHOULD SEE THE WATER IN A FEW MINUTES, MADAME COZA.
WE ALL GOOD?
KNOW THIS WAS ALWAYS EXTRA CREDIT, BUT LIFTING AND CLONING AN ACCESS CARD IS GONNA BE A LITTLE MORE DIFFICULT. MY GUY IS HEADING UP TO YOU, COMMANDER, BUT MAYBE WE LEAVE IT ALONE.
GET OUT WHEN YOU ARE SUPPOSED TO GET OUT, AGENT TOPPA---
---LEAVE IT WITH ME.
COPY THAT.
WHAT IN THE HELL IS ALL THIS?!
EVERYONE BACK IN YOUR SEATS!!!

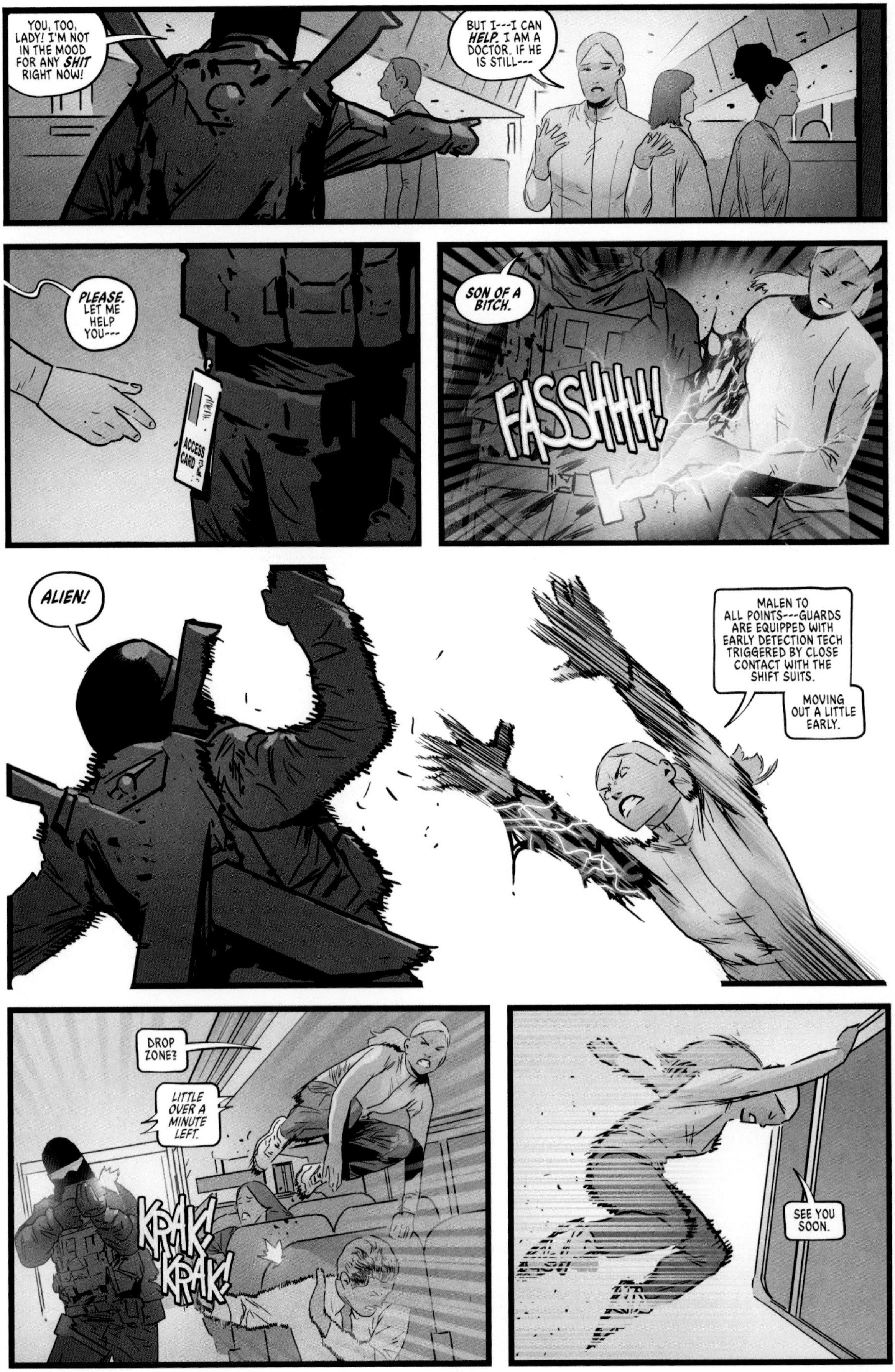
YOU, TOO, LADY! I'M NOT IN THE MOOD FOR ANY SHIT RIGHT NOW!
BUT I---I CAN HELP. I AM A DOCTOR. IF HE IS STILL---
PLEASE. LET ME HELP YOU---
ACCESS CARD
SON OF A BITCH.
FASSHHH!
ALIEN!
MALEN TO ALL POINTS---GUARDS ARE EQUIPPED WITH EARLY DETECTION TECH TRIGGERED BY CLOSE CONTACT WITH THE SHIFT SUITS.
MOVING OUT A LITTLE EARLY.
DROP ZONE?
LITTLE OVER A MINUTE LEFT.
KRAK! KRAK!
SEE YOU SOON.

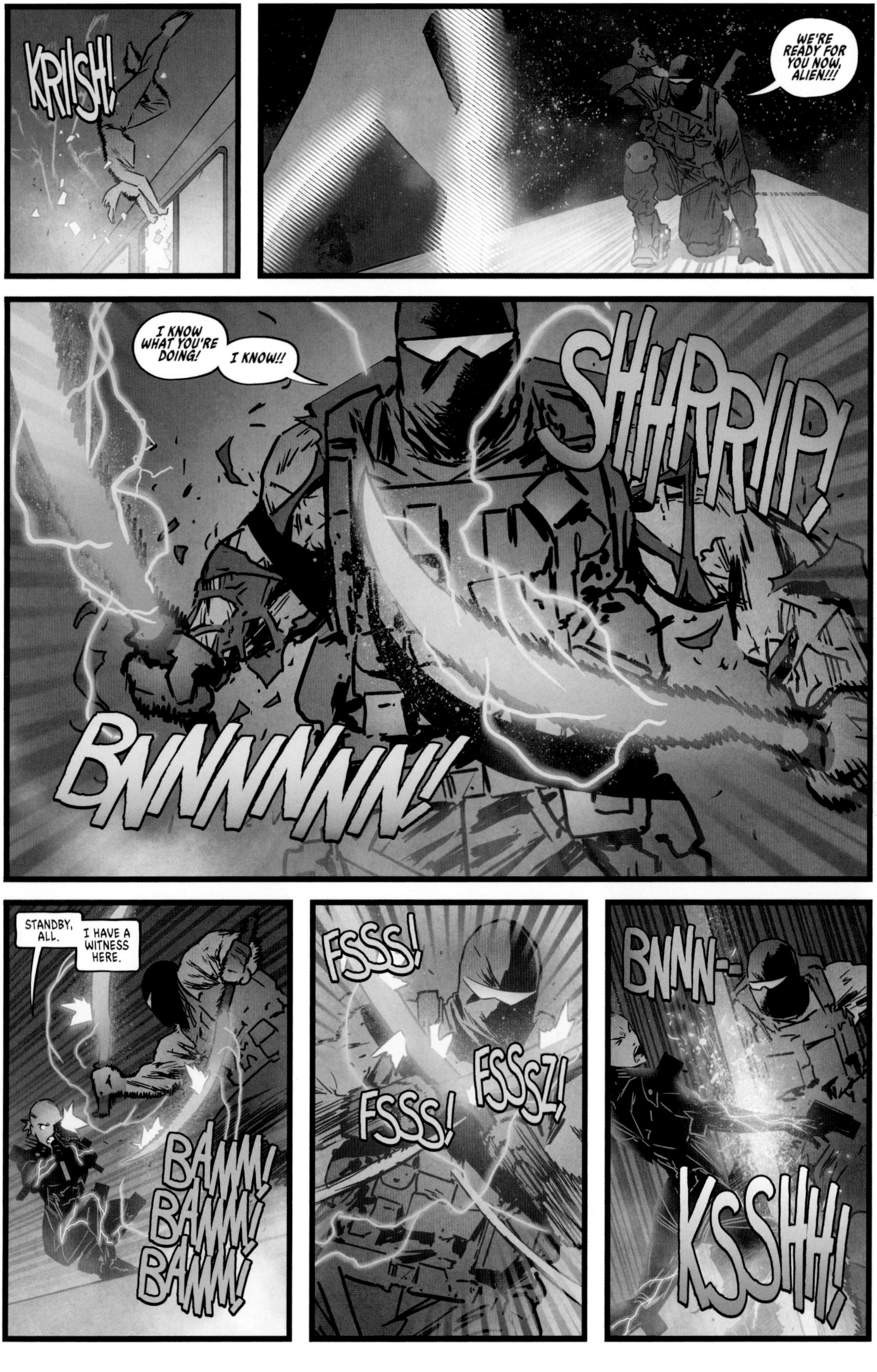
KRIISH!
WE'RE READY FOR YOU NOW, ALIEN!!!
I KNOW WHAT YOU'RE DOING!
I KNOW!!
SHRRIIP!
BNNNNNN!
STANDBY, ALL.
I HAVE A WITNESS HERE.
BAMM! BAMM! BAMM!
FSSS!
FSSSZ!
FSSS!
BNNN--
KSSHH!

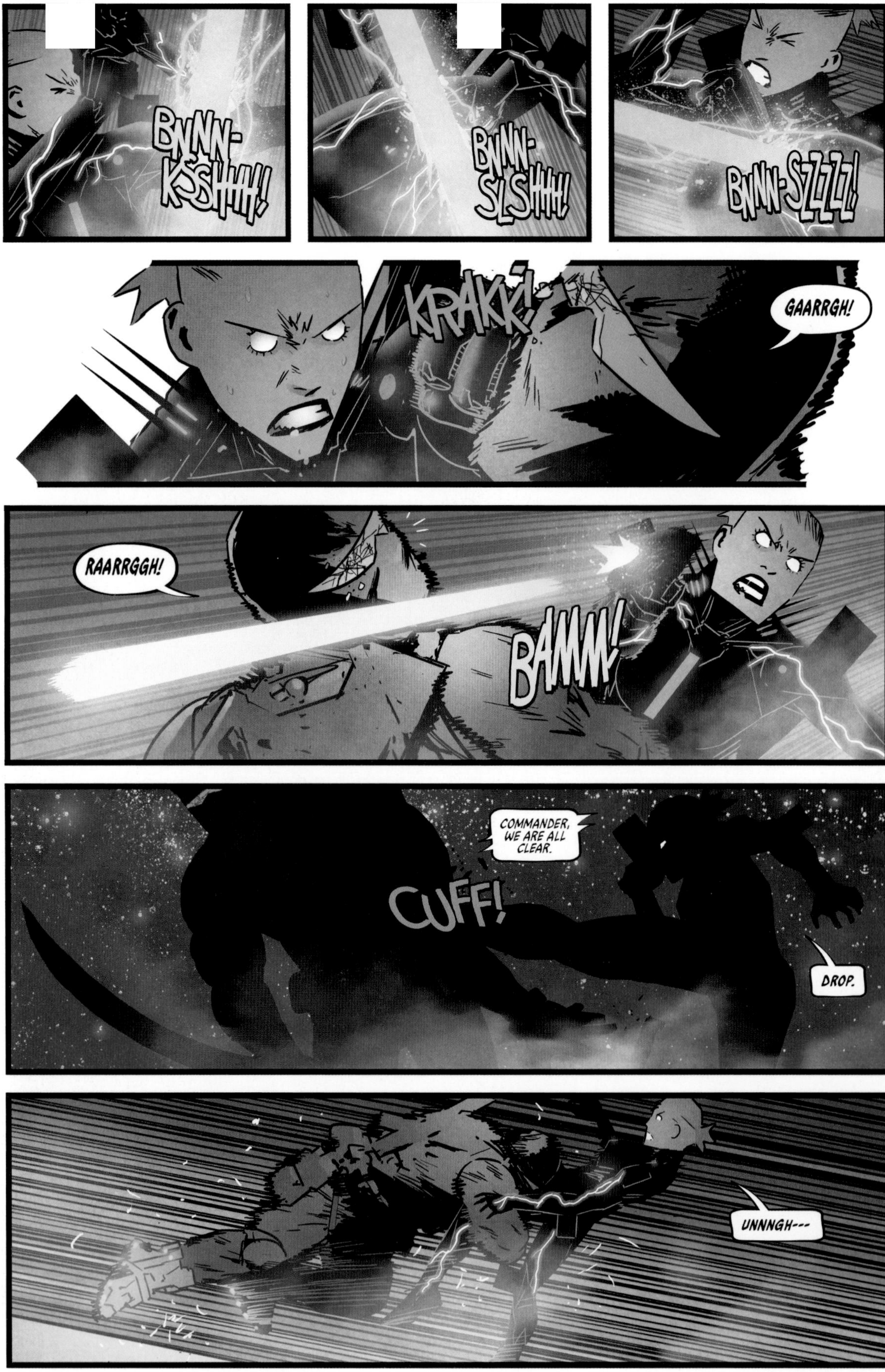
BNNN-KSHHH!
BNNN-SLSHHH!
BNNN-SZZZZZ!
KRAKK!
GAARRGH!
RAARRGGH!
BAMM!
COMMANDER, WE ARE ALL CLEAR.
CUFF!
DROP.
UNNNGH---

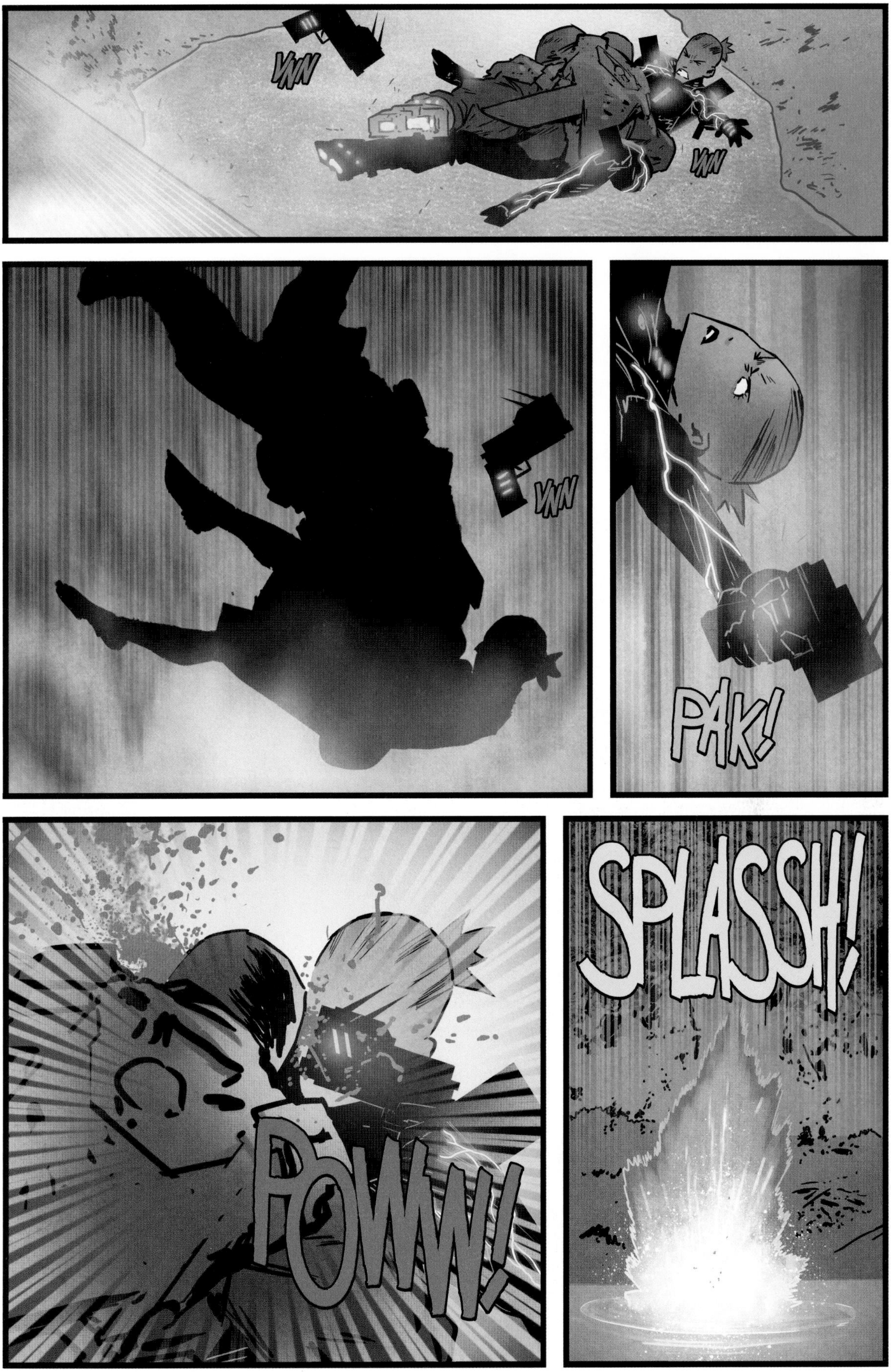
VNN
VNN
VNN
PAK!
POWW!
SPLASSH!

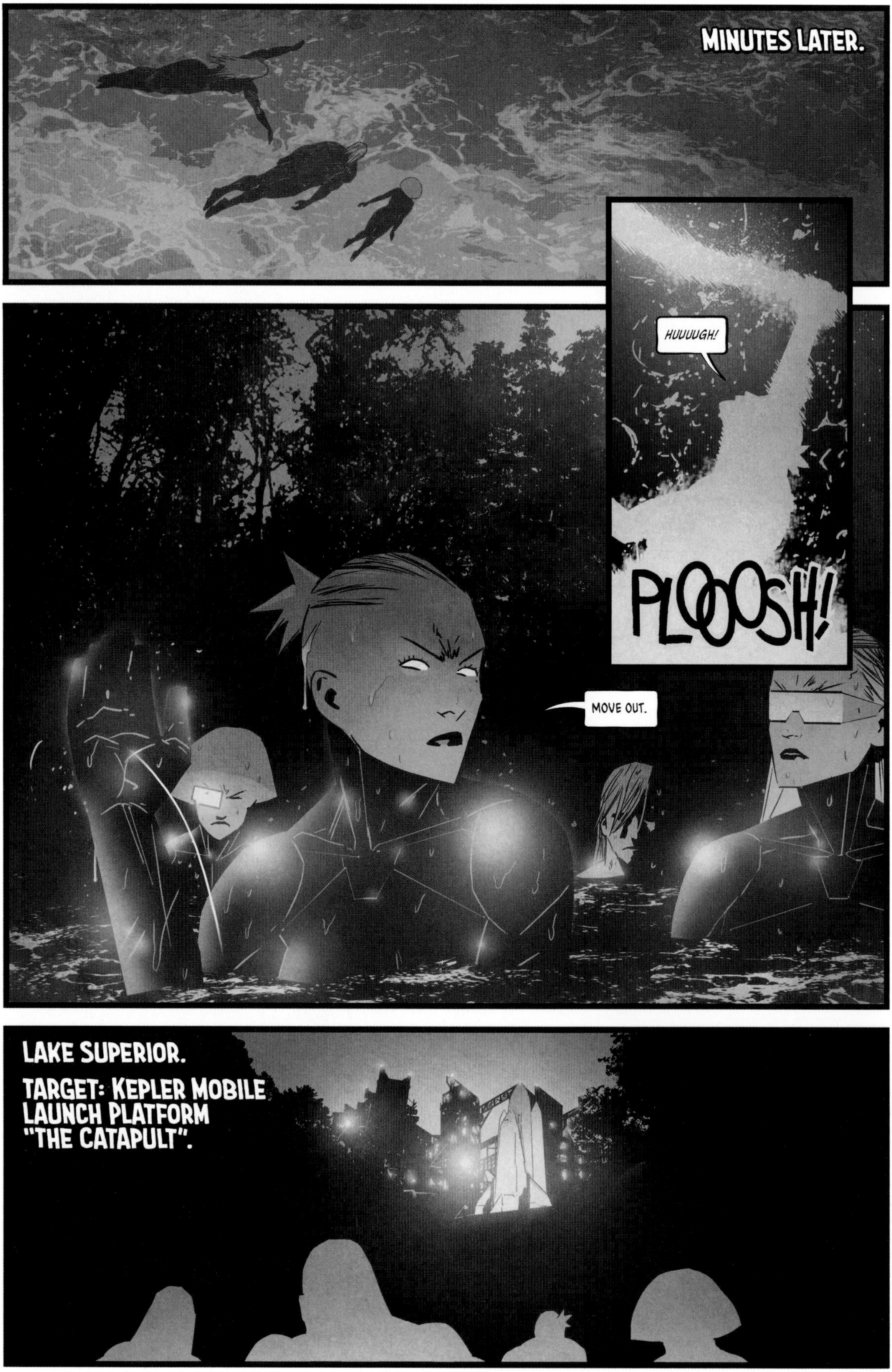
MINUTES LATER.
HUUUUGH!
PLOOOSH!
MOVE OUT.
LAKE SUPERIOR.
TARGET: KEPLER MOBILE LAUNCH PLATFORM "THE CATAPULT".

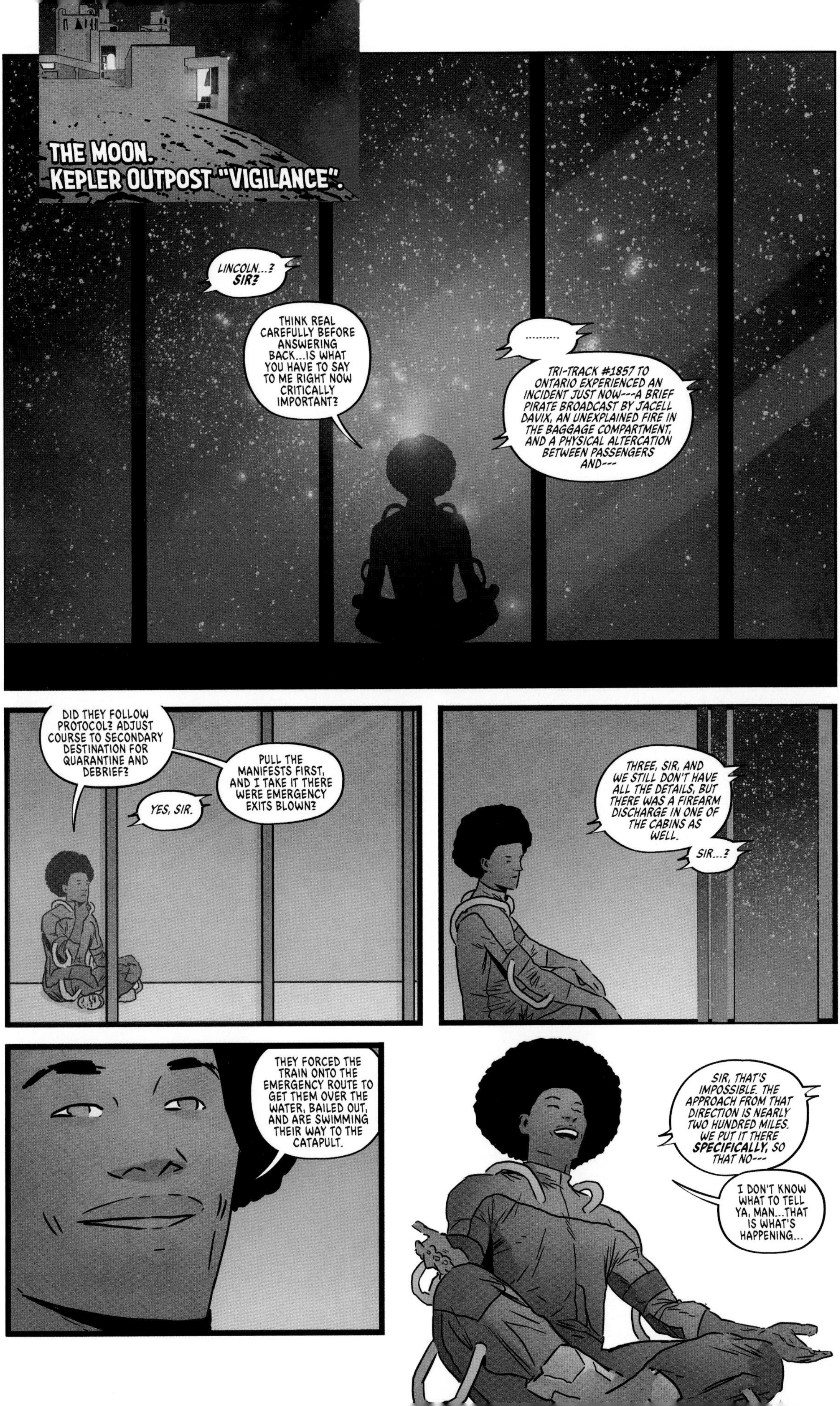
THE MOON.
KEPLER OUTPOST "VIGILANCE".
LINCOLN...? SIR?
THINK REAL CAREFULLY BEFORE ANSWERING BACK...IS WHAT YOU HAVE TO SAY TO ME RIGHT NOW CRITICALLY IMPORTANT?
....
TRI-TRACK #1857 TO ONTARIO EXPERIENCED AN INCIDENT JUST NOW---A BRIEF PIRATE BROADCAST BY JACELL DAVIX, AN UNEXPLAINED FIRE IN THE BAGGAGE COMPARTMENT, AND A PHYSICAL ALTERCATION BETWEEN PASSENGERS AND---
DID THEY FOLLOW PROTOCOL? ADJUST COURSE TO SECONDARY DESTINATION FOR QUARANTINE AND DEBRIEF?
YES, SIR.
PULL THE MANIFESTS FIRST, AND I TAKE IT THERE WERE EMERGENCY EXITS BLOWN?
THREE, SIR, AND WE STILL DON'T HAVE ALL THE DETAILS, BUT THERE WAS A FIREARM DISCHARGE IN ONE OF THE CABINS AS WELL.
SIR...?
THEY FORCED THE TRAIN ONTO THE EMERGENCY ROUTE TO GET THEM OVER THE WATER, BAILED OUT, AND ARE SWIMMING THEIR WAY TO THE CATAPULT.
SIR, THAT'S IMPOSSIBLE. THE APPROACH FROM THAT DIRECTION IS NEARLY TWO HUNDRED MILES. WE PUT IT THERE SPECIFICALLY, SO THAT NO---
I DON'T KNOW WHAT TO TELL YA, MAN...THAT IS WHAT'S HAPPENING...

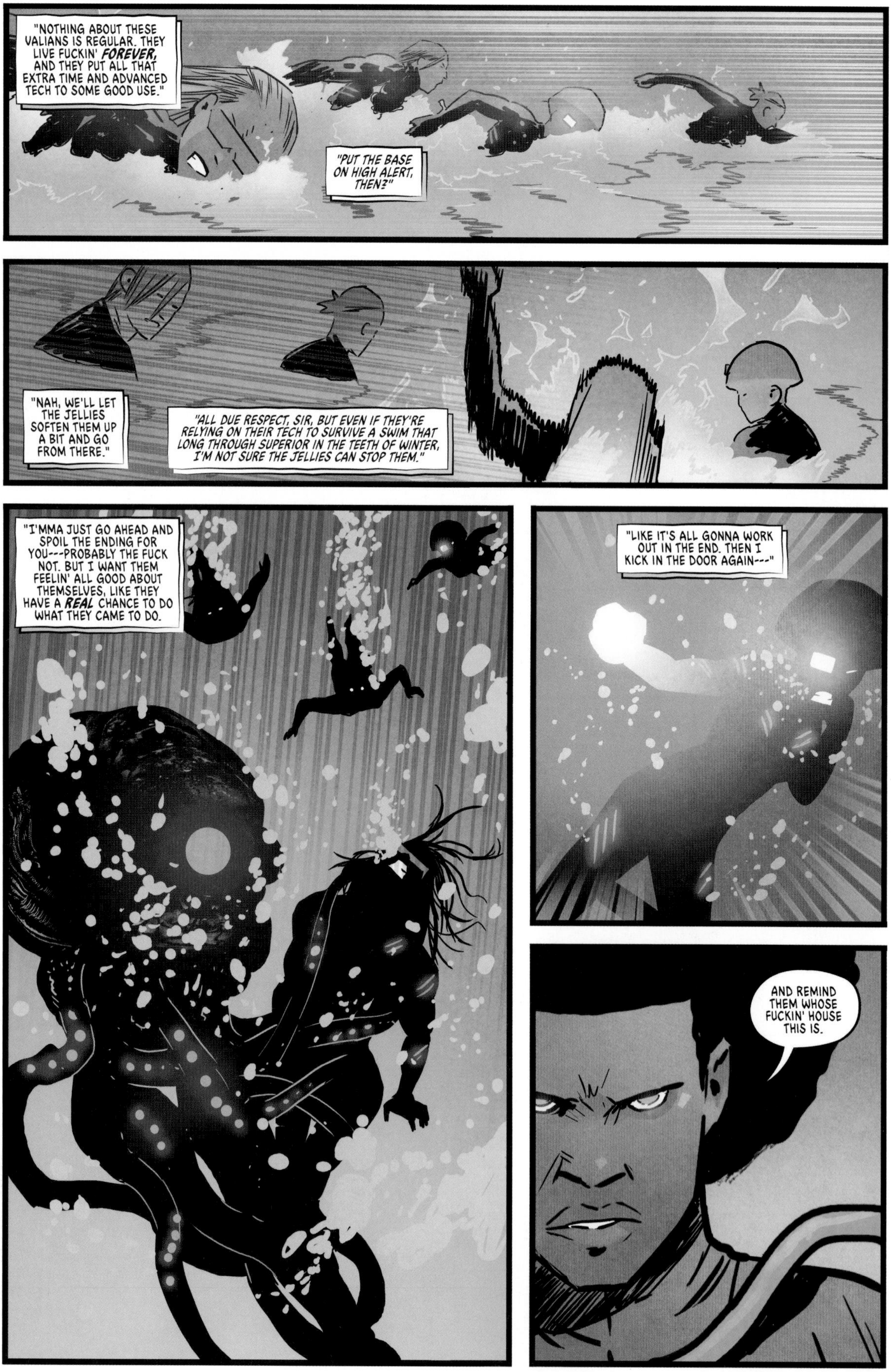
"NOTHING ABOUT THESE VALIANS IS REGULAR. THEY LIVE FUCKIN' FOREVER, AND THEY PUT ALL THAT EXTRA TIME AND ADVANCED TECH TO SOME GOOD USE."
"PUT THE BASE ON HIGH ALERT, THEN?"
"NAH, WE'LL LET THE JELLIES SOFTEN THEM UP A BIT AND GO FROM THERE."
"ALL DUE RESPECT, SIR, BUT EVEN IF THEY'RE RELYING ON THEIR TECH TO SURVIVE A SWIM THAT LONG THROUGH SUPERIOR IN THE TEETH OF WINTER, I'M NOT SURE THE JELLIES CAN STOP THEM."
"I'MMA JUST GO AHEAD AND SPOIL THE ENDING FOR YOU---PROBABLY THE FUCK NOT. BUT I WANT THEM FEELIN' ALL GOOD ABOUT THEMSELVES, LIKE THEY HAVE A REAL CHANCE TO DO WHAT THEY CAME TO DO.
"LIKE IT'S ALL GONNA WORK OUT IN THE END. THEN I KICK IN THE DOOR AGAIN---"
AND REMIND THEM WHOSE FUCKIN' HOUSE THIS IS.

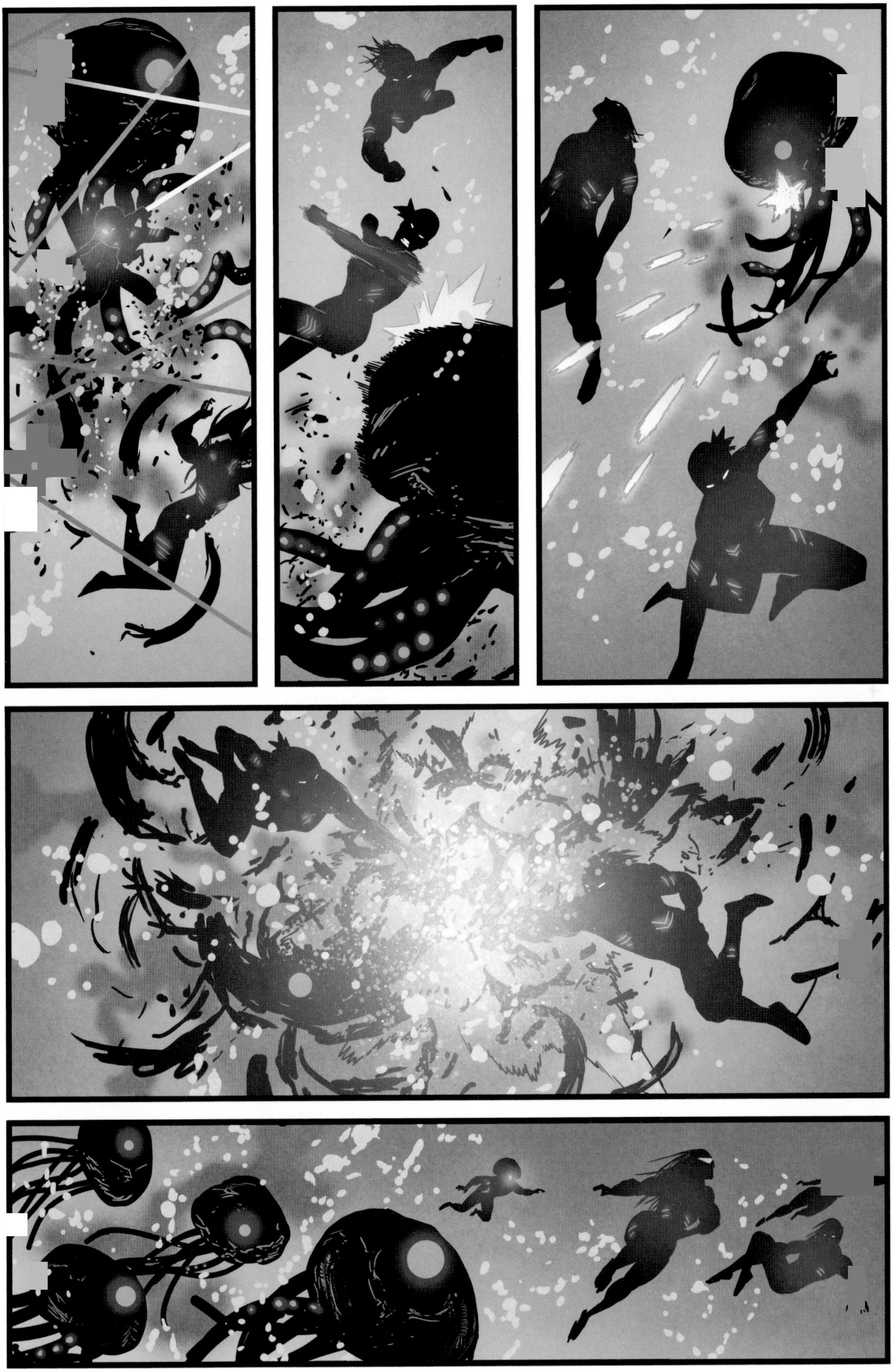

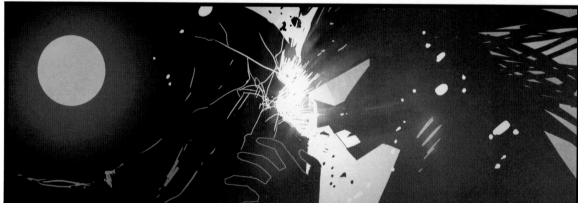

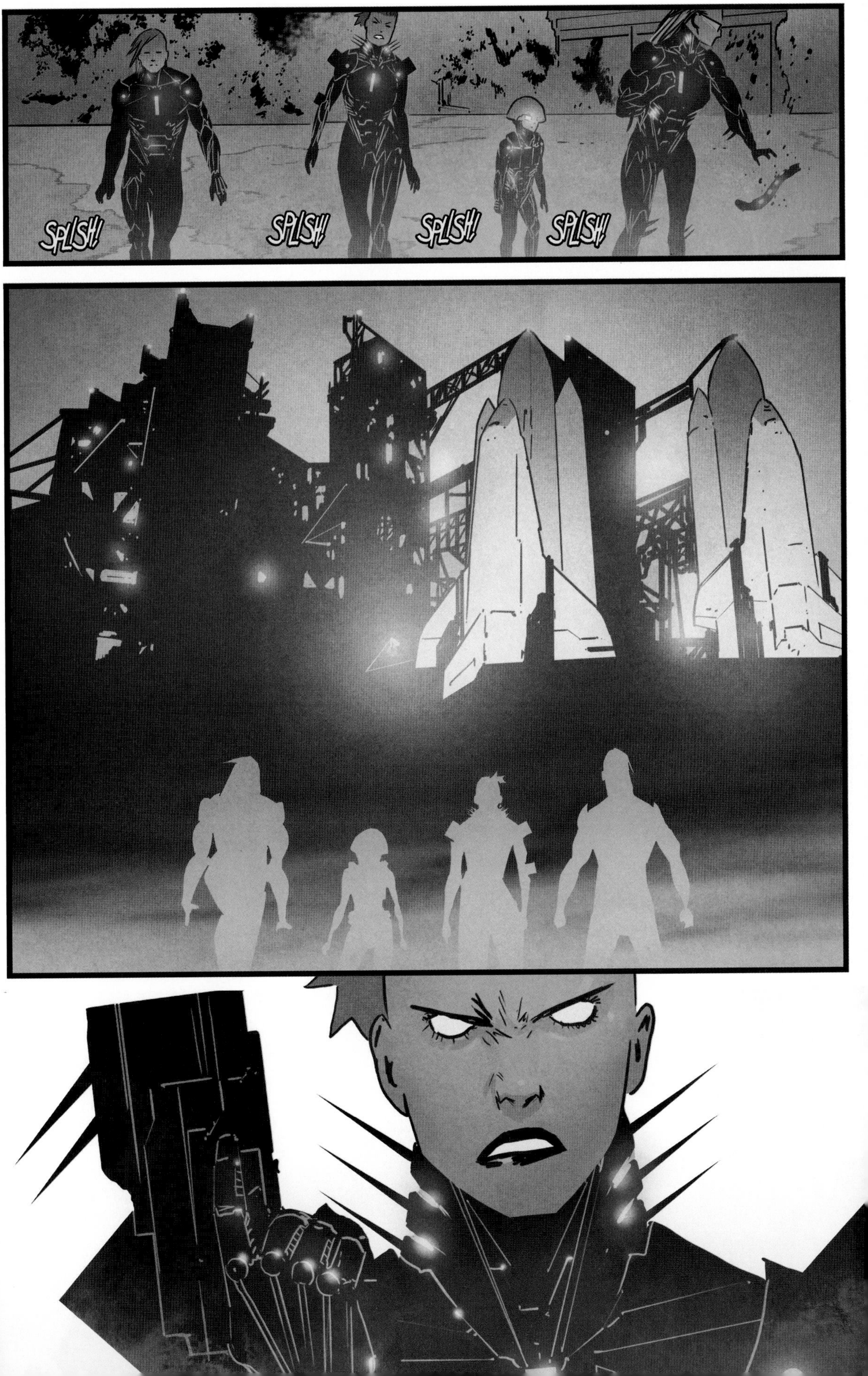
SPLISH!
SPLISH!
SPLISH!
SPLISH!

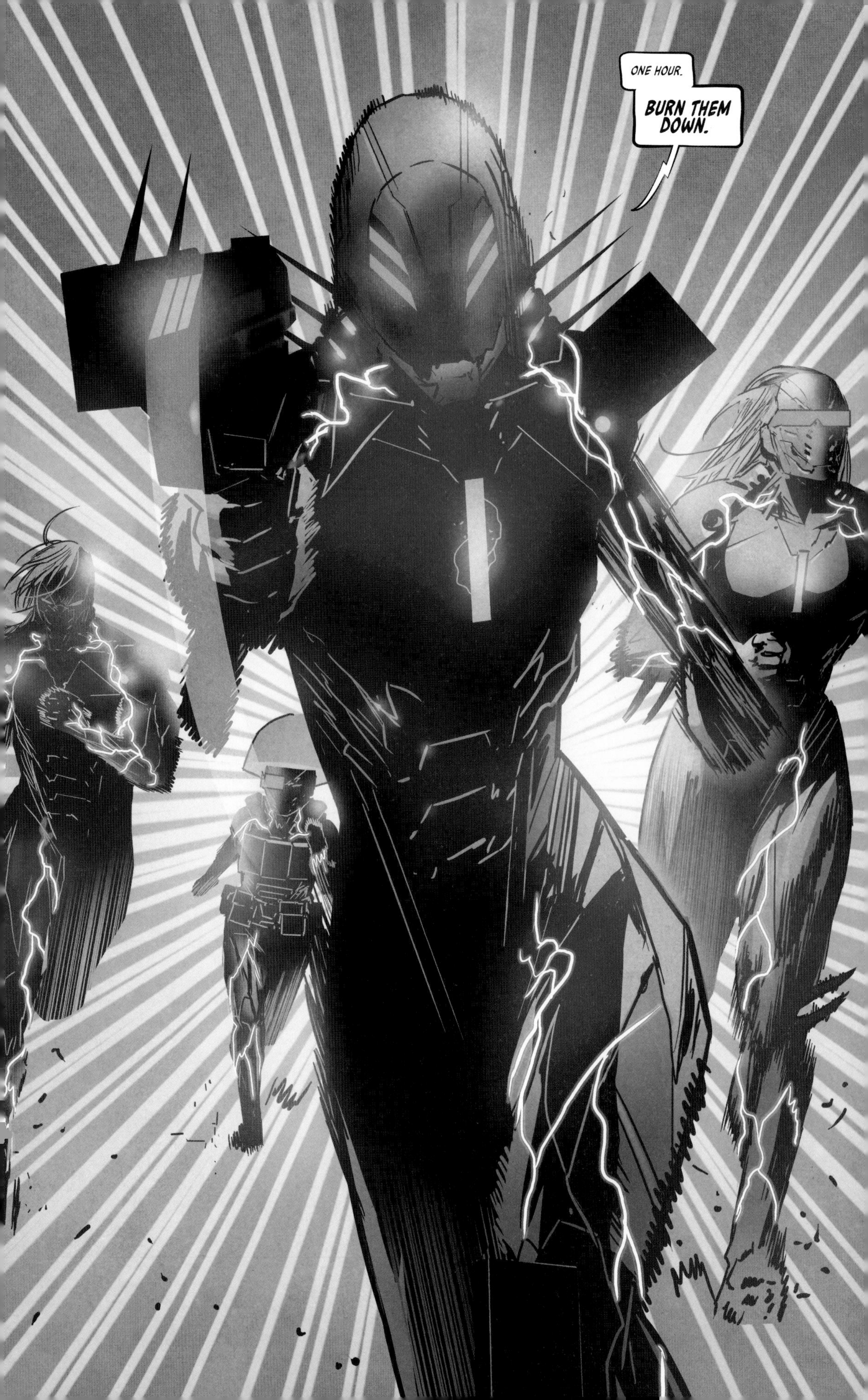
ONE HOUR.
BURN THEM DOWN.

"PREVENT THEM FROM LAUNCHING. DO WHATEVER NEEDS DOING.

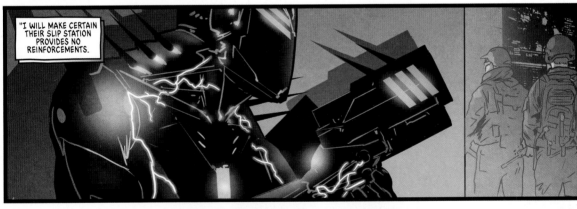

"WE MUST KNOW WHAT THEY KNOW. STRIP THEIR MAINFRAME AND THEN DESTROY IT.

"I WILL MAKE CERTAIN THEIR SLIP STATION PROVIDES NO REINFORCEMENTS.

THE MOON. KEPLER OUTPOST "VIGILANCE."

"CHECK IN EVERY TEN MINUTES. NO EXCEPTIONS.

"GOOD LUCK."

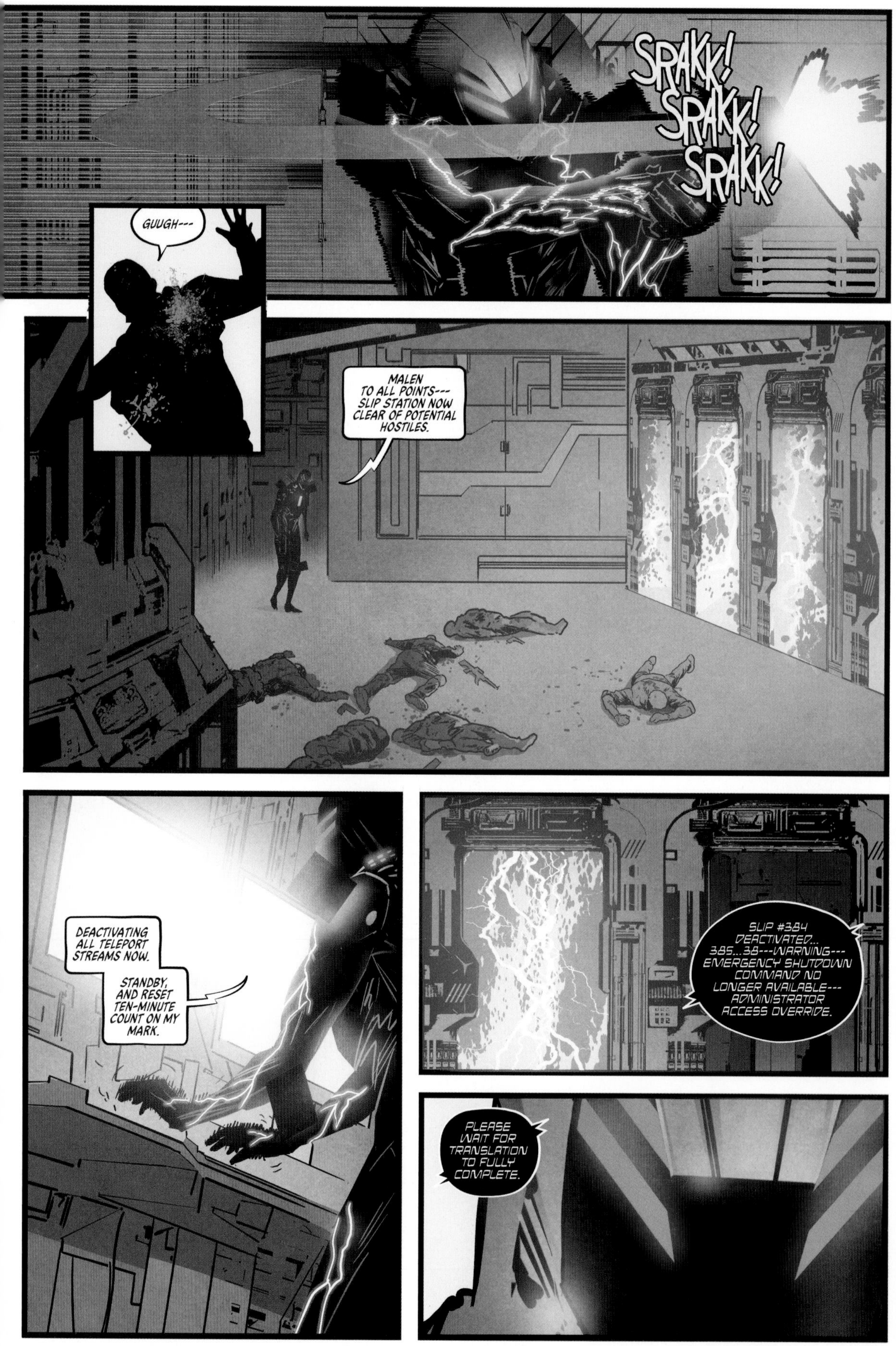
SRAKK! SRAKK! SRAKK!
GUUGH---
MALEN TO ALL POINTS--- SLIP STATION NOW CLEAR OF POTENTIAL HOSTILES.
DEACTIVATING ALL TELEPORT STREAMS NOW.
STANDBY, AND RESET TEN-MINUTE COUNT ON MY MARK.
SLIP #384 DEACTIVATED... 385...38---WARNING--- EMERGENCY SHUTDOWN COMMAND NO LONGER AVAILABLE--- ADMINISTRATOR ACCESS OVERRIDE.
PLEASE WAIT FOR TRANSLATION TO FULLY COMPLETE.

DAMMIT--- JUST SHUT *DOWN!*

COMMANDER.

YOU GOT A FEW MINUTES?

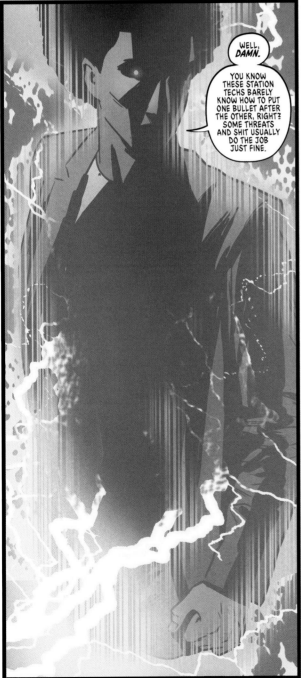

WELL, *DAMN.*

YOU KNOW THESE STATION TECHS BARELY KNOW HOW TO PUT ONE BULLET AFTER THE OTHER, RIGHT? SOME THREATS AND SHIT USUALLY DO THE JOB JUST FINE.

WHAT GAVE US AWAY?

THE TRAIN SHIT, BUT I'M ACTUALLY GLAD IT HAPPENED, BECAUSE I HAVE BEEN *DYING* FOR SOME FACE TIME WITH YOU FOR *WEEKS* NOW.

SINCE I CAME BACK TO LIFE, WHICH I GOT YOUR MAN FINN TO THANK FOR.

BUT HOLD ON REAL QUICK---LET'S MAKE SURE WE GOT A LITTLE EXTRA PRIVACY, AND YOU KNOW, AS A SHOW OF GOOD FAITH---

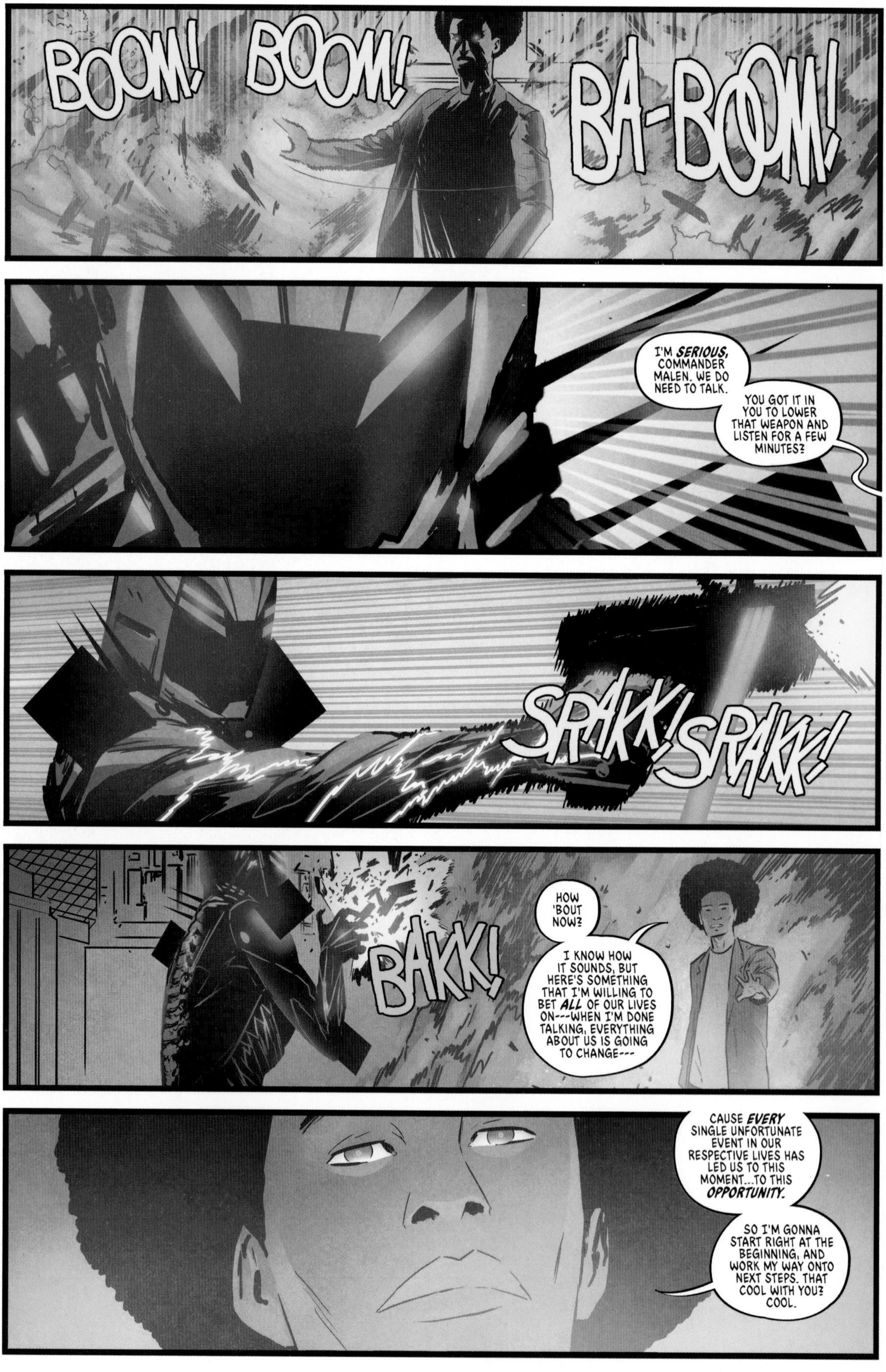
BOOM! BOOM! BA-BOOM!
I'M SERIOUS, COMMANDER MALEN. WE DO NEED TO TALK.
YOU GOT IT IN YOU TO LOWER THAT WEAPON AND LISTEN FOR A FEW MINUTES?
SRAKK! SRAKK!
BAKK!
HOW 'BOUT NOW?
I KNOW HOW IT SOUNDS, BUT HERE'S SOMETHING THAT I'M WILLING TO BET ALL OF OUR LIVES ON---WHEN I'M DONE TALKING, EVERYTHING ABOUT US IS GOING TO CHANGE---
CAUSE EVERY SINGLE UNFORTUNATE EVENT IN OUR RESPECTIVE LIVES HAS LED US TO THIS MOMENT...TO THIS OPPORTUNITY.
SO I'M GONNA START RIGHT AT THE BEGINNING, AND WORK MY WAY ONTO NEXT STEPS. THAT COOL WITH YOU? COOL.

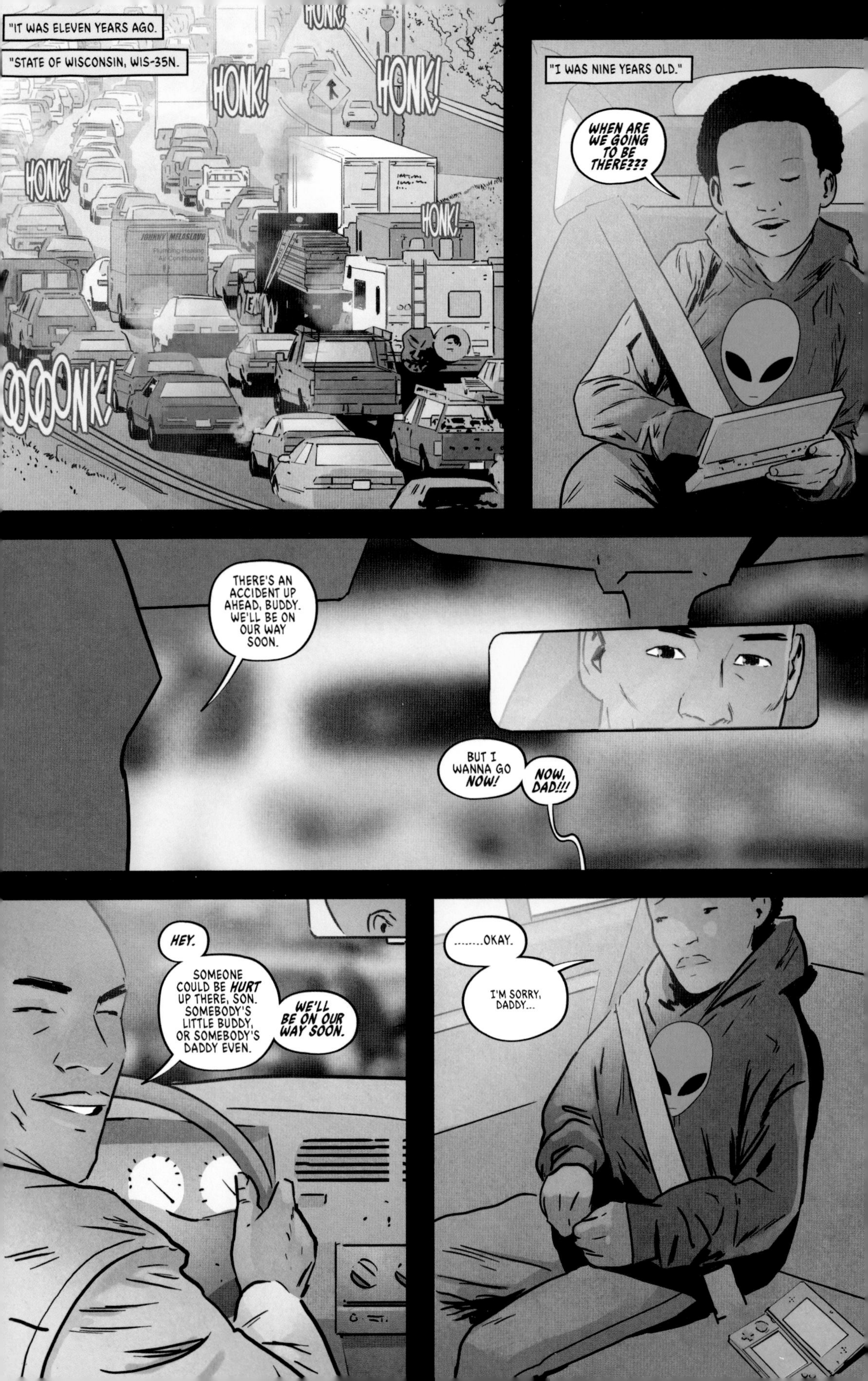
"IT WAS ELEVEN YEARS AGO.
"STATE OF WISCONSIN, WIS-35N.
HONK!
HONK!
HONK!
HONK!
HONK!
OOOOONK!
"I WAS NINE YEARS OLD."
WHEN ARE WE GOING TO BE THERE???
THERE'S AN ACCIDENT UP AHEAD, BUDDY. WE'LL BE ON OUR WAY SOON.
BUT I WANNA GO NOW!
NOW, DAD!!!
HEY.
SOMEONE COULD BE HURT UP THERE, SON. SOMEBODY'S LITTLE BUDDY, OR SOMEBODY'S DADDY EVEN.
WE'LL BE ON OUR WAY SOON.
........OKAY.
I'M SORRY, DADDY...

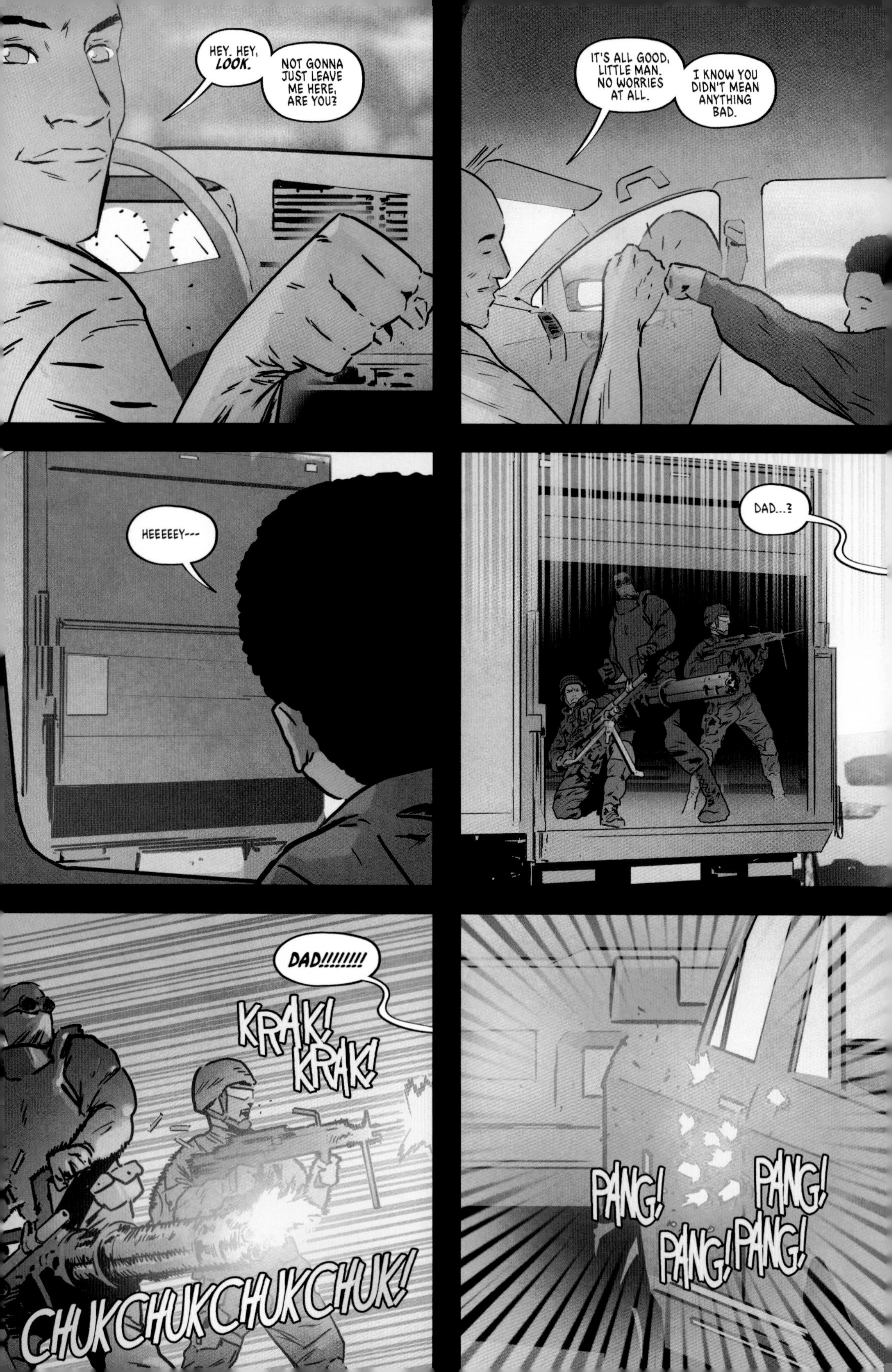
HEY. HEY, LOOK.
NOT GONNA JUST LEAVE ME HERE, ARE YOU?
IT'S ALL GOOD, LITTLE MAN. NO WORRIES AT ALL.
I KNOW YOU DIDN'T MEAN ANYTHING BAD.
HEEEEEY---
DAD...?
DAD!!!!!!!!
KRAK! KRAK!
CHUKCHUKCHUKCHUK!
PANG! PANG!
PANG! PANG!

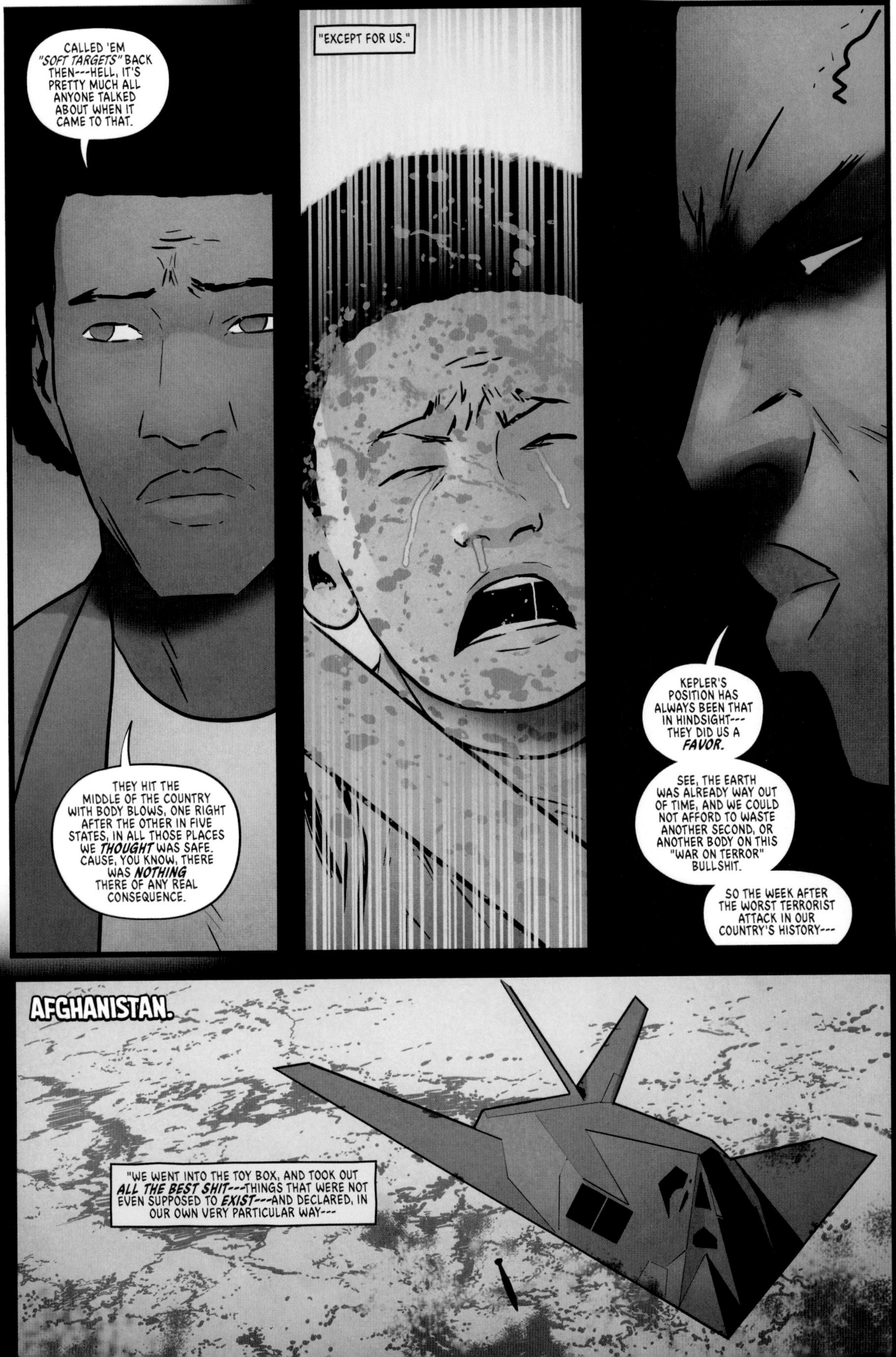
CALLED 'EM "SOFT TARGETS" BACK THEN---HELL, IT'S PRETTY MUCH ALL ANYONE TALKED ABOUT WHEN IT CAME TO THAT.
THEY HIT THE MIDDLE OF THE COUNTRY WITH BODY BLOWS, ONE RIGHT AFTER THE OTHER IN FIVE STATES, IN ALL THOSE PLACES WE THOUGHT WAS SAFE. CAUSE, YOU KNOW, THERE WAS NOTHING THERE OF ANY REAL CONSEQUENCE.
"EXCEPT FOR US."
KEPLER'S POSITION HAS ALWAYS BEEN THAT IN HINDSIGHT--- THEY DID US A FAVOR.
SEE, THE EARTH WAS ALREADY WAY OUT OF TIME, AND WE COULD NOT AFFORD TO WASTE ANOTHER SECOND, OR ANOTHER BODY ON THIS "WAR ON TERROR" BULLSHIT.
SO THE WEEK AFTER THE WORST TERRORIST ATTACK IN OUR COUNTRY'S HISTORY---
AFGHANISTAN.
"WE WENT INTO THE TOY BOX, AND TOOK OUT ALL THE BEST SHIT---THINGS THAT WERE NOT EVEN SUPPOSED TO EXIST---AND DECLARED, IN OUR OWN VERY PARTICULAR WAY---

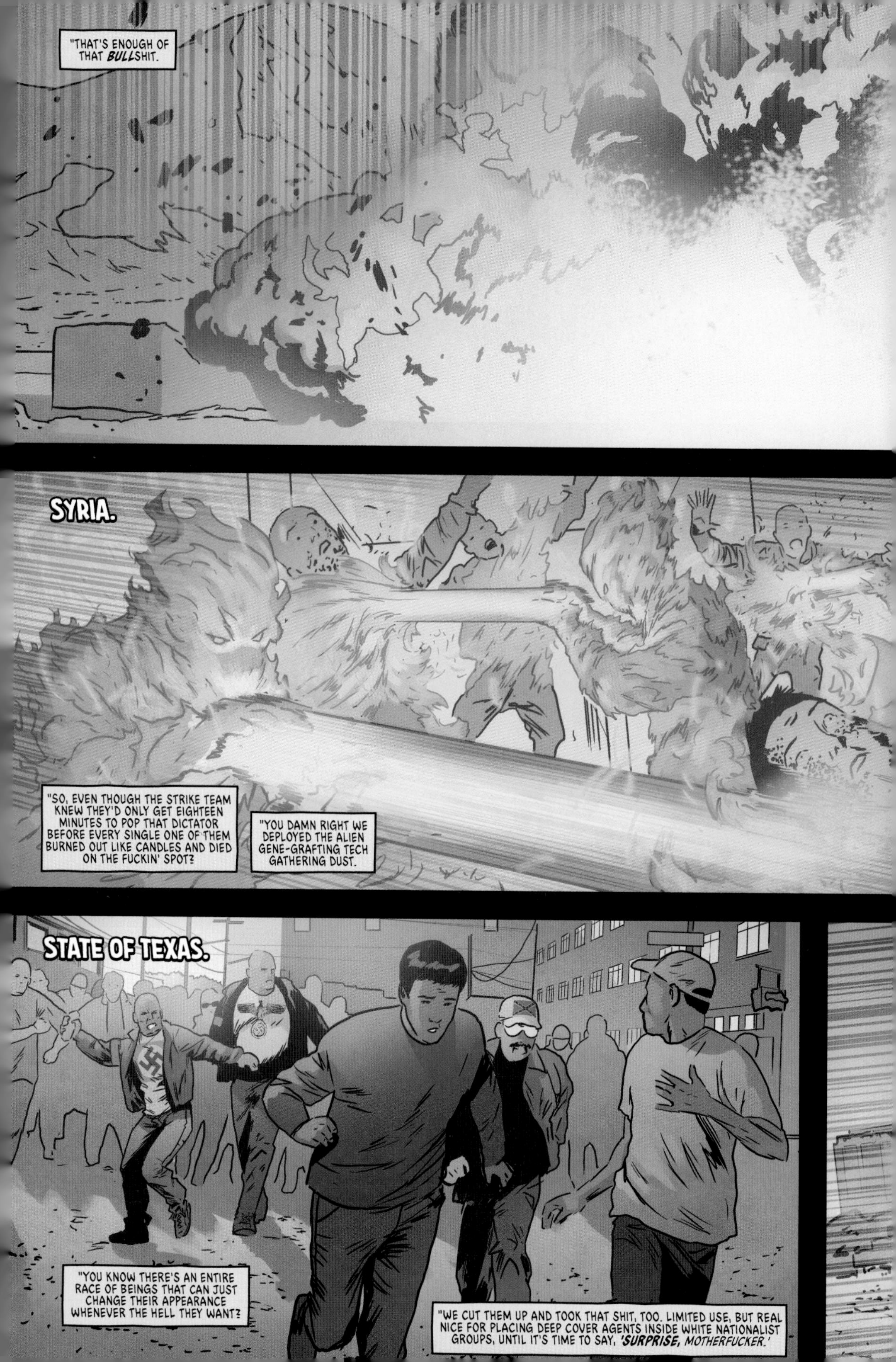
"THAT'S ENOUGH OF THAT BULLSHIT.
SYRIA.
"SO, EVEN THOUGH THE STRIKE TEAM KNEW THEY'D ONLY GET EIGHTEEN MINUTES TO POP THAT DICTATOR BEFORE EVERY SINGLE ONE OF THEM BURNED OUT LIKE CANDLES AND DIED ON THE FUCKIN' SPOT?
"YOU DAMN RIGHT WE DEPLOYED THE ALIEN GENE-GRAFTING TECH GATHERING DUST.
STATE OF TEXAS.
"YOU KNOW THERE'S AN ENTIRE RACE OF BEINGS THAT CAN JUST CHANGE THEIR APPEARANCE WHENEVER THE HELL THEY WANT?
"WE CUT THEM UP AND TOOK THAT SHIT, TOO. LIMITED USE, BUT REAL NICE FOR PLACING DEEP COVER AGENTS INSIDE WHITE NATIONALIST GROUPS, UNTIL IT'S TIME TO SAY, 'SURPRISE, MOTHERFUCKER.'

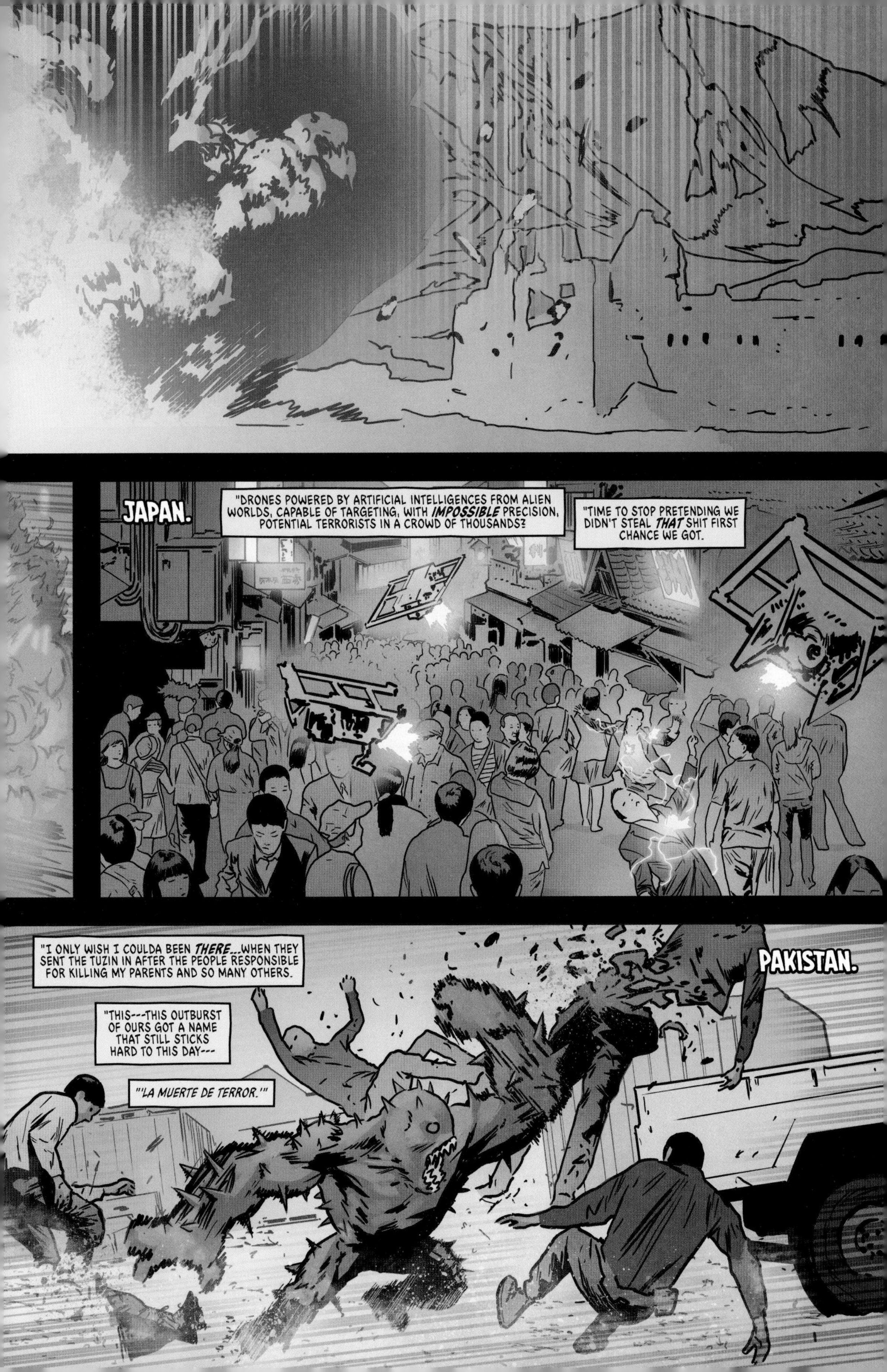
JAPAN.
"DRONES POWERED BY ARTIFICIAL INTELLIGENCES FROM ALIEN WORLDS, CAPABLE OF TARGETING, WITH *IMPOSSIBLE* PRECISION, POTENTIAL TERRORISTS IN A CROWD OF THOUSANDS?
"TIME TO STOP PRETENDING WE DIDN'T STEAL *THAT* SHIT FIRST CHANCE WE GOT.
"I ONLY WISH I COULDA BEEN *THERE*...WHEN THEY SENT THE TUZIN IN AFTER THE PEOPLE RESPONSIBLE FOR KILLING MY PARENTS AND SO MANY OTHERS.
PAKISTAN.
"THIS---THIS OUTBURST OF OURS GOT A NAME THAT STILL STICKS HARD TO THIS DAY---
"'*LA MUERTE DE TERROR.*'"

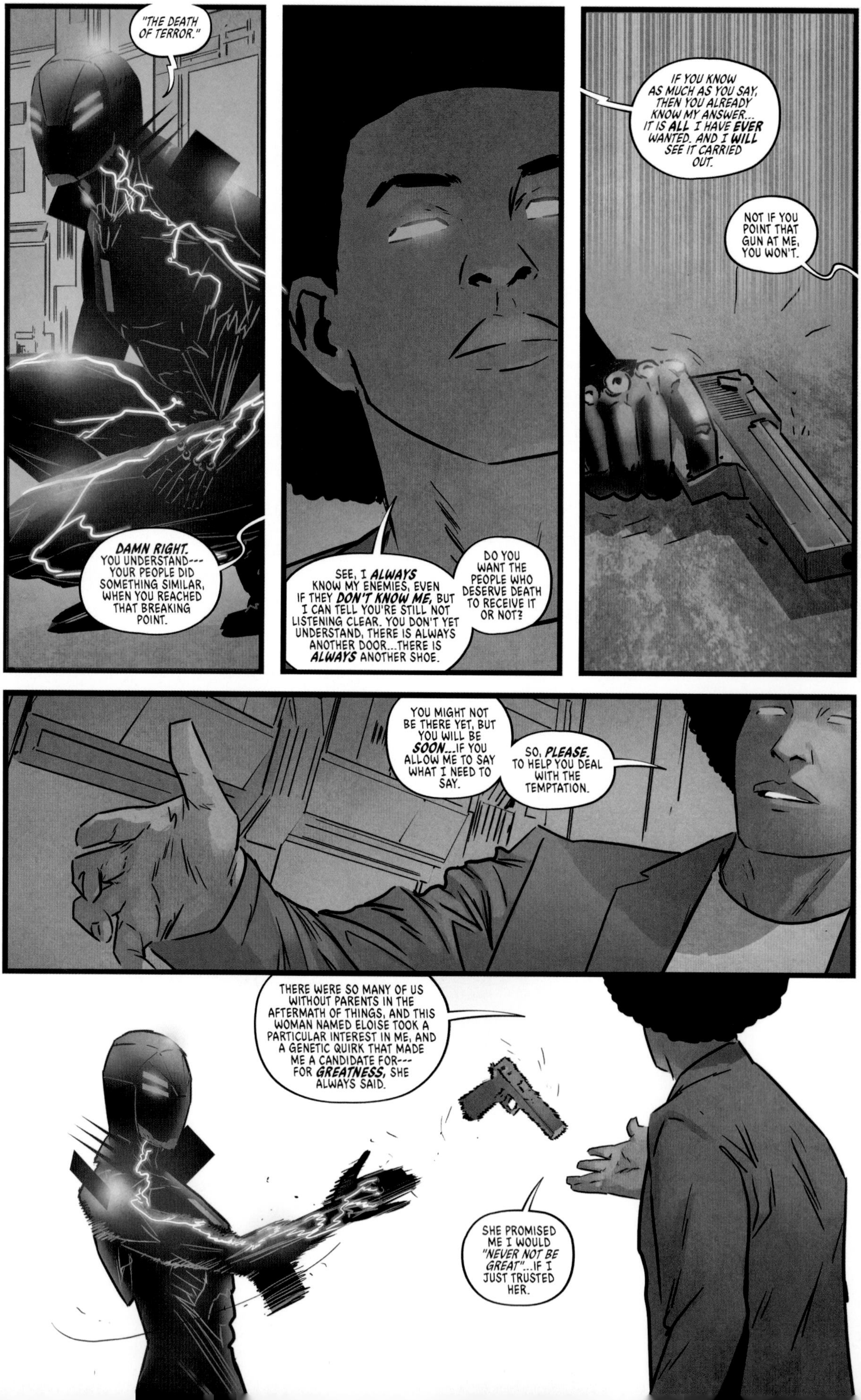
"THE DEATH OF TERROR."
DAMN RIGHT. YOU UNDERSTAND--- YOUR PEOPLE DID SOMETHING SIMILAR, WHEN YOU REACHED THAT BREAKING POINT.
SEE, I ALWAYS KNOW MY ENEMIES, EVEN IF THEY DON'T KNOW ME, BUT I CAN TELL YOU'RE STILL NOT LISTENING CLEAR. YOU DON'T YET UNDERSTAND, THERE IS ALWAYS ANOTHER DOOR...THERE IS ALWAYS ANOTHER SHOE.
DO YOU WANT THE PEOPLE WHO DESERVE DEATH TO RECEIVE IT OR NOT?
IF YOU KNOW AS MUCH AS YOU SAY, THEN YOU ALREADY KNOW MY ANSWER... IT IS ALL I HAVE EVER WANTED. AND I WILL SEE IT CARRIED OUT.
NOT IF YOU POINT THAT GUN AT ME, YOU WON'T.
YOU MIGHT NOT BE THERE YET, BUT YOU WILL BE SOON...IF YOU ALLOW ME TO SAY WHAT I NEED TO SAY.
SO, PLEASE. TO HELP YOU DEAL WITH THE TEMPTATION.
THERE WERE SO MANY OF US WITHOUT PARENTS IN THE AFTERMATH OF THINGS, AND THIS WOMAN NAMED ELOISE TOOK A PARTICULAR INTEREST IN ME, AND A GENETIC QUIRK THAT MADE ME A CANDIDATE FOR--- FOR GREATNESS, SHE ALWAYS SAID.
SHE PROMISED ME I WOULD "NEVER NOT BE GREAT"...IF I JUST TRUSTED HER.

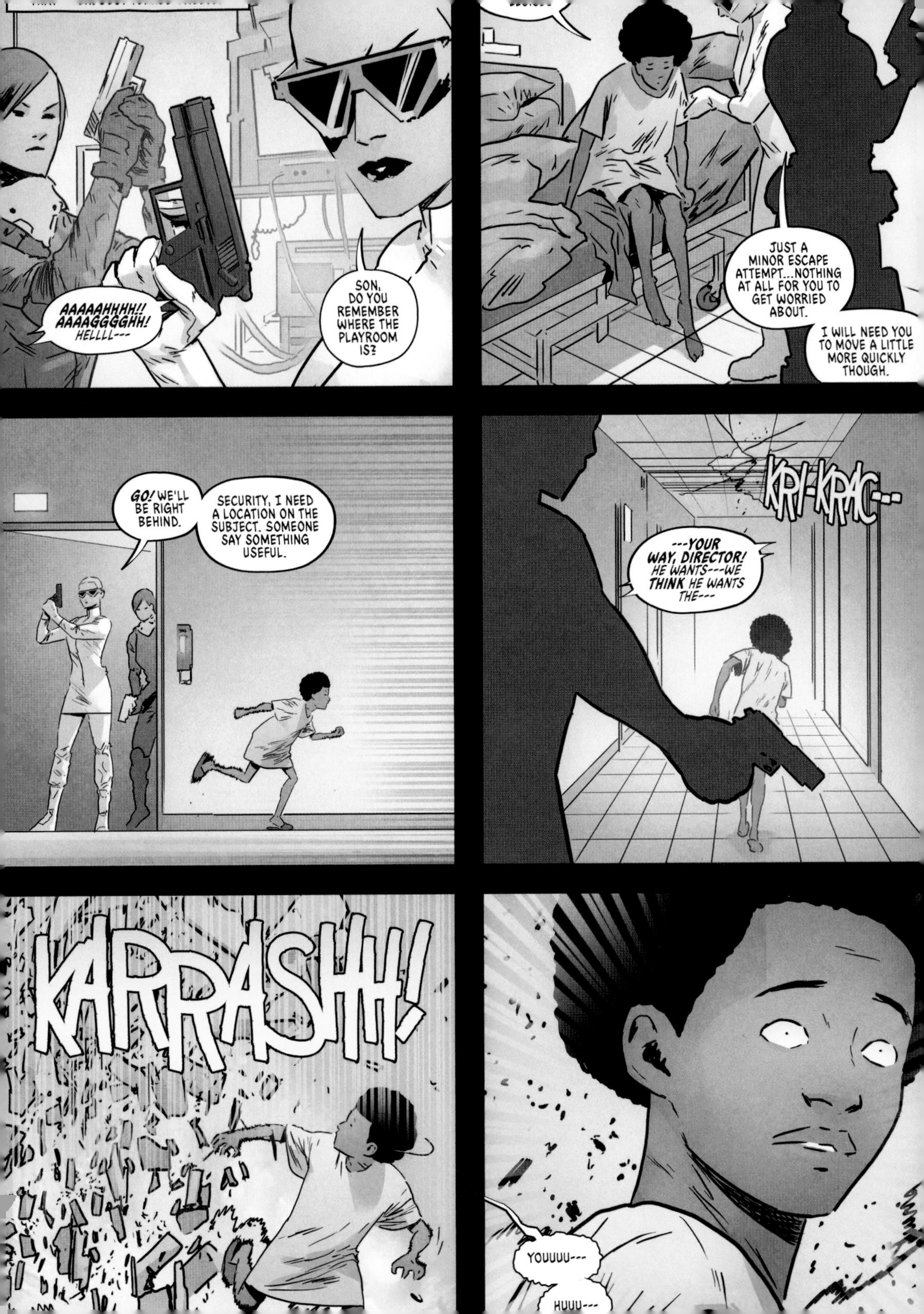

AAAAAHHHH!! AAAAGGGGHH! HELLLL---
SON, DO YOU REMEMBER WHERE THE PLAYROOM IS?
JUST A MINOR ESCAPE ATTEMPT...NOTHING AT ALL FOR YOU TO GET WORRIED ABOUT.
I WILL NEED YOU TO MOVE A LITTLE MORE QUICKLY THOUGH.
GO! WE'LL BE RIGHT BEHIND.
SECURITY, I NEED A LOCATION ON THE SUBJECT. SOMEONE SAY SOMETHING USEFUL.
KRI-KRAC---
---YOUR WAY, DIRECTOR! HE WANTS---WE THINK HE WANTS THE---
KARRASHH!
YOUUUU---
HUUU---

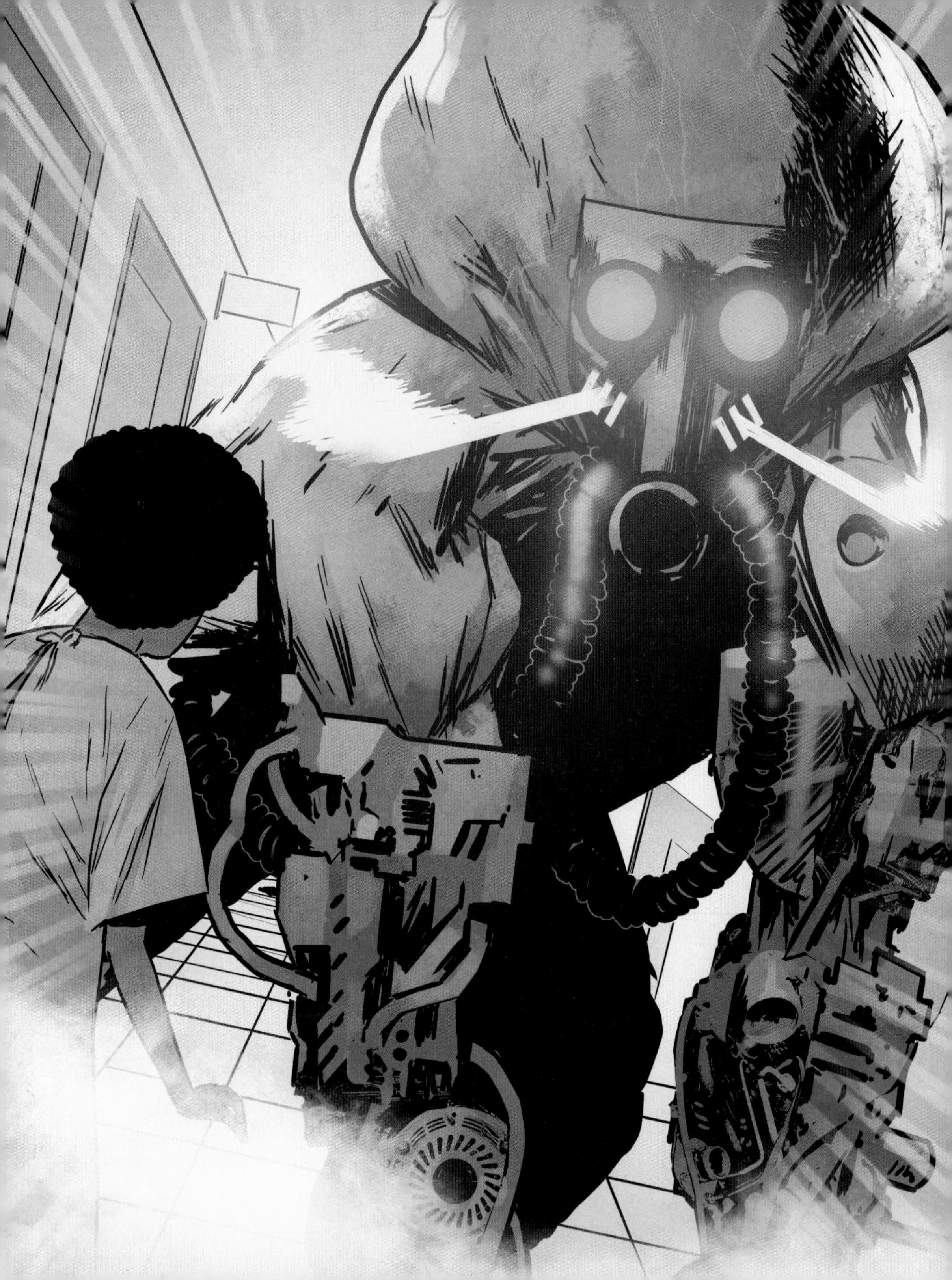

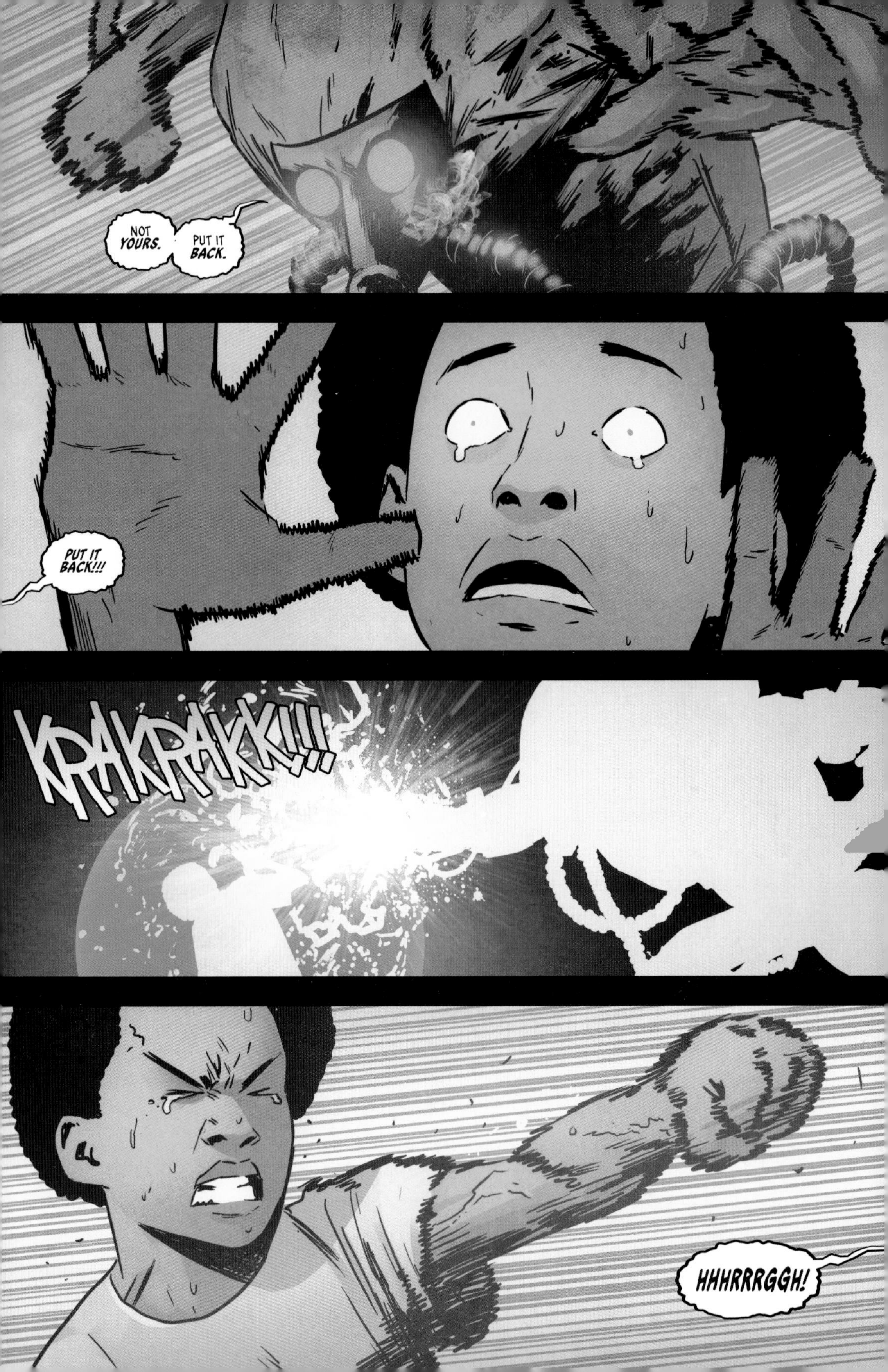
NOT YOURS.
PUT IT BACK.
PUT IT BACK!!!
KRAKRAKK!!!
HHHRRRGGH!

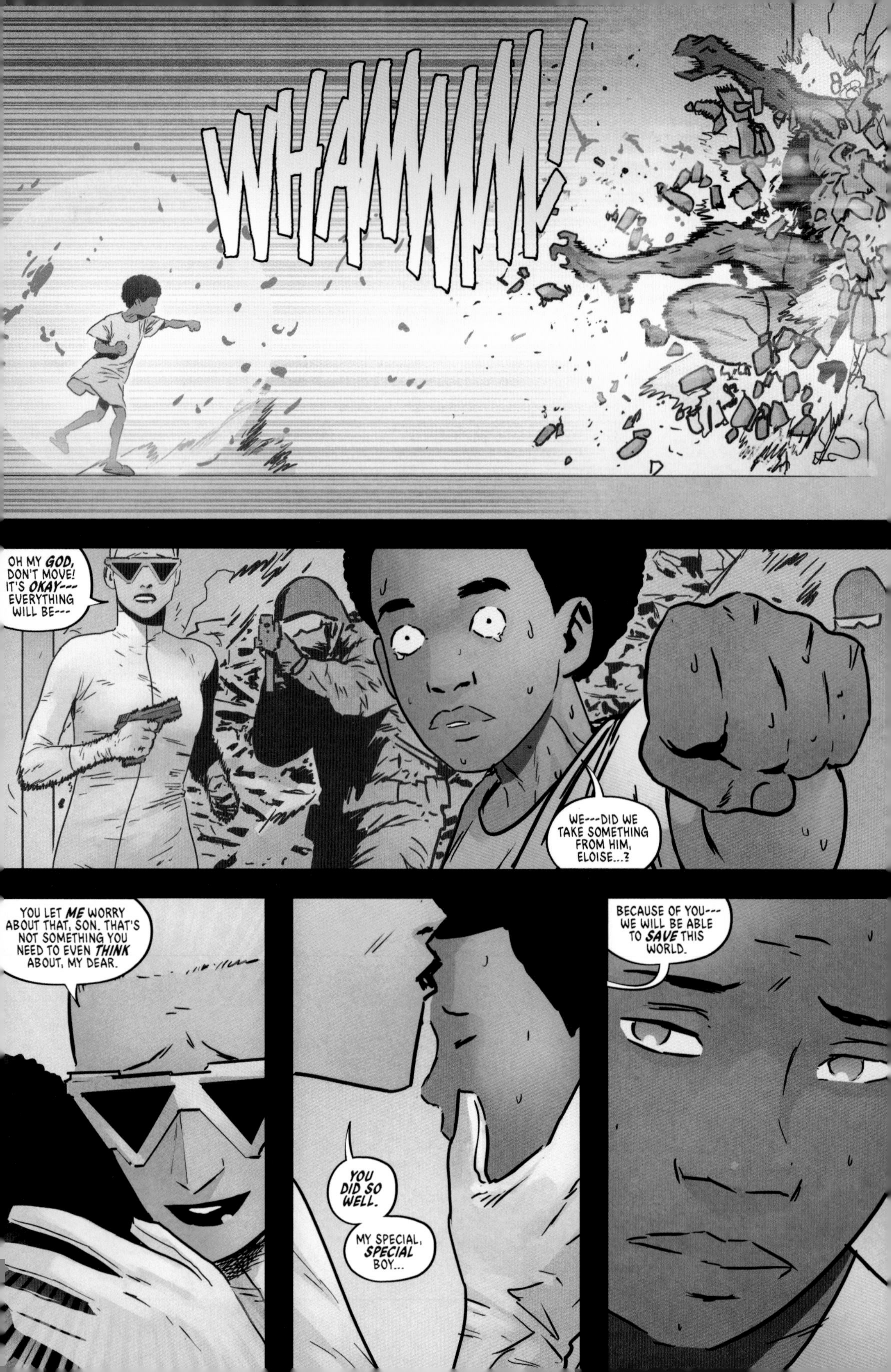
WHAMMM!
OH MY GOD, DON'T MOVE! IT'S OKAY--- EVERYTHING WILL BE---
WE---DID WE TAKE SOMETHING FROM HIM, ELOISE...?
YOU LET ME WORRY ABOUT THAT, SON. THAT'S NOT SOMETHING YOU NEED TO EVEN THINK ABOUT, MY DEAR.
YOU DID SO WELL.
MY SPECIAL, SPECIAL BOY...
BECAUSE OF YOU--- WE WILL BE ABLE TO SAVE THIS WORLD.

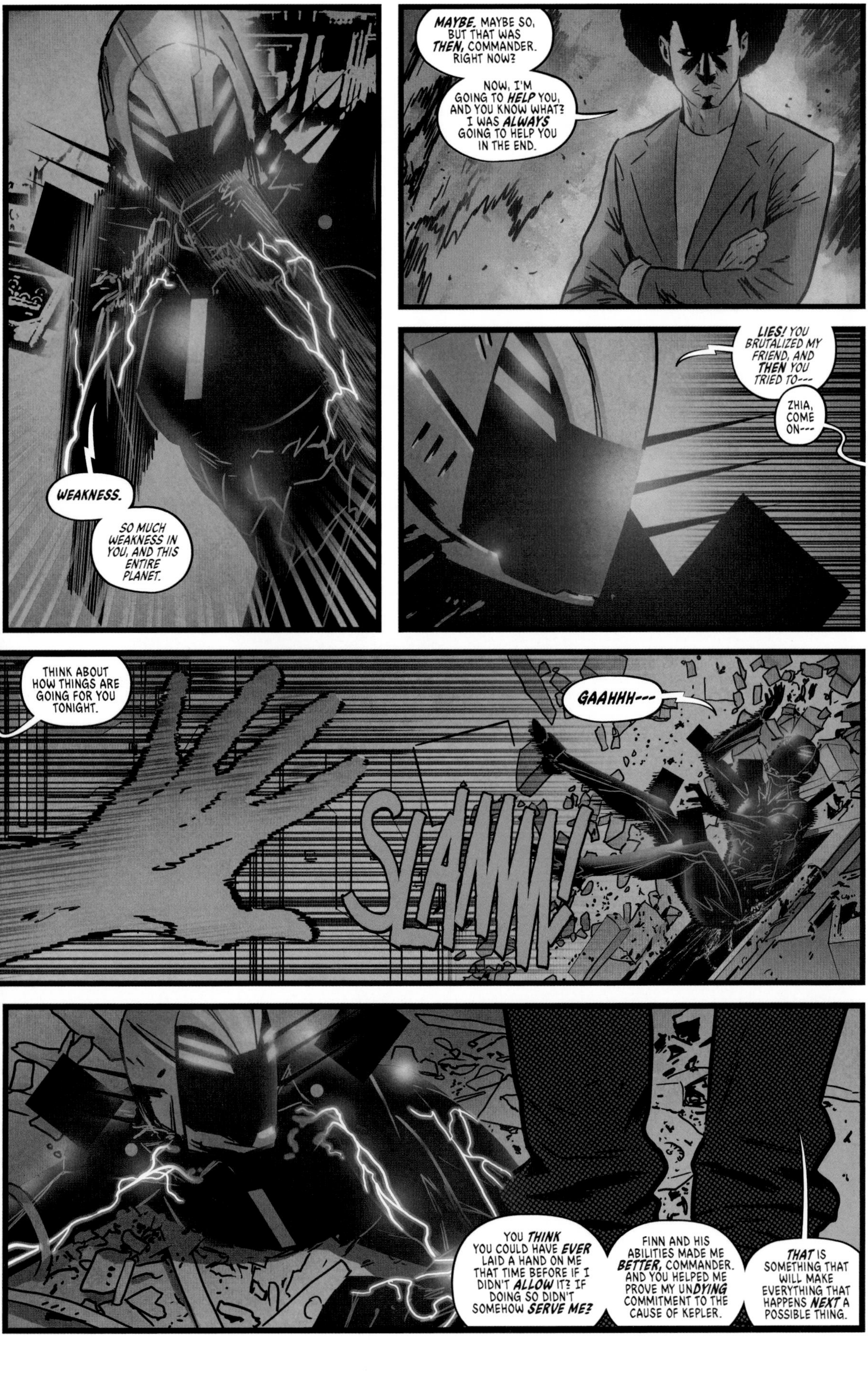
WEAKNESS.
SO MUCH WEAKNESS IN YOU, AND THIS ENTIRE PLANET.
MAYBE. MAYBE SO, BUT THAT WAS THEN, COMMANDER. RIGHT NOW?
NOW, I'M GOING TO HELP YOU, AND YOU KNOW WHAT? I WAS ALWAYS GOING TO HELP YOU IN THE END.
LIES! YOU BRUTALIZED MY FRIEND, AND THEN YOU TRIED TO---
ZHIA, COME ON---
THINK ABOUT HOW THINGS ARE GOING FOR YOU TONIGHT.
GAAHHH---
SLAMM!
YOU THINK YOU COULD HAVE EVER LAID A HAND ON ME THAT TIME BEFORE IF I DIDN'T ALLOW IT? IF DOING SO DIDN'T SOMEHOW SERVE ME?
FINN AND HIS ABILITIES MADE ME BETTER, COMMANDER. AND YOU HELPED ME PROVE MY UNDYING COMMITMENT TO THE CAUSE OF KEPLER.
THAT IS SOMETHING THAT WILL MAKE EVERYTHING THAT HAPPENS NEXT A POSSIBLE THING.

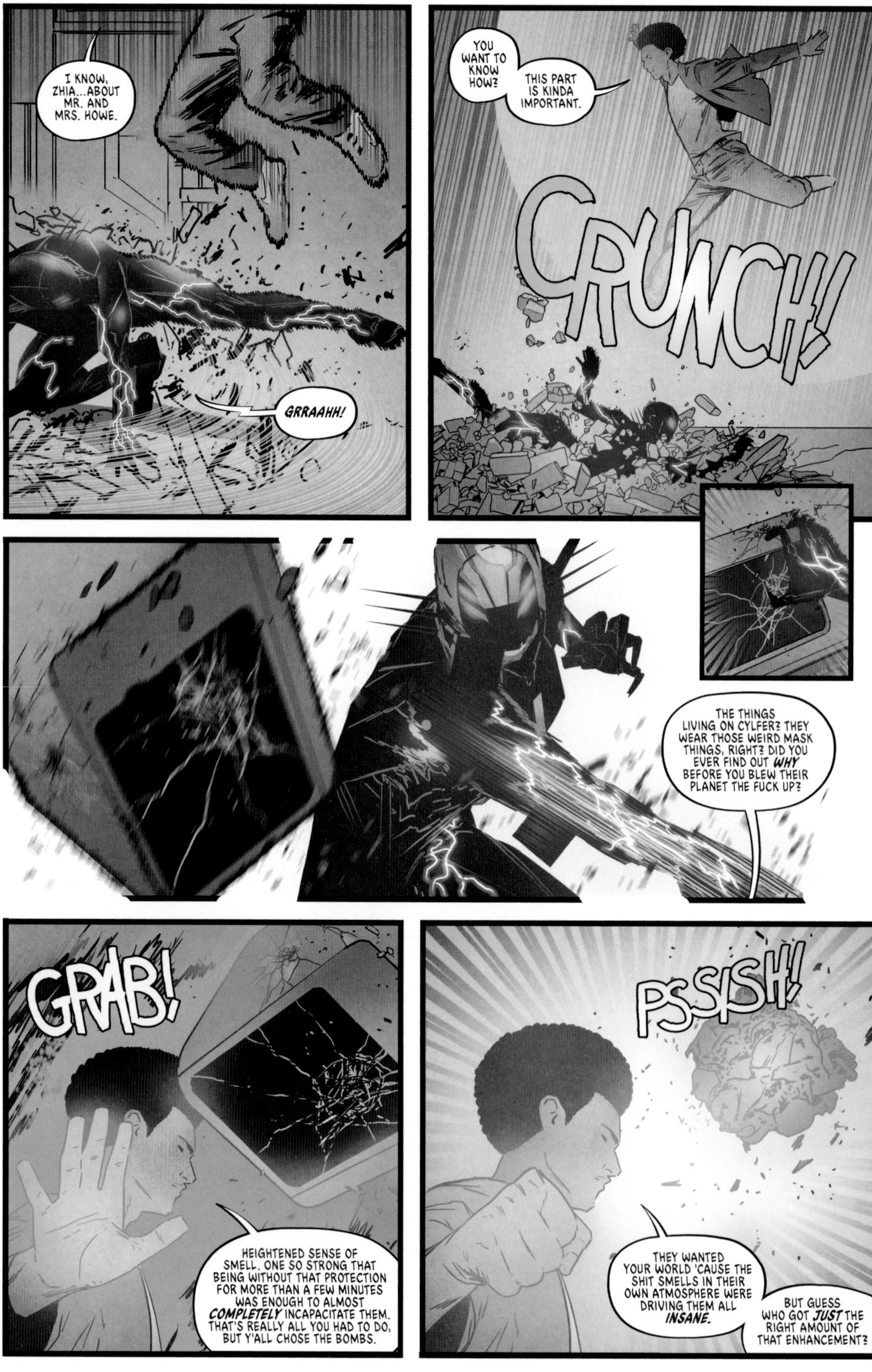
I KNOW, ZHIA...ABOUT MR. AND MRS. HOWE.
GRRAAHH!
YOU WANT TO KNOW HOW?
THIS PART IS KINDA IMPORTANT.
CRUNCH!
THE THINGS LIVING ON CYLFER? THEY WEAR THOSE WEIRD MASK THINGS, RIGHT? DID YOU EVER FIND OUT WHY BEFORE YOU BLEW THEIR PLANET THE FUCK UP?
GRAB!
HEIGHTENED SENSE OF SMELL. ONE SO STRONG THAT BEING WITHOUT THAT PROTECTION FOR MORE THAN A FEW MINUTES WAS ENOUGH TO ALMOST COMPLETELY INCAPACITATE THEM. THAT'S REALLY ALL YOU HAD TO DO, BUT Y'ALL CHOSE THE BOMBS.
PSSISH!
THEY WANTED YOUR WORLD 'CAUSE THE SHIT SMELLS IN THEIR OWN ATMOSPHERE WERE DRIVING THEM ALL INSANE.
BUT GUESS WHO GOT JUST THE RIGHT AMOUNT OF THAT ENHANCEMENT?

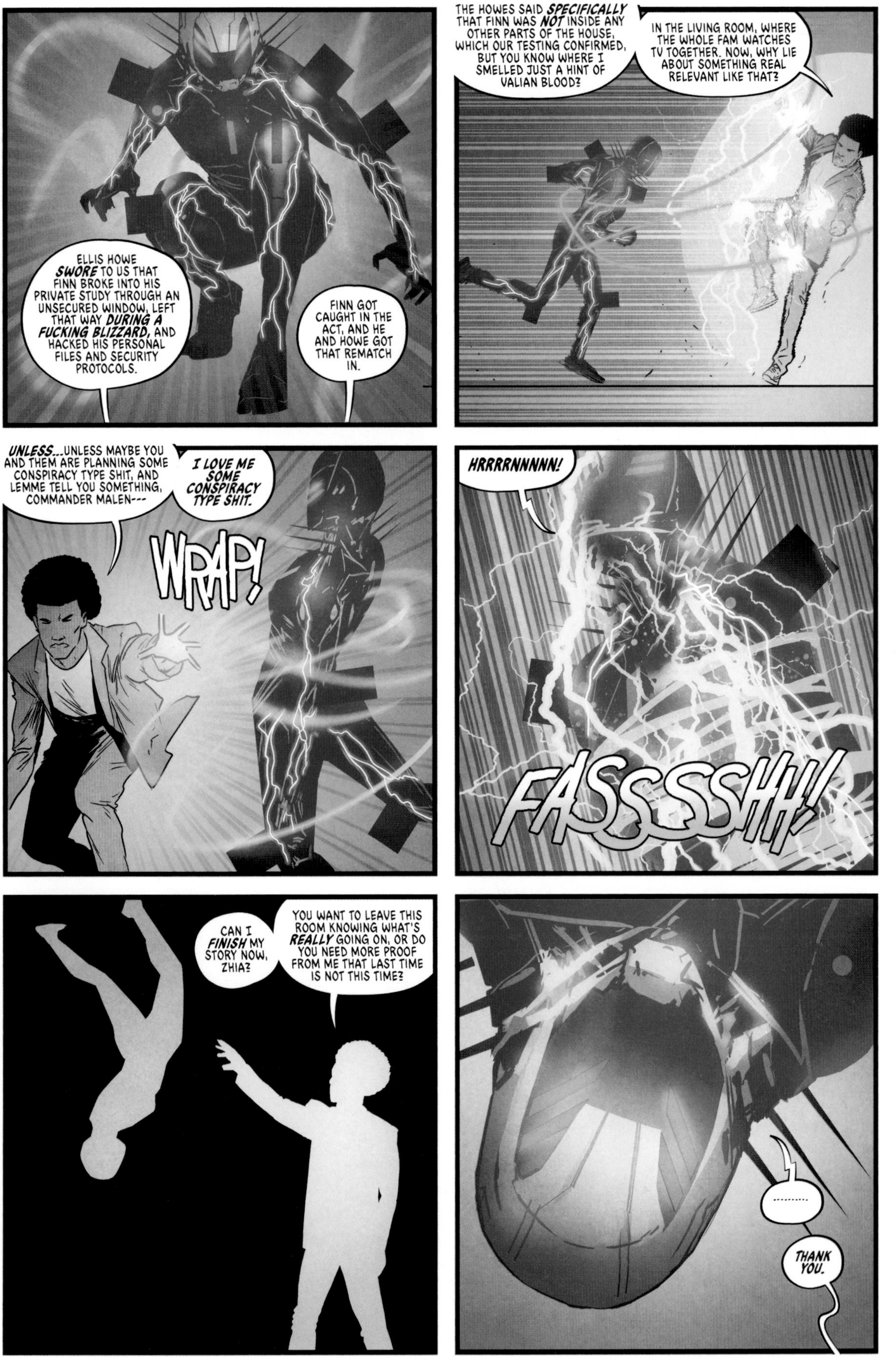
ELLIS HOWE SWORE TO US THAT FINN BROKE INTO HIS PRIVATE STUDY THROUGH AN UNSECURED WINDOW, LEFT THAT WAY DURING A FUCKING BLIZZARD, AND HACKED HIS PERSONAL FILES AND SECURITY PROTOCOLS.
FINN GOT CAUGHT IN THE ACT, AND HE AND HOWE GOT THAT REMATCH IN.
THE HOWES SAID SPECIFICALLY THAT FINN WAS NOT INSIDE ANY OTHER PARTS OF THE HOUSE, WHICH OUR TESTING CONFIRMED, BUT YOU KNOW WHERE I SMELLED JUST A HINT OF VALIAN BLOOD?
IN THE LIVING ROOM, WHERE THE WHOLE FAM WATCHES TV TOGETHER. NOW, WHY LIE ABOUT SOMETHING REAL RELEVANT LIKE THAT?
UNLESS...UNLESS MAYBE YOU AND THEM ARE PLANNING SOME CONSPIRACY TYPE SHIT, AND LEMME TELL YOU SOMETHING, COMMANDER MALEN---
I LOVE ME SOME CONSPIRACY TYPE SHIT.
WRAP!
HRRRRNNNNN!
FASSSSHH!
CAN I FINISH MY STORY NOW, ZHIA?
YOU WANT TO LEAVE THIS ROOM KNOWING WHAT'S REALLY GOING ON, OR DO YOU NEED MORE PROOF FROM ME THAT LAST TIME IS NOT THIS TIME?
....
THANK YOU.

SO I'M ASSUMING YOU KNOW SOME OF OUR *FUCKED UP* HISTORY, RIGHT? THE THINGS THAT HAVE BEEN DONE TO SOME OF US OVER THE YEARS---

---WHETHER IT WAS ENSLAVEMENT, OR THE SYSTEMIC OPPRESSION THAT FOLLOWED THAT, ALL TO ACHIEVE THE EXACT SAME OBVIOUS END---

---TO DEVALUE OUR LIVES, SO THAT ANYTHING DONE TO US WILL *ALWAYS* BE JUSTIFIED.

THE DECISIONS ABOUT WHO GETS TO LEAVE EARTH ARE *ALREADY* TAKING A VERY FAMILIAR FUCKING SHAPE, COMMANDER MALEN.

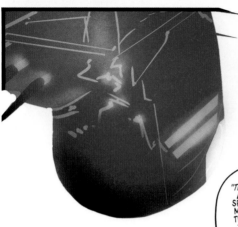

IF WE DON'T TAKE *THIS* CHANCE TO KILL OUR PAST, THEN WE *NEVER* WILL. AND I'VE BEEN WAITING *ALL* THESE YEARS FOR THE POWERS THAT BE TO *SHOW* ME SOMETHING DIFFERENT, BUT PUSH COME...THEY WANT THIS SHIT TO STAY *EXACTLY THE SAME.*

SO, *I'M* SAYING, *"THAT'S ENOUGH OF THAT BULLSHIT."* AND I'VE SPENT MOST OF MY LIFE MAKING THEM BELIEVE THAT, *ME?* I'M ONE OF *THE GOOD ONES*--- BECAUSE I CAN DO WHAT I'M TOLD, BECAUSE I CAN SMILE BACK AT THEM EVERY OTHER TIME.

BUT I'M *NOT* ONE OF THE GOOD ONES, COMMANDER MALEN, AND I *NEVER FUCKING WAS...* I'M ONE OF THE *SMART* ONES.

AND WHEN THAT TIME IS RIGHT, WHEN I DECIDE THAT IT'S TIME FOR THEM TO KNOW ME, TO FINALLY KNOW THAT I'VE BEEN PAYIN' *REAL CLOSE ATTENTION* TO THEM--- ALL THEY'VE DONE, AND ALL THEY'VE STOOD BY AND *ALLOWED* TO BE DONE IN THEIR NAME---

THEY GON' LEARN THE HARD WAY---THEY SHOULD'VE ALWAYS BEEN MORE CAREFUL WITH A ~~NIGGA~~ LIKE ME.

SMILE OR NOT.

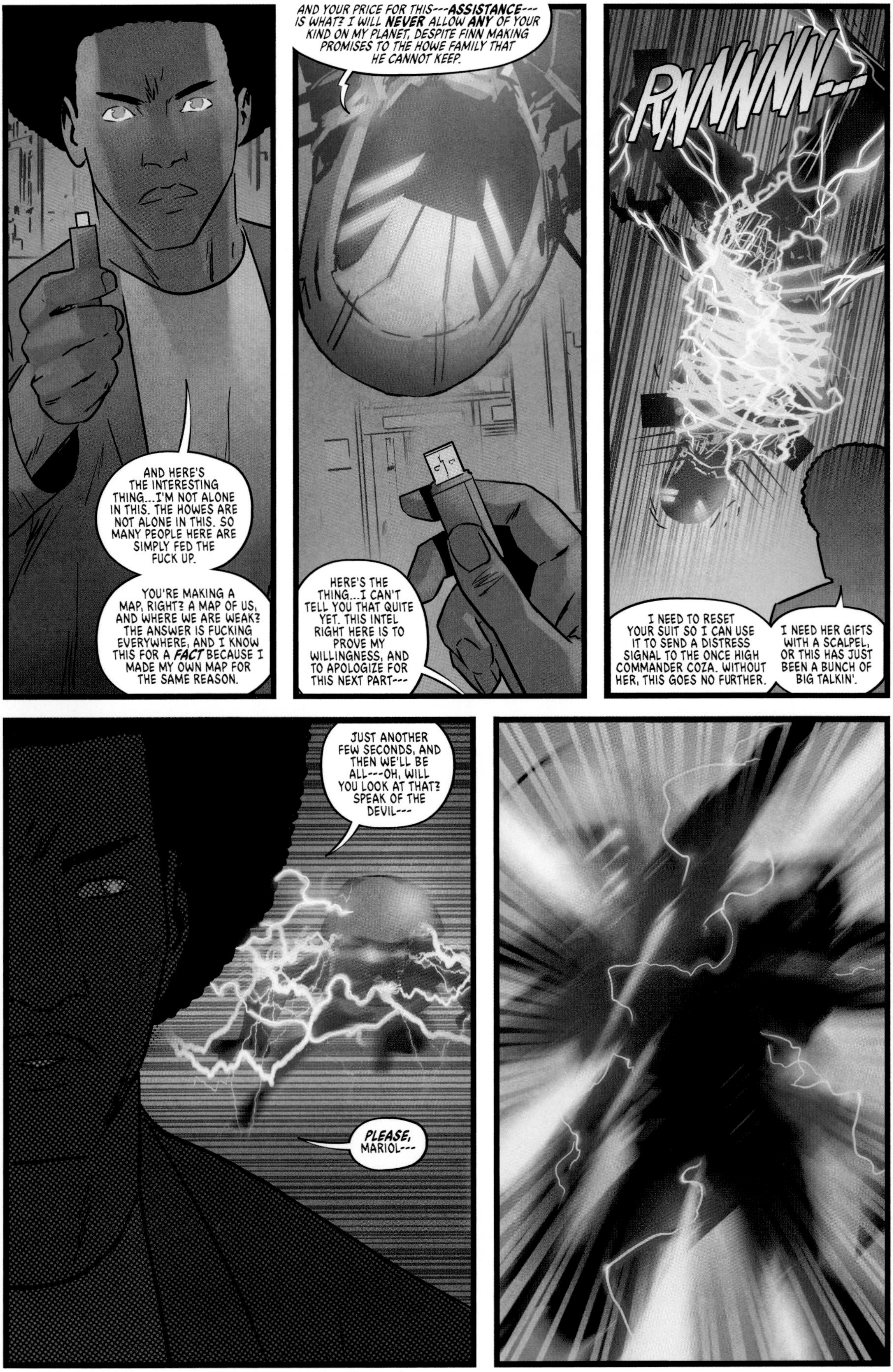
AND HERE'S THE INTERESTING THING...I'M NOT ALONE IN THIS. THE HOWES ARE NOT ALONE IN THIS. SO MANY PEOPLE HERE ARE SIMPLY FED THE FUCK UP.
YOU'RE MAKING A MAP, RIGHT? A MAP OF US, AND WHERE WE ARE WEAK? THE ANSWER IS FUCKING EVERYWHERE, AND I KNOW THIS FOR A FACT BECAUSE I MADE MY OWN MAP FOR THE SAME REASON.
AND YOUR PRICE FOR THIS---ASSISTANCE---IS WHAT? I WILL NEVER ALLOW ANY OF YOUR KIND ON MY PLANET, DESPITE FINN MAKING PROMISES TO THE HOWE FAMILY THAT HE CANNOT KEEP.
HERE'S THE THING...I CAN'T TELL YOU THAT QUITE YET. THIS INTEL RIGHT HERE IS TO PROVE MY WILLINGNESS, AND TO APOLOGIZE FOR THIS NEXT PART---
RNNNNN---
I NEED TO RESET YOUR SUIT SO I CAN USE IT TO SEND A DISTRESS SIGNAL TO THE ONCE HIGH COMMANDER COZA. WITHOUT HER, THIS GOES NO FURTHER.
I NEED HER GIFTS WITH A SCALPEL, OR THIS HAS JUST BEEN A BUNCH OF BIG TALKIN'.
JUST ANOTHER FEW SECONDS, AND THEN WE'LL BE ALL---OH, WILL YOU LOOK AT THAT? SPEAK OF THE DEVIL---
PLEASE, MARIOL---

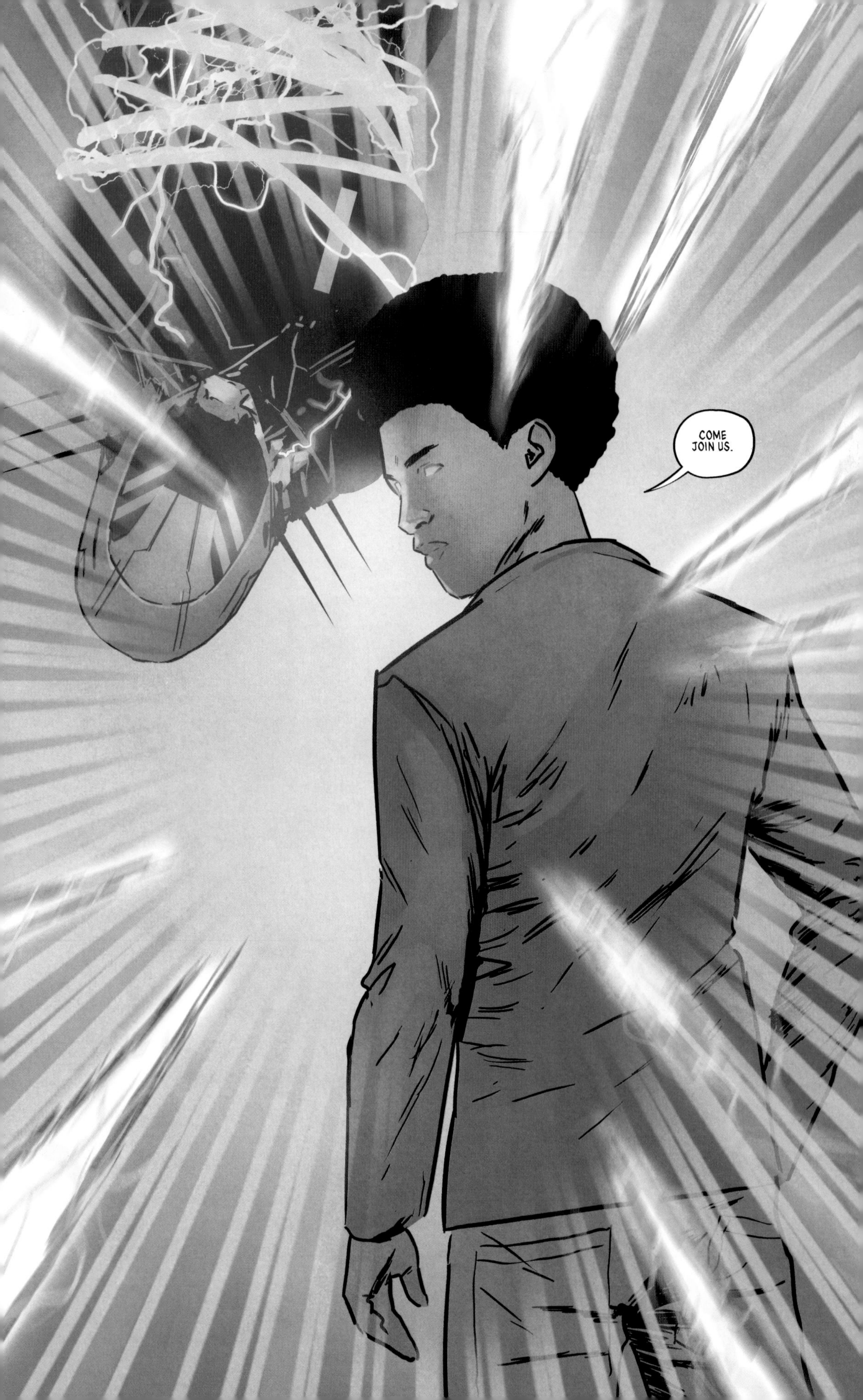
COME JOIN US.

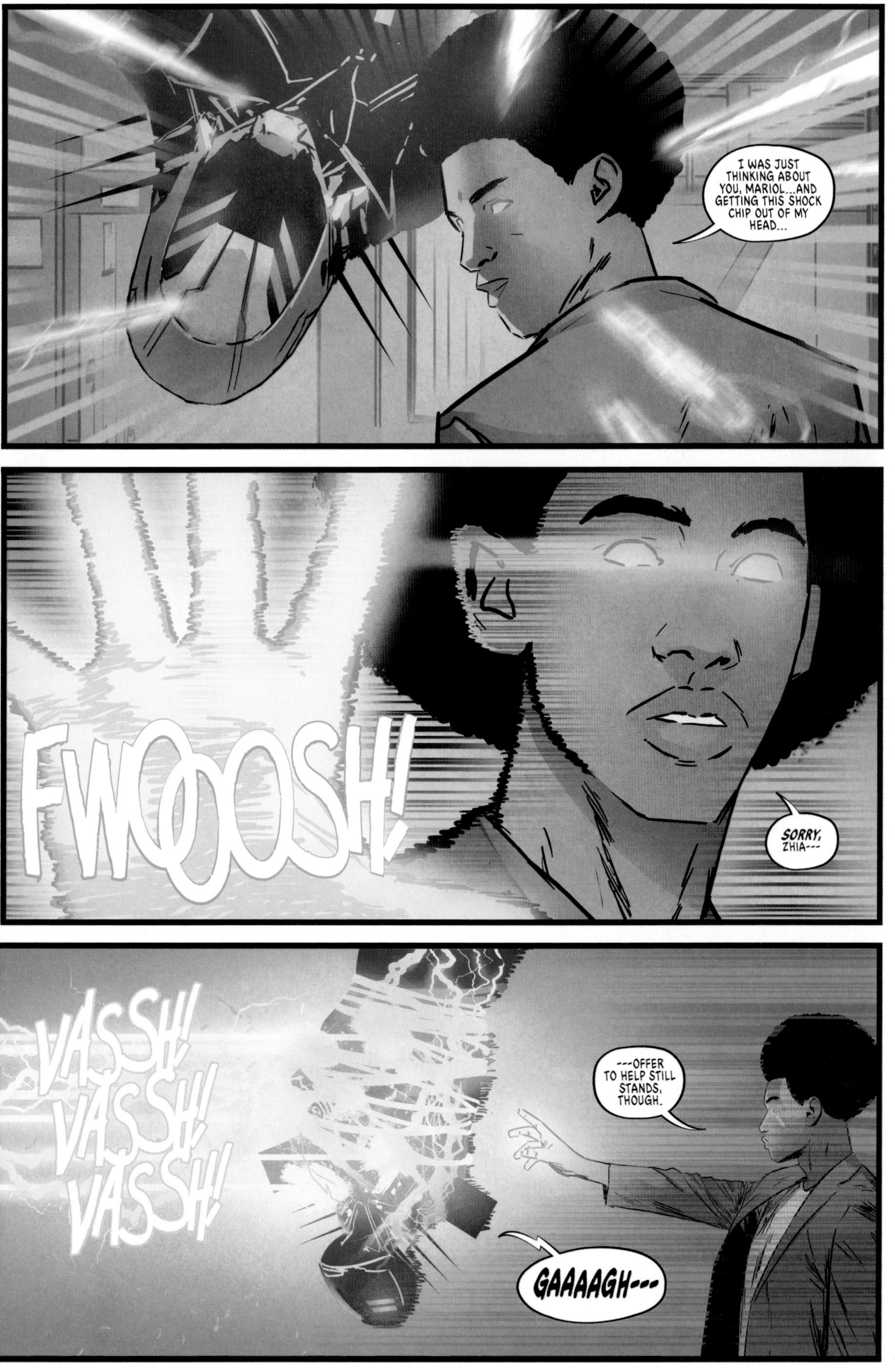
I WAS JUST THINKING ABOUT YOU, MARIOL...AND GETTING THIS SHOCK CHIP OUT OF MY HEAD...
FWOOOSH!
SORRY, ZHIA---
VASSH! VASSH! VASSH!
---OFFER TO HELP STILL STANDS, THOUGH.
GAAAAGH---

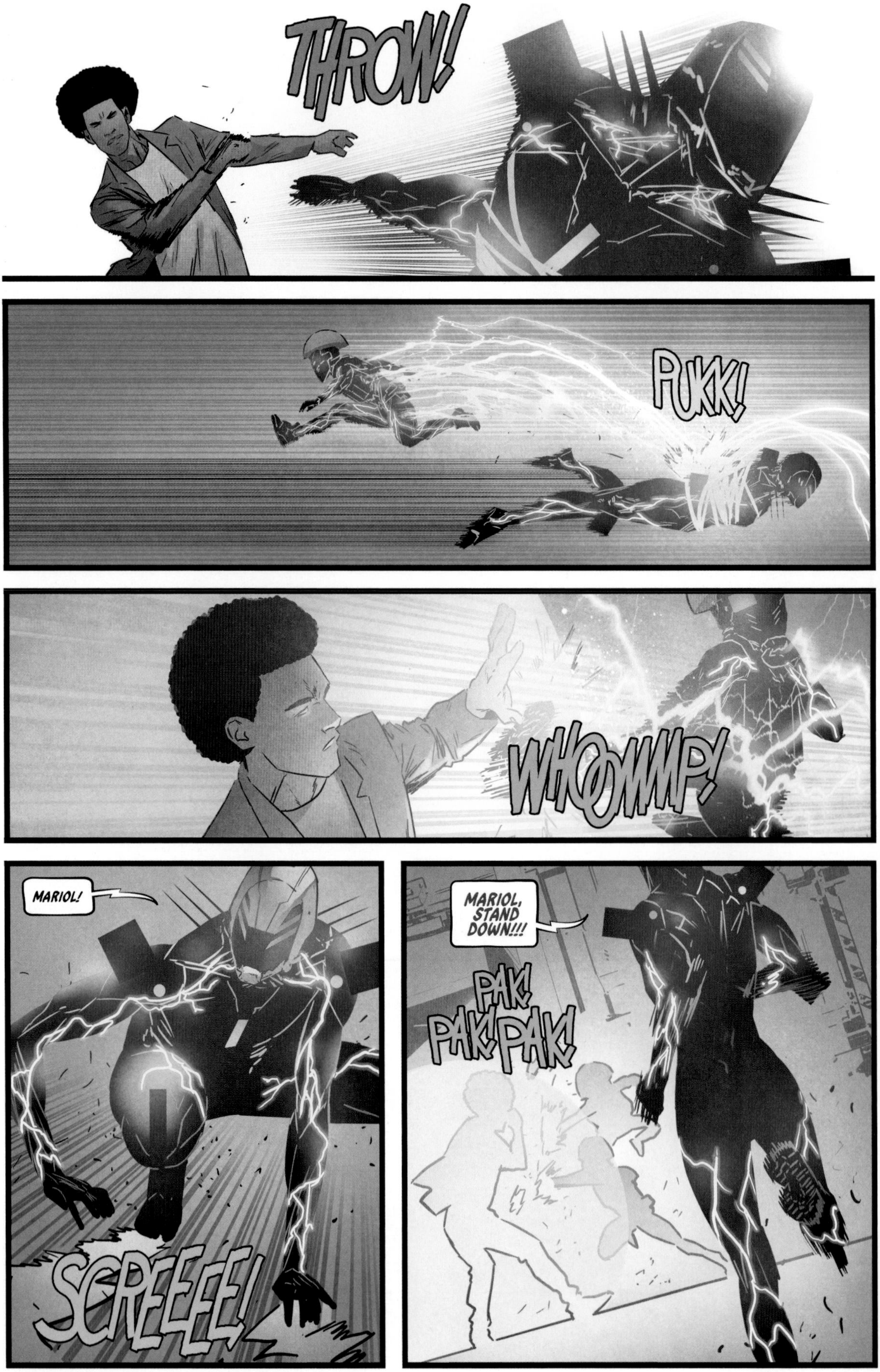
THROW!
PUKK!
WHOOMMP!
MARIOL!
SCREEEEE!
MARIOL, STAND DOWN!!!
PAK!
PAK! PAK!

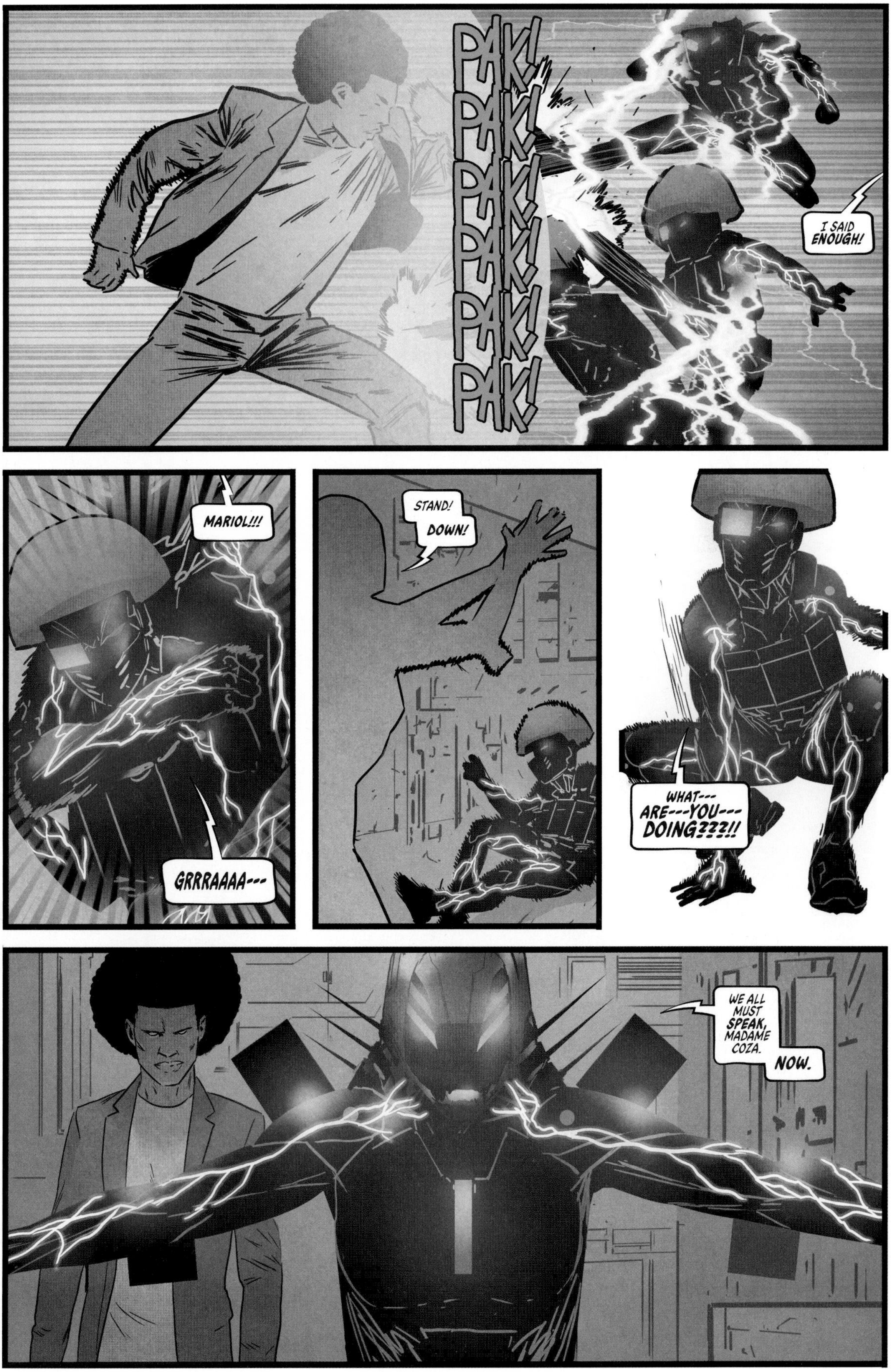
PAK! PAK! PAK! PAK! PAK! PAK!
I SAID ENOUGH!
MARIOL!!!
GRRRAAAA---
STAND! DOWN!
WHAT--- ARE---YOU--- DOING???!!
WE ALL MUST SPEAK, MADAME COZA.
NOW.

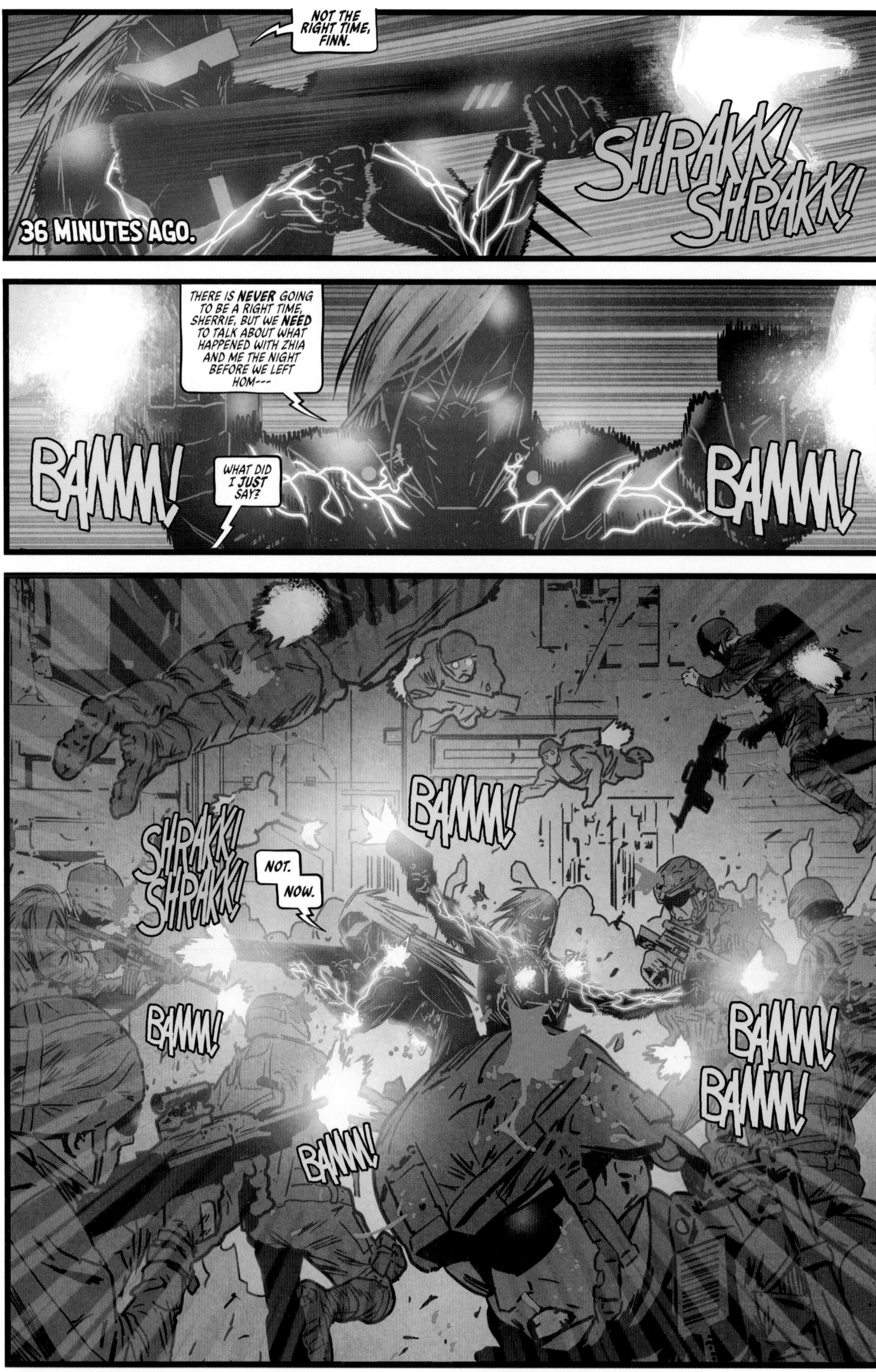
NOT THE RIGHT TIME, FINN.
SHRAKK! SHRAKK!
36 MINUTES AGO.
THERE IS NEVER GOING TO BE A RIGHT TIME, SHERRIE, BUT WE NEED TO TALK ABOUT WHAT HAPPENED WITH ZHIA AND ME THE NIGHT BEFORE WE LEFT HOM---
BAMM!
WHAT DID I JUST SAY?
BAMM!
BAMM!
SHRAKK! SHRAKK!
NOT. NOW.
BAMM!
BAMM! BAMM!
BAMM!

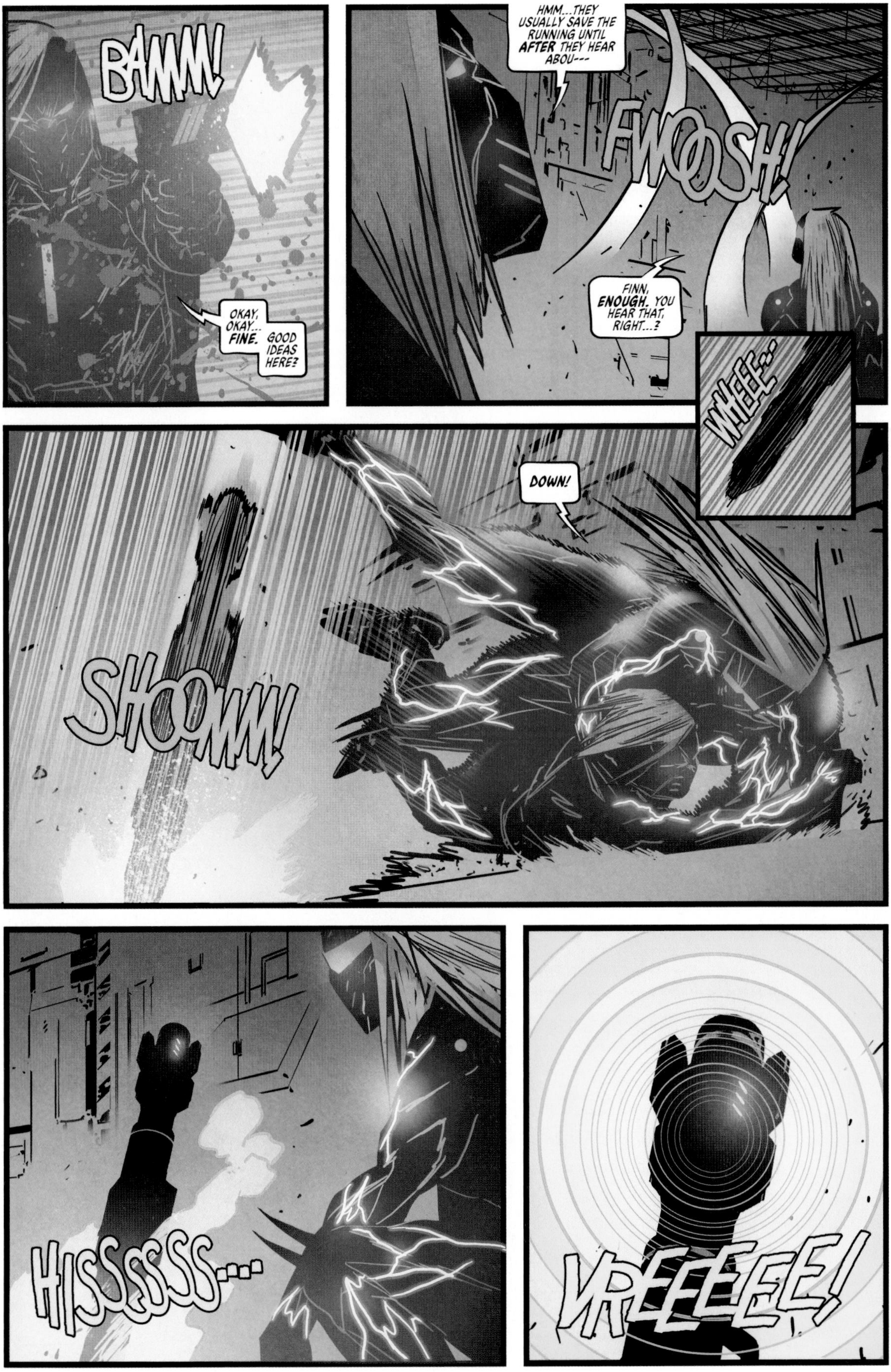
BAMM!
OKAY, OKAY... FINE.
GOOD IDEAS HERE?
HMM...THEY USUALLY SAVE THE RUNNING UNTIL AFTER THEY HEAR ABOU---
FWOOSH!
FINN, ENOUGH. YOU HEAR THAT, RIGHT...?
WHEEE...
DOWN!
SHOOMM!
HISSSSSS....
VREEEEEE!

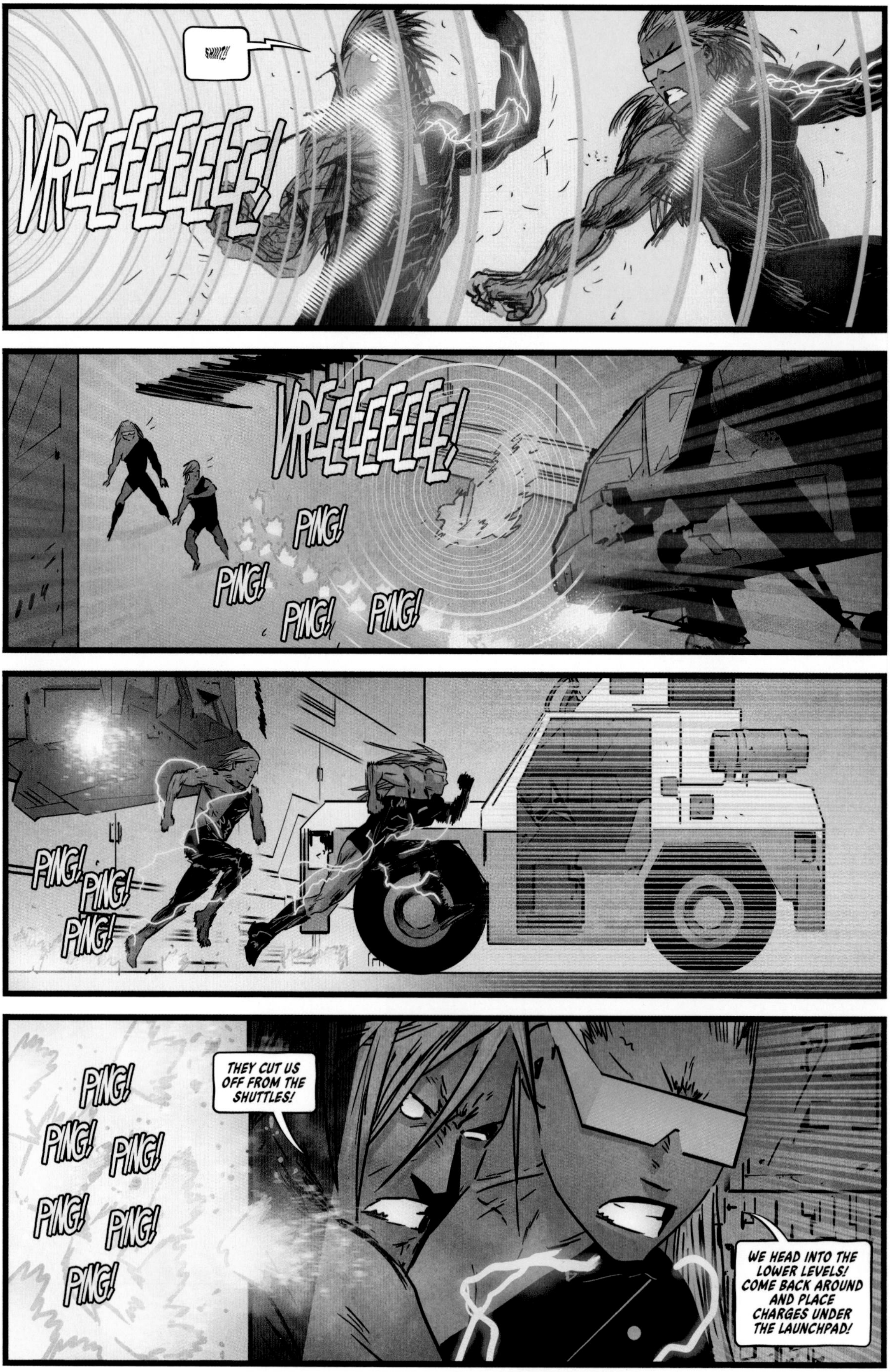
VREEEEEEEEE!
VREEEEEEEE!
PING!
PING!
PING!
PING!
PING!
PING!
PING!
PING!
THEY CUT US OFF FROM THE SHUTTLES!
PING!
PING!
PING!
PING!
PING!
WE HEAD INTO THE LOWER LEVELS! COME BACK AROUND AND PLACE CHARGES UNDER THE LAUNCHPAD!

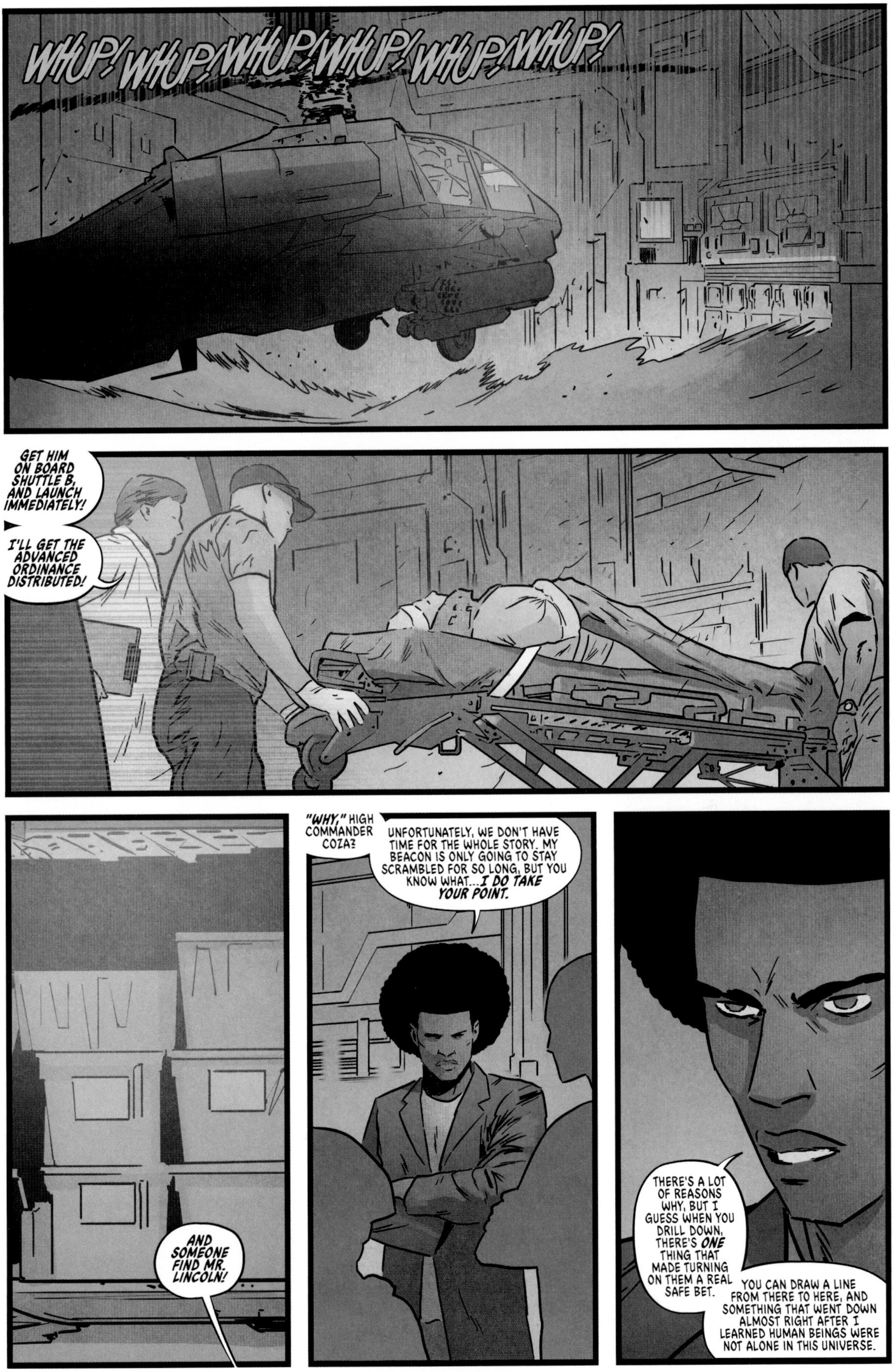
WHUP! WHUP! WHUP! WHUP! WHUP! WHUP!
GET HIM ON BOARD SHUTTLE B, AND LAUNCH IMMEDIATELY!
I'LL GET THE ADVANCED ORDINANCE DISTRIBUTED!
AND SOMEONE FIND MR. LINCOLN!
"WHY," HIGH COMMANDER COZA?
UNFORTUNATELY, WE DON'T HAVE TIME FOR THE WHOLE STORY. MY BEACON IS ONLY GOING TO STAY SCRAMBLED FOR SO LONG, BUT YOU KNOW WHAT... I DO TAKE YOUR POINT.
THERE'S A LOT OF REASONS WHY, BUT I GUESS WHEN YOU DRILL DOWN, THERE'S ONE THING THAT MADE TURNING ON THEM A REAL SAFE BET.
YOU CAN DRAW A LINE FROM THERE TO HERE, AND SOMETHING THAT WENT DOWN ALMOST RIGHT AFTER I LEARNED HUMAN BEINGS WERE NOT ALONE IN THIS UNIVERSE.

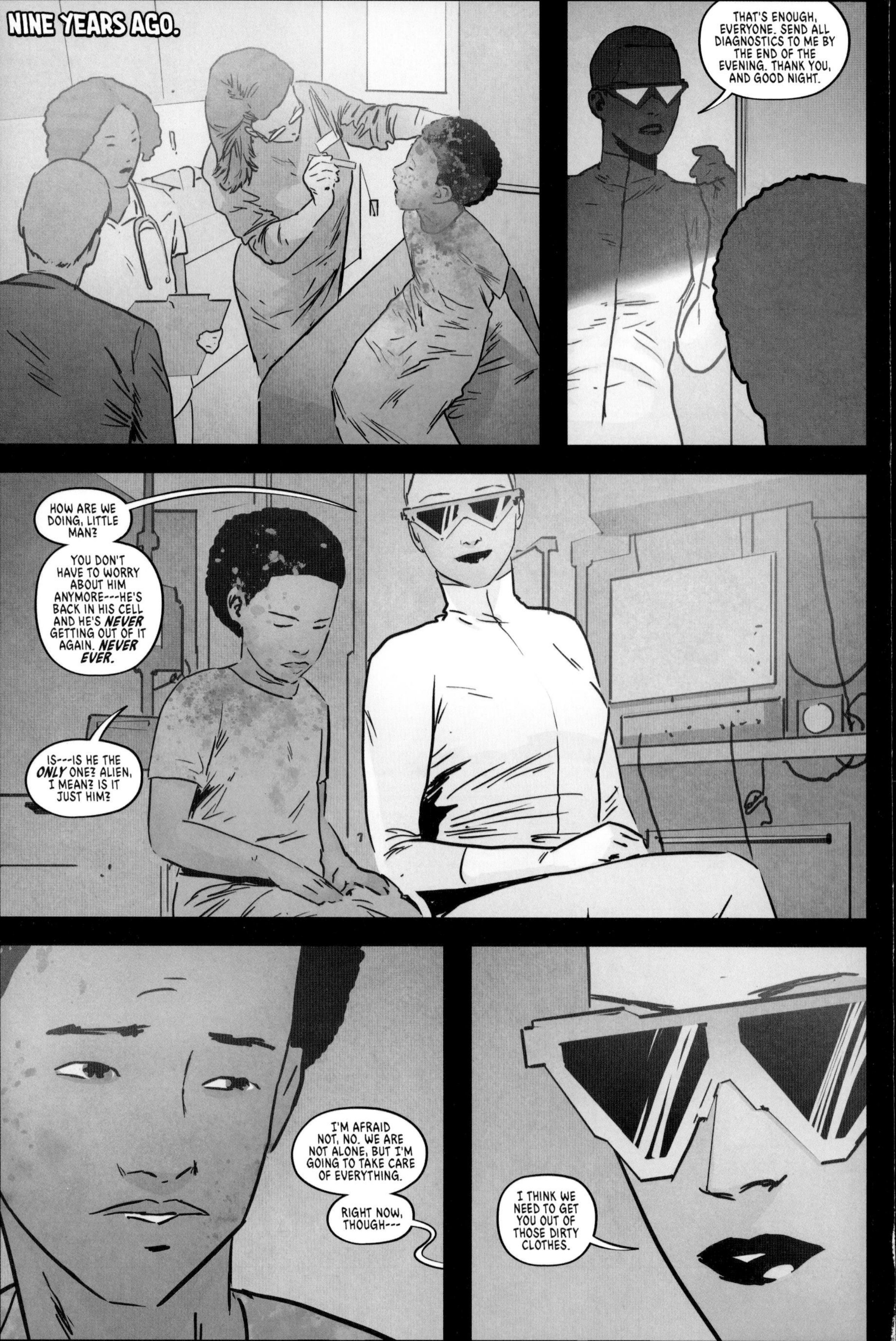

NINE YEARS AGO.
THAT'S ENOUGH, EVERYONE. SEND ALL DIAGNOSTICS TO ME BY THE END OF THE EVENING. THANK YOU, AND GOOD NIGHT.
HOW ARE WE DOING, LITTLE MAN?
YOU DON'T HAVE TO WORRY ABOUT HIM ANYMORE---HE'S BACK IN HIS CELL AND HE'S NEVER GETTING OUT OF IT AGAIN. NEVER EVER.
IS---IS HE THE ONLY ONE? ALIEN, I MEAN? IS IT JUST HIM?
I'M AFRAID NOT, NO. WE ARE NOT ALONE, BUT I'M GOING TO TAKE CARE OF EVERYTHING.
RIGHT NOW, THOUGH---
I THINK WE NEED TO GET YOU OUT OF THOSE DIRTY CLOTHES.

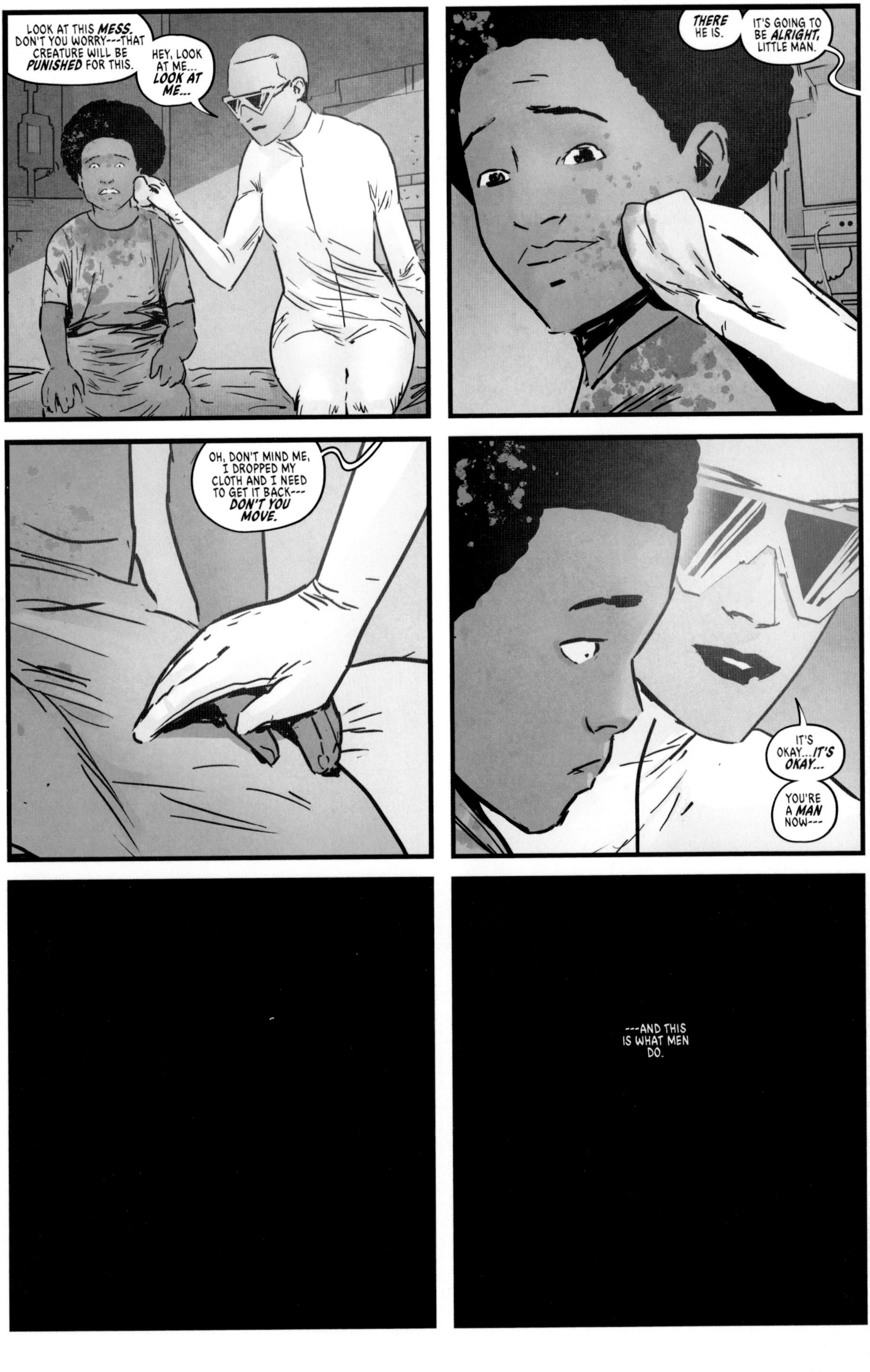
LOOK AT THIS MESS. DON'T YOU WORRY---THAT CREATURE WILL BE PUNISHED FOR THIS.
HEY, LOOK AT ME... LOOK AT ME...
THERE HE IS.
IT'S GOING TO BE ALRIGHT, LITTLE MAN.
OH, DON'T MIND ME, I DROPPED MY CLOTH AND I NEED TO GET IT BACK--- DON'T YOU MOVE.
IT'S OKAY... IT'S OKAY...
YOU'RE A MAN NOW---
---AND THIS IS WHAT MEN DO.

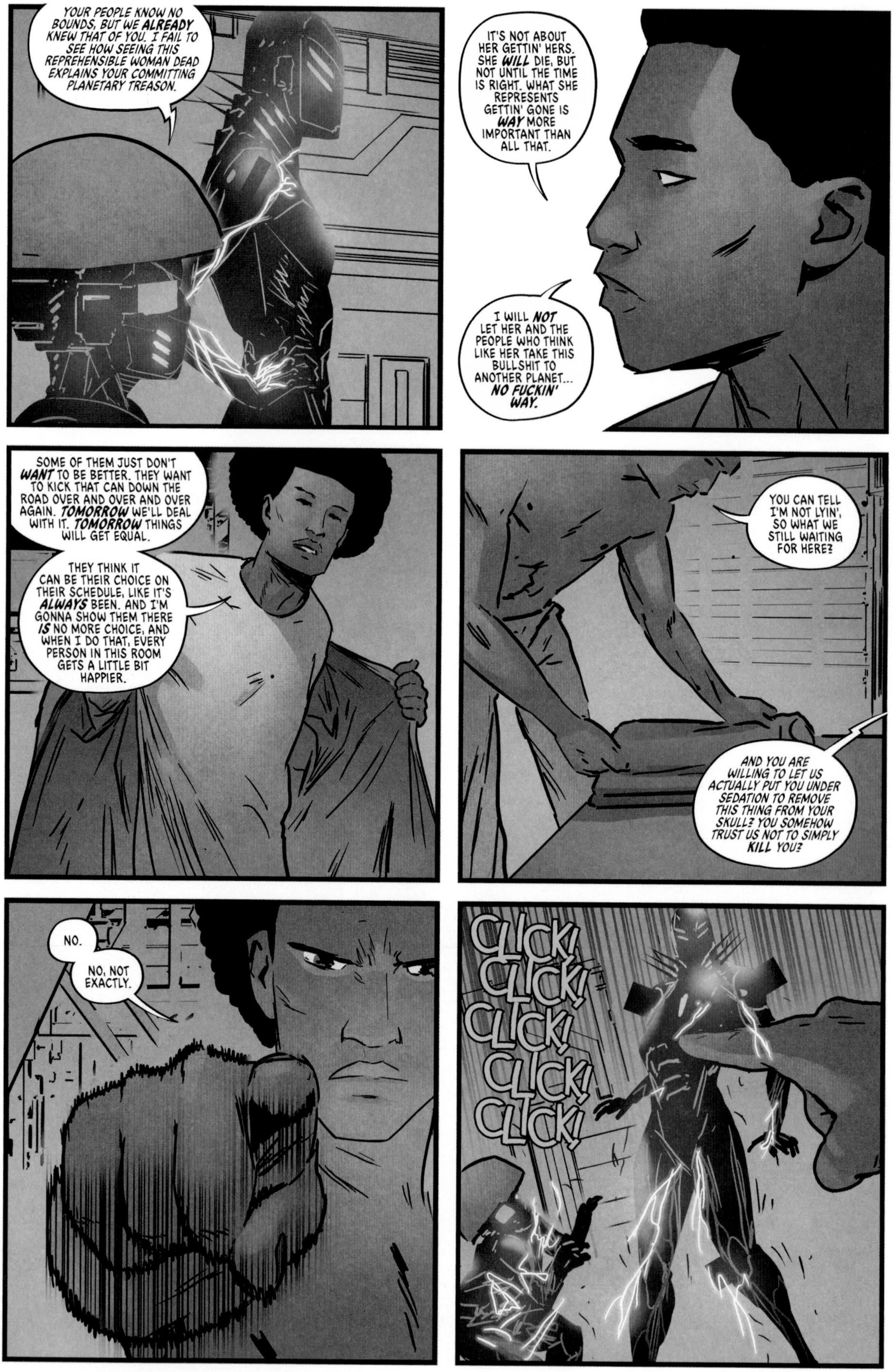
YOUR PEOPLE KNOW NO BOUNDS, BUT WE ALREADY KNEW THAT OF YOU. I FAIL TO SEE HOW SEEING THIS REPREHENSIBLE WOMAN DEAD EXPLAINS YOUR COMMITTING PLANETARY TREASON.
IT'S NOT ABOUT HER GETTIN' HERS. SHE WILL DIE, BUT NOT UNTIL THE TIME IS RIGHT. WHAT SHE REPRESENTS GETTIN' GONE IS WAY MORE IMPORTANT THAN ALL THAT.
I WILL NOT LET HER AND THE PEOPLE WHO THINK LIKE HER TAKE THIS BULLSHIT TO ANOTHER PLANET... NO FUCKIN' WAY.
SOME OF THEM JUST DON'T WANT TO BE BETTER. THEY WANT TO KICK THAT CAN DOWN THE ROAD OVER AND OVER AND OVER AGAIN. TOMORROW WE'LL DEAL WITH IT. TOMORROW THINGS WILL GET EQUAL.
THEY THINK IT CAN BE THEIR CHOICE ON THEIR SCHEDULE, LIKE IT'S ALWAYS BEEN. AND I'M GONNA SHOW THEM THERE IS NO MORE CHOICE, AND WHEN I DO THAT, EVERY PERSON IN THIS ROOM GETS A LITTLE BIT HAPPIER.
YOU CAN TELL I'M NOT LYIN', SO WHAT WE STILL WAITING FOR HERE?
AND YOU ARE WILLING TO LET US ACTUALLY PUT YOU UNDER SEDATION TO REMOVE THIS THING FROM YOUR SKULL? YOU SOMEHOW TRUST US NOT TO SIMPLY KILL YOU?
NO.
NO, NOT EXACTLY.
CLICK! CLICK! CLICK! CLICK! CLICK!

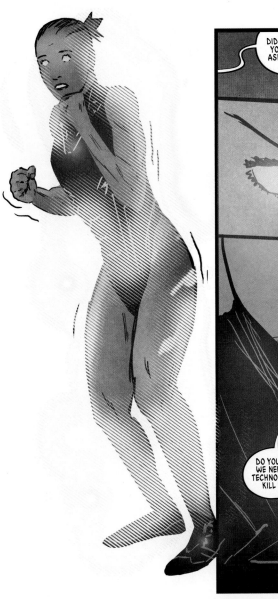

GETTING OUR HANDS ON FINN WAS JUST THE GREATEST GIFT---THAT'LL *NEVER* STOP GIVING.

THOSE SUITS ARE STILL COOL AS *FUCK*, THOUGH. OH SHIT, *SORRY---*

DIDN'T MEAN TO STRIP YOU DOWN WITHOUT ASKING FIRST---THAT AIN'T COOL---

DO YOU THINK WE NEED OUR TECHNOLOGY TO KILL YOU?

HEH...OH, I *LIKE* YOU, HIGH COMMANDER COZA. WE'RE GONNA GET ALONG *JUUUST* FINE.

ACTUALLY, I WAS THINKING THAT ZHIA IS GONNA STAY THOSE QUICK HANDS OF YOURS.

CLINK!
CLINK!

SHE'S *REAL* CURIOUS NOW, IF I CAN DO WHAT I SAY I CAN DO.

COMMANDER, FIND A TERMINAL THAT DON'T HAVE A BODY IN IT AND PLUG IN THAT MEMORY STICK, SEE IF EVERYTHING SEEMS LEGIT.

CLANG!

YOU'LL HAVE TO WORK FAST, MISS COZA, NOW THAT I HEAL LIKE YOU GUYS DO.

ALSO, I'MMA STAY CONSCIOUS SO YOU CAN TALK ME THROUGH IT--- I NEED TO BE ABLE TO DO THE SAME THING FOR SOME OTHER FOLKS. TOOLS OVER THERE NEAR MY JACKET.

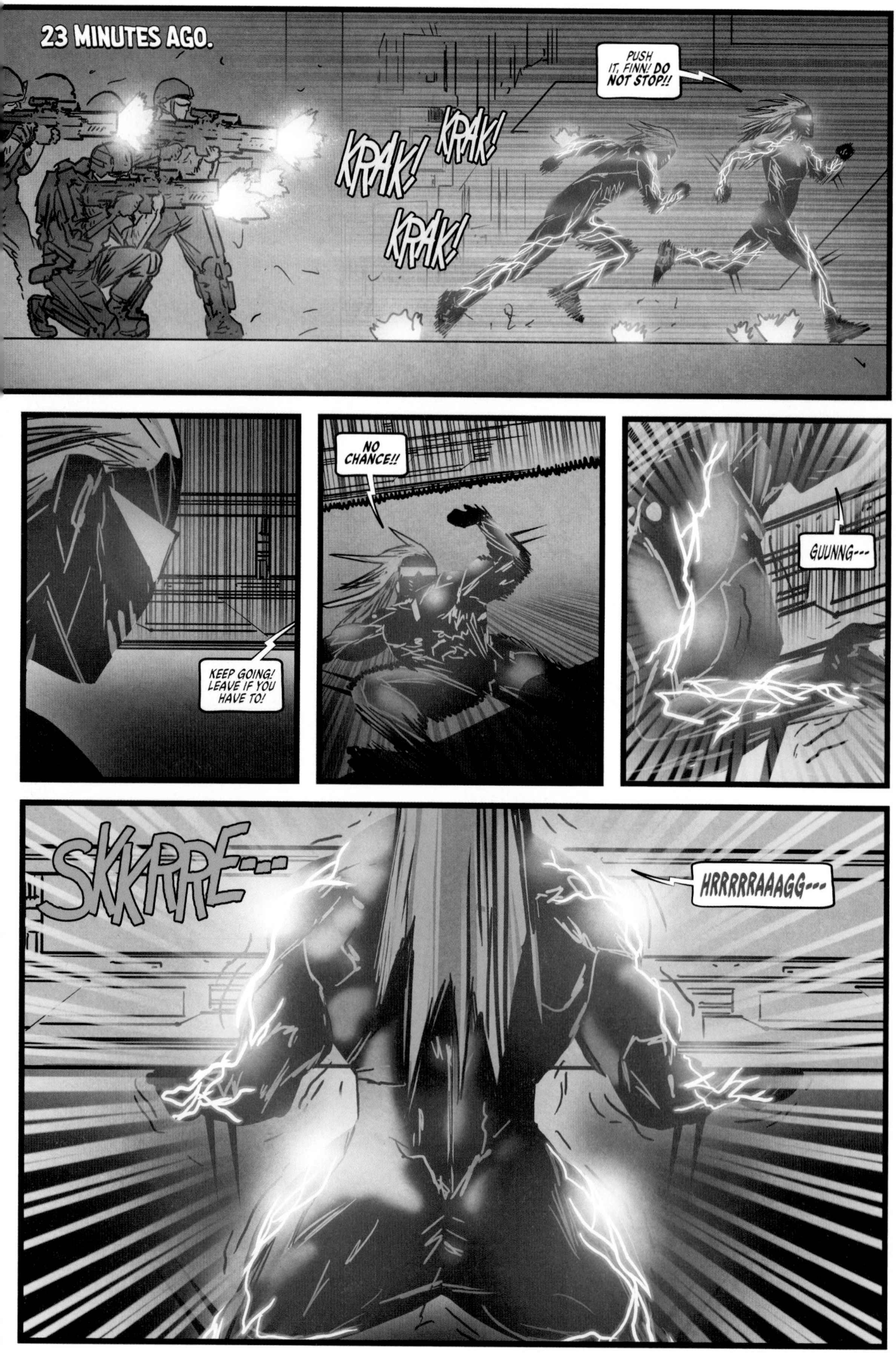
23 MINUTES AGO.
PUSH IT, FINN! DO NOT STOP!!
KRAK!
KRAK!
KRAK!
KEEP GOING! LEAVE IF YOU HAVE TO!
NO CHANCE!!
GUUNNG---
SKKRRRE---
HRRRRRAAAGG---

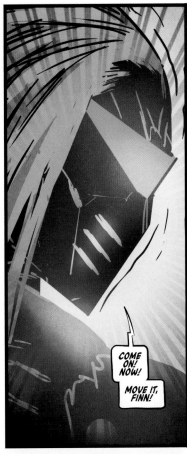

COME ON! NOW!

MOVE IT, FINN!

ALMOST THERE, SHER--- ALMOSTUNNGH---

FASSSH!

FSSSIZZ...

NOT AGAIN! WILL *NOT* TAKE ME AGAIN---

NO.

HOLD ON--- HOLD ON!

AAARRRRGGGHHH!!!!

ZNNN! ZNNN!

GET YOUR HANDS THE *FUCK* OFF HIM!!!

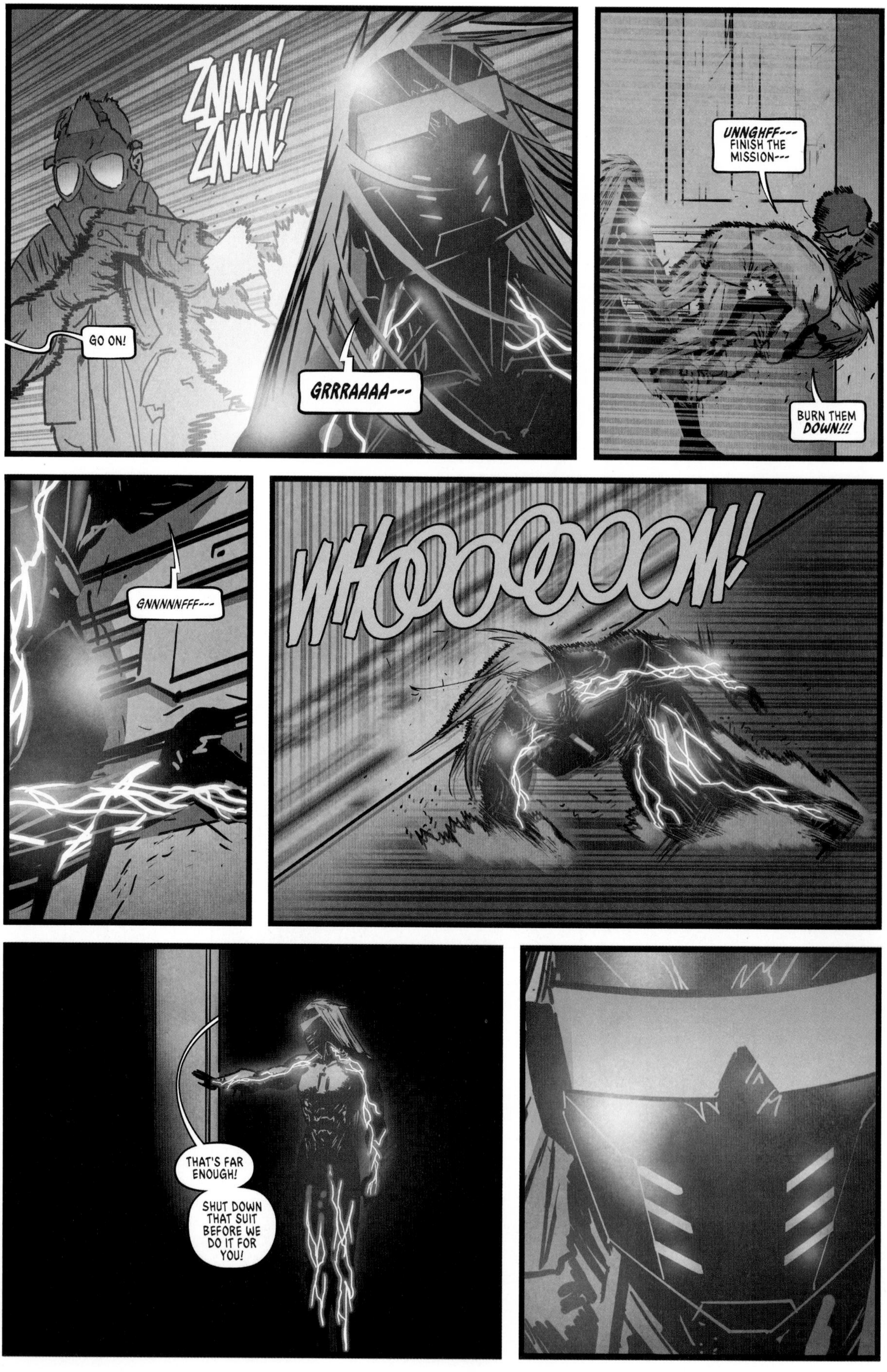
ZNNN! ZNNN!
GO ON!
GRRRAAAA---
UNNGHFF--- FINISH THE MISSION---
BURN THEM DOWN!!!
GNNNNNFFF---
WHOOOOOOM!
THAT'S FAR ENOUGH!
SHUT DOWN THAT SUIT BEFORE WE DO IT FOR YOU!

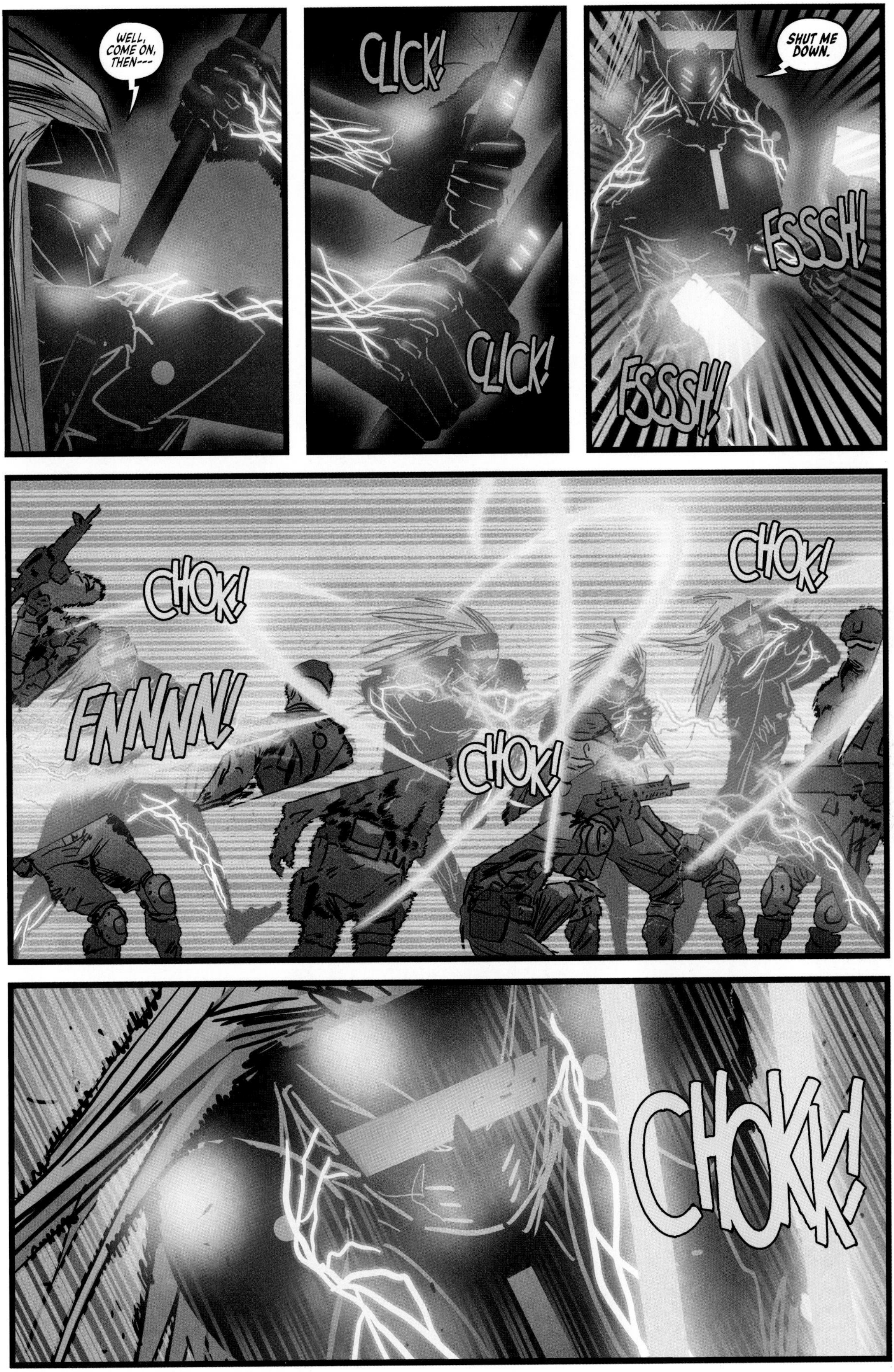
WELL, COME ON, THEN---
CLICK!
CLICK!
SHUT ME DOWN.
FSSSH!
FSSSH!
CHOK!
FNNNN!
CHOK!
CHOK!
CHOKK!

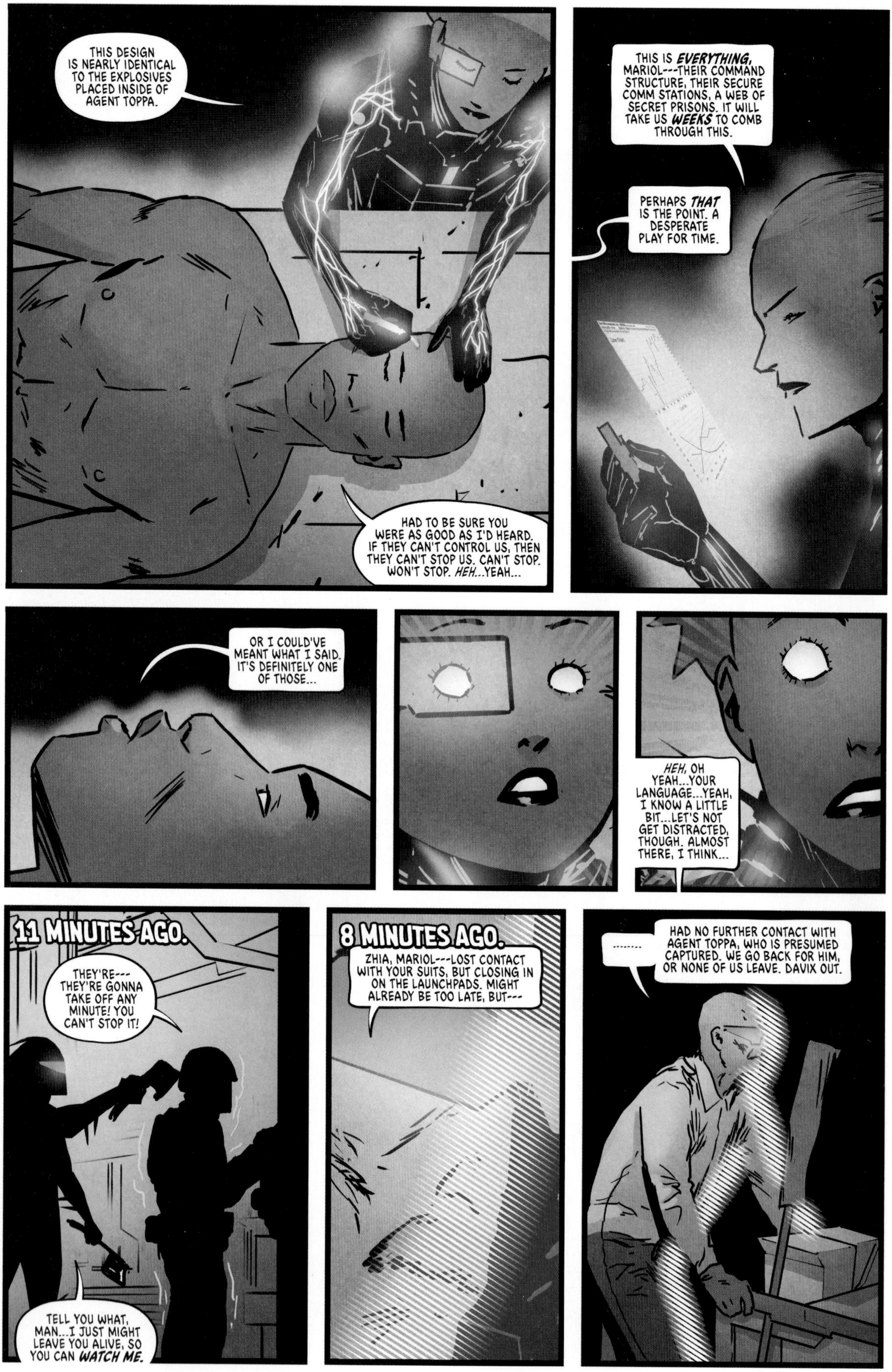
THIS DESIGN IS NEARLY IDENTICAL TO THE EXPLOSIVES PLACED INSIDE OF AGENT TOPPA.
HAD TO BE SURE YOU WERE AS GOOD AS I'D HEARD. IF THEY CAN'T CONTROL US, THEN THEY CAN'T STOP US. CAN'T STOP. WON'T STOP. HEH...YEAH...
THIS IS EVERYTHING, MARIOL---THEIR COMMAND STRUCTURE, THEIR SECURE COMM STATIONS, A WEB OF SECRET PRISONS. IT WILL TAKE US WEEKS TO COMB THROUGH THIS.
PERHAPS THAT IS THE POINT. A DESPERATE PLAY FOR TIME.
OR I COULD'VE MEANT WHAT I SAID. IT'S DEFINITELY ONE OF THOSE...
HEH, OH YEAH...YOUR LANGUAGE...YEAH, I KNOW A LITTLE BIT...LET'S NOT GET DISTRACTED, THOUGH. ALMOST THERE, I THINK...
11 MINUTES AGO.
THEY'RE--- THEY'RE GONNA TAKE OFF ANY MINUTE! YOU CAN'T STOP IT!
TELL YOU WHAT, MAN...I JUST MIGHT LEAVE YOU ALIVE, SO YOU CAN WATCH ME.
8 MINUTES AGO.
ZHIA, MARIOL---LOST CONTACT WITH YOUR SUITS, BUT CLOSING IN ON THE LAUNCHPADS. MIGHT ALREADY BE TOO LATE, BUT---
....
HAD NO FURTHER CONTACT WITH AGENT TOPPA, WHO IS PRESUMED CAPTURED. WE GO BACK FOR HIM, OR NONE OF US LEAVE. DAVIX OUT.

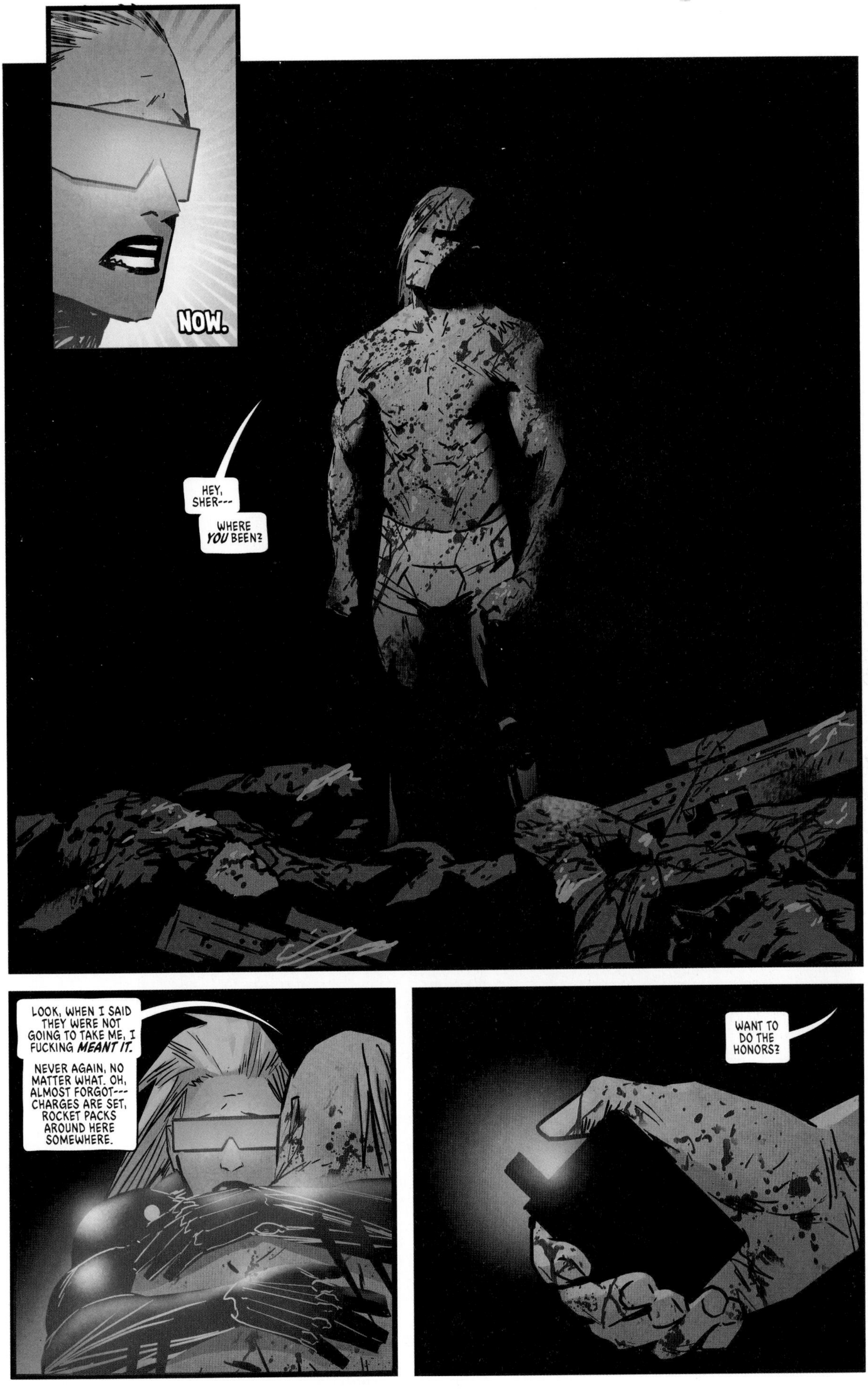
NOW.
HEY, SHER---
WHERE *YOU* BEEN?
LOOK, WHEN I SAID THEY WERE NOT GOING TO TAKE ME, I FUCKING *MEANT IT.*
NEVER AGAIN, NO MATTER WHAT. OH, ALMOST FORGOT--- CHARGES ARE SET, ROCKET PACKS AROUND HERE SOMEWHERE.
WANT TO DO THE HONORS?

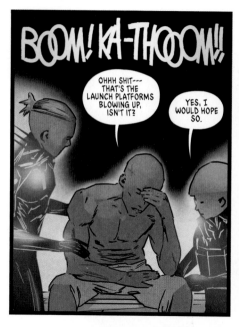

BOOM! KA-THOOOM!!

OHHH SHIT--- THAT'S THE LAUNCH PLATFORMS BLOWING UP, ISN'T IT?

YES, I WOULD HOPE SO.

PUSH!

WONDERFUL.

YOU SHOULD'VE MENTIONED *THAT*, COMMANDER. THERE IS A MAN WHO SHOULD BE ON ONE OF THOSE SHUTTLES WHO MOST *DEFINITELY* NEEDS TO LIVE. IF NOT, THEN YOUR MOMENT OF GENEROSITY HERE ISN'T GOING TO MEAN SHIT FOR US.

HOW WILL YOU EXPLAIN THE INCISION--- YOUR HAIR?

IN A FEW MINUTES, THAT'S NOT *EVEN* ABOUT TO MATTER.

LINCOLN. WHAT---WHAT HAPPENED TO YOU...IT WAS *NOT* YOUR FAULT. YOU WERE---WERE *JUST A BOY.*

YOUR SUITS SHOULD WORK JUST FINE NOW.

BE IN TOUCH.

KA-THOOOOM!

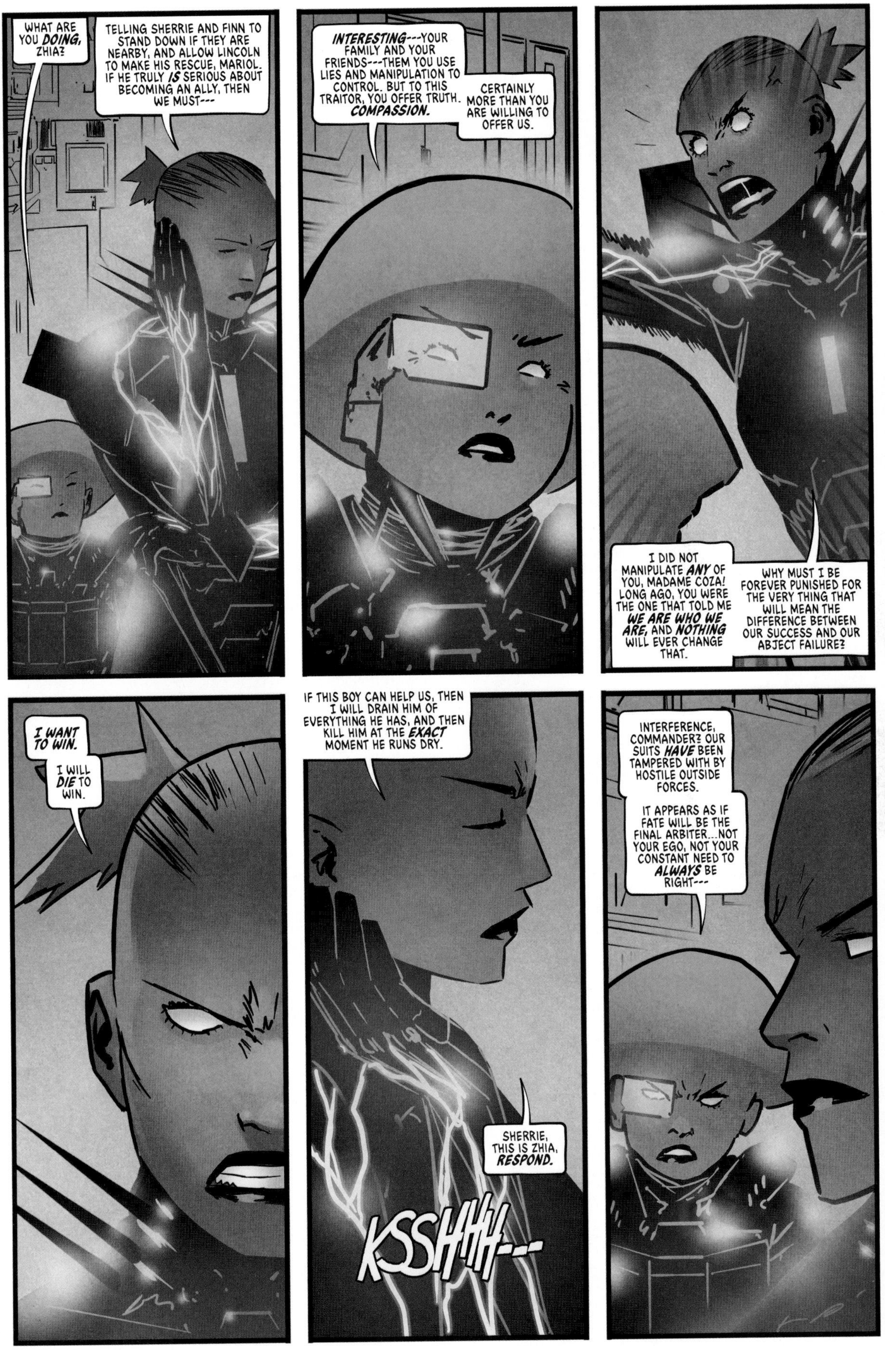
WHAT ARE YOU DOING, ZHIA?
TELLING SHERRIE AND FINN TO STAND DOWN IF THEY ARE NEARBY, AND ALLOW LINCOLN TO MAKE HIS RESCUE, MARIOL. IF HE TRULY IS SERIOUS ABOUT BECOMING AN ALLY, THEN WE MUST---
INTERESTING---YOUR FAMILY AND YOUR FRIENDS---THEM YOU USE LIES AND MANIPULATION TO CONTROL. BUT TO THIS TRAITOR, YOU OFFER TRUTH. COMPASSION.
CERTAINLY MORE THAN YOU ARE WILLING TO OFFER US.
I DID NOT MANIPULATE ANY OF YOU, MADAME COZA! LONG AGO, YOU WERE THE ONE THAT TOLD ME WE ARE WHO WE ARE, AND NOTHING WILL EVER CHANGE THAT.
WHY MUST I BE FOREVER PUNISHED FOR THE VERY THING THAT WILL MEAN THE DIFFERENCE BETWEEN OUR SUCCESS AND OUR ABJECT FAILURE?
I WANT TO WIN.
I WILL DIE TO WIN.
IF THIS BOY CAN HELP US, THEN I WILL DRAIN HIM OF EVERYTHING HE HAS, AND THEN KILL HIM AT THE EXACT MOMENT HE RUNS DRY.
SHERRIE, THIS IS ZHIA. RESPOND.
KSSHHH---
INTERFERENCE, COMMANDER? OUR SUITS HAVE BEEN TAMPERED WITH BY HOSTILE OUTSIDE FORCES.
IT APPEARS AS IF FATE WILL BE THE FINAL ARBITER...NOT YOUR EGO, NOT YOUR CONSTANT NEED TO ALWAYS BE RIGHT---

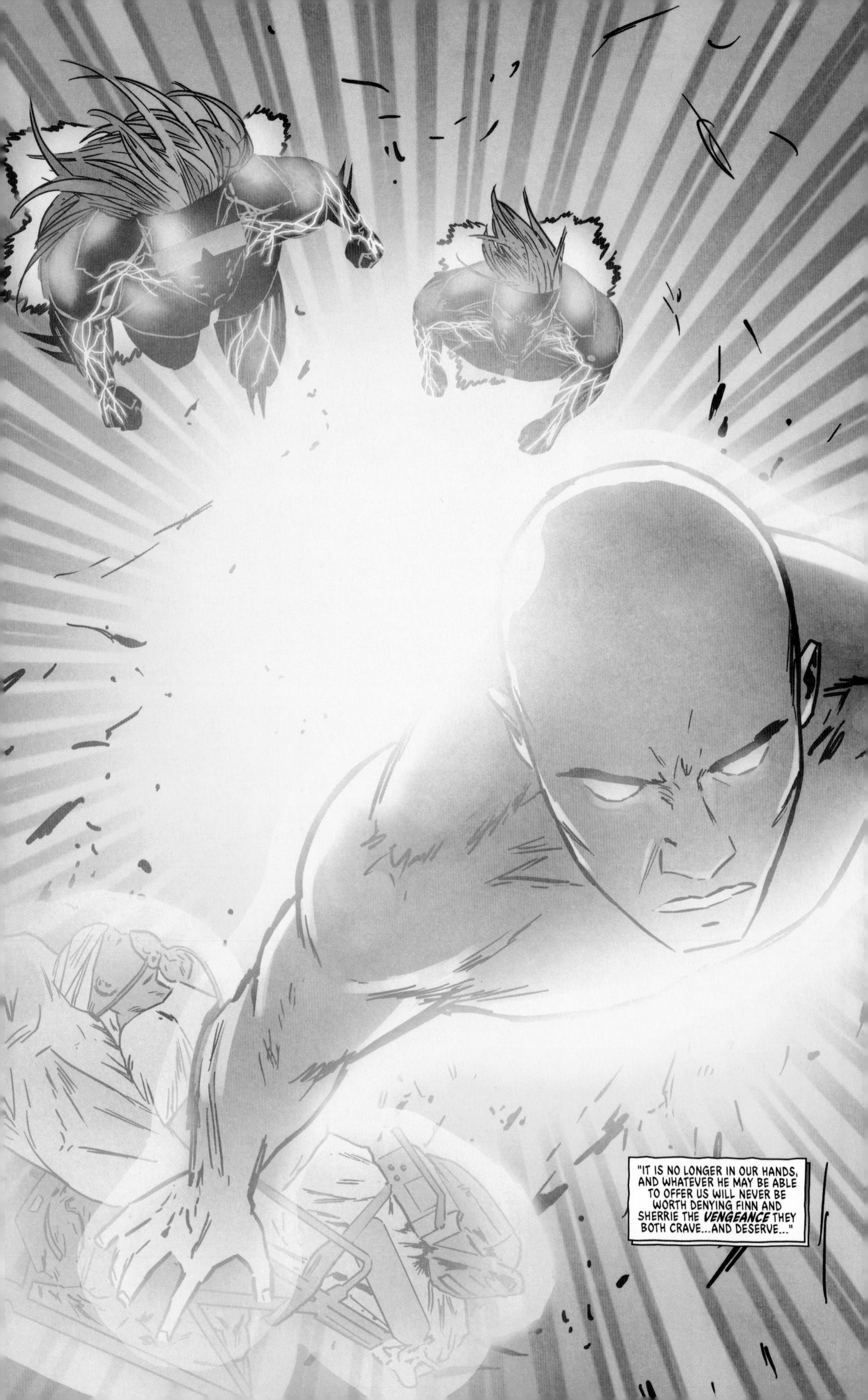
"IT IS NO LONGER IN OUR HANDS, AND WHATEVER HE MAY BE ABLE TO OFFER US WILL NEVER BE WORTH DENYING FINN AND SHERRIE THE *VENGEANCE* THEY BOTH CRAVE...AND DESERVE..."

WAIT!!!

FINN, THROTTLE THE **FUCK** DOWN BEFORE YOU BURN YOUR ROCKET PACK OUT!

FINN!

FWOOSH!

GONNA CATCH YOU AND KILL YOU FOR WHAT YOU DID TO ME---COULD HAVE GOTTEN AWAY FROM THAT PRISON IF NOT FOR---

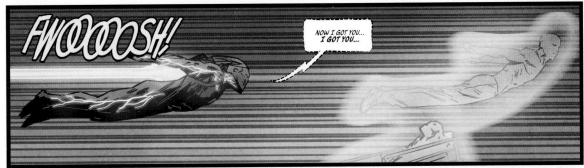

FWOOOOSH!

NOW I GOT YOU... I GOT YOU...

FWOMP---KISSHHH!

NO.

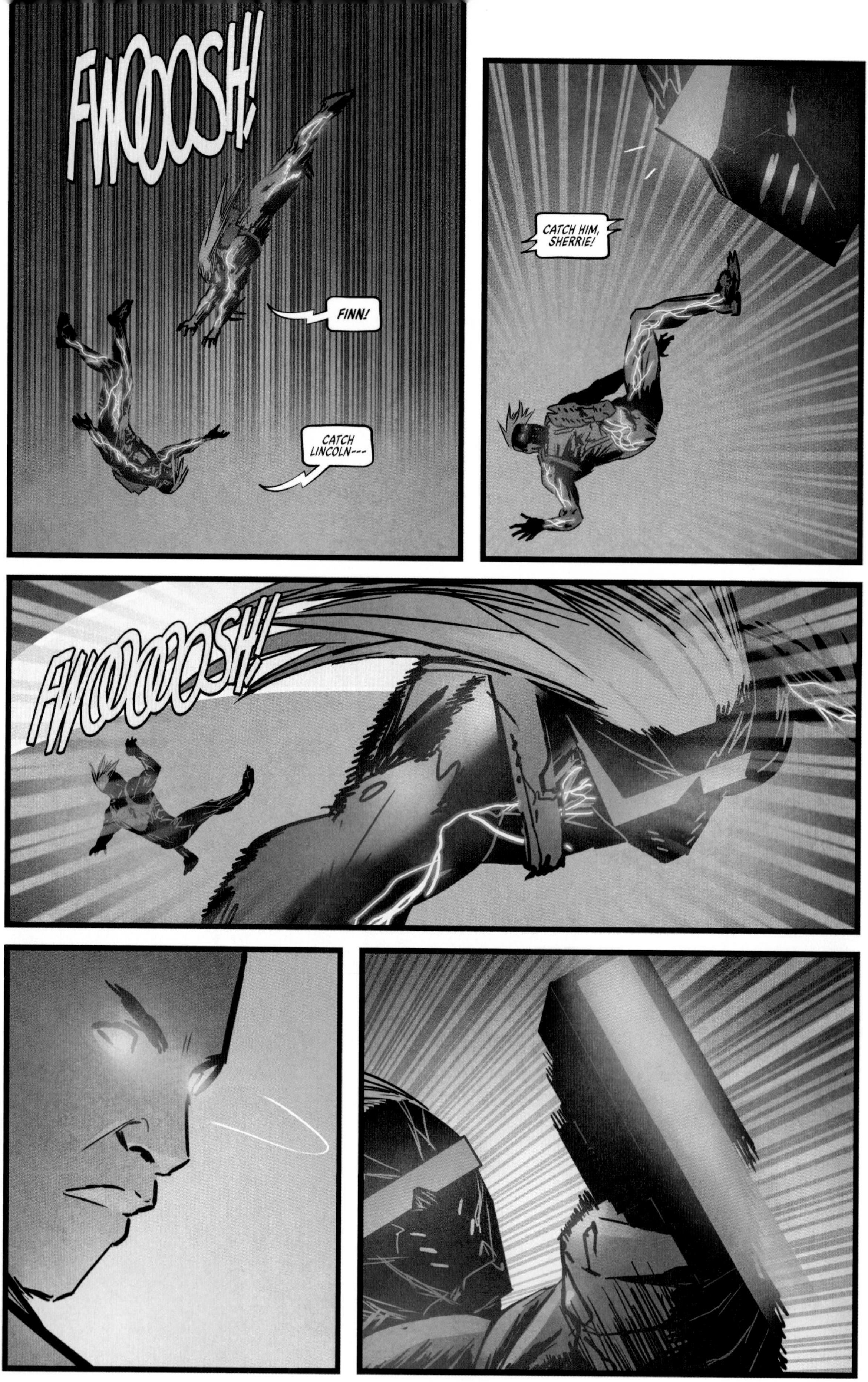
FWOOOSH!
FINN!
CATCH LINCOLN---
CATCH HIM, SHERRIE!
FWOOOOOSH!

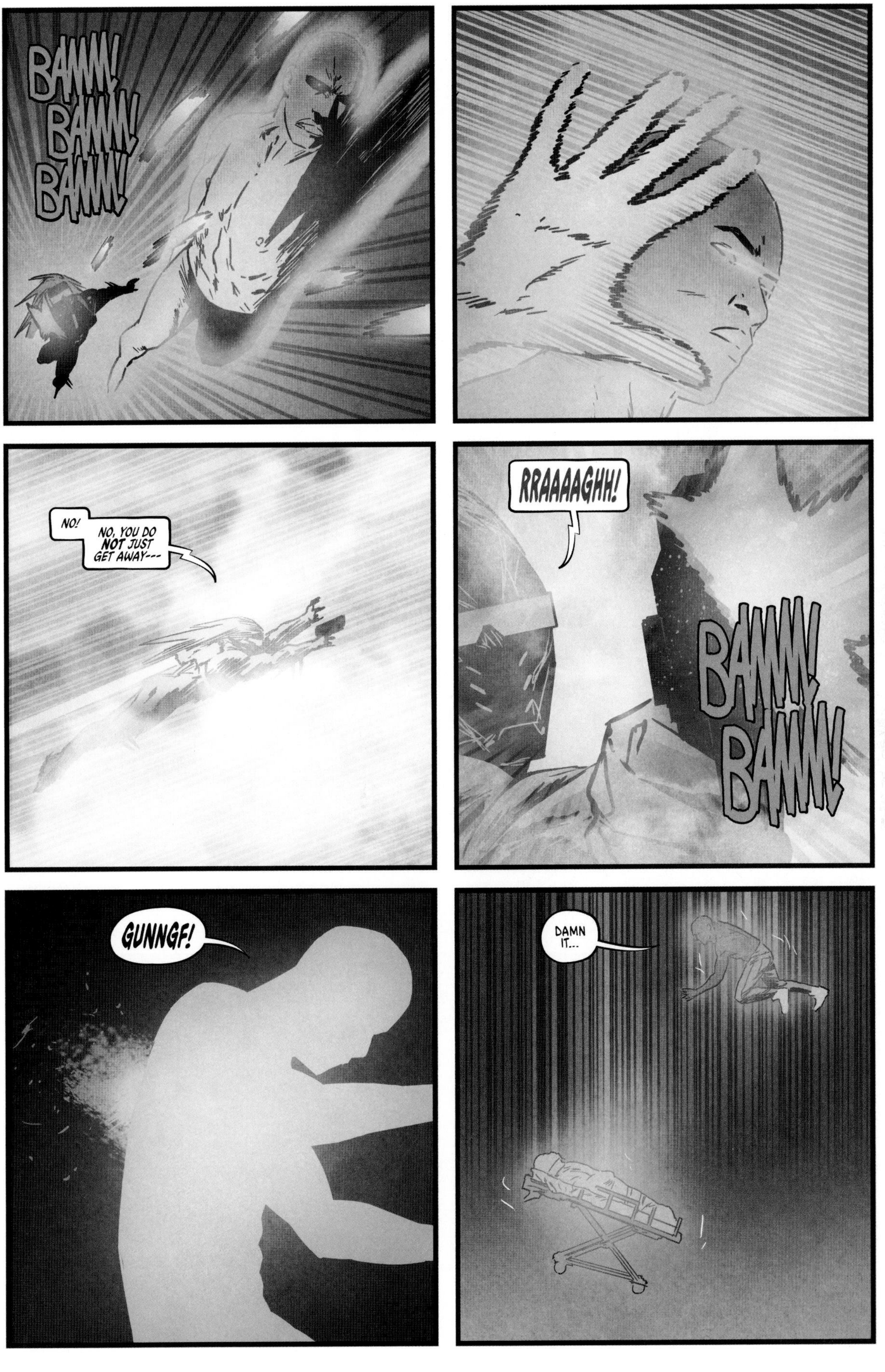
BAMM! BAMM! BAMM!
NO!
NO, YOU DO NOT JUST GET AWAY---
RRAAAAGHH!
BAMM! BAMM!
GUNNGF!
DAMN IT...

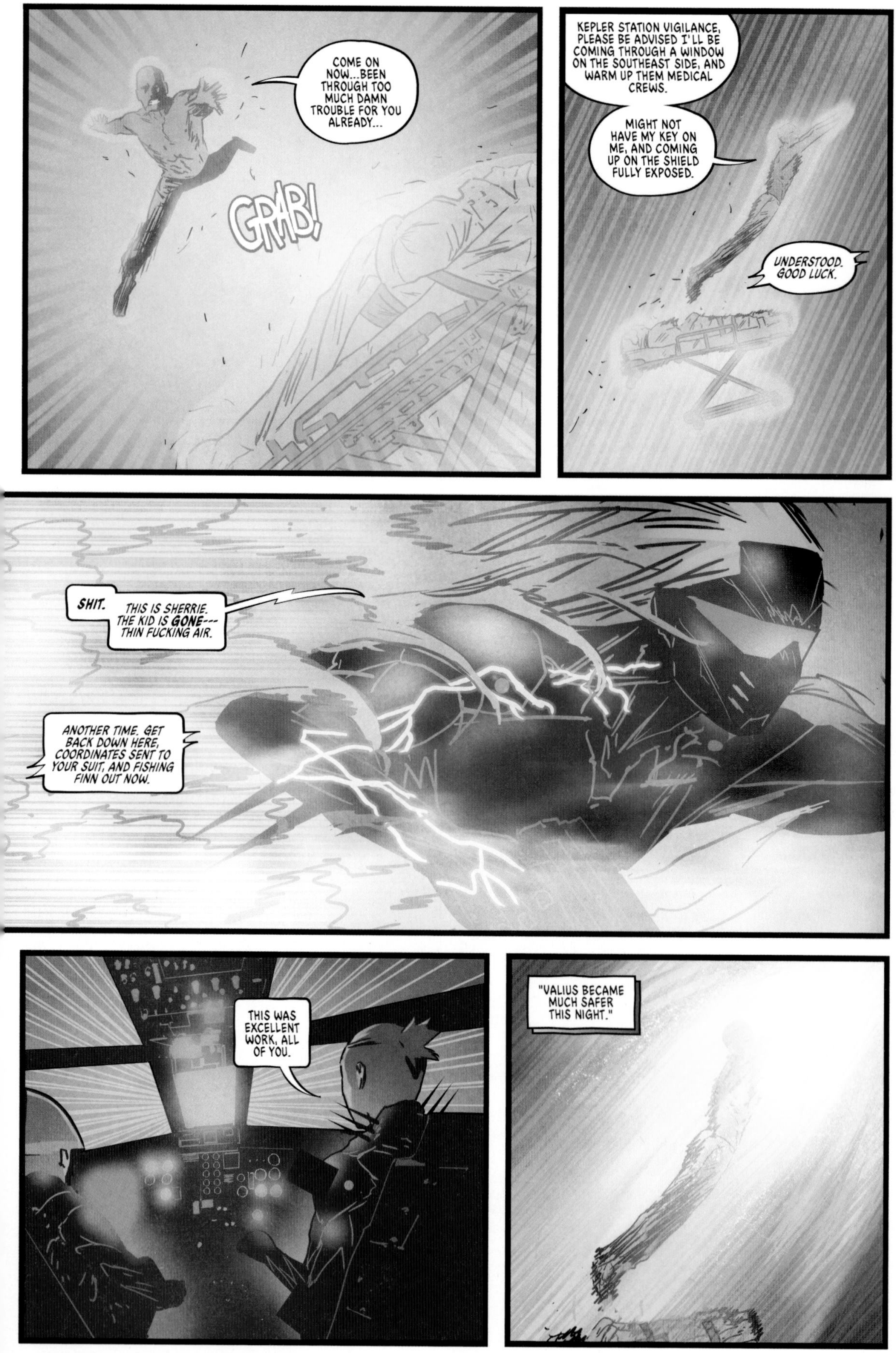
COME ON NOW...BEEN THROUGH TOO MUCH DAMN TROUBLE FOR YOU ALREADY...
GRAB!
KEPLER STATION VIGILANCE, PLEASE BE ADVISED I'LL BE COMING THROUGH A WINDOW ON THE SOUTHEAST SIDE, AND WARM UP THEM MEDICAL CREWS.
MIGHT NOT HAVE MY KEY ON ME, AND COMING UP ON THE SHIELD FULLY EXPOSED.
UNDERSTOOD. GOOD LUCK.
SHIT. THIS IS SHERRIE. THE KID IS GONE--- THIN FUCKING AIR.
ANOTHER TIME. GET BACK DOWN HERE, COORDINATES SENT TO YOUR SUIT, AND FISHING FINN OUT NOW.
THIS WAS EXCELLENT WORK, ALL OF YOU.
"VALIUS BECAME MUCH SAFER THIS NIGHT."

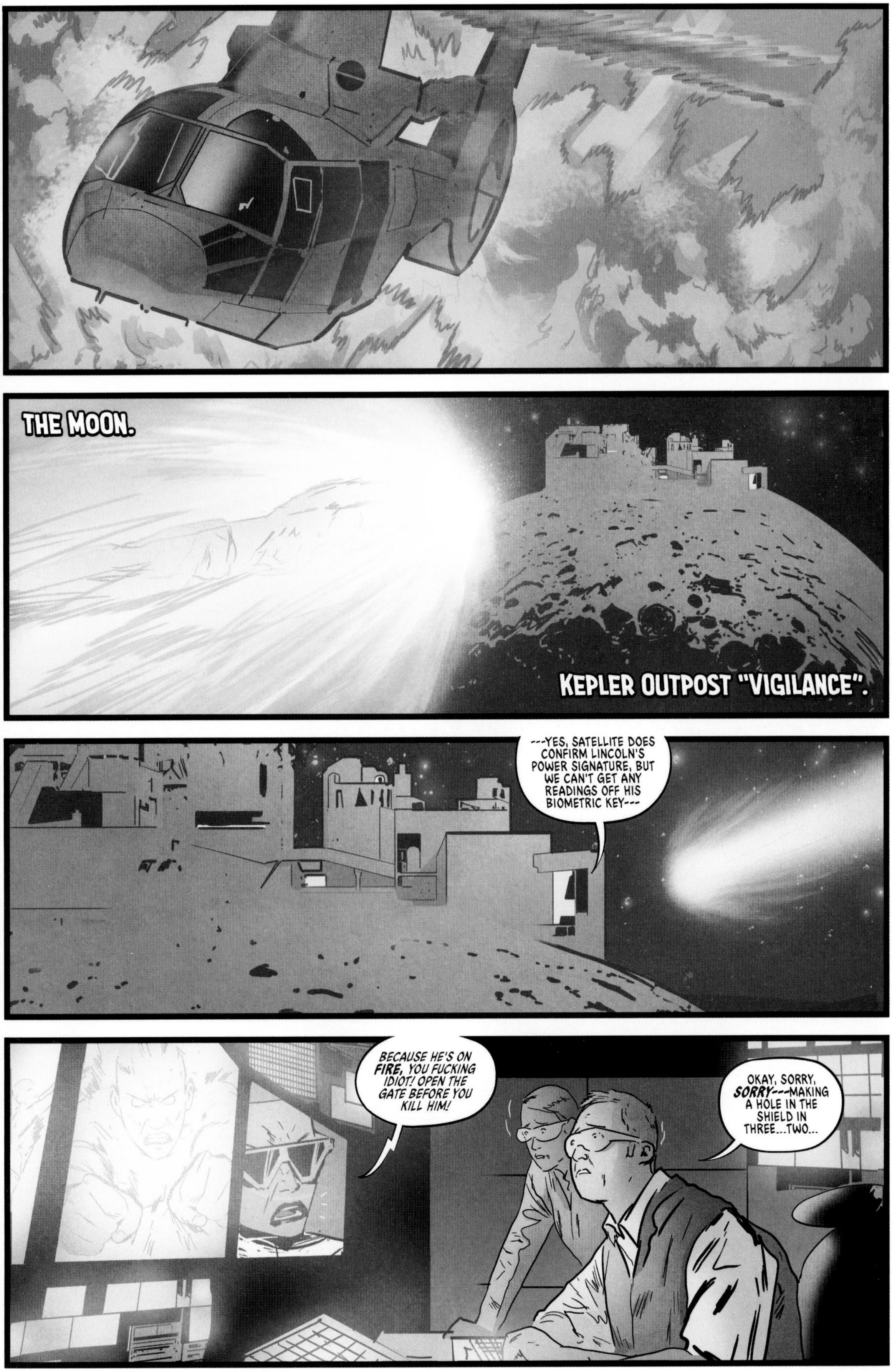
THE MOON.
KEPLER OUTPOST "VIGILANCE".
---YES, SATELLITE DOES CONFIRM LINCOLN'S POWER SIGNATURE, BUT WE CAN'T GET ANY READINGS OFF HIS BIOMETRIC KEY---
BECAUSE HE'S ON FIRE, YOU FUCKING IDIOT! OPEN THE GATE BEFORE YOU KILL HIM!
OKAY, SORRY, SORRY---MAKING A HOLE IN THE SHIELD IN THREE...TWO...

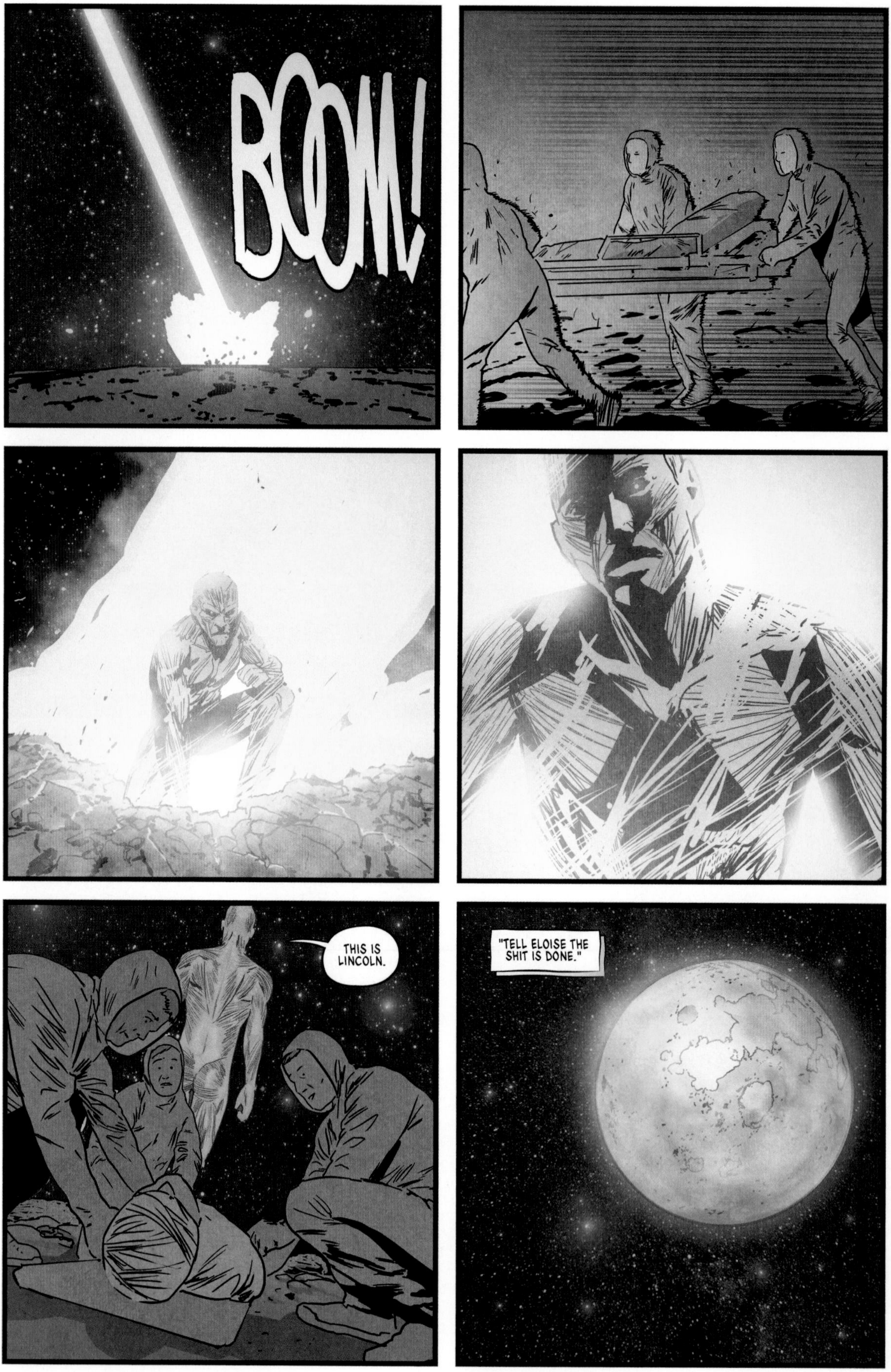
BOOM!
THIS IS LINCOLN.
"TELL ELOISE THE SHIT IS DONE."

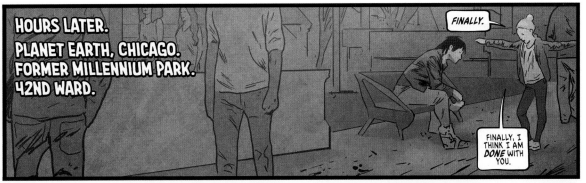

HOURS LATER.
PLANET EARTH, CHICAGO.
FORMER MILLENNIUM PARK.
42ND WARD.

FINALLY.

FINALLY, I THINK I AM *DONE* WITH YOU.

MARIOL, *PLEASE,* I--- IT IS NOT THAT---

WAS IT *ALWAYS* YOUR INTENT---TO BREAK YOUR VOW TO ME, SWORN ON THE *LIFE* OF YOUR OWN *DAUGHTER?*

NOT ALWAYS. IF I TELL YOU WHEN THINGS CHANGED, WILL YOU STAY?

WHAT LITTLE CHOICE WE EVER HAD HAS *ALREADY* BEEN STRIPPED AWAY---BY YOU, AND FOR YOUR OWN PURPOSE.

FINN---THE *MOMENT* I SAW HIM CODED RED ON THE MAP. I THOUGHT---I *KNEW* WHAT THAT LIKELY MEANT FOR US, BUT EVEN MY GREATEST FEAR WAS NOT ENOUGH.

MY MISTAKES DELIVERED HIM TO OUR ENEMIES, AND THEY USED HIM TO BECOME STRONGER. THEY STOLE OUR ABILITY TO HEAL, THEY HAVE TECHNOLOGY THAT CAN COUNTERMAND OUR OWN, AND WE NOW WAR WITH *CHILDREN.*

GIVEN *ALL* THAT...CONSIDERING WHAT WE NOW FACE, AND THE ODDS GATHERED AGAINST US...

...WHAT VOW MADE WOULD *EVER* STAND?

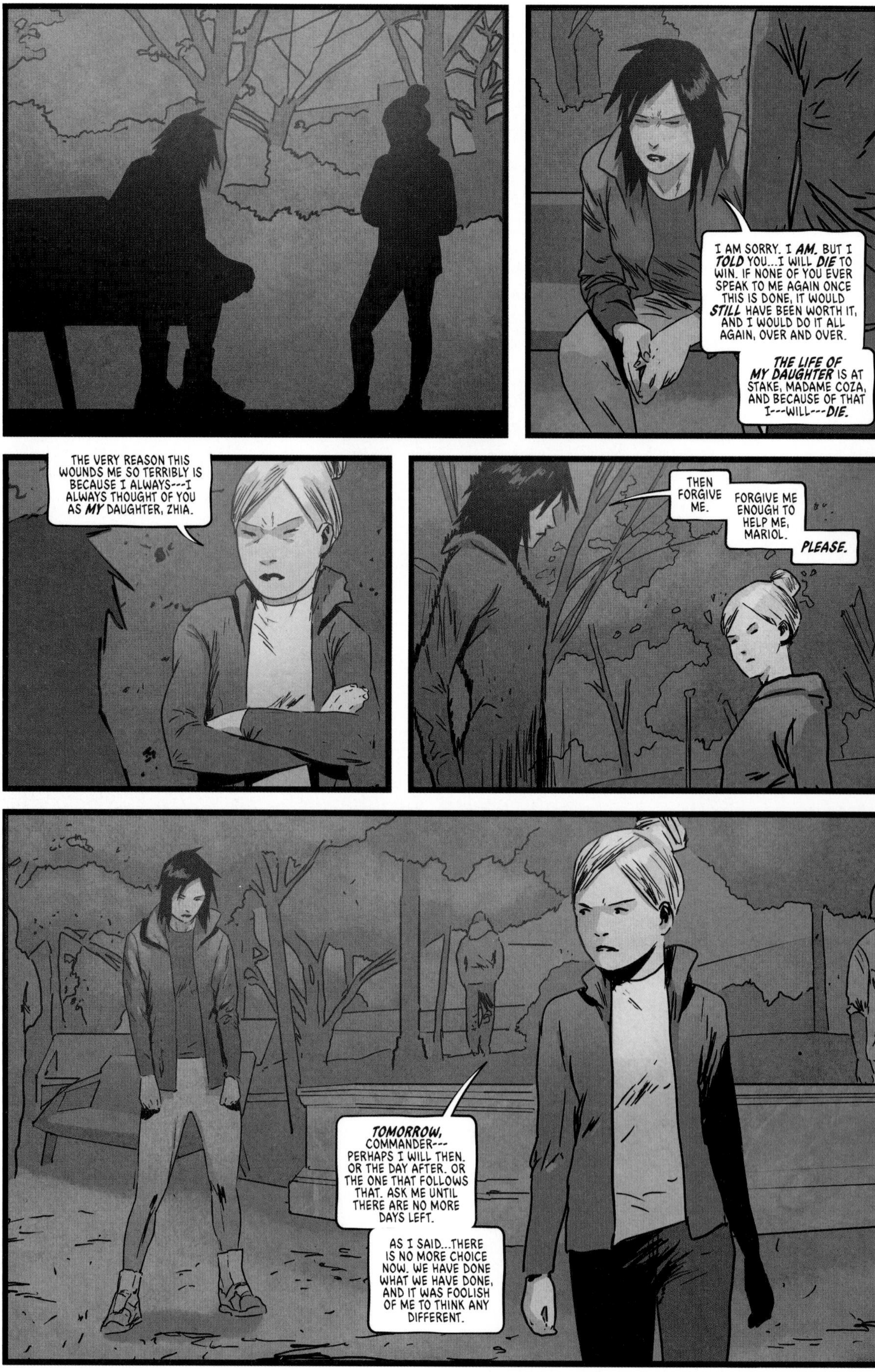
I AM SORRY. I AM. BUT I TOLD YOU...I WILL DIE TO WIN. IF NONE OF YOU EVER SPEAK TO ME AGAIN ONCE THIS IS DONE, IT WOULD STILL HAVE BEEN WORTH IT, AND I WOULD DO IT ALL AGAIN, OVER AND OVER.
THE LIFE OF MY DAUGHTER IS AT STAKE, MADAME COZA, AND BECAUSE OF THAT I---WILL---DIE.
THE VERY REASON THIS WOUNDS ME SO TERRIBLY IS BECAUSE I ALWAYS---I ALWAYS THOUGHT OF YOU AS MY DAUGHTER, ZHIA.
THEN FORGIVE ME.
FORGIVE ME ENOUGH TO HELP ME, MARIOL.
PLEASE.
TOMORROW, COMMANDER--- PERHAPS I WILL THEN. OR THE DAY AFTER. OR THE ONE THAT FOLLOWS THAT. ASK ME UNTIL THERE ARE NO MORE DAYS LEFT.
AS I SAID...THERE IS NO MORE CHOICE NOW. WE HAVE DONE WHAT WE HAVE DONE, AND IT WAS FOOLISH OF ME TO THINK ANY DIFFERENT.

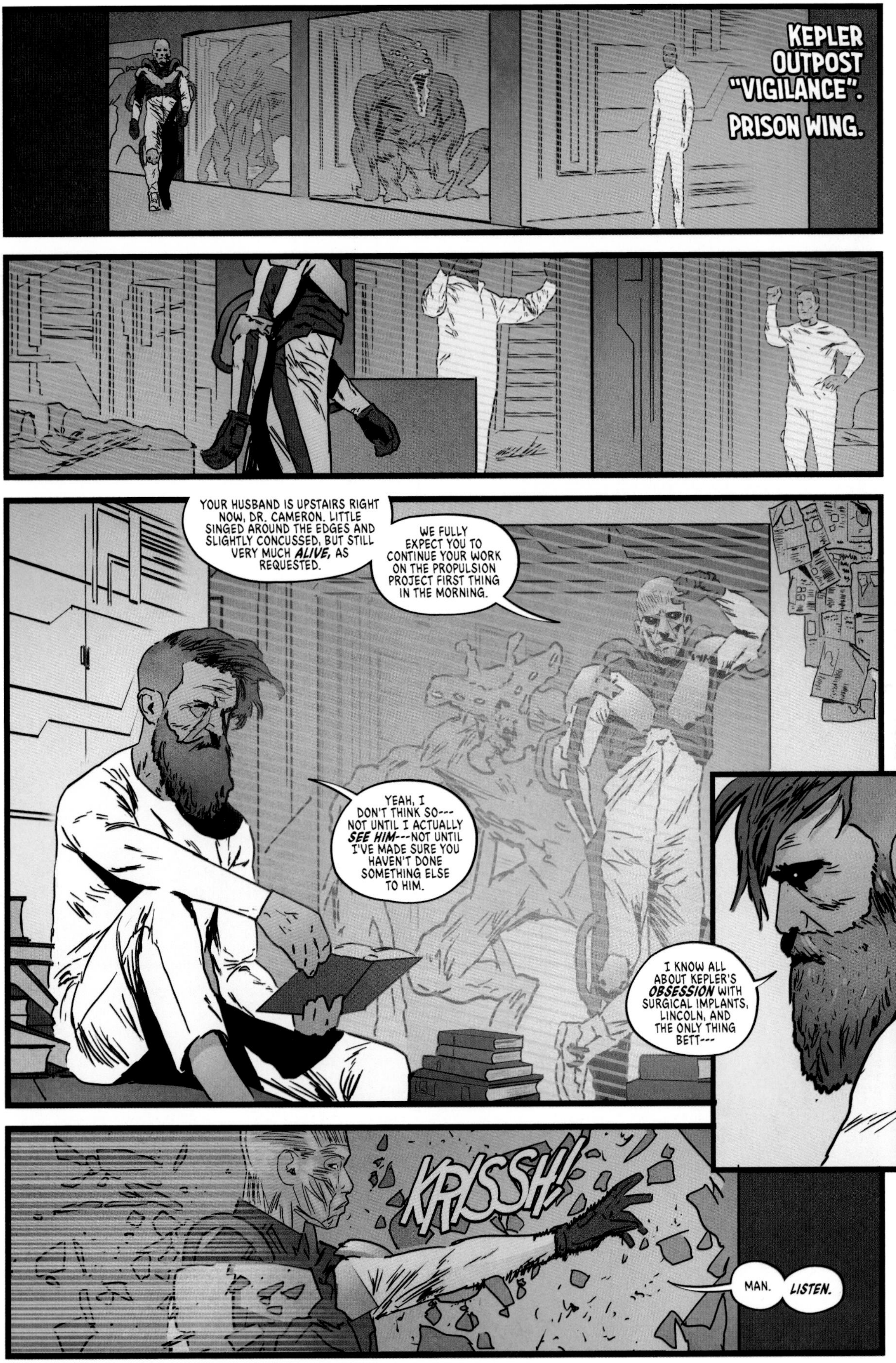
KEPLER OUTPOST "VIGILANCE".
PRISON WING.
YOUR HUSBAND IS UPSTAIRS RIGHT NOW, DR. CAMERON. LITTLE SINGED AROUND THE EDGES AND SLIGHTLY CONCUSSED, BUT STILL VERY MUCH ALIVE, AS REQUESTED.
WE FULLY EXPECT YOU TO CONTINUE YOUR WORK ON THE PROPULSION PROJECT FIRST THING IN THE MORNING.
YEAH, I DON'T THINK SO---NOT UNTIL I ACTUALLY SEE HIM---NOT UNTIL I'VE MADE SURE YOU HAVEN'T DONE SOMETHING ELSE TO HIM.
I KNOW ALL ABOUT KEPLER'S OBSESSION WITH SURGICAL IMPLANTS, LINCOLN, AND THE ONLY THING BETT---
KRISSH!
MAN.
LISTEN.

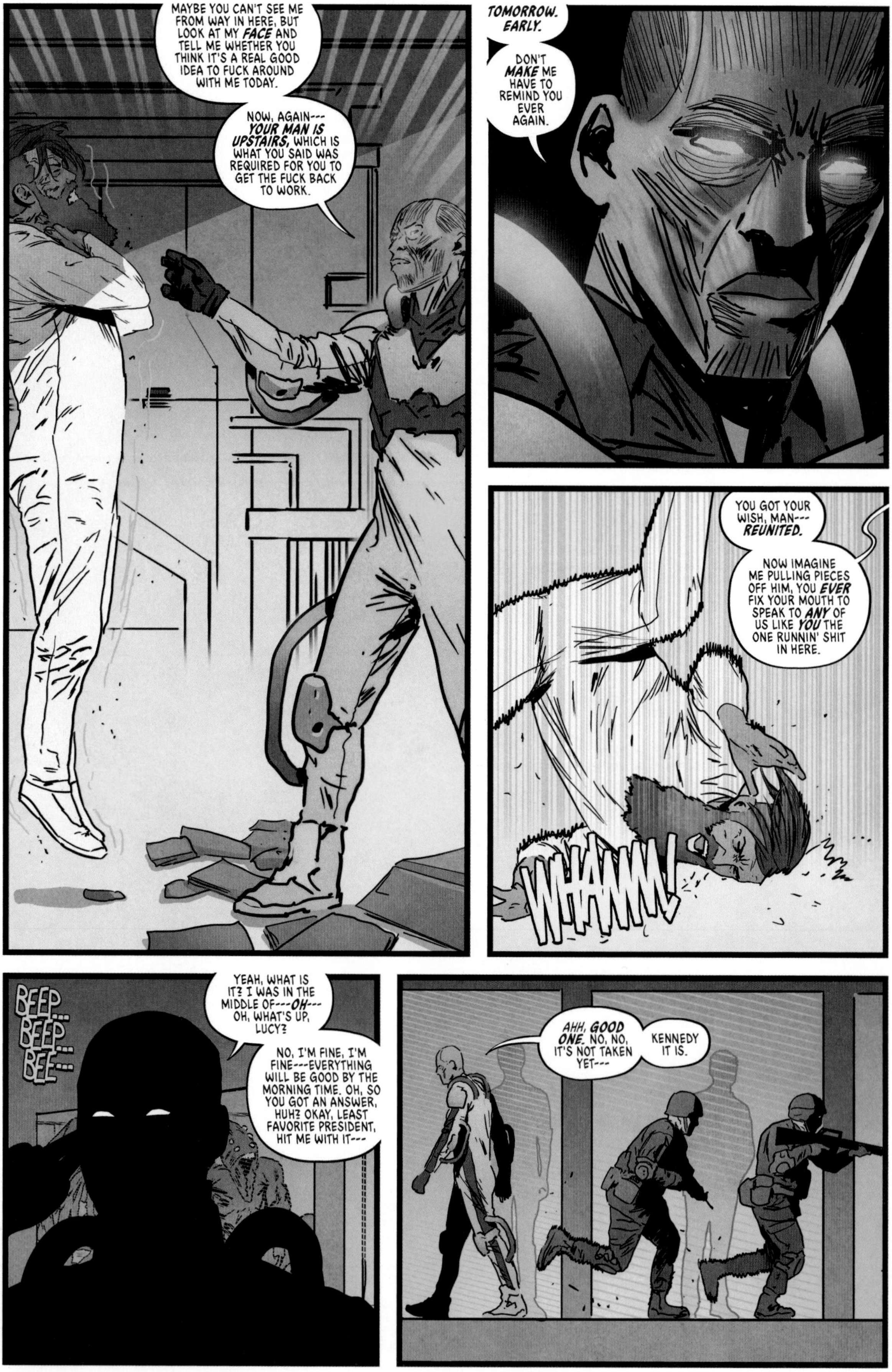
MAYBE YOU CAN'T SEE ME FROM WAY IN HERE, BUT LOOK AT MY FACE AND TELL ME WHETHER YOU THINK IT'S A REAL GOOD IDEA TO FUCK AROUND WITH ME TODAY.
NOW, AGAIN--- YOUR MAN IS UPSTAIRS, WHICH IS WHAT YOU SAID WAS REQUIRED FOR YOU TO GET THE FUCK BACK TO WORK.
TOMORROW. EARLY.
DON'T MAKE ME HAVE TO REMIND YOU EVER AGAIN.
YOU GOT YOUR WISH, MAN--- REUNITED.
NOW IMAGINE ME PULLING PIECES OFF HIM, YOU EVER FIX YOUR MOUTH TO SPEAK TO ANY OF US LIKE YOU THE ONE RUNNIN' SHIT IN HERE.
WHAMM!
BEEP... BEEP... BEE...
YEAH, WHAT IS IT? I WAS IN THE MIDDLE OF---OH--- OH, WHAT'S UP, LUCY?
NO, I'M FINE, I'M FINE---EVERYTHING WILL BE GOOD BY THE MORNING TIME. OH, SO YOU GOT AN ANSWER, HUH? OKAY, LEAST FAVORITE PRESIDENT, HIT ME WITH IT---
AHH, GOOD ONE. NO, NO, IT'S NOT TAKEN YET---
KENNEDY IT IS.

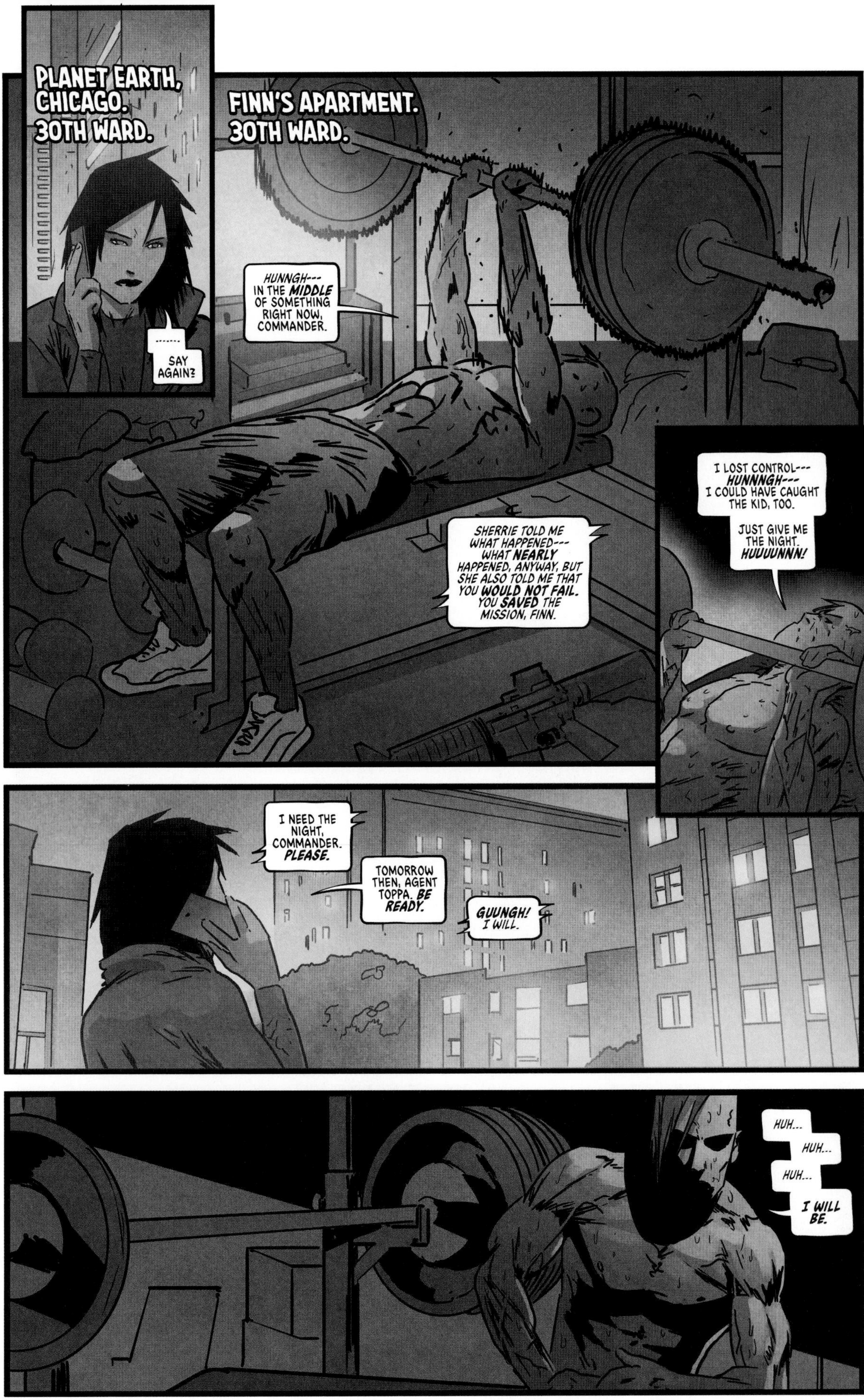
PLANET EARTH, CHICAGO. 30TH WARD.
FINN'S APARTMENT. 30TH WARD.
HUNNGH--- IN THE MIDDLE OF SOMETHING RIGHT NOW, COMMANDER.
------- SAY AGAIN?
SHERRIE TOLD ME WHAT HAPPENED--- WHAT NEARLY HAPPENED, ANYWAY, BUT SHE ALSO TOLD ME THAT YOU WOULD NOT FAIL. YOU SAVED THE MISSION, FINN.
I LOST CONTROL--- HUNNNGH--- I COULD HAVE CAUGHT THE KID, TOO.
JUST GIVE ME THE NIGHT. HUUUUNNN!
I NEED THE NIGHT, COMMANDER. PLEASE.
TOMORROW THEN, AGENT TOPPA. BE READY.
GUUNGH! I WILL.
HUH...
HUH...
HUH...
I WILL BE.

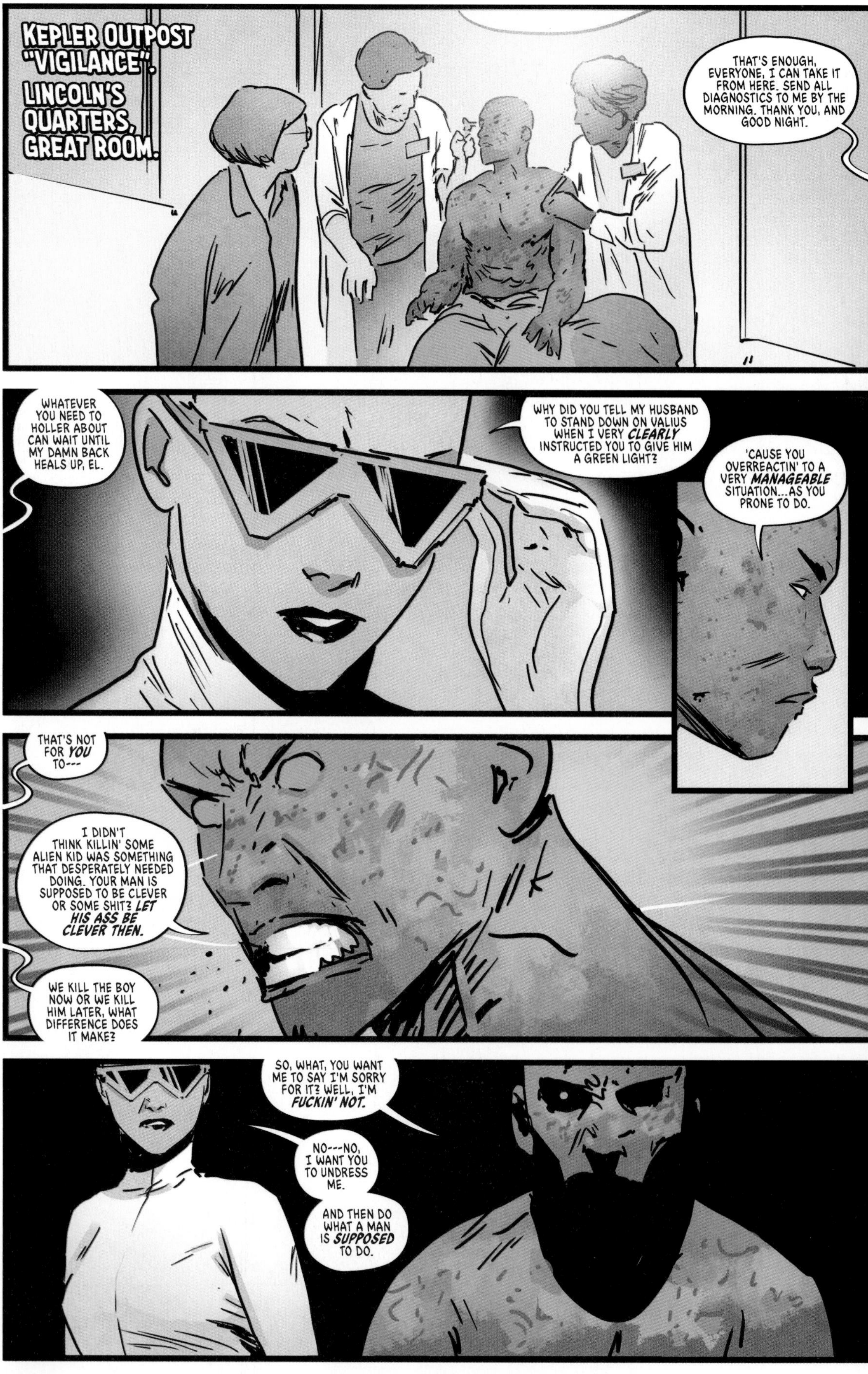
KEPLER OUTPOST "VIGILANCE". LINCOLN'S QUARTERS, GREAT ROOM.
THAT'S ENOUGH, EVERYONE, I CAN TAKE IT FROM HERE. SEND ALL DIAGNOSTICS TO ME BY THE MORNING. THANK YOU, AND GOOD NIGHT.
WHATEVER YOU NEED TO HOLLER ABOUT CAN WAIT UNTIL MY DAMN BACK HEALS UP, EL.
WHY DID YOU TELL MY HUSBAND TO STAND DOWN ON VALIUS WHEN I VERY CLEARLY INSTRUCTED YOU TO GIVE HIM A GREEN LIGHT?
'CAUSE YOU OVERREACTIN' TO A VERY MANAGEABLE SITUATION...AS YOU PRONE TO DO.
THAT'S NOT FOR YOU TO---
I DIDN'T THINK KILLIN' SOME ALIEN KID WAS SOMETHING THAT DESPERATELY NEEDED DOING. YOUR MAN IS SUPPOSED TO BE CLEVER OR SOME SHIT? LET HIS ASS BE CLEVER THEN.
WE KILL THE BOY NOW OR WE KILL HIM LATER, WHAT DIFFERENCE DOES IT MAKE?
SO, WHAT, YOU WANT ME TO SAY I'M SORRY FOR IT? WELL, I'M FUCKIN' NOT.
NO---NO, I WANT YOU TO UNDRESS ME.
AND THEN DO WHAT A MAN IS SUPPOSED TO DO.

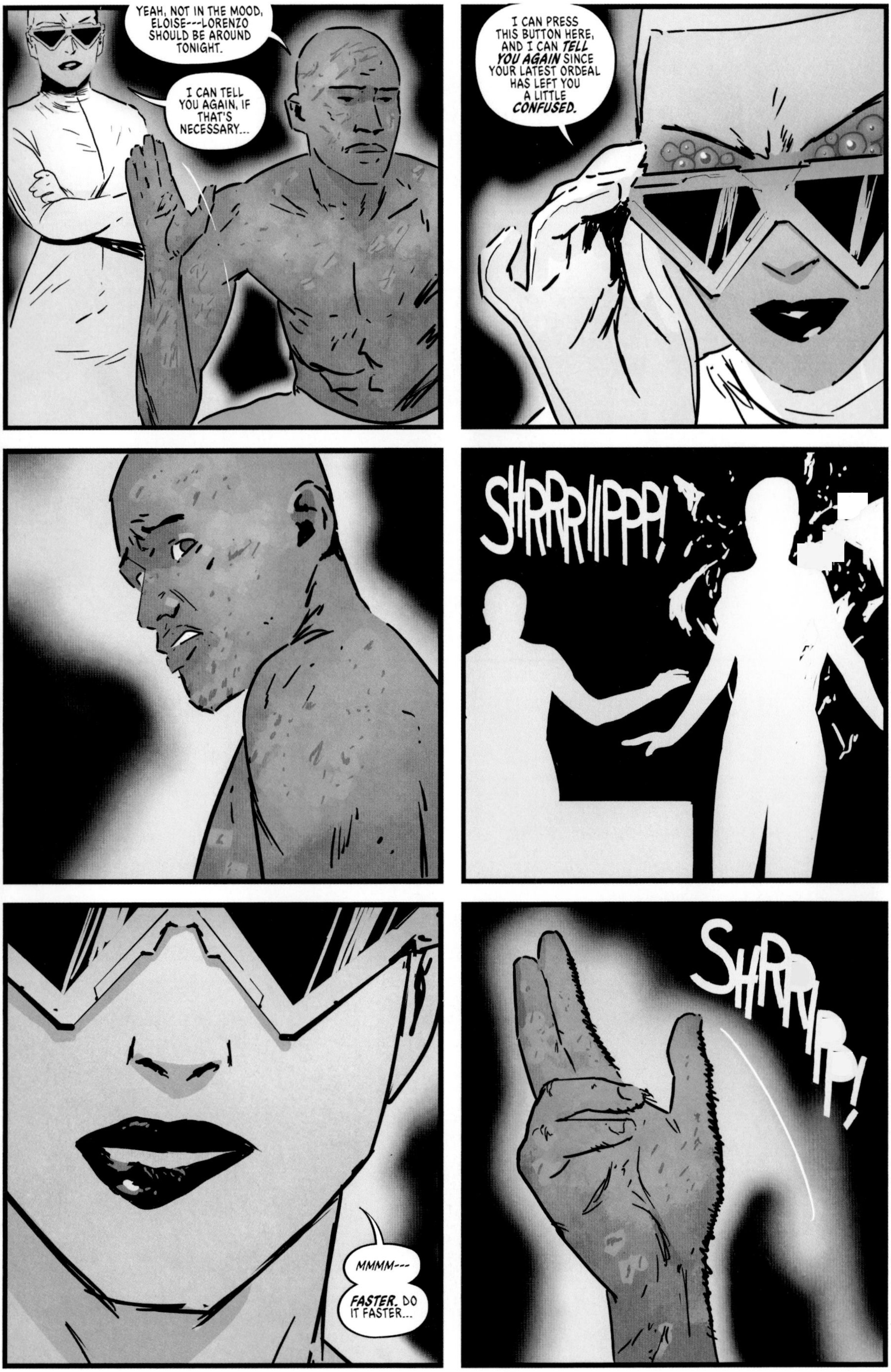
YEAH, NOT IN THE MOOD, ELOISE---LORENZO SHOULD BE AROUND TONIGHT.
I CAN TELL YOU AGAIN, IF THAT'S NECESSARY...
I CAN PRESS THIS BUTTON HERE, AND I CAN TELL YOU AGAIN SINCE YOUR LATEST ORDEAL HAS LEFT YOU A LITTLE CONFUSED.
SHRRRIIIPPP!
MMMM---
FASTER. DO IT FASTER...
SHRRRIIPP!

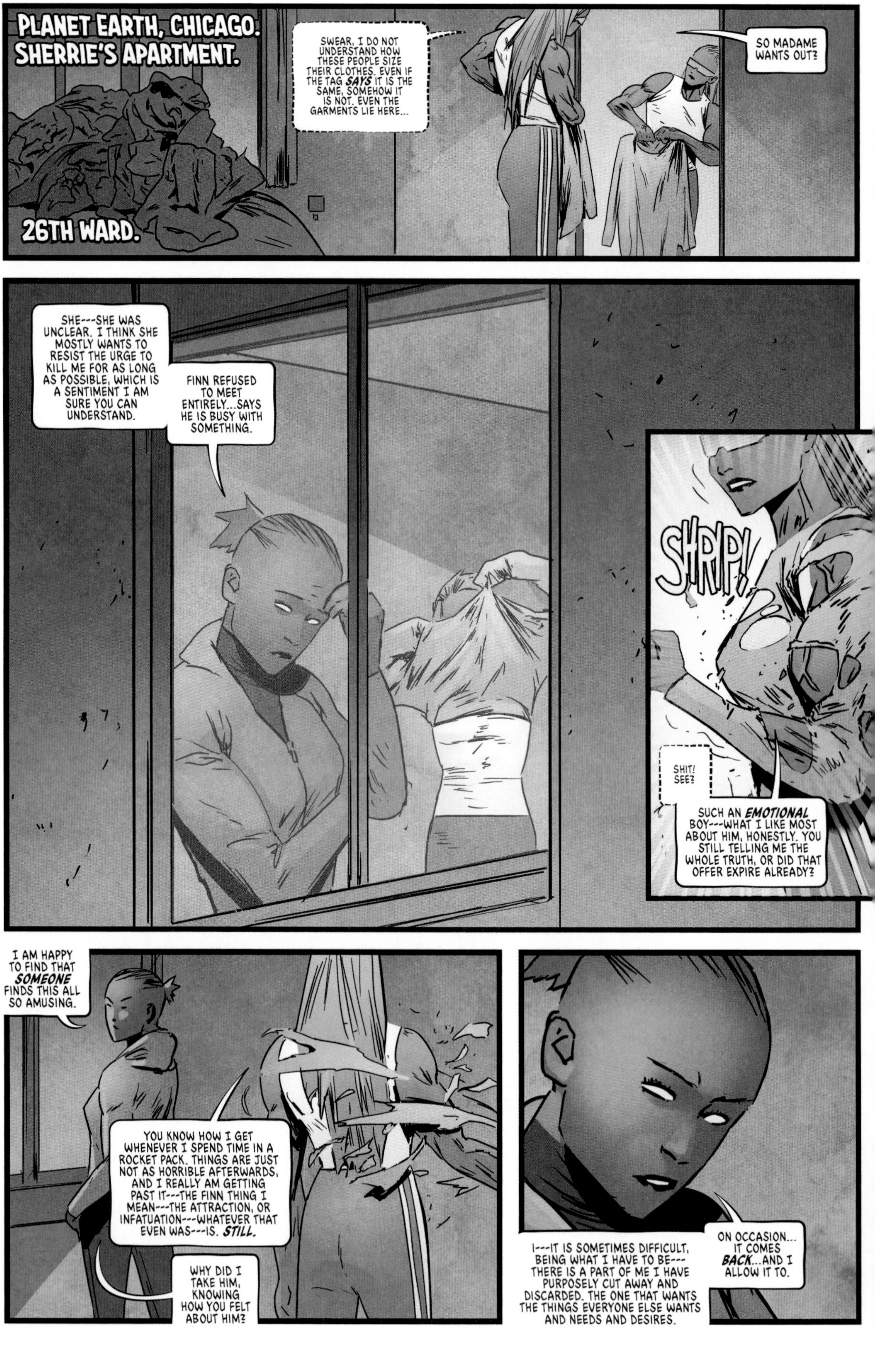

PLANET EARTH, CHICAGO. SHERRIE'S APARTMENT.
26TH WARD.
SWEAR, I DO NOT UNDERSTAND HOW THESE PEOPLE SIZE THEIR CLOTHES. EVEN IF THE TAG SAYS IT IS THE SAME, SOMEHOW IT IS NOT. EVEN THE GARMENTS LIE HERE...
SO MADAME WANTS OUT?
SHE---SHE WAS UNCLEAR. I THINK SHE MOSTLY WANTS TO RESIST THE URGE TO KILL ME FOR AS LONG AS POSSIBLE, WHICH IS A SENTIMENT I AM SURE YOU CAN UNDERSTAND.
FINN REFUSED TO MEET ENTIRELY...SAYS HE IS BUSY WITH SOMETHING.
SHRIP!
SHIT! SEE?
SUCH AN EMOTIONAL BOY---WHAT I LIKE MOST ABOUT HIM, HONESTLY. YOU STILL TELLING ME THE WHOLE TRUTH, OR DID THAT OFFER EXPIRE ALREADY?
I AM HAPPY TO FIND THAT SOMEONE FINDS THIS ALL SO AMUSING.
YOU KNOW HOW I GET WHENEVER I SPEND TIME IN A ROCKET PACK. THINGS ARE JUST NOT AS HORRIBLE AFTERWARDS, AND I REALLY AM GETTING PAST IT---THE FINN THING I MEAN---THE ATTRACTION, OR INFATUATION---WHATEVER THAT EVEN WAS---IS. STILL.
WHY DID I TAKE HIM, KNOWING HOW YOU FELT ABOUT HIM?
I---IT IS SOMETIMES DIFFICULT, BEING WHAT I HAVE TO BE---THERE IS A PART OF ME I HAVE PURPOSELY CUT AWAY AND DISCARDED. THE ONE THAT WANTS THE THINGS EVERYONE ELSE WANTS AND NEEDS AND DESIRES.
ON OCCASION... IT COMES BACK...AND I ALLOW IT TO.

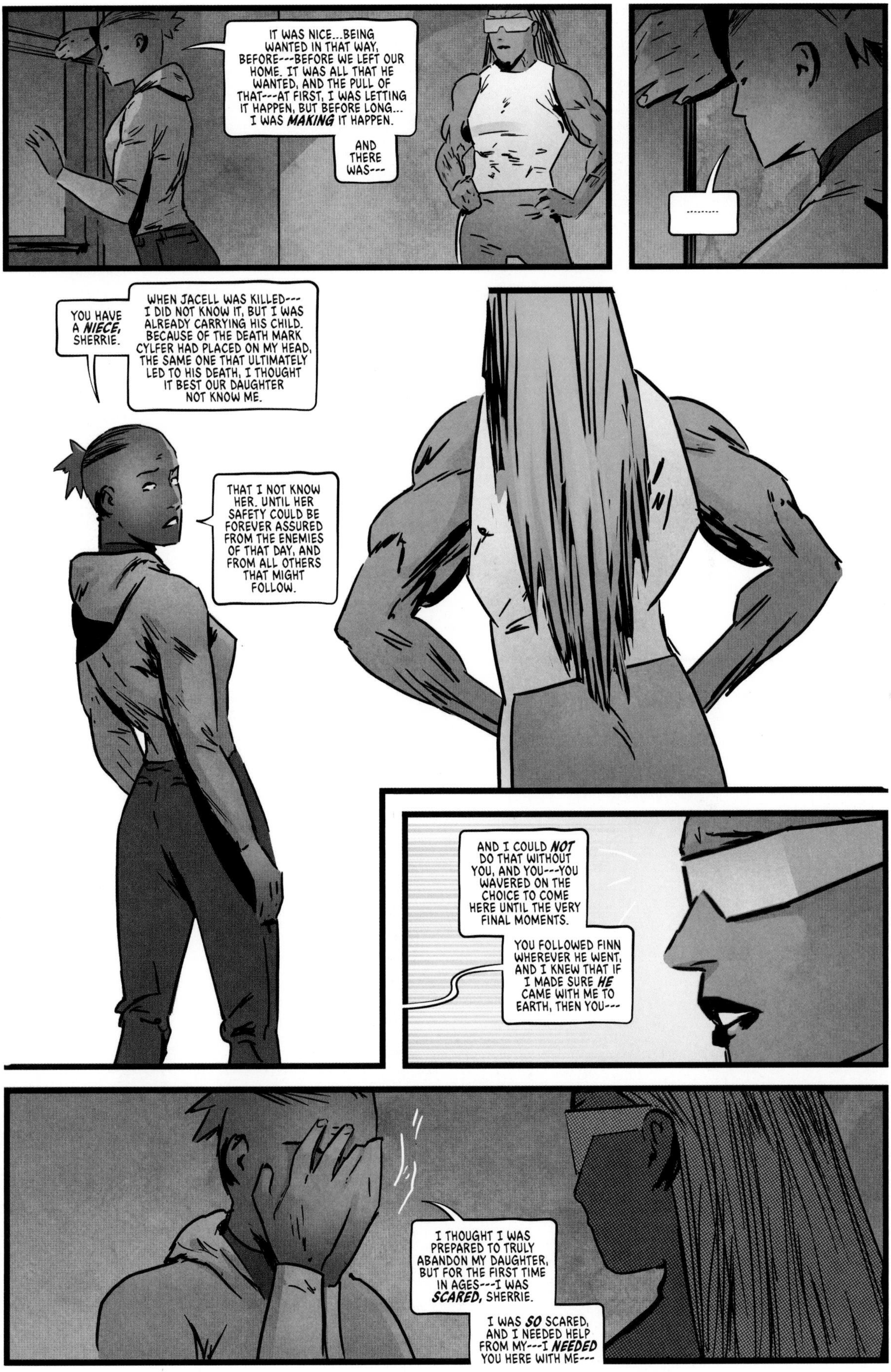
IT WAS NICE...BEING WANTED IN THAT WAY, BEFORE---BEFORE WE LEFT OUR HOME. IT WAS ALL THAT HE WANTED, AND THE PULL OF THAT---AT FIRST, I WAS LETTING IT HAPPEN, BUT BEFORE LONG... I WAS MAKING IT HAPPEN.
AND THERE WAS---

YOU HAVE A NIECE, SHERRIE.
WHEN JACELL WAS KILLED--- I DID NOT KNOW IT, BUT I WAS ALREADY CARRYING HIS CHILD. BECAUSE OF THE DEATH MARK CYLFER HAD PLACED ON MY HEAD, THE SAME ONE THAT ULTIMATELY LED TO HIS DEATH, I THOUGHT IT BEST OUR DAUGHTER NOT KNOW ME.
THAT I NOT KNOW HER. UNTIL HER SAFETY COULD BE FOREVER ASSURED FROM THE ENEMIES OF THAT DAY, AND FROM ALL OTHERS THAT MIGHT FOLLOW.
AND I COULD NOT DO THAT WITHOUT YOU, AND YOU---YOU WAVERED ON THE CHOICE TO COME HERE UNTIL THE VERY FINAL MOMENTS.
YOU FOLLOWED FINN WHEREVER HE WENT, AND I KNEW THAT IF I MADE SURE HE CAME WITH ME TO EARTH, THEN YOU---
I THOUGHT I WAS PREPARED TO TRULY ABANDON MY DAUGHTER, BUT FOR THE FIRST TIME IN AGES---I WAS SCARED, SHERRIE.
I WAS SO SCARED, AND I NEEDED HELP FROM MY---I NEEDED YOU HERE WITH ME---

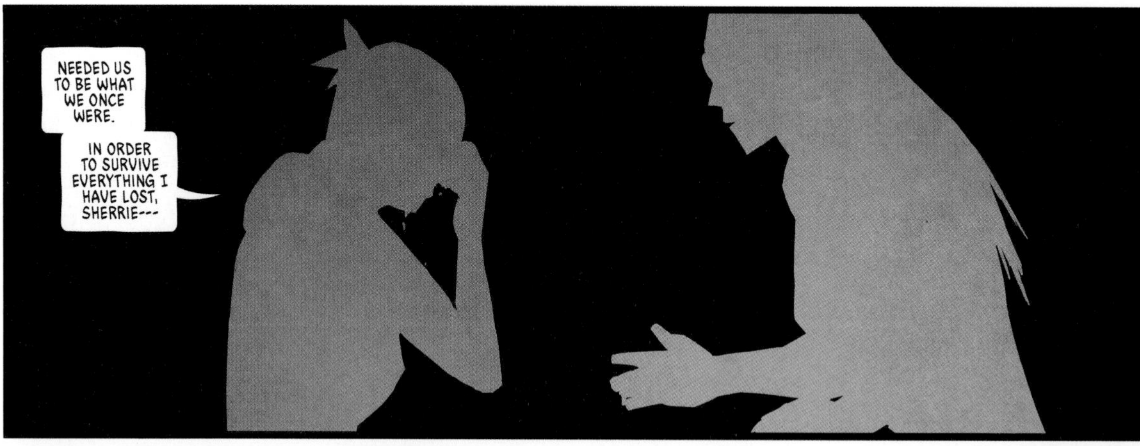
NEEDED US TO BE WHAT WE ONCE WERE.
IN ORDER TO SURVIVE EVERYTHING I HAVE LOST, SHERRIE---

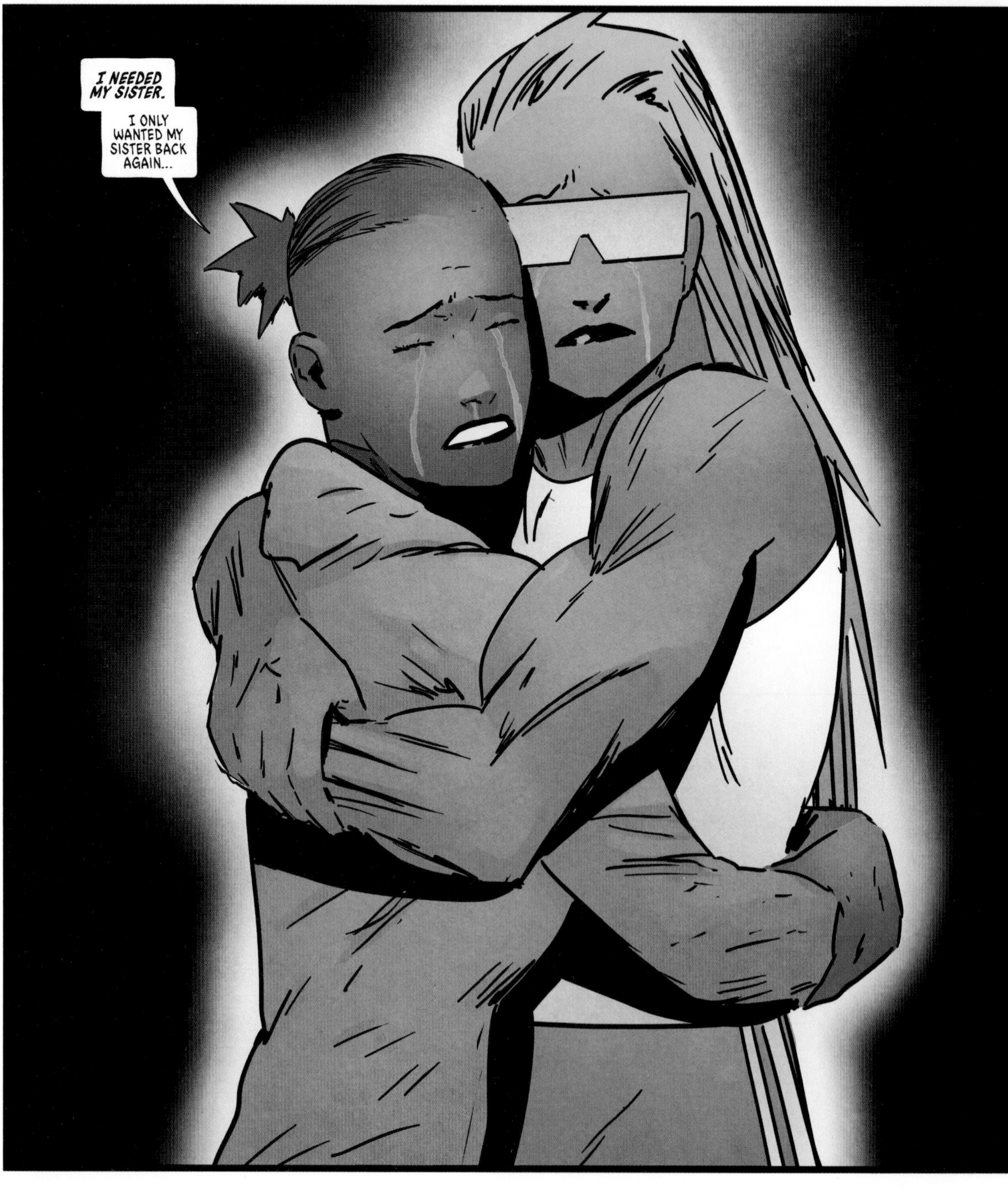
I NEEDED MY SISTER.
I ONLY WANTED MY SISTER BACK AGAIN...

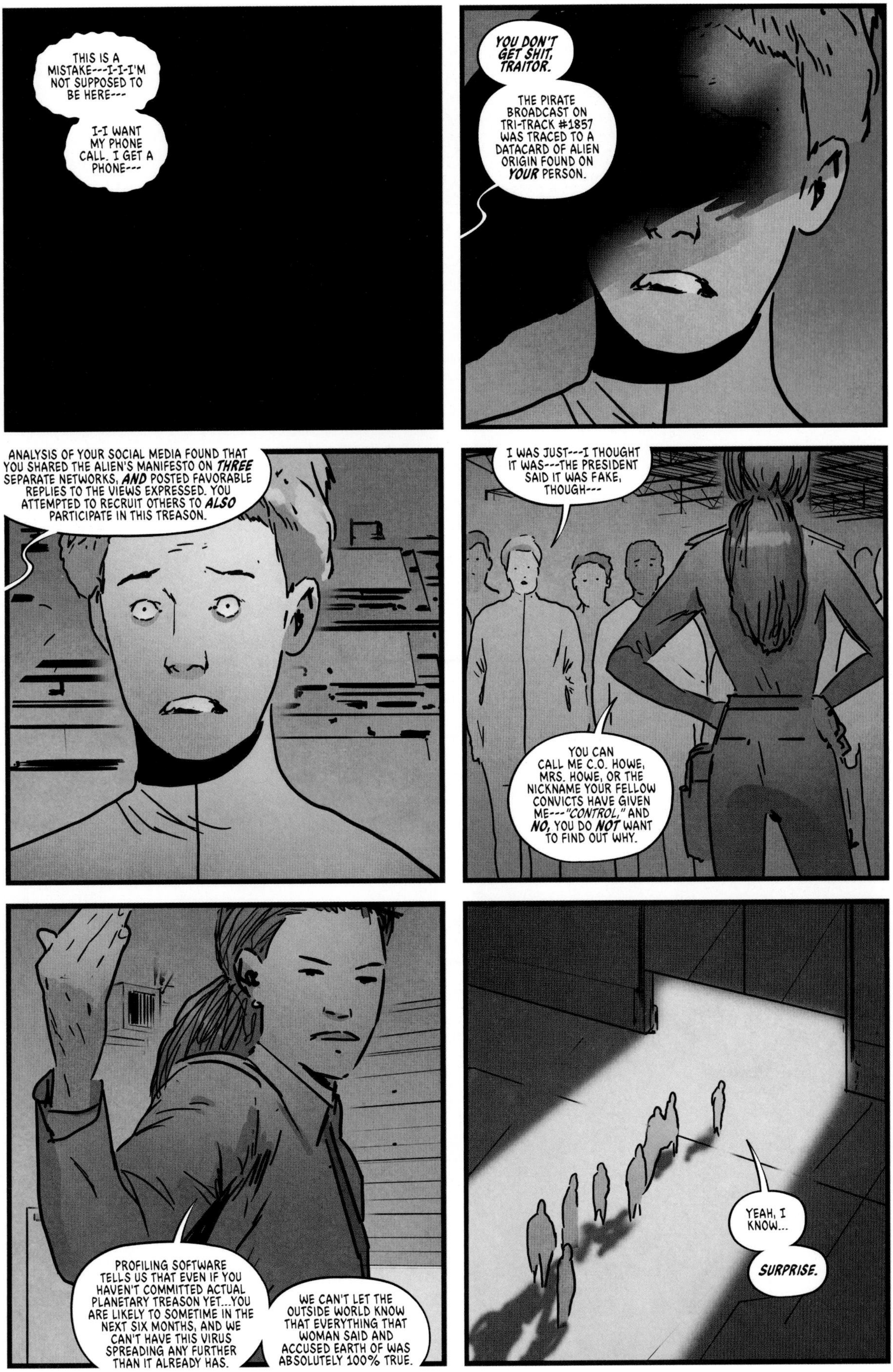
THIS IS A MISTAKE---I-I-I'M NOT SUPPOSED TO BE HERE---
I-I WANT MY PHONE CALL. I GET A PHONE---
YOU DON'T GET SHIT, TRAITOR.
THE PIRATE BROADCAST ON TRI-TRACK #1857 WAS TRACED TO A DATACARD OF ALIEN ORIGIN FOUND ON YOUR PERSON.
ANALYSIS OF YOUR SOCIAL MEDIA FOUND THAT YOU SHARED THE ALIEN'S MANIFESTO ON THREE SEPARATE NETWORKS, AND POSTED FAVORABLE REPLIES TO THE VIEWS EXPRESSED. YOU ATTEMPTED TO RECRUIT OTHERS TO ALSO PARTICIPATE IN THIS TREASON.
I WAS JUST---I THOUGHT IT WAS---THE PRESIDENT SAID IT WAS FAKE, THOUGH---
YOU CAN CALL ME C.O. HOWE, MRS. HOWE, OR THE NICKNAME YOUR FELLOW CONVICTS HAVE GIVEN ME---"CONTROL," AND NO, YOU DO NOT WANT TO FIND OUT WHY.
PROFILING SOFTWARE TELLS US THAT EVEN IF YOU HAVEN'T COMMITTED ACTUAL PLANETARY TREASON YET...YOU ARE LIKELY TO SOMETIME IN THE NEXT SIX MONTHS, AND WE CAN'T HAVE THIS VIRUS SPREADING ANY FURTHER THAN IT ALREADY HAS.
WE CAN'T LET THE OUTSIDE WORLD KNOW THAT EVERYTHING THAT WOMAN SAID AND ACCUSED EARTH OF WAS ABSOLUTELY 100% TRUE.
YEAH, I KNOW...
SURPRISE.

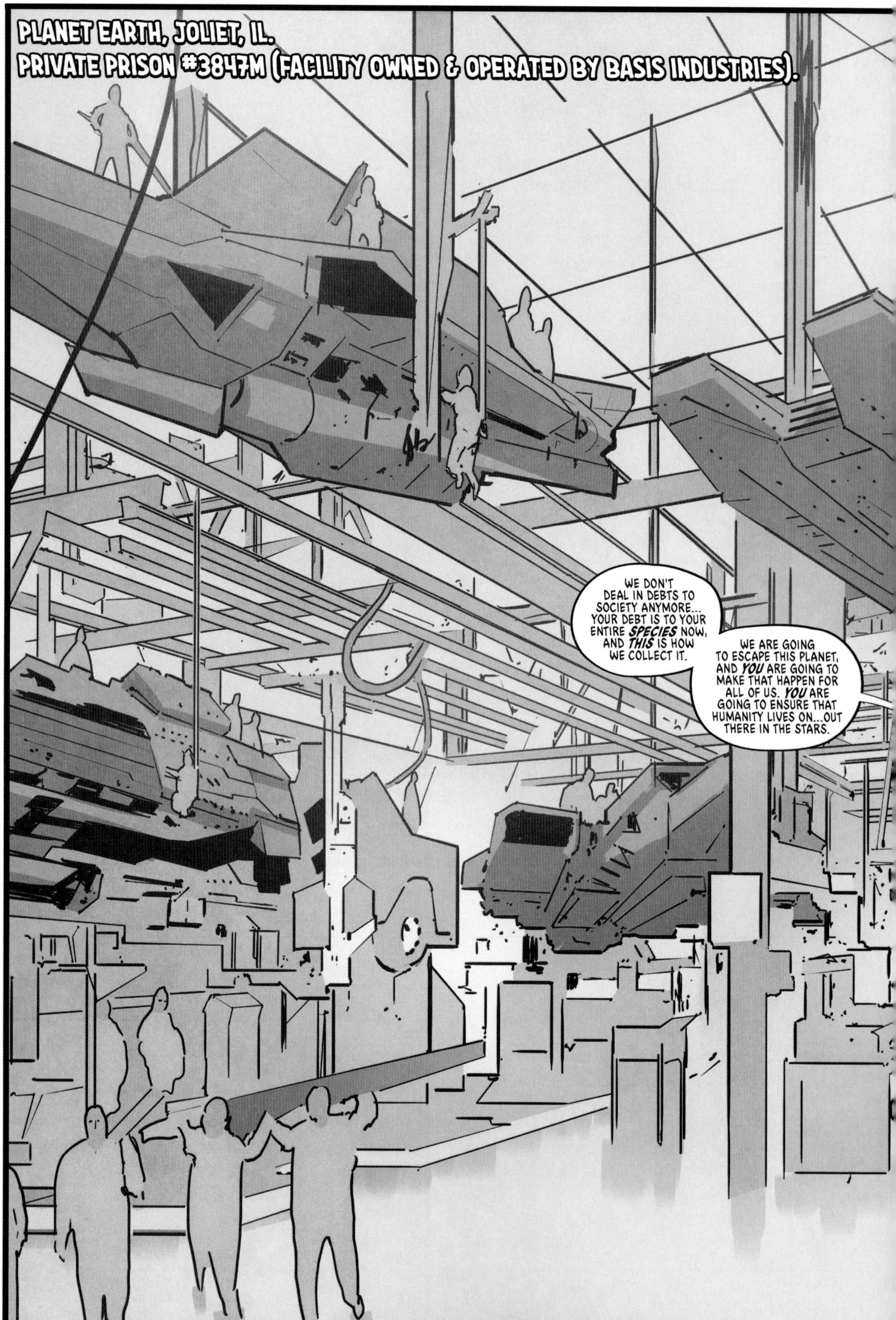
PLANET EARTH, JOLIET, IL.
PRIVATE PRISON #3847M (FACILITY OWNED & OPERATED BY BASIS INDUSTRIES).
WE DON'T DEAL IN DEBTS TO SOCIETY ANYMORE... YOUR DEBT IS TO YOUR ENTIRE SPECIES NOW, AND THIS IS HOW WE COLLECT IT.
WE ARE GOING TO ESCAPE THIS PLANET, AND YOU ARE GOING TO MAKE THAT HAPPEN FOR ALL OF US. YOU ARE GOING TO ENSURE THAT HUMANITY LIVES ON...OUT THERE IN THE STARS.

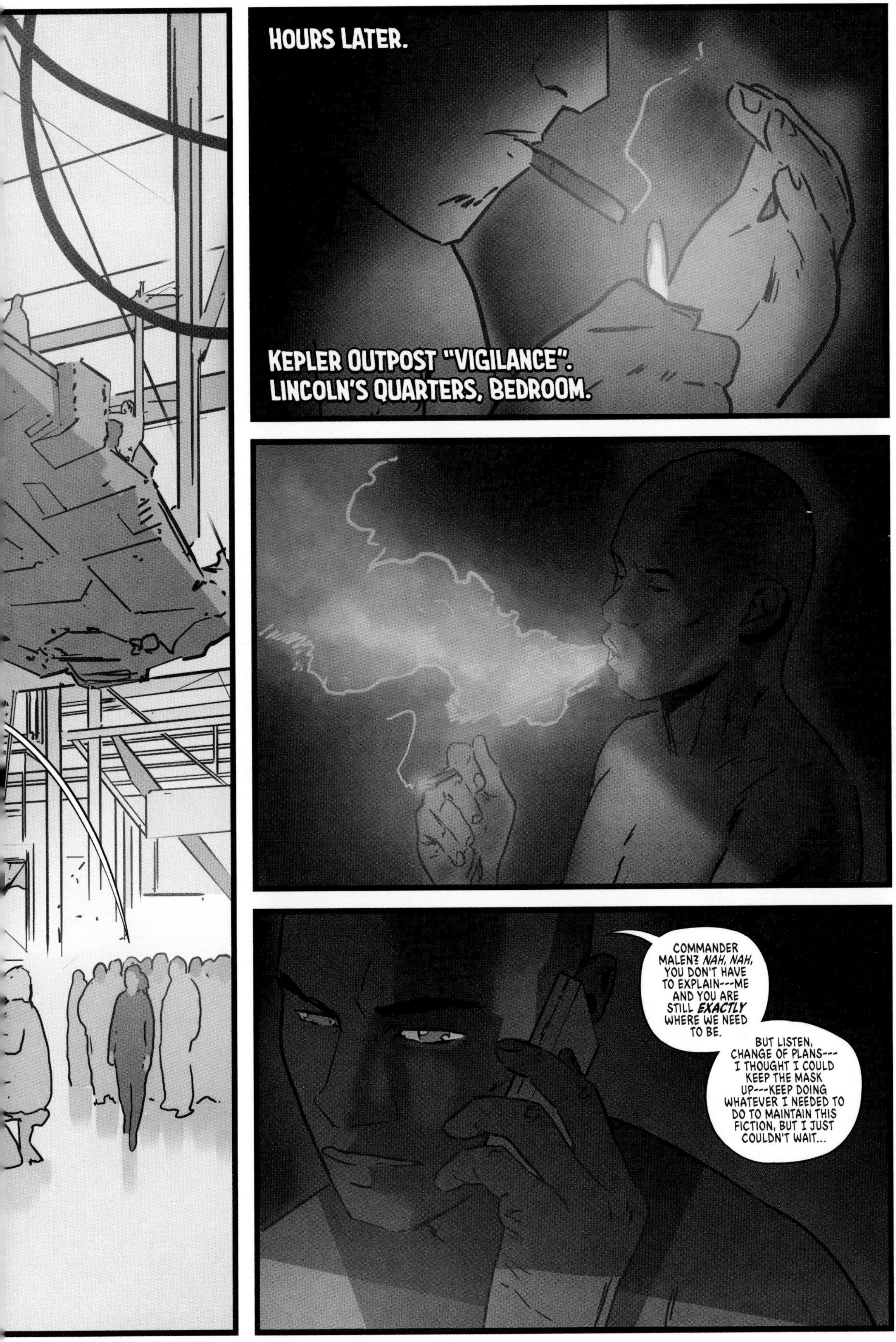
HOURS LATER.
KEPLER OUTPOST "VIGILANCE". LINCOLN'S QUARTERS, BEDROOM.
COMMANDER MALEN? NAH, NAH, YOU DON'T HAVE TO EXPLAIN---ME AND YOU ARE STILL EXACTLY WHERE WE NEED TO BE.
BUT LISTEN, CHANGE OF PLANS---I THOUGHT I COULD KEEP THE MASK UP---KEEP DOING WHATEVER I NEEDED TO DO TO MAINTAIN THIS FICTION, BUT I JUST COULDN'T WAIT...

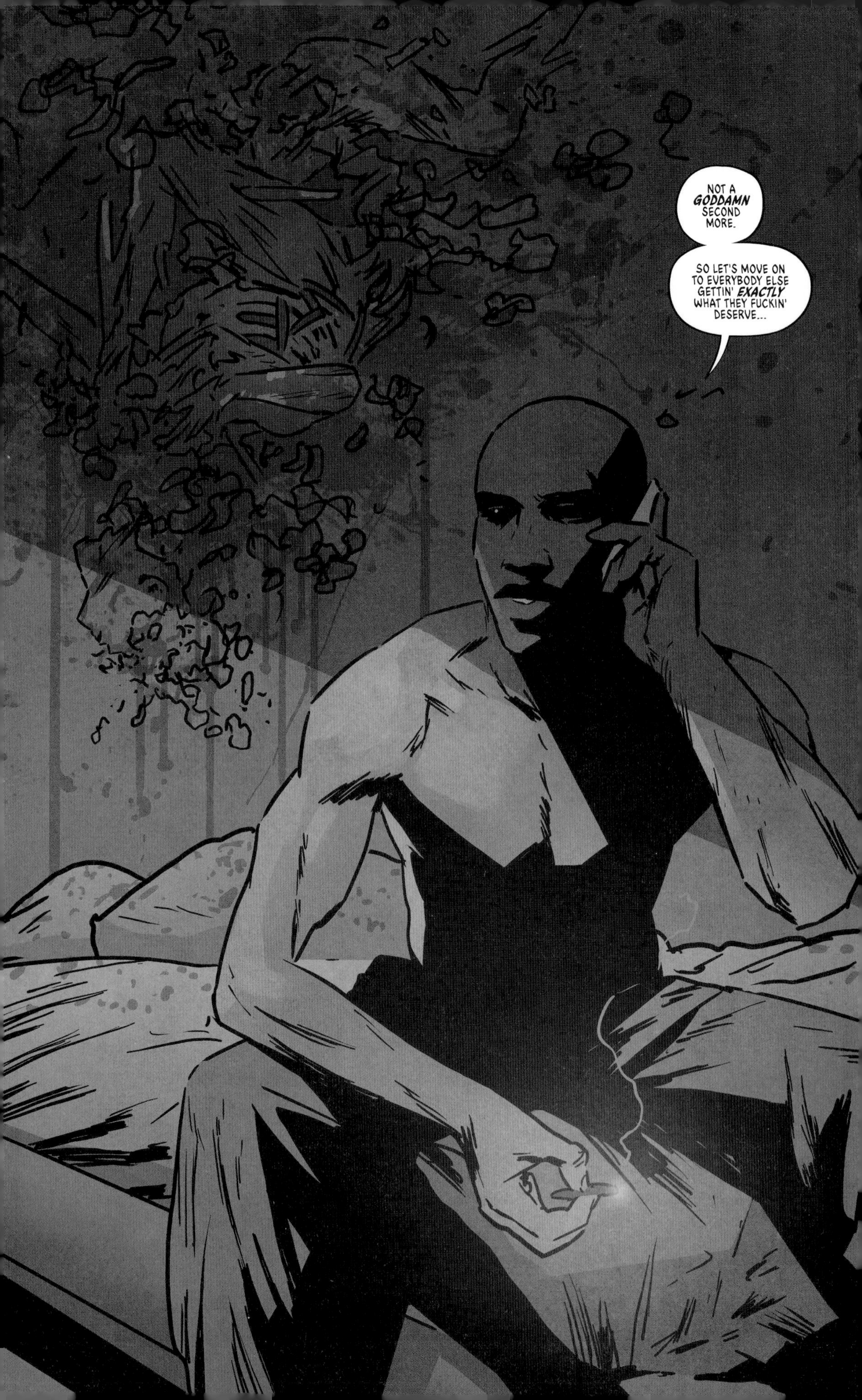
NOT A GODDAMN SECOND MORE.
SO LET'S MOVE ON TO EVERYBODY ELSE GETTIN' EXACTLY WHAT THEY FUCKIN' DESERVE...

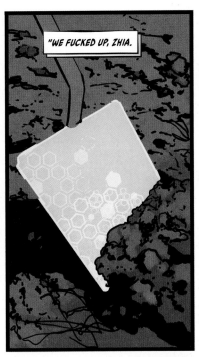

"WE FUCKED UP, ZHIA."

"WE THOUGHT WE UNDERSTOOD THE INTERESTS OF EARTH IN OUR PLANET, BUT WE WERE *SO* WRONG, AND THINGS ARE SO MUCH WORSE THAN WE *EVER* IMAGINED."

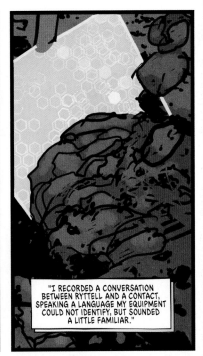

"I RECORDED A CONVERSATION BETWEEN RYTTELL AND A CONTACT, SPEAKING A LANGUAGE MY EQUIPMENT COULD NOT IDENTIFY, BUT SOUNDED A LITTLE FAMILIAR."

PLANET VALIUS. HORIZON ONE. SOLARI NATIONAL ZOO, SOUTH WING (CLOSED FOR PRIVATE TOUR OF COUNSELOR-SPONSORED ENDANGERED CREATURE EXHIBIT).

DEVIS WRACKELS (SECURITY SERVICES OPERATIVE, RETIRED/UNDERCOVER).

BECAUSE YOU HAD US LEARN SOME OF IT BEFORE YOU AND THE OTHERS LEFT---

THEY WERE BOTH SPEAKING *ENGLISH,* ZHIA... PERFECT EARTH ENGLISH.

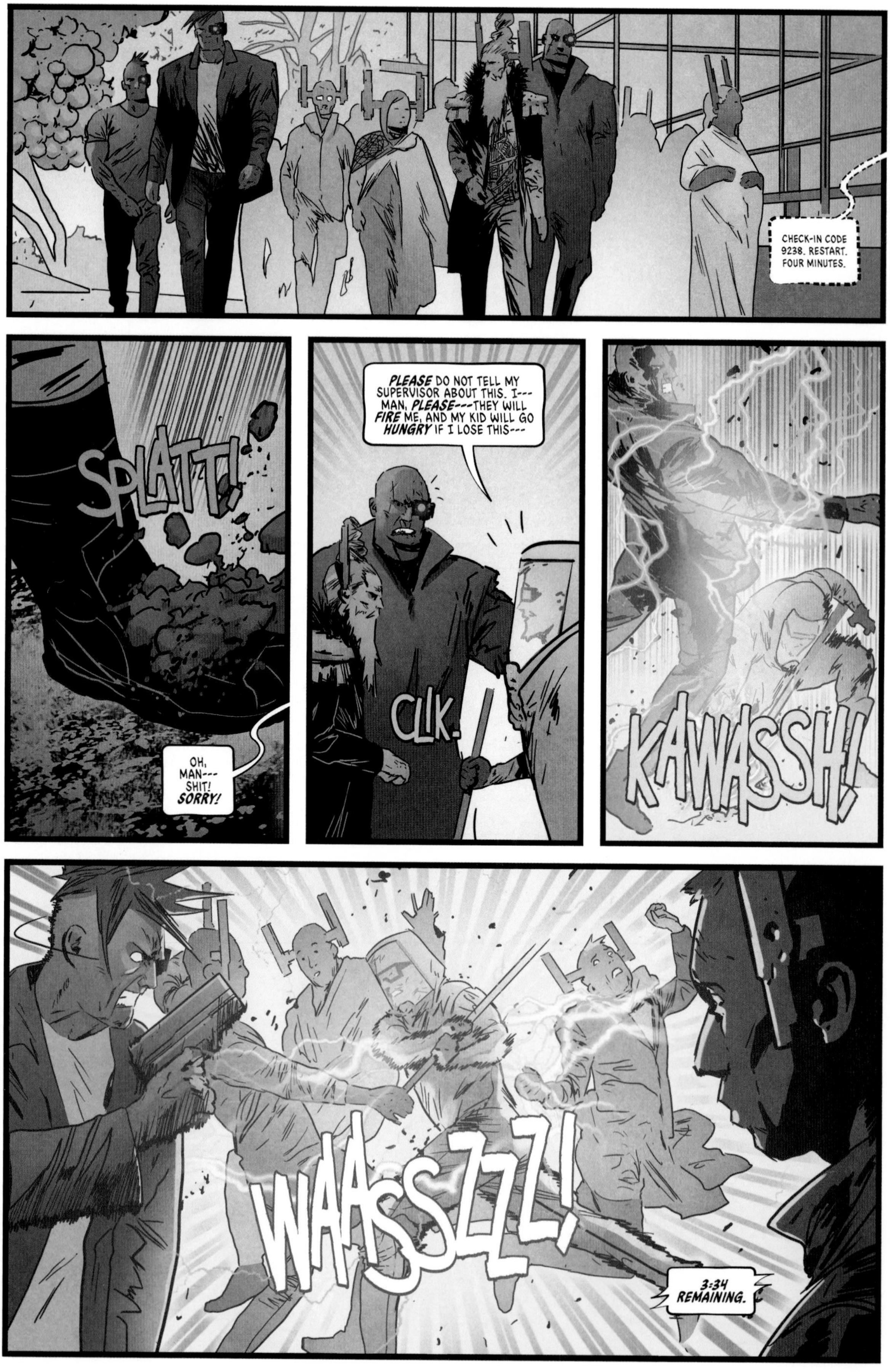
CHECK-IN CODE 9238. RESTART. FOUR MINUTES.
SPLATT!
OH, MAN--- SHIT! SORRY!
PLEASE DO NOT TELL MY SUPERVISOR ABOUT THIS. I--- MAN, PLEASE---THEY WILL FIRE ME, AND MY KID WILL GO HUNGRY IF I LOSE THIS---
CLIK.
KAWASSH!
WAASSZZZ!
3:34 REMAINING.

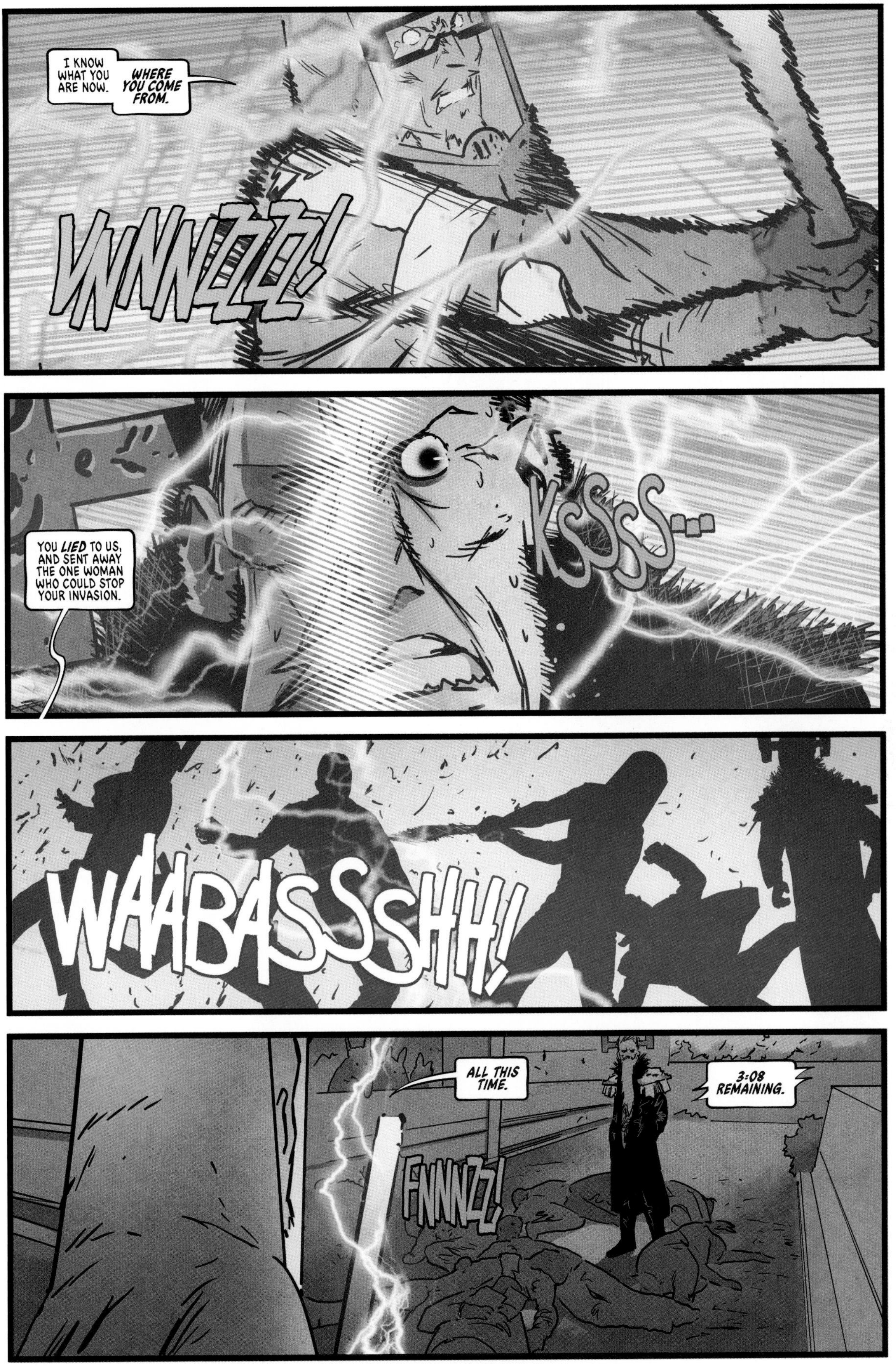
I KNOW WHAT YOU ARE NOW.
WHERE YOU COME FROM.
VNNNZZZ!
YOU LIED TO US, AND SENT AWAY THE ONE WOMAN WHO COULD STOP YOUR INVASION.
KSSSS...
WAABASSSHH!
ALL THIS TIME.
3:08 REMAINING.
FNNNZZ!

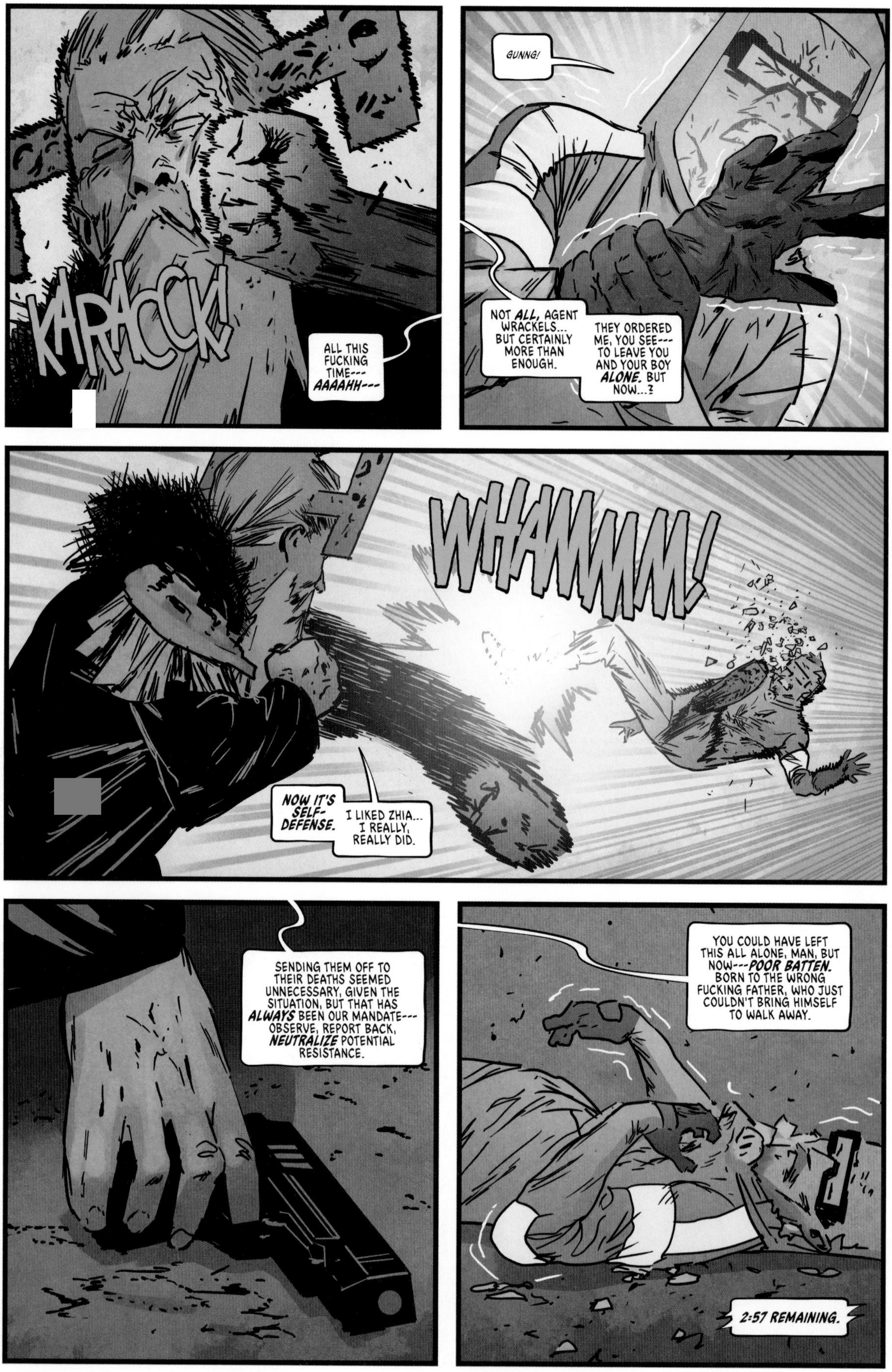
KARACCK!
ALL THIS FUCKING TIME--- AAAAHH---
GUNNG!
NOT ALL, AGENT WRACKELS... BUT CERTAINLY MORE THAN ENOUGH.
THEY ORDERED ME, YOU SEE--- TO LEAVE YOU AND YOUR BOY ALONE. BUT NOW...?
WHAMMM!
NOW IT'S SELF-DEFENSE.
I LIKED ZHIA... I REALLY, REALLY DID.
SENDING THEM OFF TO THEIR DEATHS SEEMED UNNECESSARY, GIVEN THE SITUATION, BUT THAT HAS ALWAYS BEEN OUR MANDATE--- OBSERVE, REPORT BACK, NEUTRALIZE POTENTIAL RESISTANCE.
YOU COULD HAVE LEFT THIS ALL ALONE, MAN, BUT NOW---POOR BATTEN. BORN TO THE WRONG FUCKING FATHER, WHO JUST COULDN'T BRING HIMSELF TO WALK AWAY.
2:57 REMAINING.

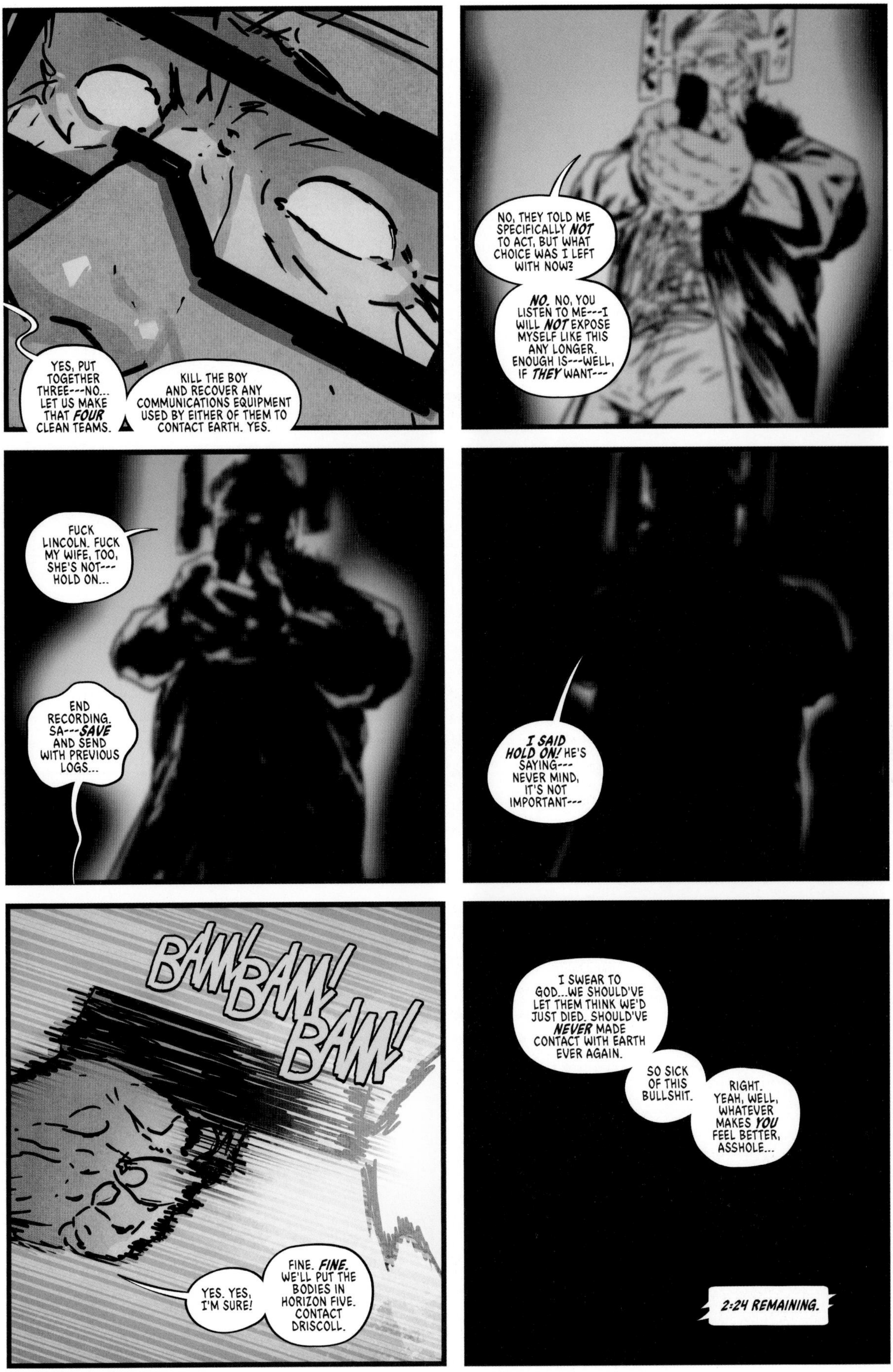
YES, PUT TOGETHER THREE---NO... LET US MAKE THAT FOUR CLEAN TEAMS.
KILL THE BOY AND RECOVER ANY COMMUNICATIONS EQUIPMENT USED BY EITHER OF THEM TO CONTACT EARTH. YES.
NO, THEY TOLD ME SPECIFICALLY NOT TO ACT, BUT WHAT CHOICE WAS I LEFT WITH NOW?
NO. NO, YOU LISTEN TO ME---I WILL NOT EXPOSE MYSELF LIKE THIS ANY LONGER. ENOUGH IS---WELL, IF THEY WANT---
FUCK LINCOLN. FUCK MY WIFE, TOO, SHE'S NOT--- HOLD ON...
END RECORDING. SA---SAVE AND SEND WITH PREVIOUS LOGS...
I SAID HOLD ON! HE'S SAYING--- NEVER MIND, IT'S NOT IMPORTANT---
BAM! BAM! BAM!
YES. YES, I'M SURE!
FINE. FINE. WE'LL PUT THE BODIES IN HORIZON FIVE. CONTACT DRISCOLL.
I SWEAR TO GOD...WE SHOULD'VE LET THEM THINK WE'D JUST DIED. SHOULD'VE NEVER MADE CONTACT WITH EARTH EVER AGAIN.
SO SICK OF THIS BULLSHIT.
RIGHT. YEAH, WELL, WHATEVER MAKES YOU FEEL BETTER, ASSHOLE...
2:24 REMAINING.

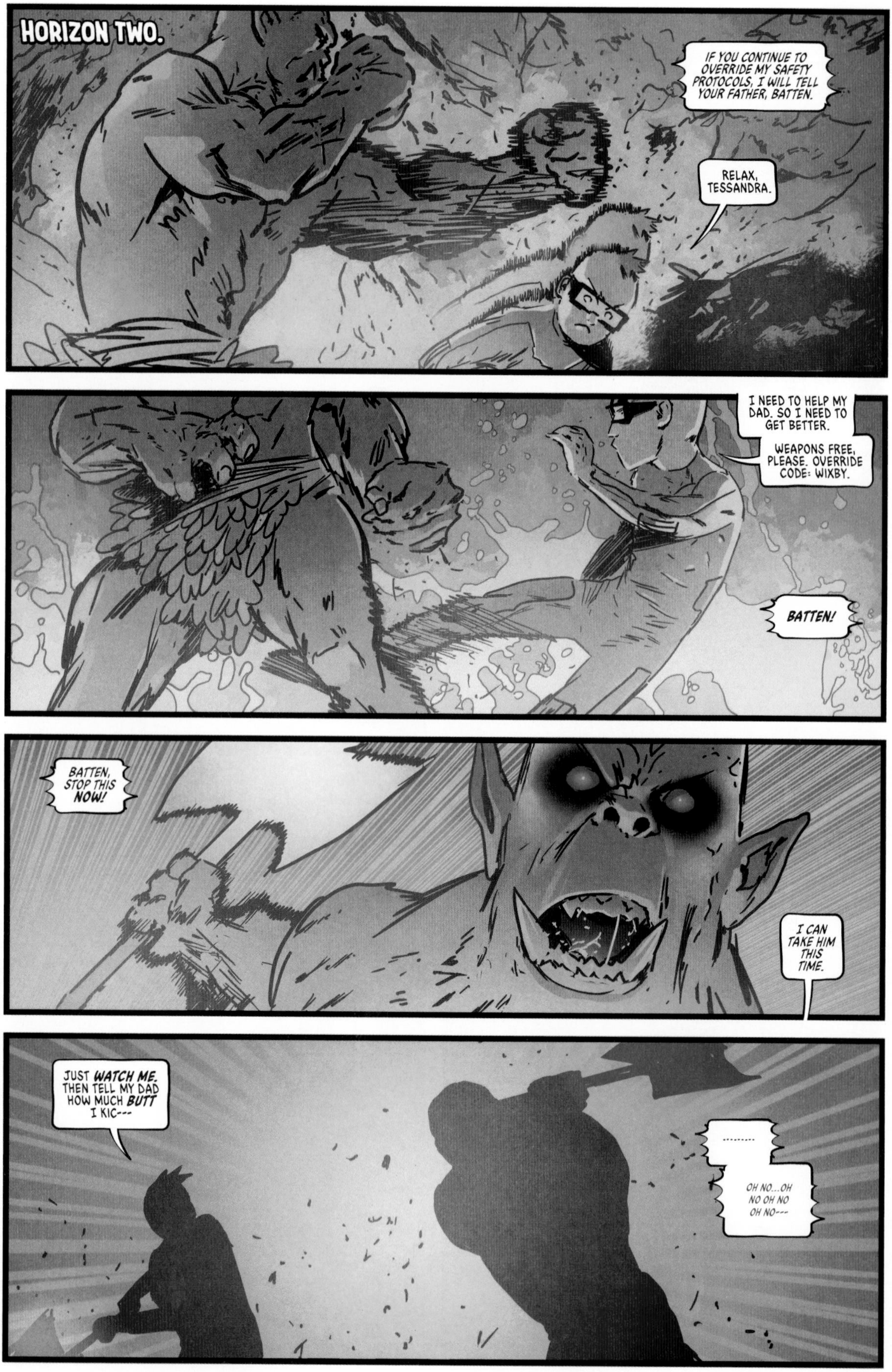
HORIZON TWO.
IF YOU CONTINUE TO OVERRIDE MY SAFETY PROTOCOLS, I WILL TELL YOUR FATHER, BATTEN.
RELAX, TESSANDRA.
I NEED TO HELP MY DAD. SO I NEED TO GET BETTER.
WEAPONS FREE, PLEASE. OVERRIDE CODE: WIXBY.
BATTEN!
BATTEN, STOP THIS NOW!
I CAN TAKE HIM THIS TIME.
JUST WATCH ME. THEN TELL MY DAD HOW MUCH BUTT I KIC---
....
OH NO...OH NO OH NO OH NO---

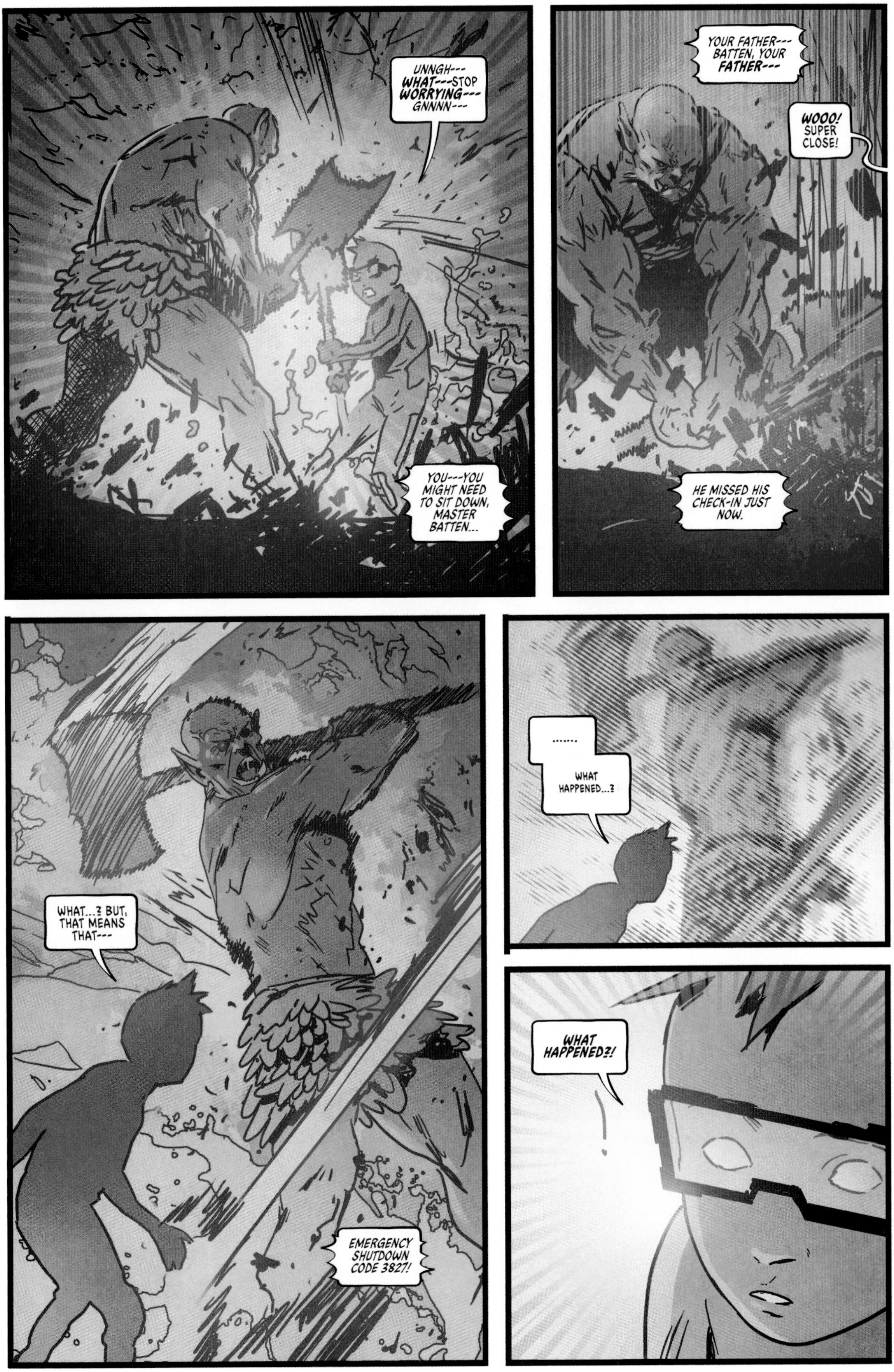
UNNGH--- WHAT---STOP WORRYING--- GNNNN---
YOU---YOU MIGHT NEED TO SIT DOWN, MASTER BATTEN...
YOUR FATHER--- BATTEN, YOUR FATHER---
WOOO! SUPER CLOSE!
HE MISSED HIS CHECK-IN JUST NOW.
WHAT...? BUT, THAT MEANS THAT---
EMERGENCY SHUTDOWN CODE 3827!
....
WHAT HAPPENED...?
WHAT HAPPENED?!

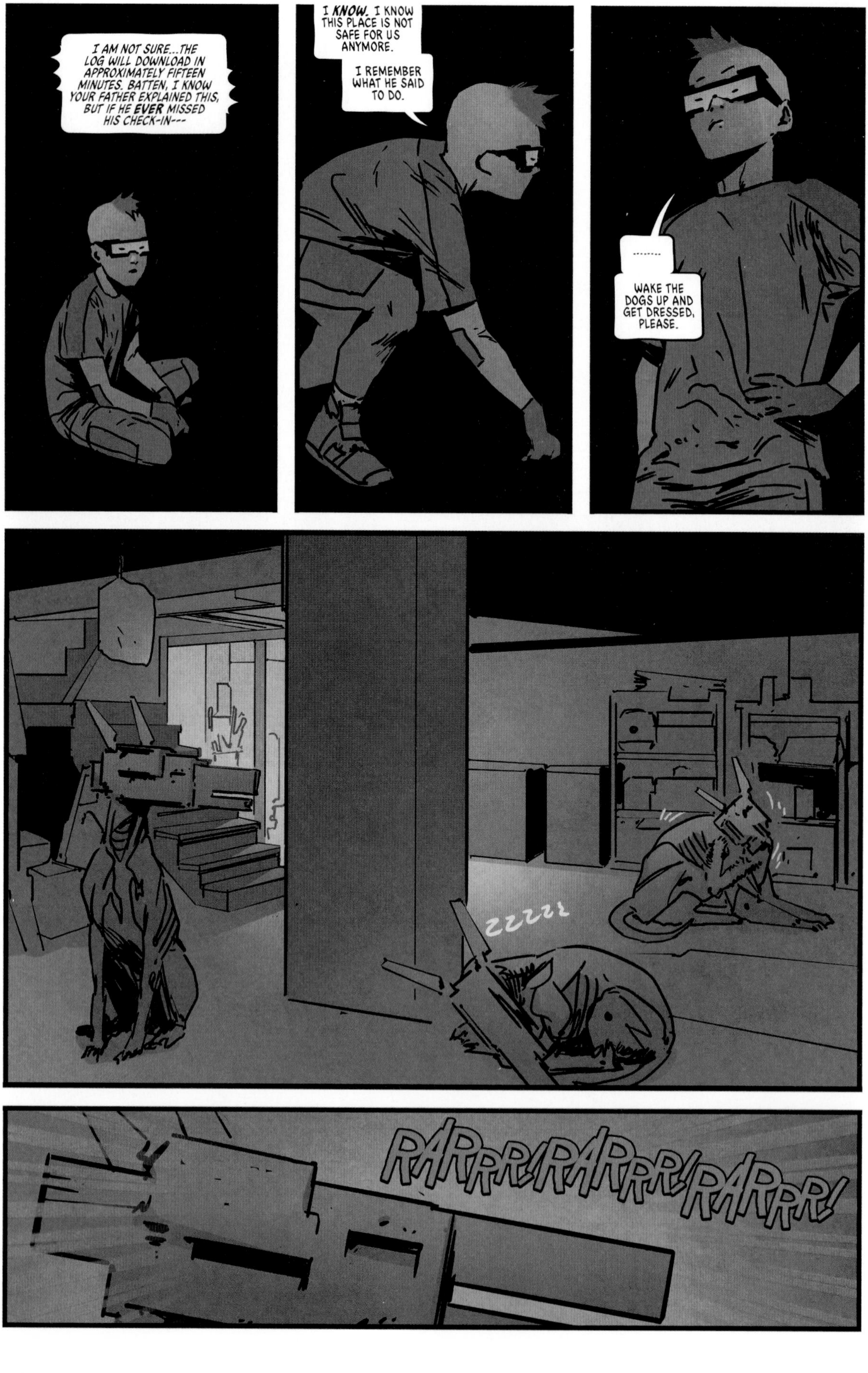
I AM NOT SURE...THE LOG WILL DOWNLOAD IN APPROXIMATELY FIFTEEN MINUTES. BATTEN, I KNOW YOUR FATHER EXPLAINED THIS, BUT IF HE EVER MISSED HIS CHECK-IN---
I KNOW. I KNOW THIS PLACE IS NOT SAFE FOR US ANYMORE.
I REMEMBER WHAT HE SAID TO DO.
....
WAKE THE DOGS UP AND GET DRESSED, PLEASE.
ZZZZZ
RARRR! RARRR! RARRR!

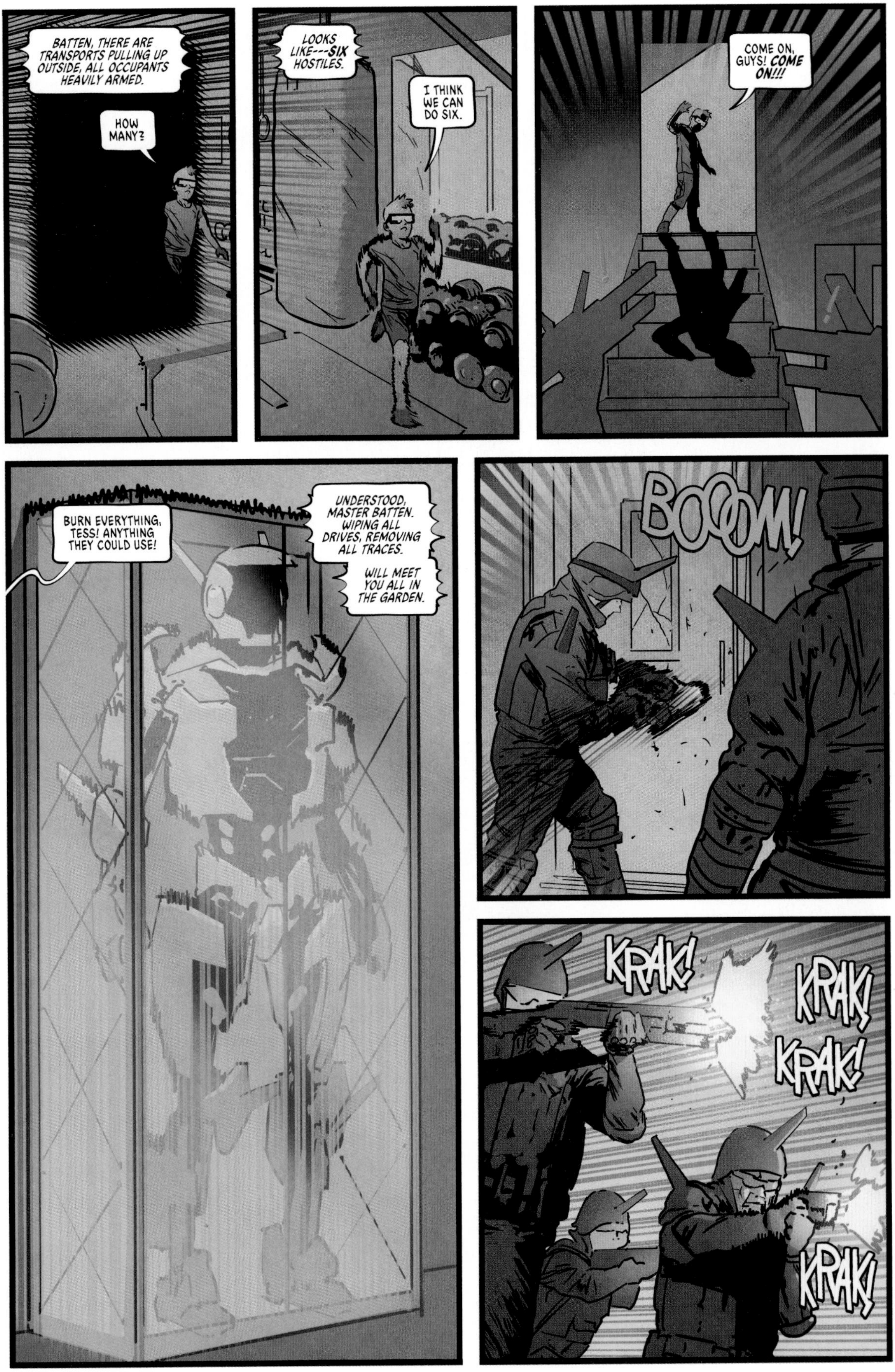

BATTEN, THERE ARE TRANSPORTS PULLING UP OUTSIDE, ALL OCCUPANTS HEAVILY ARMED.
HOW MANY?
LOOKS LIKE---SIX HOSTILES.
I THINK WE CAN DO SIX.
COME ON, GUYS! COME ON!!!
BURN EVERYTHING, TESS! ANYTHING THEY COULD USE!
UNDERSTOOD, MASTER BATTEN. WIPING ALL DRIVES, REMOVING ALL TRACES.
WILL MEET YOU ALL IN THE GARDEN.
BOOOM!
KRAK!
KRAK!
KRAK!
KRAK!

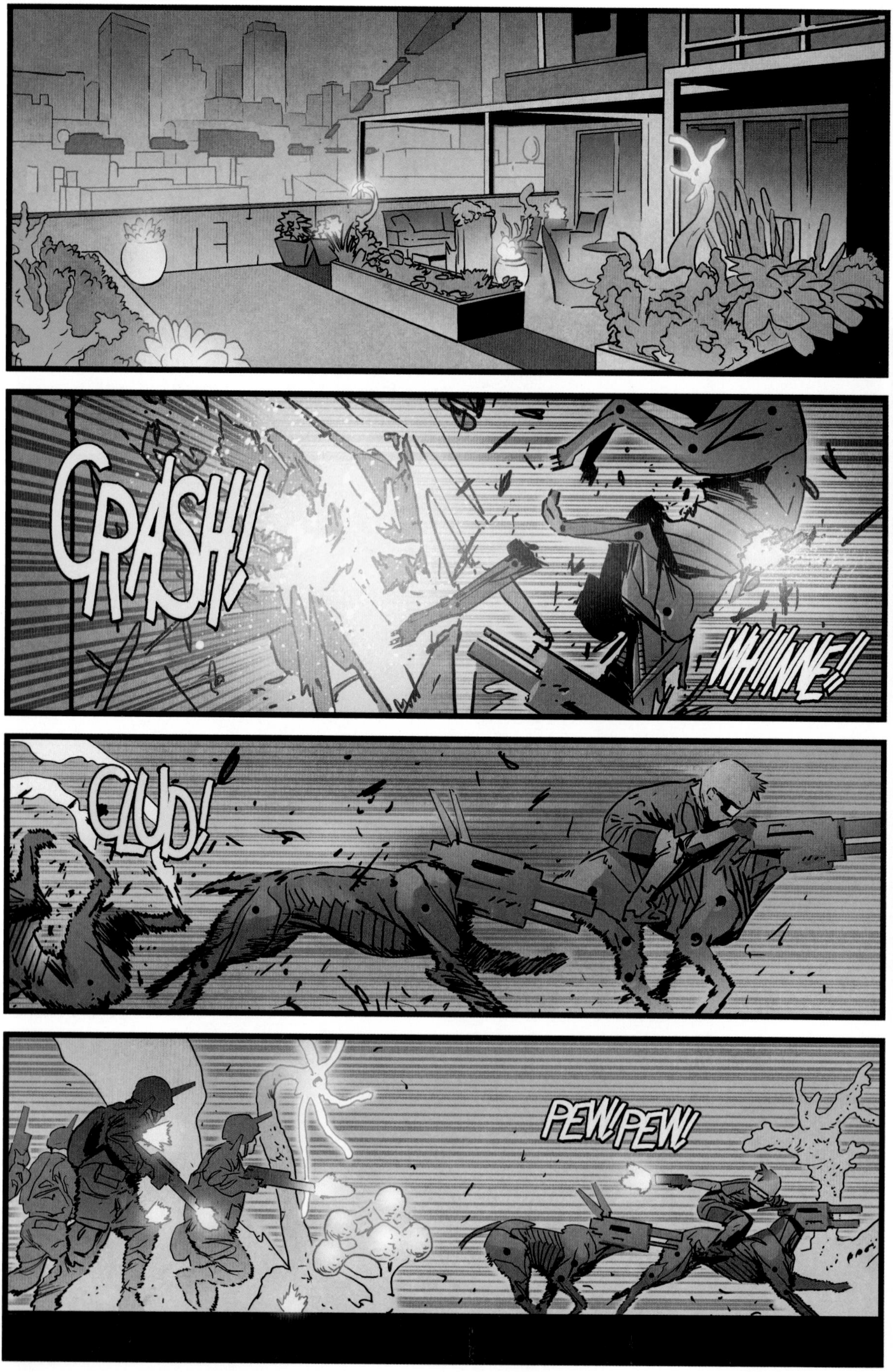
CRASH!
WHIINNE!!
CLUD!
PEW! PEW!

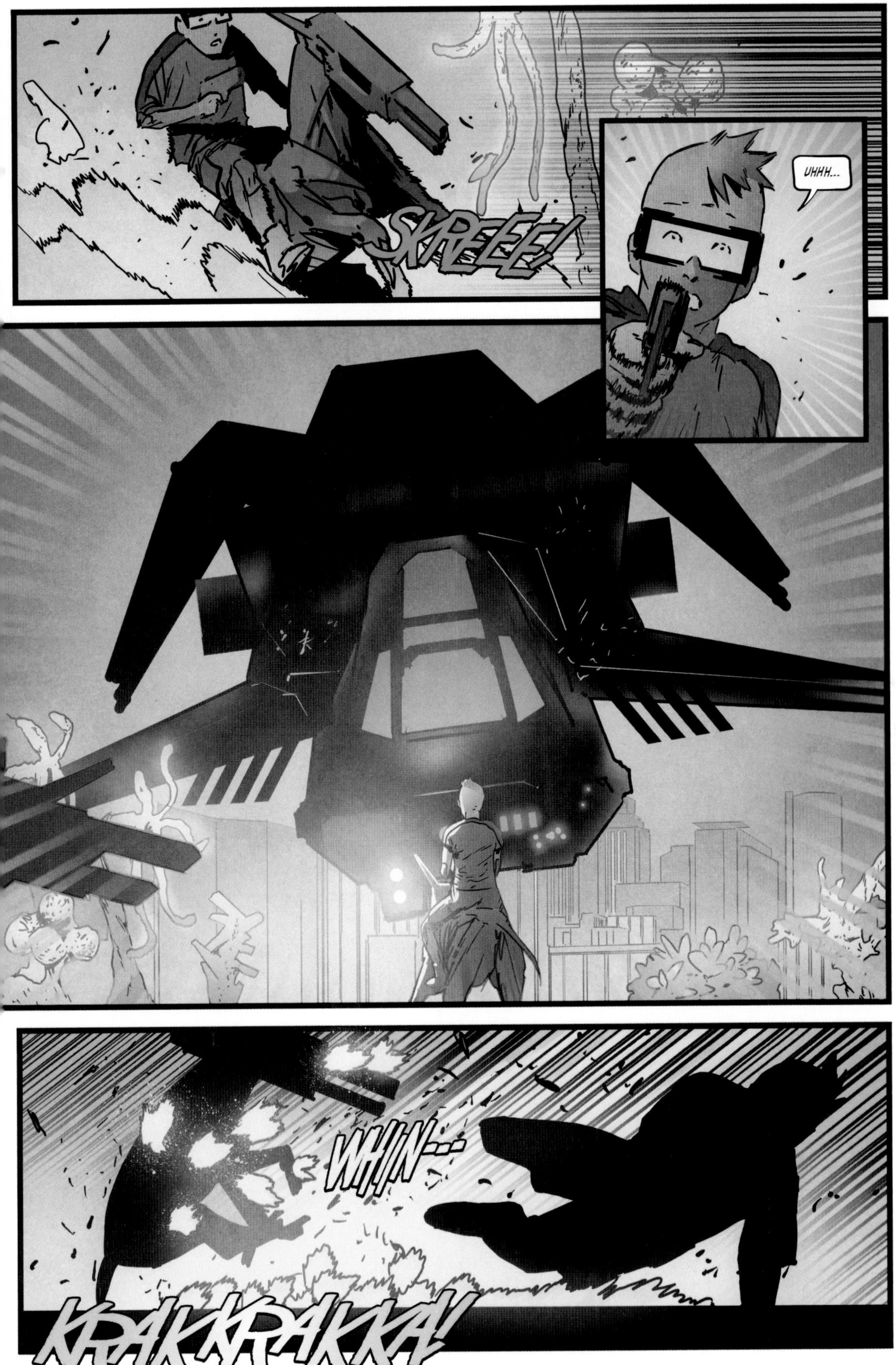
SKREEE!
UHHH...
WHIN---
KRAKKRAKKA!

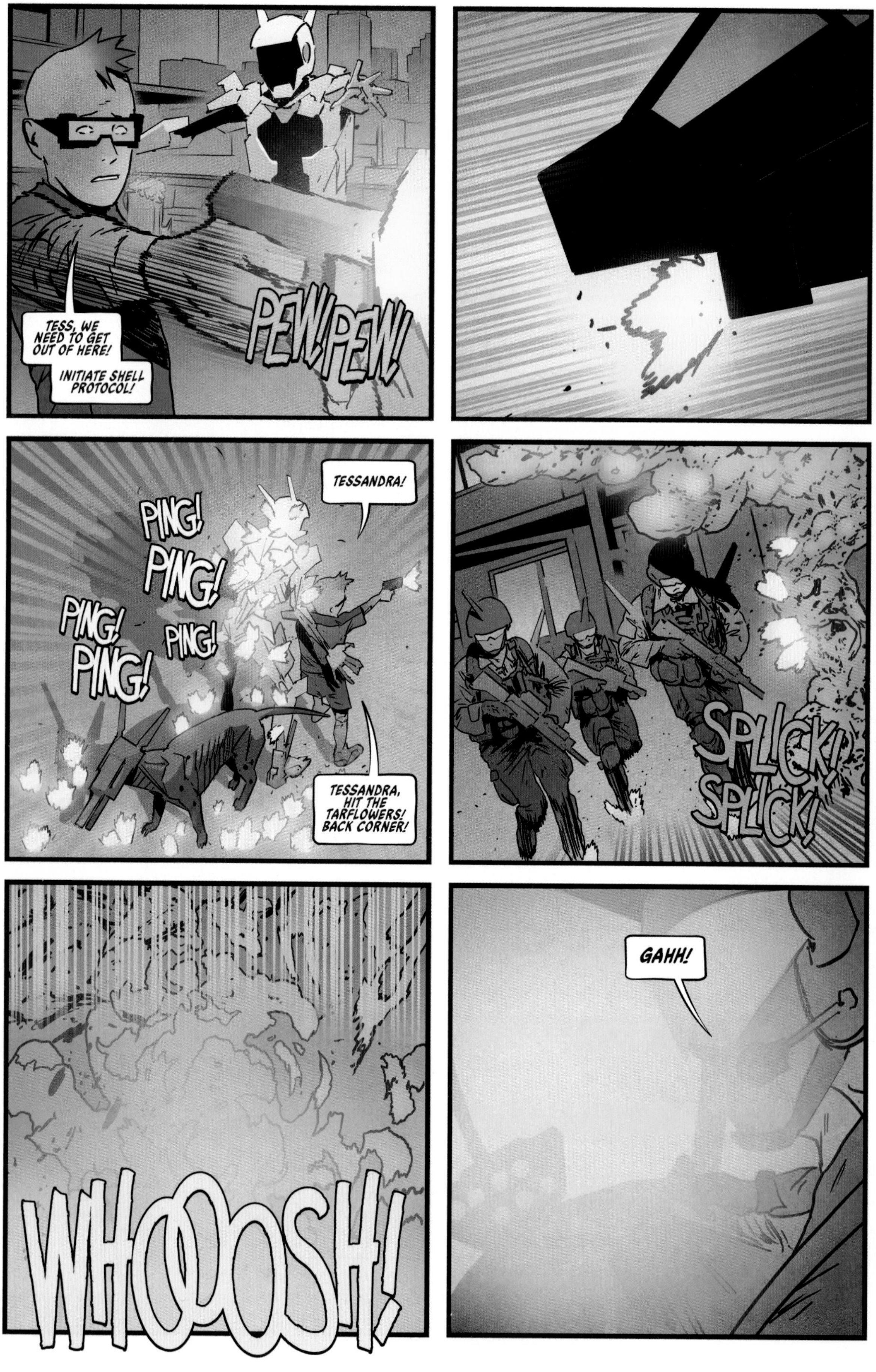
TESS, WE NEED TO GET OUT OF HERE!
INITIATE SHELL PROTOCOL!
PEW! PEW!
TESSANDRA!
PING! PING!
PING! PING!
PING!
TESSANDRA, HIT THE TARFLOWERS! BACK CORNER!
SPLICK! SPLICK!
WHOOOSH!
GAHH!

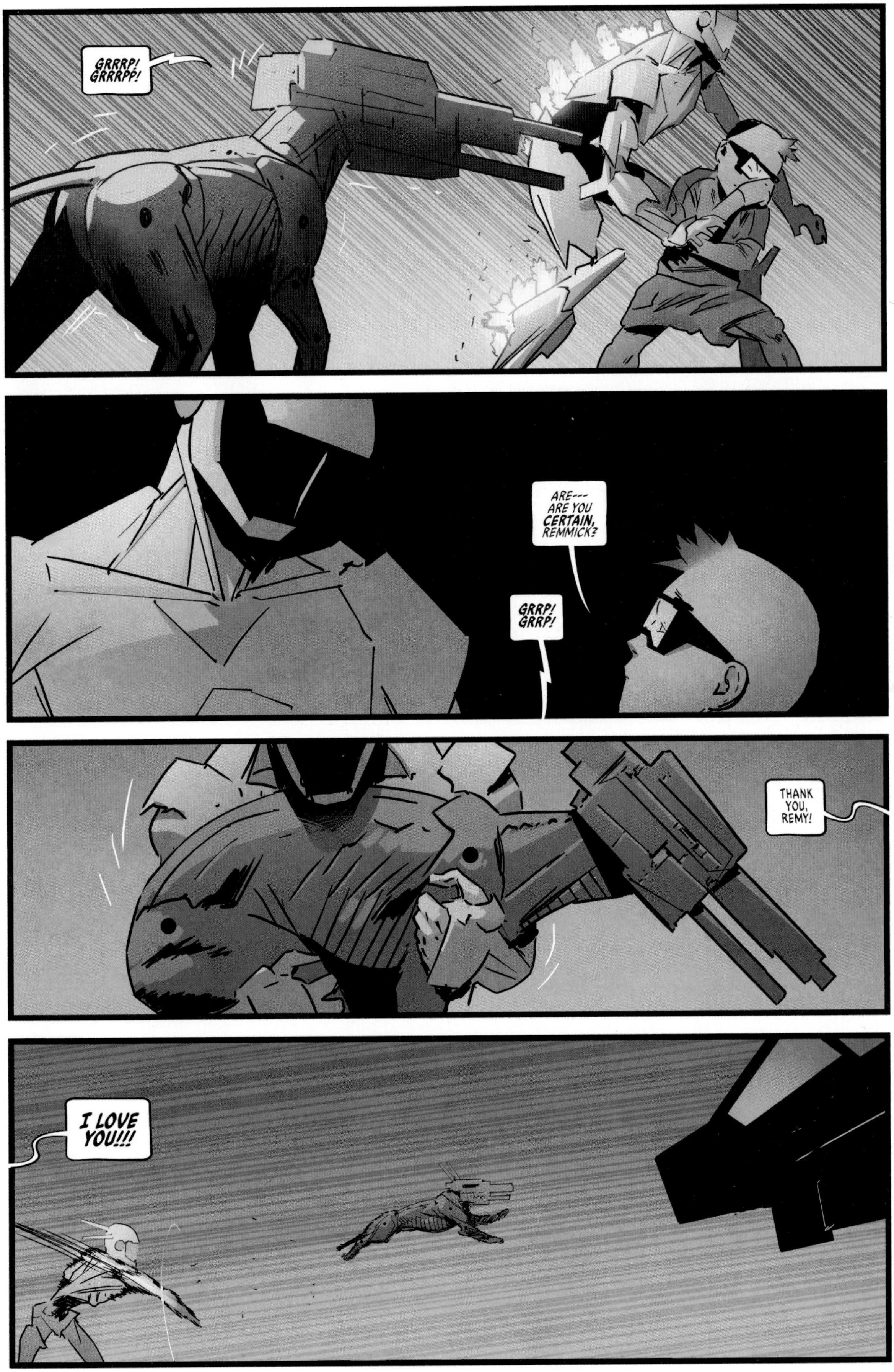
GRRRP! GRRRPP!
ARE--- ARE YOU CERTAIN, REMMICK?
GRRP! GRRP!
THANK YOU, REMY!
I LOVE YOU!!!

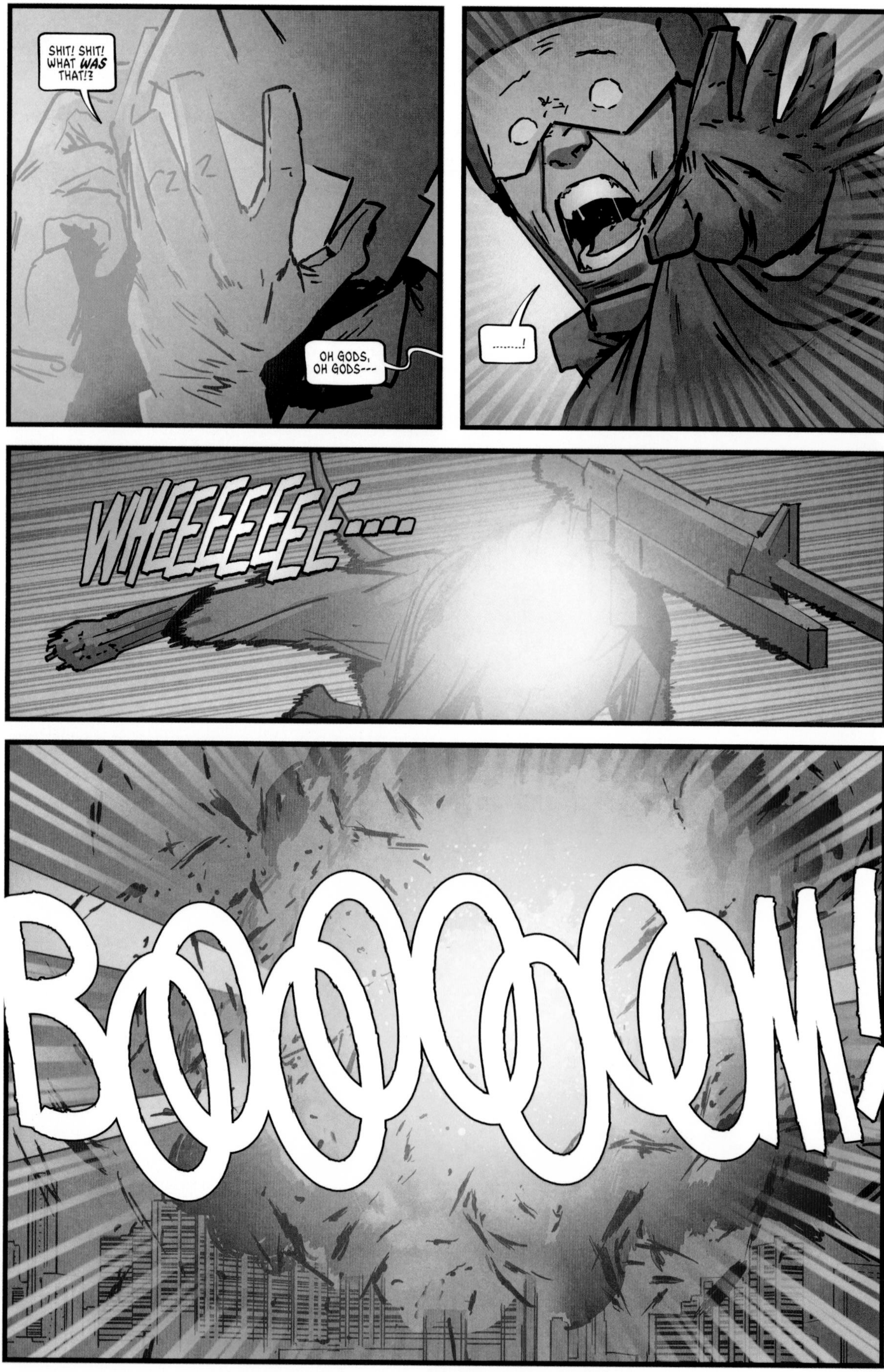

SHIT! SHIT! WHAT WAS THAT!?
OH GODS, OH GODS---
.........!
WHEEEEEEE....
BOOOOOOM!

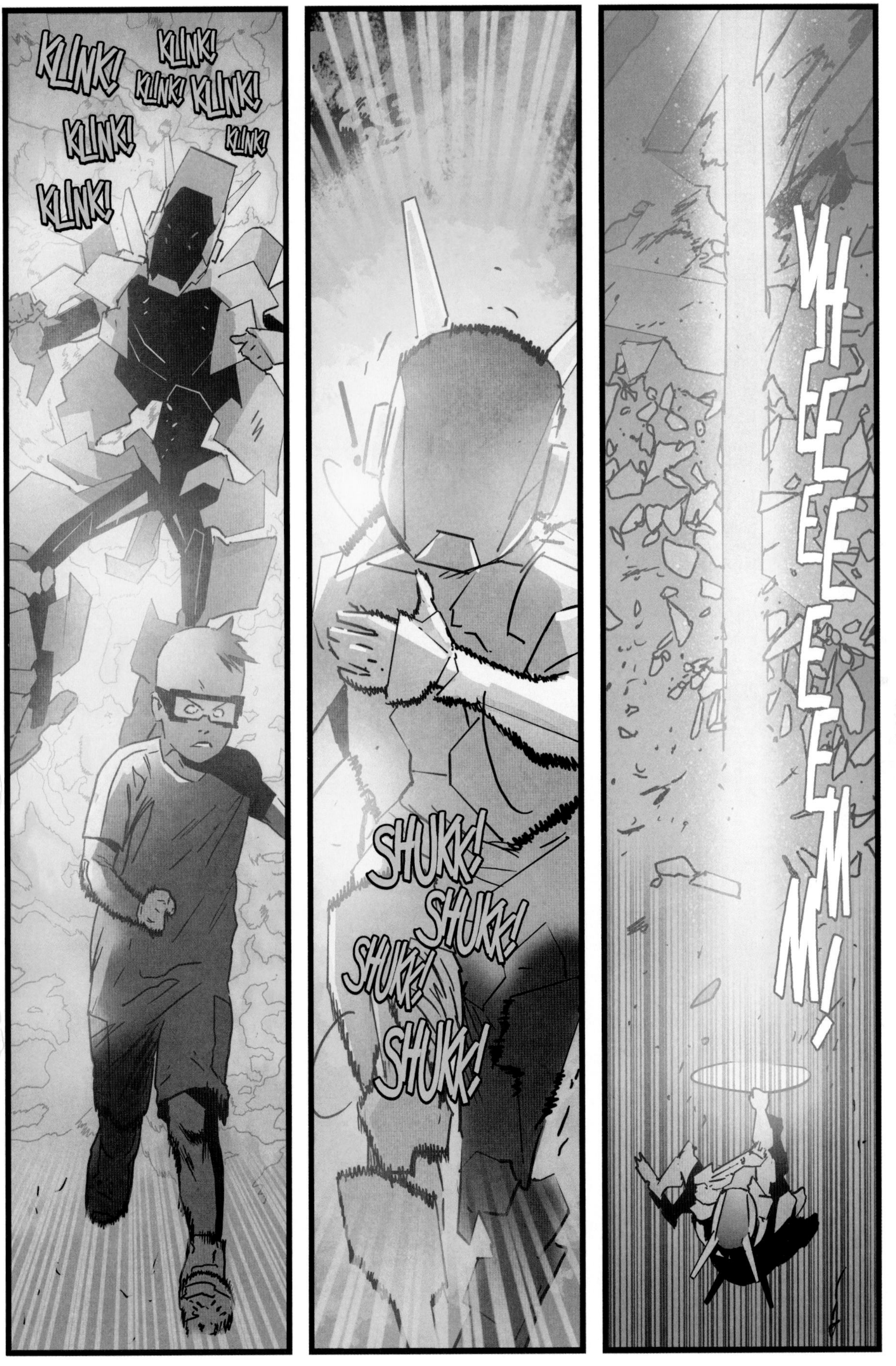
KLINK!
KLINK!
KLINK!
KLINK!
KLINK!
KLINK!
KLINK!
SHUKK!
SHUKK!
SHUKK!
SHUKK!
WHEEEEEEMM!

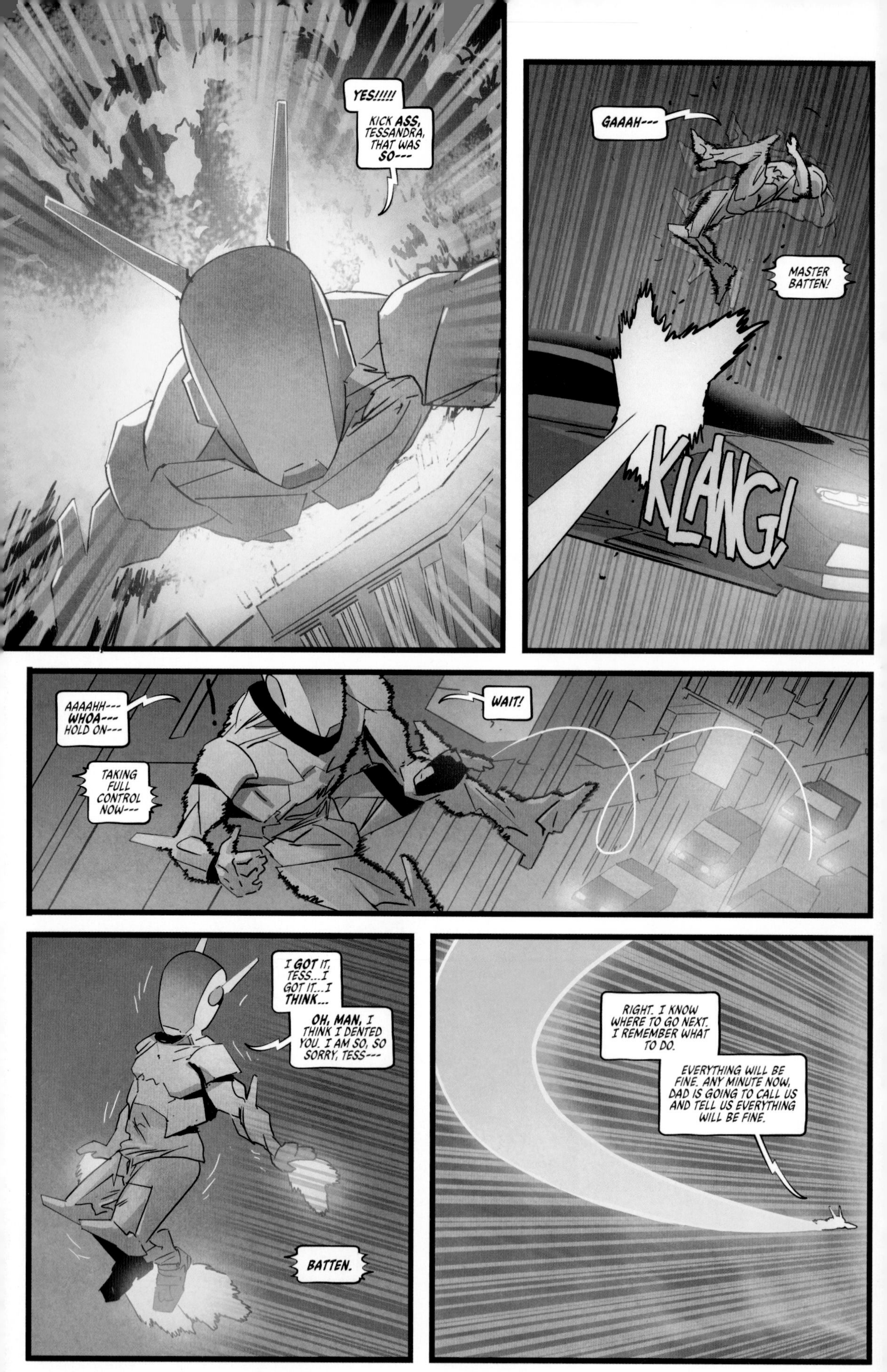
YES!!!!!
KICK ASS, TESSANDRA, THAT WAS SO---
GAAAH---
MASTER BATTEN!
KLANG!
AAAAHH--- WHOA--- HOLD ON---
TAKING FULL CONTROL NOW---
WAIT!
I GOT IT, TESS...I GOT IT...I THINK...
OH, MAN, I THINK I DENTED YOU. I AM SO, SO SORRY, TESS---
BATTEN.
RIGHT. I KNOW WHERE TO GO NEXT. I REMEMBER WHAT TO DO.
EVERYTHING WILL BE FINE. ANY MINUTE NOW, DAD IS GOING TO CALL US AND TELL US EVERYTHING WILL BE FINE.

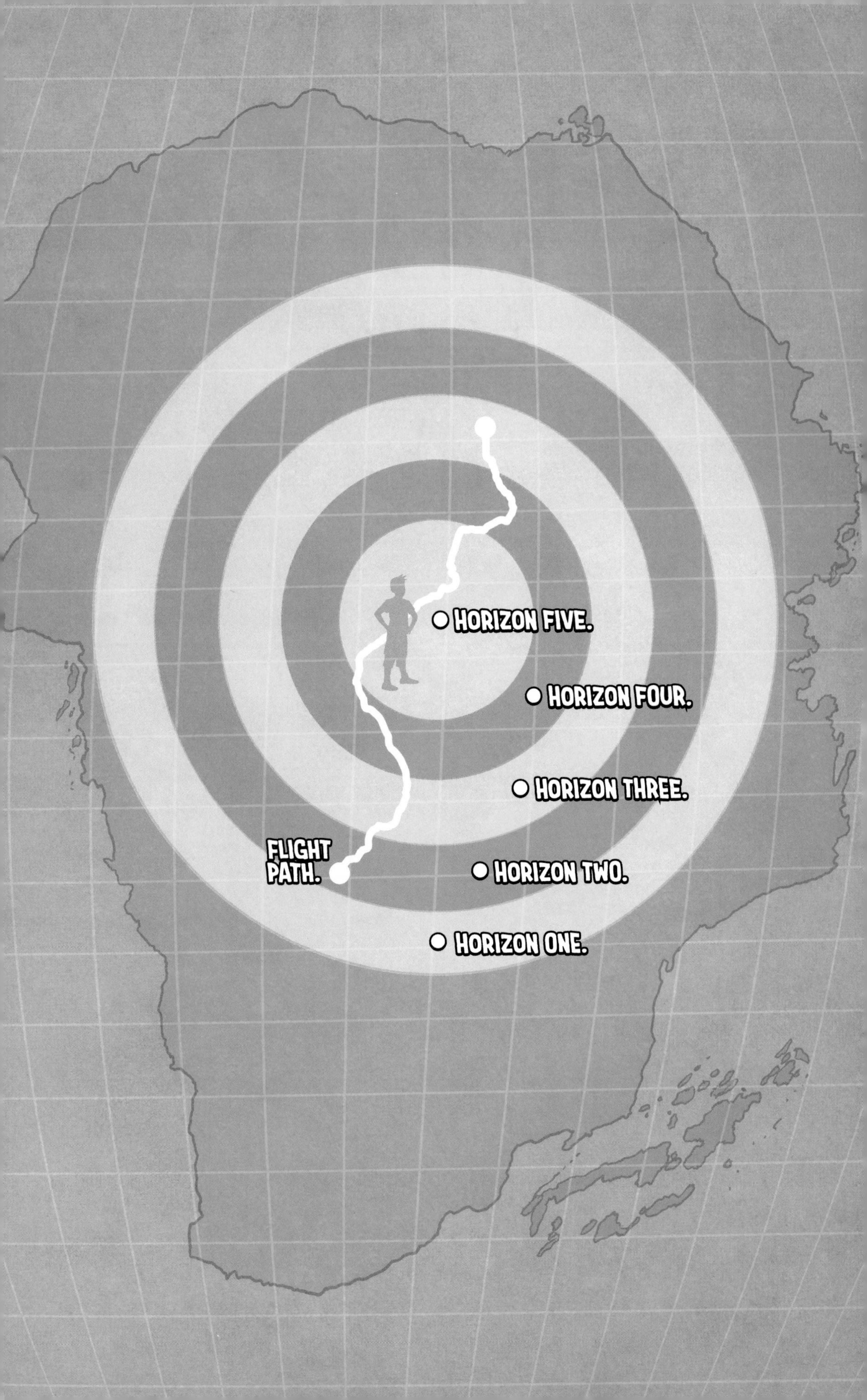
HORIZON FIVE.
HORIZON FOUR.
HORIZON THREE.
FLIGHT PATH.
HORIZON TWO.
HORIZON ONE.

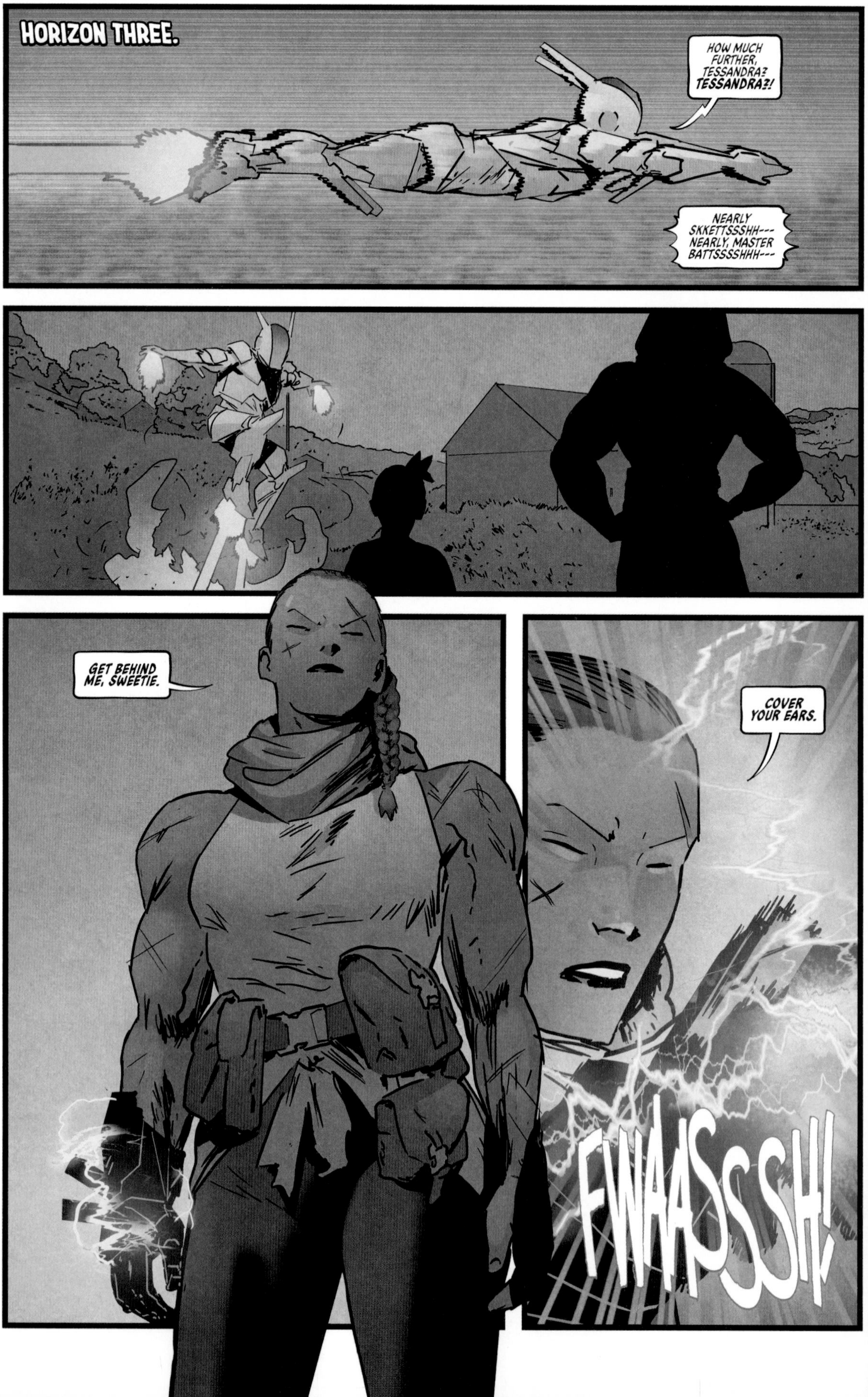
HORIZON THREE.
HOW MUCH FURTHER, TESSANDRA? TESSANDRA?!
NEARLY SKKETTSSSHH--- NEARLY, MASTER BATTSSSSHHH---
GET BEHIND ME, SWEETIE.
COVER YOUR EARS.
FWAASSSH!

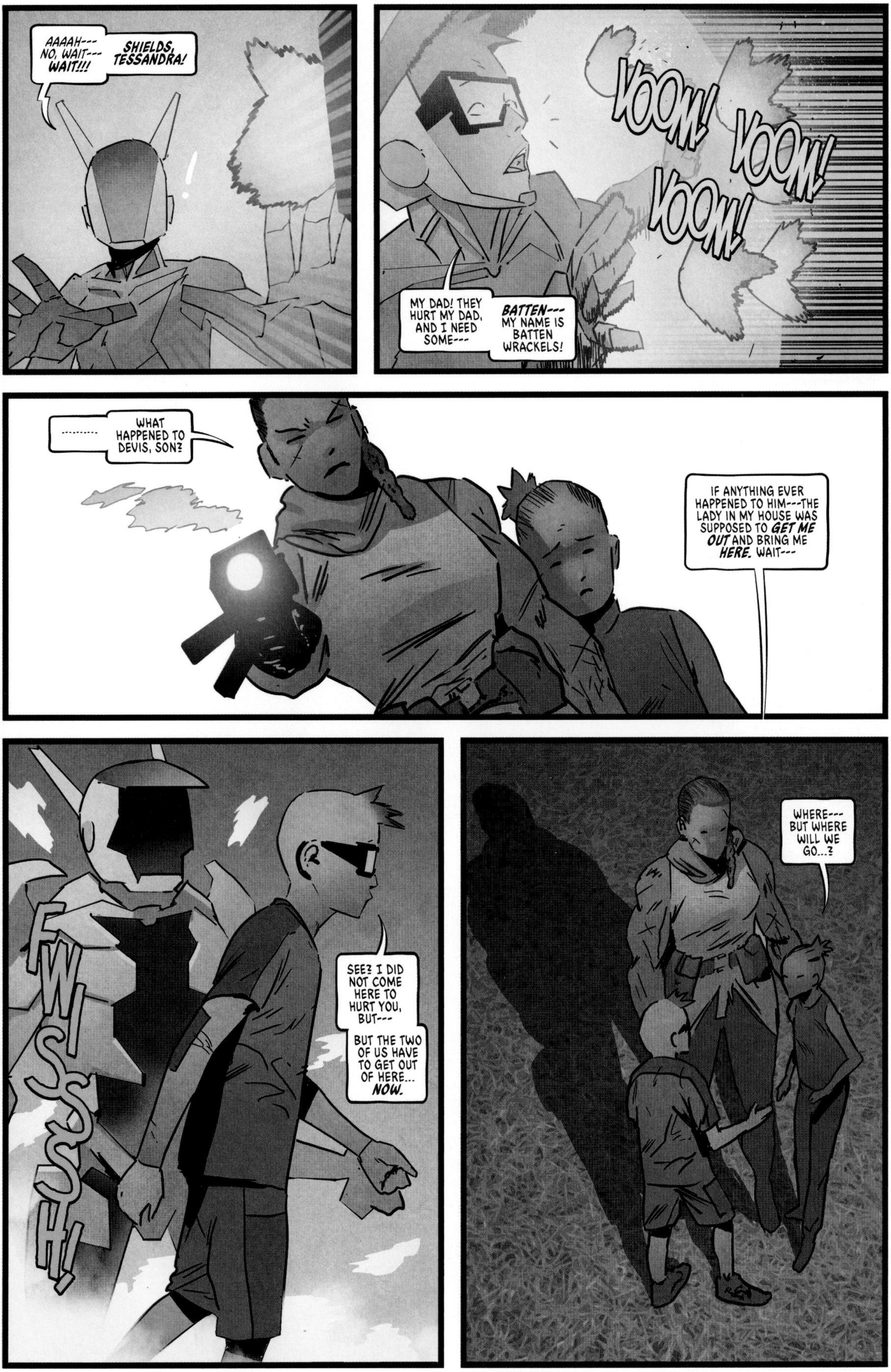
AAAAH--- NO, WAIT--- WAIT!!!
SHIELDS, TESSANDRA!
!
VOOM! VOOM! VOOM!
MY DAD! THEY HURT MY DAD, AND I NEED SOME---
BATTEN--- MY NAME IS BATTEN WRACKELS!
....
WHAT HAPPENED TO DEVIS, SON?
IF ANYTHING EVER HAPPENED TO HIM---THE LADY IN MY HOUSE WAS SUPPOSED TO GET ME OUT AND BRING ME HERE. WAIT---
FWISSSH!
SEE? I DID NOT COME HERE TO HURT YOU, BUT---
BUT THE TWO OF US HAVE TO GET OUT OF HERE... NOW.
WHERE--- BUT WHERE WILL WE GO...?

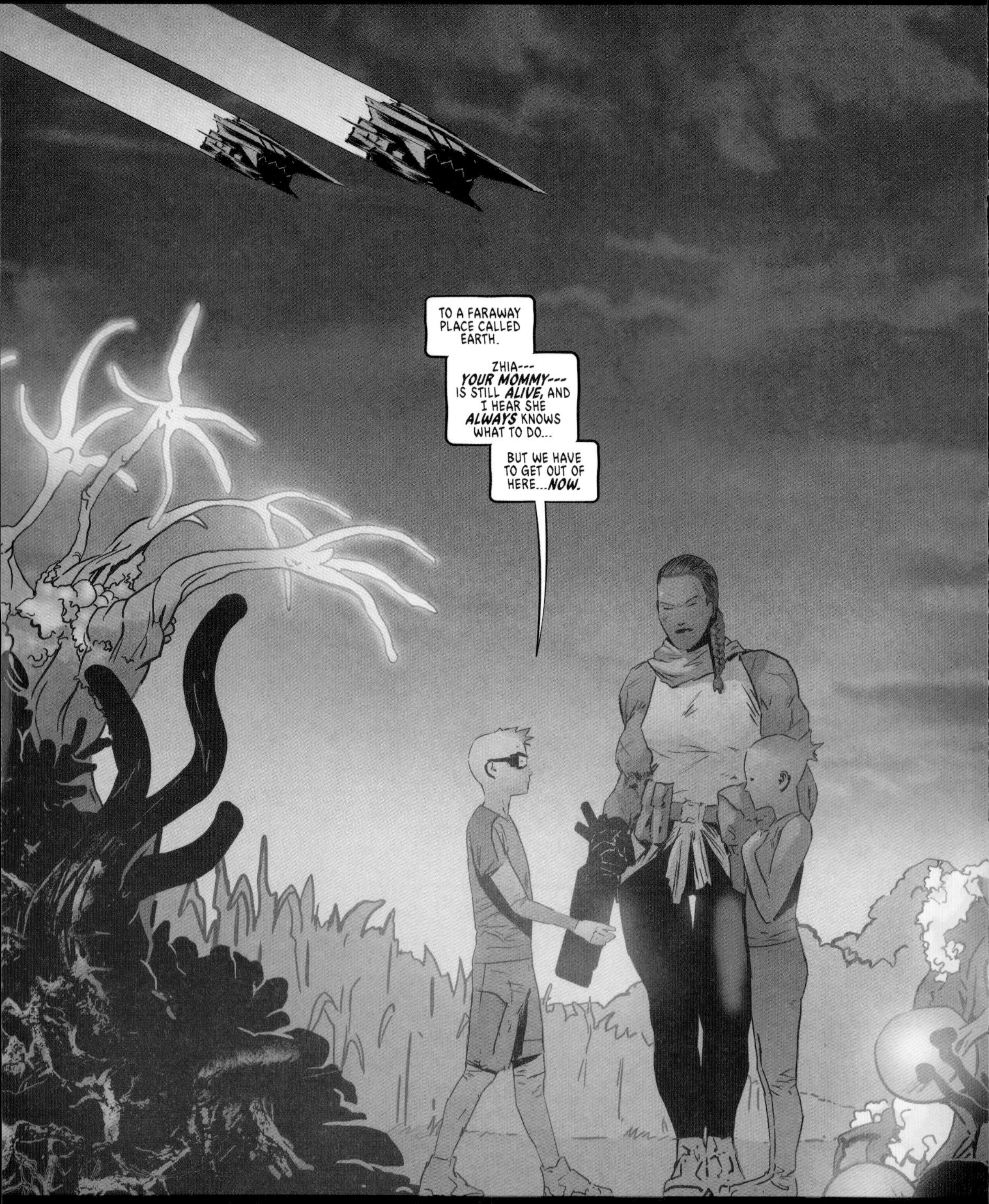
TO A FARAWAY PLACE CALLED EARTH.
ZHIA--- YOUR MOMMY--- IS STILL ALIVE, AND I HEAR SHE ALWAYS KNOWS WHAT TO DO...
BUT WE HAVE TO GET OUT OF HERE...NOW.

END BOOK THREE: REVEAL.

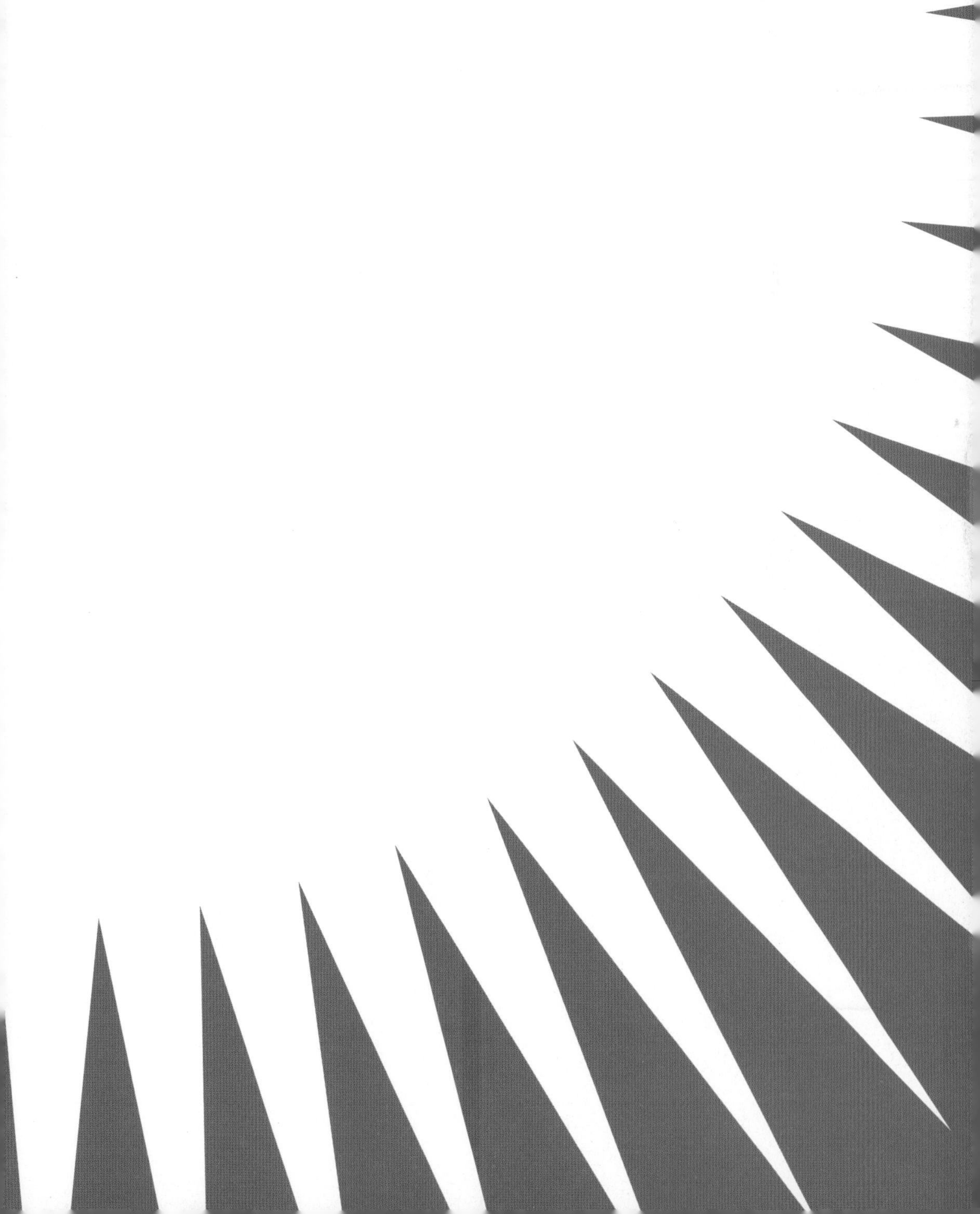

NONE OF US

HAVE THE REAL

ANSWER...

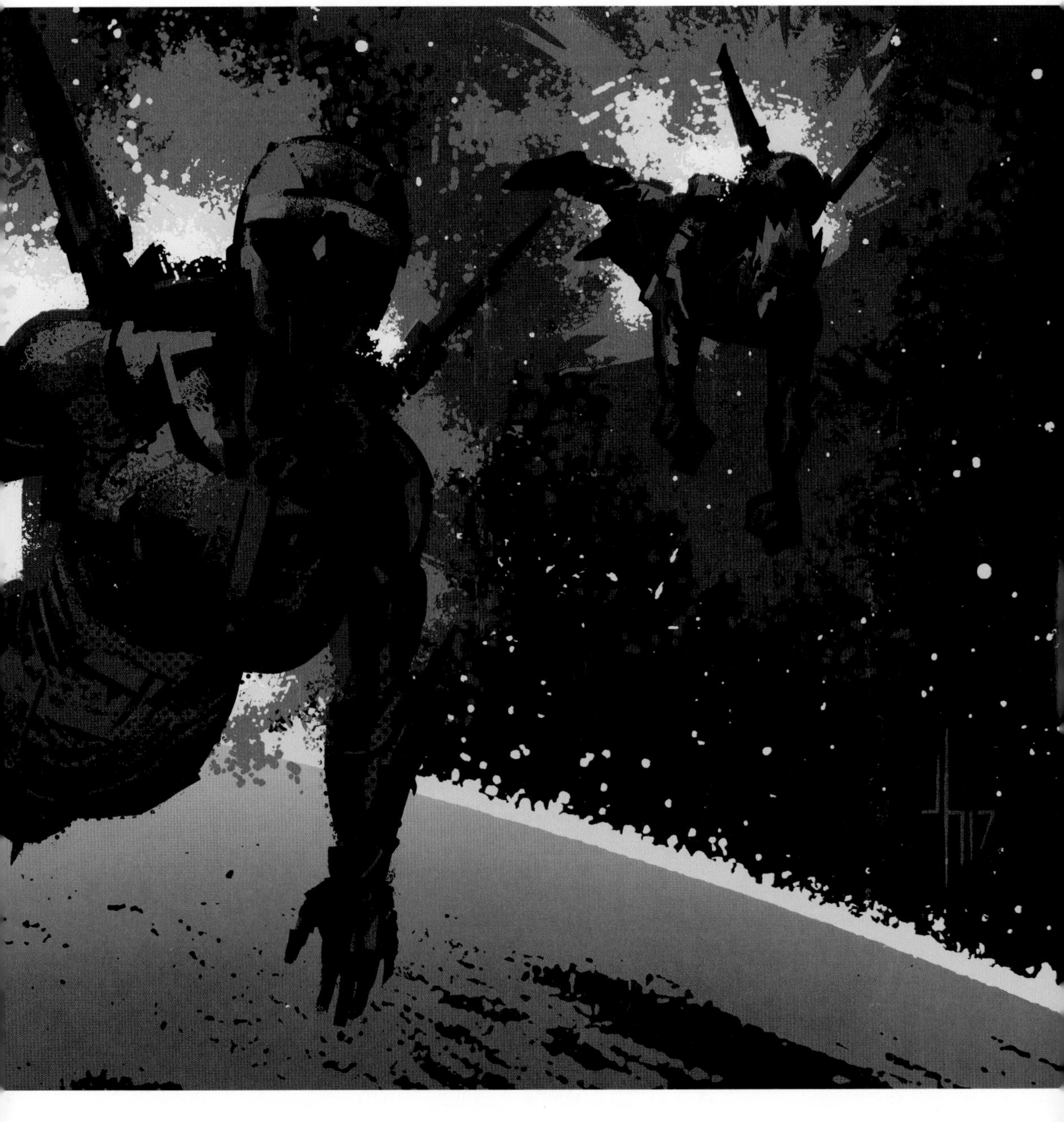

FOR MORE TALES FROM ROBERT KIRKMAN AND SKYBOUND

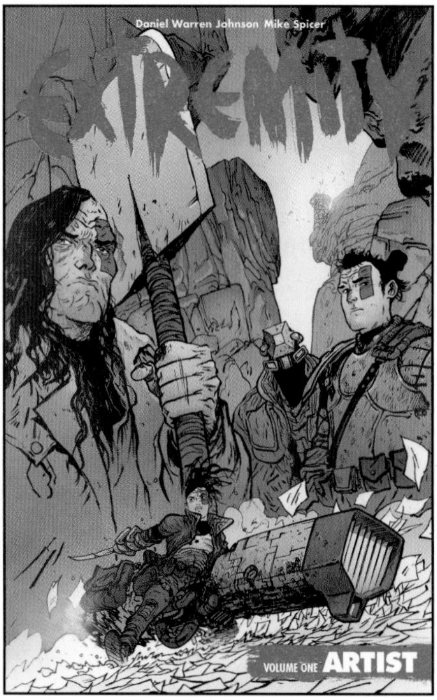
Daniel Warren Johnson Mike Spicer
EXTREMITY
VOLUME ONE ARTIST

VOL. 1: ARTIST TP
ISBN: 978-1-5343-0242-6
$16.99

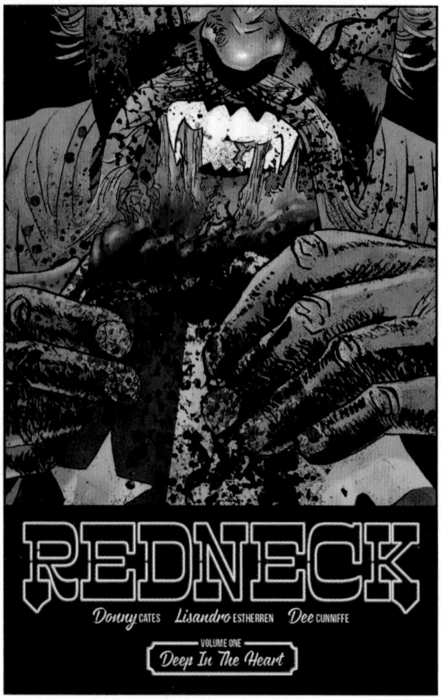
REDNECK
Donny CATES Lisandro ESTHERREN Dee CUNNIFFE
VOLUME ONE
Deep In The Heart

VOL. 1: DEEP IN THE HEART TP
ISBN: 978-1-5343-0331-7
$16.99

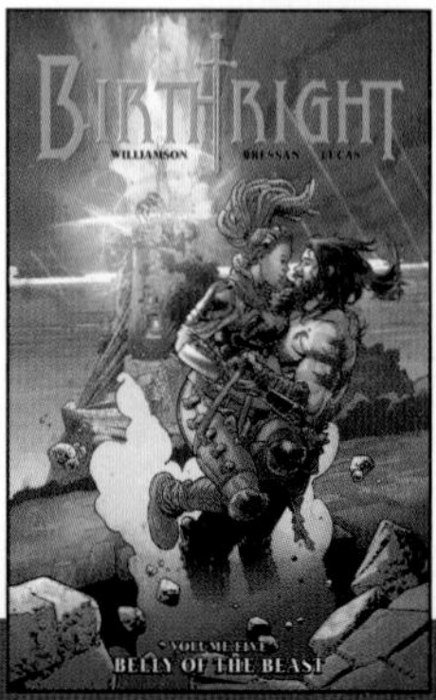
BIRTHRIGHT
WILLIAMSON BRESSAN LUCAS
VOLUME FIVE
BELLY OF THE BEAST

VOL. 1: HOMECOMING TP
ISBN: 978-1-63215-231-2
$9.99

VOL. 2: CALL TO ADVENTURE TP
ISBN: 978-1-63215-446-0
$12.99

VOL. 3: ALLIES AND ENEMIES TP
ISBN: 978-1-63215-683-9
$12.99

VOL. 4: FAMILY HISTORY TP
ISBN: 978-1-63215-871-0
$12.99

VOL. 5: BELLY OF THE BEAST TP
ISBN: 978-1-53430-218-1
$12.99

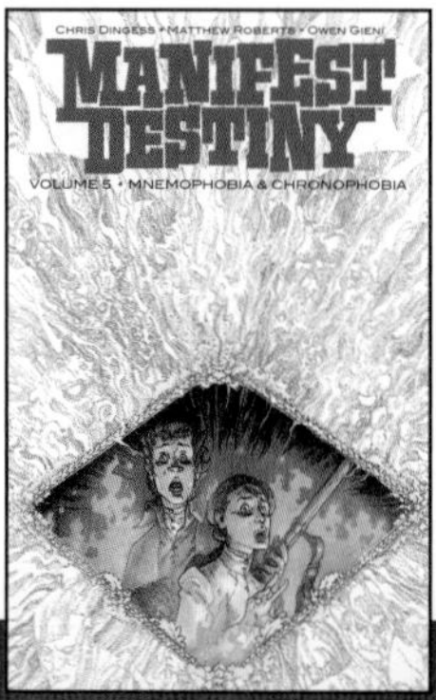
CHRIS DINGESS • MATTHEW ROBERTS • OWEN GIENI
MANIFEST DESTINY
VOLUME 5 • MNEMOPHOBIA & CHRONOPHOBIA

VOL. 1: FLORA & FAUNA TP
ISBN: 978-1-60706-982-9
$9.99

VOL. 2: AMPHIBIA & INSECTA TP
ISBN: 978-1-63215-052-3
$14.99

VOL. 3: CHIROPTERA & CARNIFORMAVES TP
ISBN: 978-1-63215-397-5
$14.99

VOL. 4: SASQUATCH TP
ISBN: 978-1-63215-890-1
$14.99

VOL. 5: MNEMOPHOBIA & CHRONOPHOBIA TP
ISBN: 978-1-5343-0230-3
$16.99

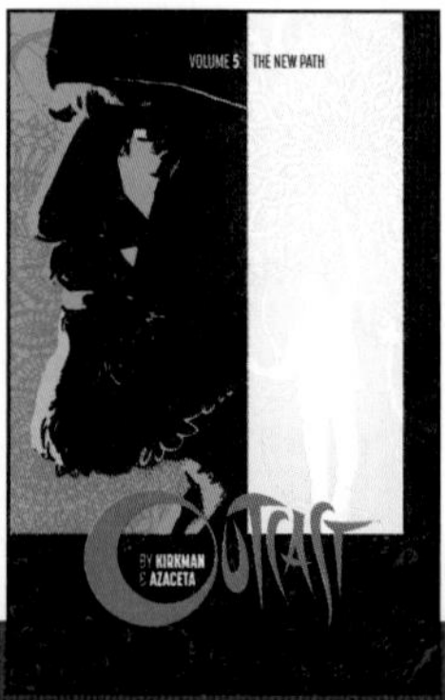
VOLUME 5 THE NEW PATH
OUTCAST
BY KIRKMAN & AZACETA

VOL. 1: A DARKNESS SURROUNDS HIM TP
ISBN: 978-1-63215-053-0
$9.99

VOL. 2: A VAST AND UNENDING RUIN TP
ISBN: 978-1-63215-448-4
$14.99

VOL. 3: THIS LITTLE LIGHT TP
ISBN: 978-1-63215-693-8
$14.99

VOL. 4: UNDER DEVIL'S WING TP
ISBN: 978-1-5343-0050-7
$14.99

VOL. 5: THE NEW PATH TP
ISBN: 978-1-5343-0249-5
$16.99

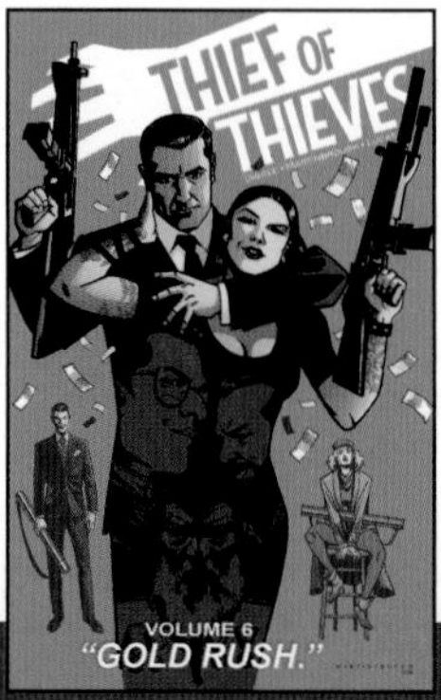
THIEF OF THIEVES
VOLUME 6
"GOLD RUSH."

VOL. 1: "I QUIT."
ISBN: 978-1-60706-592-0
$14.99

VOL. 2: "HELP ME."
ISBN: 978-1-60706-676-7
$14.99

VOL. 3: "VENICE."
ISBN: 978-1-60706-844-0
$14.99

VOL. 4: "THE HIT LIST."
ISBN: 978-1-63215-037-0
$14.99

VOL. 5: "TAKE ME."
ISBN: 978-1-63215-401-9
$14.99

VOL. 6: "GOLD RUSH."
ISBN: 978-1-53430-037-8
$14.99